A Place for Me brings to life the story of an orphan train child who settled in a small Midwestern town. In an era before mass adoption and foster care, orphanages used the nation's railway system to deliver poor children to new homes. Based on a true story, this fictionalized account humanizes the experiences of one such child, Dora Kelly. It is a fascinating tale: Dora is swept up by personal family drama, a sensationalized court trial, and her own search for love. Recommended for readers interested in popular history and juvenile fiction.

Jonathan Bean, Ph.D. is a Research Fellow at the Independent Institute and Professor of History at Southern Illinois University.

Joseph L. Murphy was a highly respected attorney and an active member of the Masonic Lodge in Canton. Sandra McKay brings his character and his love for children to life. *A Place For Me* is an enjoyable read, as it includes a lot of Canton's history, including the development of the Graham Hospital, and Fulton County's Trial of the Century. Murphy brought a little girl, Dora Kelly, home from an orphanage in Chicago. Unmothered, she became a remarkable young woman in spite of many setbacks and challenges. This is a five-part story that will appeal to people of all ages who are interested in history and the Orphan Train, and to young people seeking role models that have transitioned challenges into opportunities.

Terry Seward, Past Grand Master of Masons in Illinois

During my childhood I learned my Aunt Dora came to Canton on the Orphan Train. This was just a nugget of family history, and I never understood her amazing journey until her granddaughter Sandra brought it to life. I so enjoyed reading her story and stories like these are a reminder of what our ancestors did and achieved to give us the lives we have today.

Vicky Turl, Dora Kelly's niece and lifelong educator.

a Place for Me

AN ORPHAN'S JOURNEY HOME

by

Sandra McKay

First US Edition 2021
Printed in the United States of America

Paperback: ISBN 978-0-9966566-6-5
Library BISAC Codes:

FIC045020	FICTION / Family Life / Siblings
HIS036090	HISTORY / US / State & Local / Midwest (IA, IL, IN, KS, MI, MN, MO, ND, NE, OH, SD, WI)
JUV013050	JUVENILE FICTION / Family / Orphans & Foster Homes

Book cover and book design by Patrise Henkel
website: www.patrise.com
Author photo by Sunnie Brookbank

Published 2021 by Storyweaving Press
PO Box 739, Accokeek, MD 20607
Editor by Carol Burbank
website: www.storyweaving.com

Contact Information:
Sandra McKay
website: AuthorSandraMckay.com
email: dorabysandramckay@gmail.com

This book is dedicated to
My husband,
Donald McKay
Who encouraged me to write Dora's story

And in memory of
Dora Belle Kelly Moss
And her lost brothers,
Jack and Louis Kelly

Contents

Foreword

A Place for Me: An Orphan's Journey Home

S andra McKay entered my life more than a year ago via a message on social media. A fan letter of sorts, she wanted to share with me how much she enjoyed reading my second book, Maggie: A Journey of Love, Loss and Survival. This award-winning work of historical, biographical fiction originated from family stories and written documents relating to my great-grandmother's tumultuous life. Sandra soon informed me she had embarked upon her own work of historical fiction, based on her grandmother Dora's life in the early 1900s.

Sandra and I both value the importance of preserving family histories. Our grandmothers' stories were simply too compelling to be lost to the distant past. This shared belief resulted in each of us, at different times, deciding to put pen to paper (or in today's world, fingers to keyboard). That mutual love of family history brought us together, and we began an email dialogue, sharing information focusing on the writing process, along with a splash, now and then, of personal information. Although Sandra lives in Illinois and I'm in Montana, she promptly proved the adage the world is indeed a small place after sharing her only sister passed away in 2018 in a town only sixty miles from where I live.

The premise of Sandra's story drew me in and piqued my interest in her work. She clearly knows her subject well and despite obstacles, has remained tenacious in the telling, not to mention possessing the drive to stick with it through the sometimes-daunting steps to publication. I am impressed by her resolve and commitment to sharing her grandmother's captivating story.

A Place for Me: An Orphan's Journey Home transports the reader to the American Midwest in the early 1900s. We meet eight-year-old Dora and her two younger brothers at the moment strangers arrive to forcibly remove them from their mother's arms. After the untimely death of her husband, she's not able to support her family. Amidst the children's cries of terror, the men place each child in a separate carriage, while their mother weeps in anguish, helpless to stop them. Six days later, after an overland carriage ride to St. Louis, Dora boards one of the infamous orphan trains to Chicago.

Soon settled into an orphanage, Dora somehow adjusts to her new life, only to have it upended when a man with a long-white beard takes her away. She becomes the ward of Joseph Murphy, a wealthy bachelor, and for the next five years enjoys a life of privilege until Mr. Murphy passes away. A well-reported and contentious trial decides the fate of Mr. Murphy's disputed fortune, leaving Dora to face a Cinderella-like life— only this time, the wicked stepmother takes the form of Mr. Murphy's last housekeeper. You'll cheer for Dora as she strives to overcome her fate, and quite possibly experience compassion for what she endures. And I suspect by the time you turn the last page, you'll applaud the remarkable woman she becomes.

Close to Sandra McKay's heart, there's no doubt that she is the best person to tell Dora's extraordinary story. Her narrative affirms the indomitability of the human spirit and is a tale begging to be told, reminding us not to forget the lives of our ancestors. Cheered on by her extended family, Sandra spent two years of research for this labor of love and who better to bring the story alive today than the protagonist's granddaughter?

This work of historical, biographical fiction will appeal to readers, both men and women, as well as youth who have an interest in history and specifically stories of the orphan trains that crossed the United States between 1854 and 1929.

Vicki Tapia

Vicki Tapia is the author of *Somebody Stole My Iron: A Family Memoir of Dementia* (2015 Finalist for the High Plains Books Awards) and *Maggie: A Journey of Love, Loss and Survival* (Solo Medalist: 2018 New Apple Literary Awards for Historical Fiction; Finalist: 2019 Next Generation Indie Book Awards; Finalist: 2019 Book Excellence Awards). Currently, she's preparing for the release of her third book, *Harry & Grace: A Dakota Love Story*, written from stories her father shared about his parents, unexpected homesteaders in western North Dakota in the early 20th century.

Prologue

November 7, 1902, Ullin Village, Illinois. A dreary day.

Eight-year-old Dora, five-year-old Jack and two-year-old Louis are sleeping late, keeping warm together. Louis has a cold, breathing heavy with a soft baby snore. Dora wakes up to loud talking in the kitchen; her mother, Ella, is shouting and crying.

The door to the bedroom opens suddenly. The light behind him frames a large man's body, making it difficult to see his face. Dora lifts Baby Louis from his cradle to protect him. He starts to cry, and Dora holds him close as she leans back into the shadows.

Her mother screams from the kitchen. "No! Get out!"

The man crosses the room to Dora, and he pulls Louis from her arms. Startled, Louis shrieks. Jack wakes up and he sees the man, so he starts crying, too. Dora runs past him towards her mother. but another man in a heavy coat and a wide-brimmed hat catches her around her waist and picks her up.

"So, this is the little girl." He turns her head so he can see her face. "Pretty one she is. Someone will want her – she won't be in the home for long." He turns to her mother. "Stop crying! They'll be fine!"

Ella follows, crying out, as the man carries Dora down the stairs and puts her, struggling, into a carriage. "I've changed my mind! Let her stay! I can make it work!"

The man just shakes his head. Wearing only her night shirt, Dora is cold, so the man wraps her in a blanket. The other two men come out of the house carrying Jack and Louis and they put them into separate carriages.

"Where are you taking my brothers? Where are you taking me? Why is Mama crying?" The man ignores Dora's questions. He climbs into the carriage with Dora, and she hears the crack of a whip as the carriage moves down the hill, north, leaving town. Dora starts to cry hard, looking back out the window to see her mother collapse to the snowy ground in tears.

"Hush, now," said the man, pushing Dora back onto the seat and adjusting her blanket. "I'm not going to listen to your wailing all the way to St. Louis. Besides, you are going to a nice place. Better than back there! And there are lots of other little girls like you there, and nice ladies will take care of you. Call me Mr. Fields. I'll take care of you. Hush, now!"

Dora can't stop crying, although her sobs turn to sniffles. They stop around noon to pick up food. There are people walking about, women with children, yet no one seems to see Dora, or hear her cry for help. At the end of the day, they stop at a tavern.

"How much for two cots and supper for me and the girl?"

"Thirty cents and that includes breakfast in the morning."

The aroma of pork frying floats out from the kitchen, and Dora wipes her runny nose with the edge of the blanket. She's suddenly hungry. They find a place at a long table and Dora wolfs down her supper of fried pork, potatoes, warm bread and butter, and a tall glass of milk. Mr. Fields belches and orders another shot of whiskey. After supper they head to a large room on the second floor, where there are cots and people sleeping on bed rolls on the floor.

The next morning after breakfast, they go outside to look for their coachman, Whip. He has already changed horses and is waiting to resume their six-day journey to St. Louis. Dora loses count of the days. Every day is the same, two meals a day and Whip changes the horses for their trip the next day. Each day they eat the same meals, fried pork at dinner and bacon, eggs and cornbread for breakfast. Bone weary, Dora falls into a deep sleep on the tavern cot, dusty from the trip and still in the same nightshirt worn when she left home.

Finally, at the train depot in St. Louis; Dora shrinks back against Mr. Fields.

She has never seen so many people. She trembles when Mr. Fields takes her by the hand and pulls her towards the station. Dora looks for her mother, like she has everywhere, hoping she would have followed. She starts to cry again. They walk up to a long table where a woman is sitting.

"Here's the girl from Ullin," Mr. Fields takes a receipt and gently but firmly pushes Dora up to the table. "Stop crying. You'll be all right."

The woman takes Dora's hand and brings her to a back room with no window and little light. The woman reminds Dora of a witch in a black dress and her hair in a tight bun, a stern face and hard hands. The woman rummages through a box to find a set of clothes and shoes for Dora. Dora's crying has calmed down to quiet sobs.

The woman takes off her Dora's filthy nightshirt to put on under garments and a heavy white flour sack play dress.

"My goodness, child, you need a bath." Her face still wet, Dora pulls on knee high cotton socks and leather slippers that the woman hands to her.

"Here - here is a nice wool coat for your ride on the train to Chicago."

"I don't want to go to Chicago. I want to go back to Ullin. I want my mama and Maggie Ann."

"You don't have a mother anymore, little girl. You're an orphan now. When you get to the home you'll understand. Now put on your new coat." Half dragging her, the woman walks Dora towards the train.

A man is shouting, "Children's Aid Society, check in here!" He is holding a book and pen and it looks like he's eating chocolate candy, but then he spits a brown liquid in Dora's direction. Yuk! Chewing tobacco! She tries not to cry again while stepping over the mess.

"This is Dora Kelly."

"Open your mouth, girl." The check-in man sticks his dirty finger into her mouth and rubs it over her teeth. "This one looks healthy." He checks Dora's name off the list.

Then he picks her up and carries her up the steps onto the train. He sets her on a bench, and hands her a bag with bread and cheese. "Stay here."

She stays. A boy next to her says, "Hi," but she looks down and bites her lip.

Most of the children are sleeping, some on the benches and some on the floor of the train. Dora hears the whistle and the puffing of the locomotive, the lurch as the train moves forward. She stands up to look out the window. Her mama is still not there, Mr. Fields is gone, the tobacco man is talking with the witch. She watches them get small, and then the train station disappears, and there are only warehouses and ugly brick buildings as the train leaves out of town. She keeps looking, though, back towards her past not knowing what is ahead.

PART ONE

Ullin Village

*"Clouds come floating into my life,
no longer to carry rain or usher storm,
but to add color to my sunset sky."*

Rabindranath Tagor —Stray Birds

Home

1901, Ullin Village

My story starts in southern Illinois, with my parents and brothers, Baby Louis and Jack. Life in Ullin Village is simple and we're happy. People in Ullin are born, live, and die here, near family without the thought of going anywhere else. We children run and play at the edge of the Cache River. I am only seven, but every day I go by myself across a large arched bridge into town to take lunch to my Daddy and Uncle Jasen at their barbershop.

Ullin is a railroad town, dirt roads fanning out from the train depot. On the way to town, you pass the Fruit Belt Service Company and the Phoenix Flour Mill down from the James Bell Sawmill. Sometimes, you can see the horses and oxen hauling the trees cut near the Cache Bottomlands before they're floated to the mill for sawing. Daddy told me the blue limestone of the hills above fill the lime kilns every day, then limestone is shipped by rail to all parts of the country. Men work hard at back breaking jobs, at the coal mine, and at the sawmill, the flour mill, the limestone quarry, and the railroad, while women cook, scrub, wash and hang clothes on clothes lines to dry, all the while taking care of us children and babies. Some of my friends have another sister or brother every year.

People tell me I am lucky to live in Ullin, that life is easy in our small village. Some complain that Ullin is small, but it doesn't seem small to me. It's my whole world. Sunday is my favorite day -- our day of rest. Everyone goes to the Methodist Church in the morning, and the rest of the day is spent with family.

I like the people in Ullin. They care about one another, and they help one another when things get hard, or when another baby is born. Billy Swank's mama died when she had Baby Jessica. Billy was sad and he missed school for a while, but the Pastor told us that new life is a gift, and death is simply part of God's plan.

Spring is so beautiful in the village, there on the edge of Cypress Creek National Wildlife Refuge. I always wake up to birds chirping and the coo-ah coo coo-ah of mourning doves. Bluebells pop up under shade trees and violets bloom through the grass as if God had spattered lavender paint on our front yard.

We live on the quiet side of town, in a three-room cabin on the edge of the Cache River. Our cabin is made from logs and clay from the Cache Basin. There is a porch outside the kitchen door, and a big lawn that slopes down to the river. My daddy Curtis Kelly and Uncle Jasen own a barbershop, the second shop on the other side of the bridge from our cabin. They know everyone and everyone likes them too.

I feel the warmth of the morning sun on my face as it creeps into the corner of the kitchen. I watch as the lace curtain transfers its silhouette onto my cot. I jump up and nudge Jack. Excited, we run outside to the privy, and we come back inside to wash our hands in the basin, and to splash water on our faces. We hang our nightshirts on hooks above our cots and pull on our play dresses. Hungry and eager to play outside, we run to the kitchen for breakfast.

"Mama, can Jack go with me to the barbershop this time?"

"Well, I suppose he's old enough. Jack, you must mind your sister!" Like every other morning in the summer, Mama spreads honey on slices of fresh bread, and she adds sugar and cream to our steaming cups of tea.

After breakfast, we run outside to play. There are no clouds, and the blue sky is a perfect backdrop for the morning sun which forms a perfect circle the color of melted butter.

Jack is distracted by a flutter of sparrows in our willow tree, so I run to the box in the shed to get the soccer ball Uncle Jasen gave us. We kick the ball back and forth, sometimes missing it, but Jack always catches it before it rolls down into the river.

Mama calls us, "Dora, Jack, it's time to be on your way!"

She gives me two cloth sacks to carry, one filed with pieces of stale bread, and a larger sack with warm bread, a hunk of cheese, and a jar of apple butter.

"Follow me, Jack, let's go feed the ducks!" As we run down towards the river, we can see the ducks swimming towards the riverbank to get their daily treats. The water is so clear that we can see the rocks and small fish swimming at the bottom of the stream. I sit on my favorite boulder at the river edge and Jack stands next to me, throwing the pieces of stale bread that float until they are devoured by the ducks.

We spend almost an hour feeding them, then we take our shoes off to wade in the shallow edge of the river. After a while, I put on my shoes and sit under a shade tree to look for four-leafed clovers. Jack is already bored so he starts to play at the base of the bridge. He comes when I call him back, but then he starts to throw rocks at the ducks.

"C'mon, Jack, it's time to go." The sun is high in the sky, so I know it's close to lunch time. I stand up with my bouquet of four-leafed clovers in one hand, and Daddy's lunch sack in the other.

As we cross the bridge, the sounds of downtown Ullin grow louder and louder and we laugh, taking turns to imitate the sounds of the tugboat whistle, the drumbeats of the steam locomotives at the depot, and the constant buzz of the sawmill. There's a horse drawn sawmill truck speeding towards us from the bridge, so we have to zig zag to get out of the way. Excited and out of breath, we charge through the door of the barbershop.

Uncle Jasen is sweeping hair, and a breeze follows us through the door catching the hair in dancing circles in the air before scattering it back across the floor.

"Well, there's our darlings! So, Dora, you brought your little brother along today. C'mon, Jack, I'll take you for a spin." He laughs and we close the door.

Uncle Jasen leans his broom by the corner cabinet and he lifts Jack onto the barber chair. Jack hangs on with dear life to the arms of the chair as Uncle Jasen spins the chair around and around. Jack giggles so hard, he gets the hiccups.

Daddy is laughing as he crosses the room. "Stop, Jasen, let's have lunch before you make him sick. You need to get married and have some young 'uns of your own, so you have someone to play with!"

I hand the lunch sack to Daddy, and I take the broom to sweep up the hair so I can take it outside to the garden.

"Thank you for bringing us lunch, Dora, and thanks for sweeping up the hair and putting it in the garden. It keeps the rabbits from eating our vegetables."

I come in the back door and I give Daddy a big hug.

He winks at me. "Now, scoot home you two, or Mama will worry. "

When we get home, Mama is sitting in her rocking chair on the porch snapping beans for dinner the next day. We can smell cabbage soup cooking on the stove.

"Here, Mama, I picked these for you!" She takes the bouquet of four-leafed clovers and puts them in a small glass of water on the kitchen table.

"Thank you, Dora. The good Lord surely gave you a special gift. I don't know anyone who can find four-leafed clovers like you."

It's usually dark when Daddy comes home from the barbershop. The shop is only three blocks away, so we can see when he blows the oil lamps out, and we know he's on his way home. Mama has us bathed and in our nightshirts and we wait patiently, leaning our elbows on the table, waiting for Daddy to finish eating his supper.

When Daddy is done eating, it's playtime!

"C'mon, you ragamuffins! I'll sing and you can dance like angels in your nightshirts." Jack and I tap dance gracefully around the room while Daddy's tenor voice fills the air.

"In Dublin's fair city,
Where the girls are so pretty,
I first set me eyes on sweet Ruby Malone,
As she wheeled her wheelbarrow,
Through streets broad and narrow,
Crying, Cockles and mussels, alive, alive, oh!'

After a while it's time for bed. Mama carries Louis to his cradle, and Daddy picks Jack and me up, one under each arm, to carry us to our cots. Then the room becomes quiet, and we whisper our bedtime prayers:

Now I lay me down to sleep...

I stop in the middle of my prayer, "Daddy, do angels sing and dance?"

"Why, of course they do! Now, finish your prayers and have sweet dreams."

Every day, we play by the river and feed the ducks. Blue gill and bass have returned to the bottomlands. We laugh at the baby ducks swimming behind their mothers, dunking their heads in the water towards the silvery glimmer of fish.

The iceman, Mr. Magee, delivers ice on Wednesdays, and he chips chunks of ice for us and the other children in the neighborhood. Summers are so busy -- church on Sunday, and picnics and potluck dinners celebrating weddings, baptisms, graduations, birthdays, or any other good reason to get together.

Towards the end of June, the whole town gets ready for the big Fourth of July celebration, and all the Kelly women start planning the annual holiday picnic. Snow and cold usually keeps folks inside with their families at Christmas, so the Fourth of July is the only holiday to really celebrate with friends and neighbors.

Everyone including our aunts, uncles and cousins, gather at the park for the annual Fourth of July celebration. Like every other year, the parade kicks off the day's events, then families have picnics. We are excited to run and play games.

It's early when we cross the bridge and walk towards the park, but we want to be in time for the parade at ten o'clock. Daddy is carrying Jack and the picnic basket and Mama carries Louis and a lantern. I run ahead across the bridge towards downtown, trying not to drag our quilt. We walk up a grassy hillside towards the park, and Daddy points to the rounded crown of a tall pin oak tree. Our favorite picnic spot!

"Look, here comes Uncle Jasen!" Jack and I run to greet our Uncles Jasen, James, Henry, and John. Aunts Dora, Maggie and Elisa and cousins, Orella and Halforson, trail behind. Mama and our aunts spread quilts on the lawn. We all jump up when Halforson calls out for a game of tag.

"Mama, will the parade start soon?"

"Soon, very soon!" The park is filled with people laughing and talking, and children squealing and chasing each other.

My mama and daddy look so happy and handsome. Everyone says hello to them. Today, mama has curled her flaxen hair and her dress matches her blue eyes. She sings along with the band in the gazebo – I can see why she is a soloist in the church choir! Daddy is suntanned with deep-set eyes and a boyish smile, and I love the way he pulls mama tight.

"Look, Ella," as he points to a tree down the street, "someone put up the American flag stitched by you ladies and your friends for the Ladies Aid Society."

Soon, we hear the beat of the parade drummers. Leading the parade is a Civil War veteran with his five-year-old grandson marching by his side. There are wagons and horses including some mares with their colts, followed by the drum and fife corps from Mound City. Then the mayor gets out of his carriage covered with flags and red, white and blue ribbons, and he climbs onto the bed of a wagon to give a speech, but we can't hear him over the cheers.

Mama calls us to eat our special picnic of fried chicken, sweet potato croquettes, and vegetables from the garden. We laugh at Baby Louis who crows happily, sitting on a quilt with sweet potatoes all over his face.

"Here, Ella, you can use this to wash his face." Aunt Maggie hands a wet cloth to Mama.

After we eat, Daddy walks down the road to join the men in a game of horseshoes, leaving us behind to play and Mama to visit with neighbors and the aunts. I play hide and seek with Orella and Halforson, and Jack plays marbles on the path with some of the older boys from the neighborhood. Even though Jack is the youngest, he can keep up with the older boys, and he even wins every now and then.

After a while, I coax the girls, including Cousin Orella, to sit with me and to look in the grass for four-leafed clovers.

"Dora, I never find any. We looked last year, remember? There aren't any here."

"Well, there are too. Look here, I found four and look at this one, it has five leaves!" I carefully put the clovers into my pocket to add to my collection.

It's getting late and Jack and I are tired. Mama starts to wonder when Daddy will be back. She looks up to see him coming up the road waving a golden horseshoe, his fourth trophy for winning the annual horseshoe tournament. "Here, Ella, this is for you to add to your collection on the kitchen wall."

Even though he's hot and sweat is dripping down his forehead, Daddy grabs Mama around the waist and he gives her a big kiss.

The park is getting quiet. The red sun gets bigger as it disappears under the horizon and one-by-one campfires are lit for storytelling later in the evening. The lamplighter sings as he walks down the street to light the oil street lamps. Our family shares cakes and cupcakes. Mama and the other women drink cider and the men down pints from the local pub. Soon the flickering white lights of campfires and lamps are like dappled sun light on the lawn, giving a sense of calm to day's end.

Daddy helps Mama as she stands up to call us, "Dora, Jack, it's time to go home.".

Daddy waves at the neighbors to let them know we're leaving. "God Speid, Jasen!"

Uncle Jasen waves as he walked towards home. Everyone exchanges handshakes, hugs and kisses and one-by-one we all leave the park, wishing we could stay and watch the stars come out.

Daddy is smiling and happy, but tired from the heat. His bronzed muscles flex beneath his undershirt and his blonde hair curls from the humidity. A curl falls down to the center of his forehead.

"C'mon, sweetheart, let's get our angels home and tucked in for the night!" Daddy carries Jack and the picnic basket and Mama carries Louis, while I trail behind helping Mama with the quilt and picnic basket as we walk across the bridge to our cabin.

It's been a good day.

Boyo!

"**D**addy, something's wrong with Jack!" I run into the barbershop in a panic.

Jack stumbles through the door, into the barbershop crying and shaking his head. Uncle Jasen picks him up and he sits him in the barber chair. He steps on the pedal to make the chair higher so he can examine Jack's ears and nose.

Daddy stops trimming Mr. Keagen's beard to cross the room. "Where does it hurt, Jack?"

Jack wails non-stop, shaking his head. It hurts to see my little brother crying, so I start to cry, too.

Uncle Jasen leans Jack's head back. "Why look here, Curtis, it looks like he shoved a small stone up his nose." Uncle Jasen gets a can of pepper from the closet, "Let's see if we can make him sneeze!"

He throws a small handful of pepper into Jack's face. Jack sneezes but the stone remains firmly lodged in his nose.

Daddy picks Jack up by his ankles, turning him upside down and shaking him as he holds him by his feet. Scared, Jack screams even louder. But shaking him doesn't work; the stone does not come out.

Daddy shouts above the noise, "Jasen, you finish Mr. Keagen and we will go up the street to Doc Donovan's. Sorry, Walt, but I know you understand."

Daddy is carrying Jack while I trail behind, both of us wailing loudly all the way up the street towards Doc Donovan's office. By the time we reach his porch, a crowd has gathered to see what's wrong. Doc Donovan meets us at the door with open arms.

"Doc, it looks like Jack shoved a small stone up his nose and we can't get it out!"

Doc Donovan carries Jack inside and sets him on a table. "Let's see here...." He looks up Jack's nose carefully. "Sure enough! It's only a little one. Only take a minute!"

Doc crosses the room to a cabinet, where he takes a tiny silver spoon from a drawer. In no more than a minute, he removes the stone from Jack's nose.

Jack laughs, and I stop crying and reach out my hand. "That's such a cute spoon! Doctor, where can I get a little spoon like that? It's just the right size for my dolly."

Doc hands the spoon to me, "Here, Dora, you can have this one."

"What do I owe you, Doc?" Daddy pulls out his wallet.

"Nothing, Curtis. How about no charge for a haircut and shave when I come in next time?" They shake on it, and we head home. Daddy carries Jack while I hold the tiny spoon tight in my hand.

After we cross the bridge, I run ahead and grab Mama in the kitchen. "Mama, Jack put a stone up his nose and Doc Donovan gave me this little spoon for my dolly!"

"Well, that was very nice of the doctor, but you've been crying. Curtis, what happened?"

Mama is busy cooking sweet potato stew, so Daddy sits down on a kitchen chair, and he pulls Jack onto his lap. "Ella, we tried everything to get that rock out of Jack's nose. Jasen threw pepper in his face to make him sneeze, and I held him by his ankles upside down, but it was just plain stuck. What a sight we must have been. Jack was shaking and wailing, and Dora was crying louder than I'd ever heard her! By the time we got to Doc Donovan's half the town was following us! Doc fixed it, though, and next thing you know, Jack was laughing!"

Mama gives Jack a stern look. He knows he's in trouble, so he slips down off Daddy's lap, and we run outside.

While Jack gets the ball, I listen at the door, because we're both worried. But they're not mad at all – it's just mushy stuff. Just in case, I listen, and what a surprise – even better news!

"Ella, this is my family." Taking her arm, he pulls her close. "Something you and I created together."

"I love you, Kurt."

"Ella, I have loved you from the first time I saw you covered in mud from trying to catch that baby pig at the county fair. I told Jasen, I'm going to marry that girl!" They laugh. "By the way, Ella, I have a surprise for you. I've been thinking about adding a room on the back of the cabin, so the children will have their own place to sleep. What if I build a perfect room for our angels? Would you like that?"

"Can we do that? That would be wonderful, but can we afford it?"

Daddy pulls a paper from his front pocket. "Here's the design I have in mind. I think we can afford it. Jasen and John will help, and we can get logs from the sawmill. It will give us more privacy as well."

"Oh, Kurt, I can hardly wait to tell the children. Dora and Jack will be so excited! Think of it – a four-room house!"."

"Well, we have to get started right away! Tomorrow, I'll go to the sawmill and order the logs, and I'll ask Jasen and John to help so the new room can be done before cold weather sets in. We will have plenty of room for our three angels!"

Mama calls us in for supper and I don't let on that I heard them talking. I'll wait until they tell us all about our own new room and maybe even a new bed!

We are hungry and ready to dive into the stew and biscuits. Daddy folds his hands to give the blessing.

> *"Thank you, Lord, for Doc Donovan,*
> *and for getting the rock out of Jack's nose.*
> *We also thank you for our family, this good food,*
> *and for the good life you have given us. Amen."*

"Amen!" I say loudly.

Summer's winding down and the days are getting shorter. Daddy, Uncle John and Uncle Jasen have been working hard to build our new bedroom on the back of the cabin. We watch as they work together every night after work, and all day on weekends, only taking time off to go to church Sunday morning.

Jack and I are so excited, but we miss our nightly playtime with Daddy. Every night I ask, "how soon will it be done, Daddy?" At first, he answers with weeks, then days.

The new room is finished just in time in October, when there is a chill in the air and little time to work late in the day, before night sets in.

We have a real bed with feather ticking sewed by Mama. The bed, along with a small chest to hold our clothes and a water basin, fill the tiny room with just enough space at the foot of the bed for Louis' cradle. Small as it is, Jack and I are so excited. We no longer sleep on cots in the corner of the kitchen. We have our own bedroom!

Mama invites Uncle Jasen and Uncle John and his family for supper on the porch on Sunday to celebrate the new room. We sit down to eat, and everyone becomes quiet, looking at Daddy to say grace.

"Thank you, God for this good food and for my bráthairs. I could not have built the new room without their help nor without your help, Amen."

"Now, let's eat!"

After supper, the sun is setting so Mama and Aunt Maggie carry the dishes into the kitchen for cleanup. Mama lights the oil lamps so she and Aunt Maggie can visit in the parlor while the Daddy and my uncles stay on the porch to watch us play hide and seek. They rehash family stories passed down about life in Ireland, each trying to outdo the others.

We come inside and one by one, we all fall asleep on the floor. John calls Maggie to the parlor, "C'mon, Maggie, it's getting late. Let's go home so these people can go to bed." John shakes Orella and Halforson and pulls them to their feet to walk them to their buggy for the short ride home. After thanking Ella for the good food, Jasen leaves for the short walk to his cabin, and we go off to our beds, sleepy and full.

Life is good in Ullin Village. Mama and Daddy love one another, and we all live in a nice home filled with happiness. We have all that we need and would not have it any other way.

As I am dropping off, I see Mama and Daddy checking in on us.

"Our angels are so sweet! And that was a great supper, Ella. Did you see Jasen, he ate two slices of your apple pie! I'm proud of you and my family..." As they hug, I see him wipe away a little tear from her cheek. "Are you tired, sweetheart? What's wrong?"

"Oh, I don't know.... I love you and I am proud of our family too, but – oh, you'll laugh! Kurt, our life is so perfect, and I just have a strange feeling that something bad is going to happen."

"Nonsense! You're just tired. What could possibly go wrong?"

Daddy might be right, but I will collect more four-leaf clovers as extra protection, just in case.

Winter passes and the seasons intertwine with cool spring nights and hot summer days. As fall rolls around again, we buy a pumpkin from a farm wagon crossing the bridge towards downtown. Mama has been canning and making jellies, while Daddy gathers logs to lay in for the winter. Life at the Kelly home has settled down to a routine of chores, work, school, church, and evening meals in front of the fireplace, followed by Daddy singing Irish melodies while we float around the room in our nightshirts like angels. But soon we'll find out that Mama was right, and everything would change.

Daddy's been sick, so I don't know what's going to happen at Christmas. Mama told us we're not going to Uncle James' and Aunt Dora's for dinner on Christmas Day unless Daddy gets better. He's been coming home early from the barbershop and he goes straight to bed. Mama says he has a cold, but he just keeps getting worse.

Mama and Daddy try to make light of it because they don't want to spoil our Christmas. We get to open our presents in front of the fireplace on Christmas Eve.

"It's Christmas! It's Christmas!" Jack and Louis are running around the room, squealing with excitement as they see the presents piled up.

"Jack! Louis! Sit down. Let's see what Santa brought this year," Mama calls, and they settle down a little. Jack rips open his package to find a new bag of marbles and a carved wooden horse. Louis bounces his new blue ball across the room towards the kitchen. Daddy surprises Mama with a delicate tatted collar from Mrs. Treece's dry goods store. She says she'll wear it with her grey dress when she goes to church on Sunday. Daddy always knows what to expect; Mama always gives him a jar of homemade fudge.

Mama takes a package from under the tree, tied with a red ribbon, and she hands it to me, "Here, Dora, this is for you."

I open the package to find a doll with yellow yarn hair and a blue ruffled dress. She has blue button eyes and a red heart-shaped mouth.

I recognize Mama's handiwork right away. Knowing she made the doll for me makes her even more special. "Oh, I love her so much, thank you!"

Daddy pipes in, "Why, Dora, she really is beautiful. What's her name?"

I knew her name as soon as I saw her, "Why, Maggie Ann after our Aunt Maggie. She is my Maggie Ann!"

December in southern Illinois is cold and damp and the house is always especially cold in the evening. Daddy asks me to go outside to fetch wood 'cuz sometimes he doesn't feel up to facing the weather. Once he loads the wood I gather enough for the night and a little for the morning fire, he goes right to bed at the same time we do. In the morning when we wake up, Jack and I crawl under the feather ticking, waiting for Daddy to stoke the fire and warm up the house. Once the cookstove is going, we roll out of bed to the aroma of sausage and warm biscuits.

This morning, like every other morning, Jack and I run to the kitchen window and pull back the curtain, expecting to see another cold and dreary day, but a miracle happened while we slept – the sun glares off the new snow. The trees have been dusted white and Jack spots a bright red cardinal, sitting in the undergrowth near the bank of the river. We can hardly wait to go outside, to ride on our sled down the bridge which slopes towards our cabin.

Mama calls us to the table, "Dora, Jack, get dressed and eat your breakfast, then you can go outside to play!"

With a weak voice, Daddy calls from his bed, "Don't make anything for me, Ella, I don't feel like eating."

"I wish you would eat something. This cold has lingered on too long. Just try to eat a bite or two." Mama fixes a small plate of food and takes it to the bedroom. She touches Daddy's forehead, "Curtis, you're burning up! You have a fever!"

He is so sick, so I don't think he feels like disagreeing with her. He takes one bite of sausage, and a bite of biscuit. Then he just lays his head back on the pillow.

"Children, go out to play. Let your father rest!" Mama looks worried, but we're so excited by the snow that we don't mind.

The next morning, we wake up to hear Daddy moaning. I run to their bedroom to find him holding his belly in pain. As soon as I approach the door, I'm confronted with the stench of vomit which floats through the air into the kitchen and the rest of the house.

"Dora, get dressed and go outside to get some wood for the cookstove," Mama says, not looking up from cleaning around their bed. I bring in as much as I can.

While waiting for the stove to heat up, Mama puts a large pot of water on so she can clean up the mess and she starts our breakfast. We're not very hungry with the smell, and Mama crying, and Daddy being so sick.

"Can I help, Mama?" She looks so worried!

"No, my angel. Go out and play. And watch your brothers!" She sends us out the door with an extra biscuit and a hug. When we come in a few hours later, the house doesn't smell so bad, and Daddy is sleeping.

Doc Donovan has been stopping by every day since Daddy stopped going to work at the barbershop. His face is pasty and yellow, and he's not getting better. One day, instead of sending us off to our room, Mama calls us to the kitchen table where she and the doctor are talking. Louis is napping, which turns out to be for the best.

"What's wrong, Mama?"

"Oh, your daddy is very sick." Mama pulls Jack and me close.

"Stop crying, Mama. If we sing, will Daddy feel better?"

"No, we must be very quiet so he can sleep. Maybe, oh, my babies! How will we live without Daddy?"

Doc Donovan takes her hand and says, very gently, "Children, your daddy has typhoid fever. You and your Mama are doing everything that can be done, feeding him hot liquids and keeping him warm, and making sure he gets rest. But he's very, very sick. Your uncles and aunts will be here to help, and you should do everything you can to help your mama. I will be here every day, too, but you have to be strong for your mama."

I suddenly feel very afraid. "What do you mean? Is Daddy going to die like Billie Swank's mama did?"

Mama holds me close. "We don't know, honey. I don't even want to think about that. I don't know. I just don't know. Oh, Doctor, what am I going to do with these three angels?"

"We'll help you all through this, Ella. You too, children." The doctor pats her hand.

Mama sits up straighter, and she gives me a stern look. "Dora, I need you to help by taking care of Jack and Baby Louis. You need to keep them quiet so Daddy can rest. We can all pray he'll get better. And whatever happens, we will just have to be brave."

Da!

January 1902

I don't understand why Daddy is sick or what to expect, but I know from the look on Doc Donovan's face that it's bad. I turned eight this week, but everyone is so worried about Daddy, that they forgot my birthday. I guess it was just another day and I'm still eight years old. Maybe we can celebrate if Daddy feels better soon.

All I want to do is run, I don't know where to, but somewhere away from whatever's happening. I feel like crying but I need to be brave for Mama, Jack, and Louis. Mama looks so tired from taking care of Daddy. I'm the oldest, so I need to take charge. I can't sit or sleep, so I decide to take the rug from the parlor outside to the clothesline, where I beat it with Mama's double heart rug beater, over and over again. When I can't beat it anymore, I fall to the ground crying, feeling deep inside that life will never be the same.

The next morning when Doc Donovan comes in through the door, we can hear Daddy's heavy breathing. "Ella, how long has he been like this?"

"It started last night. Doctor, there are times I don't think he knows who I am, and other times he sees things that are not there. Last night, he told me to get the chickens out of his room! He's sleeping now and he will sleep most of the day, then we will be awake with him all night."

"How are you doing, Ella? Do you need help from the Ladies Aid?"

"Goodness, no, the last thing I need is for those women to be in my house when it needs to be cleaned. Besides, I am not in the mood for company. Thank you, though. Dora is a big help and Curtis' brothers have been delivering meals, so I don't have to cook. They leave them on the porch, so they don't have to come into the house." She glances over at us, peeking in the front door. "I don't know how to explain to Dora and Jack that they can't to go into the room to see Curtis anymore."

"Ella, why don't you let Dora and Jack in the room to see their father, then send them to stay with an aunt and uncle until this is over?"

I put Louis on the floor. "Until what is over? I don't want to go away. I want to stay here and help Mama."

Mama straightens up, "Dora, it will help me if you go to Aunt Maggie's and take care of Jack and Louis, so all I have to worry about for now is taking care of your daddy. Now, put some clothes in a sack so you can say goodbye to Daddy before you leave."

I want to look pretty for Daddy, so I put on a clean dress and comb my hair. Jack's eyes are big, and I choke back tears as we go into their room. Daddy opens his eyes, "Why, there's my angels! Where's the baby?" There's blood on his pillow and blanket, and it looks like his tongue is bleeding.

I want to make him feel better. "Daddy, we miss you. We are sorry you feel sick. We've tried to be quiet so you can sleep, and I've been bringing in wood every day. Mama is getting Louis dressed so we can go for a visit with Aunt Maggie and Uncle John."

"I know, Dora. Thank you. I miss singing for you at night. You are the big sister, so I want you to be brave and do what your Mama -- says." Then Daddy's face turns white, and he vomits blood. I call Mama, and she rushes us out of the room. Everyone's crying, and Jack and I just sit on the stairs praying and staying very quiet. I hold Jack's hand tight and watch Louis so he doesn't get his nice clothes dirty.

Uncle John is coming after he has finished milking. He parks his buggy next to our porch steps. He walks past Mama and goes to the bedroom to see Daddy, but he only stays only a few minutes.

Mama wraps us up in blankets for the buggy ride. Aunt Maggie greets us at the door and Orella and Halforson come running from a back room when we get there. It's getting late, so we eat supper, and Aunt Maggie carries Louis to a cradle that she brought down from the attic. With Louis tucked in, she goes to the parlor to make up a bed for Jack and me.

Jack's eyes are as big as saucers, "What's that?"

She explained, "Why, it's a davenport. See how it opens up to make a bed?"

Jack jumps onto the bed, "I've never seen a davenport before!" We change into our night shirts and hunker down under a blanket and feather ticking. Some pin feathers float in the air and tickle our noses. We laugh for the first time in a while, and soon we are fast asleep.

The next morning, we wake up at the sound of Pasquale the rooster crowing at the morning sun. Jack and I race to the privy. He wins, but he lets me go first. When we get back to the kitchen, Baby Louis is sitting in a highchair, smiling and happy with a milk mustache and porridge all over his face and in his hair.

Uncle John pulls up a chair, "Come, children, let's eat! Orella, it's your turn to say grace."

After breakfast, Uncle John takes us outside to feed the chickens. We laugh when Jack backs away, scared when the chickens run up to him for more feed. Uncle John hands the basket to me, "Here, Dora, I'll show you how to find and gather the eggs."

He shows me a brown egg tucked under some hay in a nest where the chickens roost to lay their eggs. He gives me the egg. It's still warm so I hold it in my hand for a minute before gently placing it in the basket.

That evening after supper, Aunt Maggie pulls me onto her lap. I start to cry. "Aunt Maggie, will God hear me if I ask Him to make my daddy well again?"

"Of course, He will if He thinks it best. But if He thinks your daddy will be better up in heaven with him, He will take your daddy into His arms just like your daddy hugs you. You know your daddy is very sick."

I guess I know daddy might die, but I don't want to think about it. I scoot down to the floor and Aunt Maggie crosses the room to pick up Baby Louis. She rocks him to sleep, humming a lullaby.

A winter storm is approaching, and the wind is howling outside. I look out a window to see the snow, so fresh and white, kicked up in whirls in the moonlight. Orella and Halforson have already gone to bed. I lie next to Jack on the floor in front of the fireplace. The warmth and crackling of the fire make us sleepy, but I don't want to go to bed because I don't know how to pray tonight. I'm warm and comfortable and too tired to get up. Later, I half wake up when Uncle John carries us to the davenport.

"Dora, Dora, wake up!" I try to hide my head under my pillow, but Aunt Maggie is shaking me. "Wake up, Dora, you and Jack need to get up and get dressed. Doc Donovan is here to take you home!"

I'm confused because it's still dark outside, but I nudge Jack awake. Still in our nightshirts, Aunt Maggie bundles us up in blankets for the buggy ride home. Uncle John and Doc Donovan carry Jack and me to the buggy, and Aunt Maggie lifts Louis to me, so I can hold him on my lap. Doc Donovan pulls our blankets tight to make sure we will stay warm.

"Your mother needs you, Dora. You will have to be brave. Help your brothers, promise! There's a good girl." She looks worried.

Other than Baby Louis crying, no one talks on the way home. Doc does not explain, and we don't ask any questions. The January wind cuts through our blankets, so the three of us huddle together. The sky is dark and there are only whispering clouds across the moon, casting black shadows under the trees and on the road ahead. It's kind of scary but all we care about is keeping warm.

We pull up in front of our porch and Doc Donovan takes Louis while Jack and I jump down from the buggy and run into the kitchen. The house is warm from the cookstove. Everyone is in the parlor and all of the lamps are lit. Mama is sitting in her rocking chair, crying. Aunt Dora holds her arms out to us, then she takes our hands, leading us to the bedroom to see Daddy. I make Jack tiptoe into the room, thinking he must be resting or fast asleep. It's so quiet and peaceful. He's not coughing anymore.

I put my hand on Daddy's cheek and jump back. "He is so cold. Aunt Dora, bring some more blankets. He needs to be warm."

When I see her sad face, I start to cry, realizing there's probably nothing I can do to make Daddy warm. Mama is standing next to us. She takes us back to the parlor where she returns to her rocking chair, hugging us onto her lap, and she holds us close, wiping her tears with the hem of her dress. Suddenly, I have a feeling that something really bad has happened. I feel sick and tears bubble up from inside me.

Mama tries to comfort me while her tears fall like big raindrops on the top of my head. "Dora, please don't cry. Your daddy was sad whenever his baby angels cried."

I try to push myself away from her, but she is hugging me too tight. I finally break away and stand up, remembering Daddy said I should be brave and take care of Mama and my brothers. "Mama, what is wrong with Daddy?"

"God has taken your daddy to live with him in heaven. He will never be sick again."

"Will he be warm in heaven?"

"Yes, he will feel the warmth of the sun all the time! But the four of us will have to find happiness without him. No more daddy singing and dancing with his little angels in angel night clothes." She cries even harder, and Aunt Dora leads us all gently to our bedroom

Louis is already asleep in his cradle. We all crawl onto our bed, Mama, Aunt Dora, Jack and me. I hear the whistle of a faraway train. I quickly fall asleep.

January 13, 1902. Daybreak

An ear-piercing scream wakes me up, and I jump down to the floor and run to the kitchen. Two strange men are carrying my daddy out the door. Mama screams and screams, and she sinks to her knees with gasping wails.

I run to her. "Don't cry, Mama. Please, don't cry!" I pat her face, trying to comfort her. She takes my hand from her face and holds it to her breast. She looks up at me, but she is still sobbing and shaking. The men have Daddy in the back of a wagon parked in front of our porch. When I look up again, they are gone. I am alone with my mama, crying on the floor.

During the next two days, the clock on the mantle ticks loudly, but it seems like everything is happening in slow motion. People around me are always cooking and cleaning and I help when they tell me what to do, but sometimes they have to shake my shoulder to get my attention – it's like a dream.

I keep thinking that this feeling can't last forever. Daddy is laid out in a pine box in the parlor, and our neighbors and the women from the Ladies Aid Society in their hats with flowers who come in and out, bringing more food and saying nice things to Mama.

It seems like we are never alone, and I wonder when everyone will just go home. Maybe this is what Mama needs but I want things to go back to normal. Why is Daddy sleeping in the parlor? Will he wake up? I know he can't be dead, and he'll get up soon then everyone will go home. I feel so sad and wonder if we will ever be happy again.

Finally, we all go in a parade of black-draped buggies to the hill behind Uncle John's barn. It's cold and windy, so Mama holds us close to shelter us from the wind. Everyone is praying together at the gravesite. The pallbearers, Doc Donovan and my uncles, grab ropes to lower the pine box into a grave that is under a dead tree. Why would they put him there?

I can't believe they're putting a box with my daddy inside into a hole in the ground! Seeing the box disappear into the dark hole, I scream! Uncle Jasen picks me up and he carries me to Uncle John and Aunt Maggie's house where everything is already set for the funeral dinner. I try not to cry too hard.

People start to come in, a few at a time, at first talking in whispers. They stand in the kitchen near the warmth of the cookstove, and a few come into the parlor and hover near the fireplace. After everyone arrives, the rooms become silent except for the sounds of the crackling fire and Mama and me sobbing. Uncle John breaks the silence with "Let us pray...."

I wonder why Uncle John is still talking to God. Even if He answers, what could he have to say to someone who took our Daddy away from us? I look around the room at all the people I don't know who are holding plates of food in their hands. He should just let them eat. Someone gives me a cookie, and Uncle John just keeps praying. Jack is running around, so I grab him by his collar and take him to Mama. I let go just as Uncle John says, "Amen."

The Bucket!

March 30, 1902

Mama cries every night in her room, but during the day, we develop a routine and things feel a little more normal. We're crying less and when Uncle Jasen comes by and he makes jokes, I decide it's okay to try to be happy.

Spring arrives with a promise of a new beginning. The crisp air smells like clean sheets fresh off the clothesline, and the pink crab apple trees that line the other side of the road smell so sweet. Jack sees the first robin, and the blue and yellow crocus look like tiny fairy princesses dancing at the base of the porch.

It's Saturday, the day before Easter, but it seems like such a short time since Daddy died, maybe because Spring is early this year. It's still cool in the morning, so Mama fires up the cookstove for heat. She makes biscuits for breakfast, the first time since she started cooking at the hotel.

"Dora, Louis is running around and getting in my way. Why don't you and Jack take him outside to play." I take Louis by the hand and Jack runs ahead to get the ball out of the shed. Jack tries to get Louis' attention by bouncing the ball, but Louis heads straight for our flower bed.

By the time I catch up with him, he's holding a blue crocus in one hand and he's reaching for a yellow daffodil, "No, Louis, we don't pick Mama's flowers! Come with me, let's play ball with Jack."

After a while, Mama calls us to the porch, with a plate of sandwiches. We eat, sitting on the porch steps. The sun is shining, and the warm bread and cheese makes me feel good all over. Mama goes back to the kitchen, and she brings a bucket of boiling water so we can pluck a chicken for Easter dinner, setting it on the top step of the porch.

She goes back into the house to get another pail for the feathers and Jack jumps up, kicking the pail. I let out a scream as the boiling water spills onto my lap.

Mama comes running out the kitchen door, "Dora, what happened? Oh, Lord Jesus!" She picks me up and she carries me to the kitchen table. It feels like my legs are on fire and I want to throw up. Mama pulls me upright to a sitting position and a white light explodes in my head before I lose consciousness.

"Jack, run fast, get Uncle Jasen!"

When I wake up, Mama is taking off my dress and I hear Uncle Jasen's boots hit the porch floor running. I'm awake but I'm trying to be quiet. Uncle Jasen takes one look at me and goes to the pump for some cold water.

He pours handfuls of water on my legs. "Lord, help us! What happened?"

Mama just yells at him. "Jasen, fill the washtub with cool water and help me to lift her into the bath, then go get Doc Donovan!"

Jack is hysterical. "Mama, I'm sorry I forgot it was there!" In the excitement, everyone forgot that Louis is alone outside but just when I am trying to tell Mama, he comes into the kitchen and he grabs Mama's leg.

By the time Doc Donovan arrives, everyone is crying. The cold water has little effect on the pain. When I look down, I see blisters the size of my hand puffing up on my legs.

Mama tells him, "Doctor, there was an accident with a bucket of boiling water, and Dora has been scalded!"

"My goodness, Ella, these are bad burns. Let's pat her dry and get something on her legs to block out the air. That will help to ease the pain. It will be important to keep the burns sealed and moist. Do you have a new can of lard? Also, we will need some clean white cloths to wrap around her legs. We can use clean diapers left over now that Louis is potty trained?"

Mama gets the lard tin from the cupboard while Jack digs through dresser doors to find some soft diapers. Doc Donovan scoops handfuls of lard and he is carefully spreading it on my legs. I scream when he touches me. Mama's afraid to touch me, but Doc Donovan urges her on, "Ella, if you wrap her legs, it will block out the air. The pain will not go away, but it will not be as bad." She carefully wraps my legs with the soft white cloths. After drying the rest of my body, Mama dresses me in a clean white nightshirt and Doc Donovan carries me to my bed.

I feel a little better when I stay still. I can hear Doc Donovan talking to Mama in the kitchen, "Now, Ella, you must be careful and try not to break the blisters or she can get an infection. I'll come by every day to help you, until she is better."

"Oh, Doctor, I feel so guilty. I should not have set the pail outside until I was ready to use it."

"There, there Ella, accidents happen. She will be all right in a couple weeks. You just need to forgive yourself. You'll see, you will be able to put this behind you when she is better and playing outside again with her brothers. Just make sure you do not break her blisters."

"Will she be scarred?"

"We don't know, yet. I know you probably heard me the first time, but you can't hurry the healing process with burns -- let the blisters break on their own. Oh, and it will be best if she sleeps alone, so you should bring Jack and Louis to your bed to sleep with you."

I hear Aunt Maggie and Uncle John come just as Doc Donovan is leaving. I know I'm supposed to go to sleep. I start to cry again.

Aunt Maggie hears me and comes to sit on the bed. "Oh, you look so tiny, my sweetheart!" I start to wail even louder. I can't help it. I hear Jack start to cry again, too.

"It really hurts, Aunt Maggie!"

"I know it does, Darling. Are you cold? You are shaking!" I nod yes, so Mama brings a quilt from the daybed in the parlor so she and Aunt Maggie can spread it loosely over my body. I pull the quilt up to my chin, trying to get warm.

Aunt Maggie asks, "Dora, is there anything I can do for you?"

Suddenly I feel tired. "No. I just want to sleep so when I wake up the burns will be gone and I won't hurt anymore. Tell Jack not to cry. I'll be better tomorrow."

As I drift in and out of sleep, I can hear them all talking in the kitchen. Uncle John says, "Dora can't take care of Jack and Louis anymore. She needs you now."

Maybe she will stay home like before, but she told us she needs to go to work. Maybe she will leave me here alone. I still feel cold.

Then Uncle Jasen says, "We'll help." I hope they bring over some fresh milk and some of the blue speckled eggs from their chickens.

Everyone seems to be crying again, but I'm finally starting to feel better.

Then John says, "Let's pray, and in the silence, I finally fall asleep for real.

I don't know how many days have passed and all that has happened because I sleep as much as I can. Every morning, Mama brings tea and biscuits to me in bed, but I can't eat, knowing what will happen next.

Doc Donovan comes every morning so he and Mama can bathe my legs. They try to be gentle when removing the loose skin from the blisters, but it really hurts, even the slightest touch and even when they apply a cooling salve and wrap my legs in clean bandages. I try not to scream because Jack cries and covers his ears to block out the sound of my crying. Eventually, I don't not cry as much, and Jack and Louis come to my room for little visits. Sometimes they make funny faces, trying to make me laugh. One day they do a funny dance, and I start to laugh, and it doesn't hurt so much when I move. I just want to get out of this bed and put on a play dress so I can go outside.

I decide to ask Doc Donovan if I can get up and go outside.

He looks happy and takes my hand. "I've been waiting for you to ask. Of course, just take it easy. Maybe you should start by just sitting on a quilt. You can play with your doll, and I hear you like to look for four-leafed clovers."

After a couple weeks, I start to help again, and Mama returns to work at the hotel, leaving me to take care of Jack and Louis. Still, she comes home earlier, she says until I'm completely healed. We spend most of our time on a quilt under the red oak tree, playing house with Maggie Ann and Baby Louis.

At first, Jack is on his best behavior, but he has discovered a newfound freedom. He likes to wade at the edge of the river, and he plays stick ball with the Flannery boys next door. Mrs. Larsen, from across the street, stops by every day for a few minutes and sometimes she brings a plate of cookies, so he behaves when she's here. But sometimes he wanders a little too far and he takes too long to get back. I try to get him to understand why we shouldn't worry Mama.

One day, I look up and Mama is coming down the bridge towards home. She looks tired, and she's all hunched over. She isn't pretty anymore. I wonder when she will start to feel better. I can move around more, but I get tired.

Jack is sitting on the porch steps with three boys who live across town. They are older and they have dirty faces. "Mama, my friends want me to go with them to play marbles. They say there's a good place to play marbles behind the train depot." The boys try to force smiles and look nice, but their rotting teeth are just plain ugly.

Mama looks worried. "No, Jack, I don't know these boys and, besides, they're too old for you to be playing with. You boys go on home now, it's supper time." Jack looks at the boys, and they just laugh and run off. They wait by the tree and later, when she goes into the kitchen, he follows them down the road.

Mama calls out from the house, "Dora, Jack, sandwiches are almost ready so come on in."

"Mama, Jack isn't here. He left with those boys." Jack has never left the yard without one of us before.

Mama sets Louis on the floor, "Dora, you watch, Louis." I hug the baby when I see her break a long thin branch off the burning bush at the corner of the house. Mama takes off towards the bridge with her switch in hand. Before long, I can hear Jack yowling as they come across the bridge.

Mama is switching Jack's legs all the way to the porch, then she pulls him by his ear into the kitchen. "Now, go to your room and stay there!"

Jack is wailing, so Louis and I start crying, and pretty soon Mama drops onto a kitchen chair, her face in her hands, crying.

"Mama, will you let Jack have supper?"

"Of course, Dora, but he'll have to stay in his room and eat from the chair."

I know it's going to be a long night. Mama is very quiet, and so are we.

The next morning, we all have breakfast before Mama leaves for work. I make a special effort to clean up, so I don't notice that Jack must have left after Mama was gone. I can't go look for him until Louis is down for a nap, but I suspect he's playing marbles with the boys behind the train depot.

I stomp my foot, "Jack, c'mon, we're going home."

"No, you're not my boss!' The older boys smirk and pretend they're ignoring me.

"C'mon, Louis is home alone, so you have to come home now!" I grab Jack by his arm and drag him through town towards home. Once inside the kitchen, I push him into our bedroom and slam the door shut. Jack tries to open the door, so I push the bolt lock, locking him in. I can hear him crying but after a while he's quiet, so I guess he cried himself to sleep.

Mid-afternoon, Jack wakes up. "Dora, let me out!"

"No, Jack! Mama told you that if you ever go away without permission again, she would lock you in your room until you say you're sorry."

Jack is still in his room when Mama comes home from work. "Mama, Jack went with those boys to the train station, so I locked him in his room, and he still hasn't said he's sorry."

"You are a good big sister. It's OK." Mama grins and hugs me.

Mama unlocks the door, "Jack, get out here! Do you want me to get a switch again?'

"No."

"Then you apologize to your sister, and don't you ever do that again or I'll throw your marbles in the river. Those boys are too old for you and it's not safe to play near the railroad tracks."

Maybe because he knows she will throw his marbles in the river, Jack hasn't run with those boys again. And they haven't come around anyway. He plays with the Flannery boys and sometimes he and Louis play with the blue ball.

Mama works every day, and I make beds and clean house while Jack and Louis play outside, except on rainy days when they play on the porch. Mrs. Larsen still stops by every afternoon and sometimes she helps me to change beds and we dust and clean the parlor. Mama starts coming home later each day then eventually, only after dark. But I am feeling better, so I don't mind. I think Daddy would be proud of me. Sometimes I hum the songs we used to sing together when I'm making lunch.

Little Big Sister

One day I'm in our bedroom, and Doc Donovan stops by to talk to Mama. I go to the door to listen.

The doctor sounds serious. He says, "Dora is still a little girl, and she is too young to have full responsibility to take care of Jack and Louis."

I think that's silly. I'm being a good big sister, but Mama says we can move to an upstairs apartment, at the back of Doc Donovan's house, that is being cleaned up and freshly painted, so I start to get excited. I really don't want to move, but it sounds nice, and he says his wife can help us. Besides, Doc Donovan is a nice man.

Mama agrees. The apartment will be ready next week. And tomorrow we all get to go visit with Aunt Maggie and Uncle John on the farm! We haven't seen them for a while. Mama sounds happy, too.

There's lots of things to do on Aunt Maggie's farm. We can play with Orella and Halforson, and I love the farm animals.

This is my third visit, so Uncle John has given me some chores to do, gathering eggs and spreading dry feed for the chickens. I love the animal babies, and I have named each of the little baby ducks. They follow me around like I'm their momma!

Uncle John brings Jack to the barn to see the horses. Jack squeals with excitement, and he scares the horses. Uncle John shows him how to approach the horses slowly and quietly, cautioning him not to stand behind a horse lest he gets kicked. By Wednesday, the horses recognize Jack, and they greet him at the fence, knowing he will pet them and give them apples.

Every day after breakfast, Aunt Maggie throws a quilt over the clothesline, so Orella and I can play with our dolls while we watch Louis.

Aunt Maggie peeks her head into our playhouse, "Girls, would you like to help me tomorrow to get ready for a family picnic? Everyone's coming! Dora, your mama is coming with Uncle Jasen, plus all of the other aunts, uncles, and cousins."

I've been worrying that people might forget Jack's birthday. "I'll help! Is it going to be a birthday party for Jack?"

Aunt Maggie laughs, "You remembered! Yes, we decided to make it a family celebration. After the picnic you'll go home with your mama and the next day. Y'all will be movin' to your new home over Doc Donovan's."

I wish we could always stay on the farm. "Aunt Maggie, why can't we just live here with you?"

"You need to be with your mother, Dora. She misses you."

I hope the new place is as nice as Doc Donovan's. But I have to tell my ducklings that I will be leaving, and they should be good.

Pasquale is crowing at the rising sun. I jump up from the davenport and hurry through the kitchen in my bare feet, past Aunt Maggie and out the door to the privy in back. When I return to the kitchen, everyone's already eating, chowing down on fried potatoes and eggs.

"Aunt Maggie, what are we going to make for the picnic?"

"Well, after you and Orella get dressed, we need to go to the garden to get some snap beans. Then we will all put on aprons, and I'll show you how to roll out biscuits so they will be fluffy and tender. Jack, we want to make some salads. Will you go to the garden for three cucumbers and four tomatoes? Be careful when you pick them, so you don't break the vines and pick the ripe ones like I showed you!"

Jack and I run to pull our satchels from the closet and to get dressed. Jack and Louis go outside to the garden where Uncle John is picking beans, "Jack, make it four big cucumbers for good measure. Jack, you show Louis how to pick a tomato. Remember, pull it gently off the vine so it doesn't break. Now, you try."

Louis pulls a big red tomato, and he holds it high for everyone to see. "That's it! Good boy!"

Aunt Maggie and I cross the lawn to the garden. Jack puts the cucumbers and tomatoes in my basket, and Uncle John dumps his sack of beans onto Aunt Maggie's outstretched apron.

After returning to the kitchen, Orella and I watch as Aunt Maggie ices a cake she baked the day before for Jack's birthday. We dip our fingers into the icing a couple times, leaving just enough to finish icing the cake.

We snap the green beans and before long, the kitchen is filled with the aroma of a big pot of beans simmering with potatoes and side meat. The cookstove is hot and we bring Aunt Maggie a towel from the laundry. "Aunt Maggie, you are really sweating!"

"Dora, remember this, horses sweat, ladies sparkle! While the cookstove is hot and I have your help, why don't we make some cornbread to go with the beans. It will only take a few minutes. Then the cornbread can bake while we roll out the biscuits."

I go to the icebox for eggs. Aunt Maggie cracks them into a bowl, and she adds the cornmeal and a couple hands of flour with some baking powder and salt. She puts the bread in the oven, and she calls out the kitchen door, "John, where are the boys? Are you and Jack looking after Louis?"

"Yes, last I looked he was sleeping on the blanket in the playhouse."

Aunt Maggie mixes the dough for the biscuits, folding the dough over and over. "Orella, use this lard to grease the baking sheets. Dora, you are going to need an apron. Here, I have one that is just your size." She scatters flour on the table, and she hands me the rolling pin. I stand on a chair so I can reach the table and Aunt Maggie shows me how to hold flour in my hand to dust the rolling pin, and to roll the dough out evenly, about one inch thick. Then she hands drinking glasses to Orella and me, so we can cut the biscuits that we place three fingers apart on the baking sheets. Just in time, 'cuz the cornbread is done, and we pop the biscuits into the oven.

Orella and Aunt Maggie laugh. I have flour all over, on my dress, on my face and some in my hair. Aunt Maggie pours some water into a basin so I can clean up at the kitchen sink. I start to go outside but Aunt Maggie stops me, "Where are you going?"

"I'm going outside to see if Louis is awake and to play with Jack."

"Well, check on Louis, but come back in. We're not done. A cook always cleans up after cooking and baking."

Aunt Maggie is hot and sweat is dripping off her forehead, but she has a happy smile on her face. It's really fun to work with her and Uncle John at the farm. Everywhere I look, I can see the love that Uncle John has for farming, the cleanliness of the barn, the garden and neat rows of corn, and the plow sitting next to the horse corral. I get a warm feeling when I go to their house. I hope we never have to leave.

The Kelly's start arriving soon after the noon meal, one family at a time. Jack is so excited! It's his birthday and we have boy cousins that play marbles. At first, we play Catch Me If You Can! Then I look up to see Uncle Jasen and Mama crossing the lawn. Jack, Louis and I run to her, and she kneels down to pull us close. Uncle John crosses the lawn, "Welcome, Ella, the children have missed you." Mama smiles, but I'm sure she knows that we have fun living on the farm, if only for a week.

Uncle John has set up long tables with benches on the lawn covered with tablecloths that Aunt Maggie gave him, all with different prints, so it looks like a big patchwork quilt. The women have gone out of their way to show off their favorite recipes. There are baskets of fried chicken, potato salad, casseroles, cookies and pies.

At four o'clock, Uncle John rings the dinner bell and everyone gathers around the tables. Uncle John addresses the crowd, "Let us pray."

> *"Father, thank you for allowing us to share this meal together,*
> *And thank you for bringing Jack into our lives and making*
> *this birthday so joyful.*
> *Bless this good food and thank you for all of your blessings.*
> *Amen"*

"Amen!"

After the meal, everybody sings Happy Birthday to Jack, and we eat cake and all the wonderful desserts. Everyone brought presents for Jack – carved horses, trucks, and of course, more marbles. The boys play marbles on the porch while we clean up and too soon, everyone heads home.

Mama comes into the house with Aunt Maggie to gather our belongings while Uncle Jasen shoos us towards his buggy. I'm trying to hold back my tears. When I look back, I'm blinded by the setting sun, a burst of gold melting into the horizon. It feels scary, like I want to hold on to something, but there's nothing to hold onto. We fall asleep holding each other as the buggy sways towards our new home.

Uncle John and Halforson came with their wagon to move everything from the house to the apartment. I'm sad 'cuz we're leaving the house Daddy built, but Doc Donovan's house is the nicest building in downtown Ullin. The two-story house is painted sunshine yellow with green shutters. There's a green door and a "Doctor" sign hanging on the wood awning that covers the front porch. There's a tinted window on each side of the door, each with a lace tie-back curtain. Doc's office is in the front and he and his family live behind. The stair to our apartment is also at the back of the house.

Uncle John turns the key, and we run into the new apartment, which is sunny, bright and clean. All three rooms have been freshly painted white but still, it's really hot. I ask for the bedroom that has a window with a bench, where I can read and play with Maggie Ann. There are cots in the gathering room for Jack and Louis.

Doc's house has a high fence bordering the backyard where we can play while Mama's working. The only thing we quietly gripe about is that the privy is out back so we will have to go down a flight of stairs to go outside.

Uncle John and Halforson start moving the furniture and heavier boxes up the stairs, then some men across the road look our way. Soon, a few new neighbors help with the furniture. Mama, Jack and I carry lighter items including pillows, blankets, and satchels and we put Louis in charge of getting our toys upstairs, except I make sure Maggie Ann is settled in on our reading bench so she feels at home.

Everything's unloaded when Mrs. Donovan brings sandwiches and lemonade. "Welcome, everyone! I bet you're hungry. I'll bring a plate of cookies for later, too."

Uncle John and Halforson are dripping with sweat. Uncle John takes the pitcher of lemonade, "Thank you, lady, this is real nice. We needed this, it's hot up here!"

Mama walks her to the door, "Thank you, Mrs. Donovan..."

"Oh, just call me Beth. Let me know if you need anything."

Under Mama's direction, Uncle John and Halforson put the furniture in place. I'm happy 'cuz I got the bedroom I want, and our bed just fits into the corner. But when our movers leave, we suddenly feel sad, because it's different and so hot, and it doesn't feel like home at all. Suffocating silence fills the room and I can hardly breathe. I'm tired of waiting all the time for life to get better. I want to just go home, but I decide it's probably best to just be quiet. Mama sits down on a kitchen chair, and she starts to cry.

"Well, look at us," she finally says, when everyone starts sniffling. "Dora, Jack, let's put things where they belong so we can make this our new home."

The next day, Mama goes to work. Everything is in its place, even the pictures on the walls, including Daddy's golden horseshoes. We stay alone all day except when Mrs. Donovan stops in for a few minutes to check on us, so I make lunch and watch Jack and Louis. We like her. She always brings cookies or a snack, and her visits cheer me up.

The next Saturday, Mrs. Donovan comes to the backyard where we are playing, "Would you like to come into the house for a little party? It will just be with me and the girls. They made cookies and we thought it would be fun to have a tea party.:"

I'm thrilled and start to say yes but then I look down at Jack and Louis and my dirty play dress. "That will be so much fun, but we have to clean up. I want to put on a clean dress if we are coming to a party. Can I bring Maggie Ann?"

"Is Maggie Ann your doll? Of course, she can come. In fact, I think we still have a little chair for dolls, so she will have a special place to sit! And we'll wait to start until you're ready. Just come downstairs when you're dressed."

I take the boys upstairs and I put on my prettiest play dress, pink with tiny blue flowers and a ruffle around the bottom. Jack and Louis are waiting for me in the kitchen. "Jack, your face is still dirty!"

"No, it isn't! I washed my face."

"Yeah, I see, you washed your face with one finger!" There's a clean white circle around his face but everything else is smudged with dirt. I giggle. "You have to wash all of your face, like this!"

I wash Jack's face and we go downstairs where the Donovan girls, Mary and Margaret, have set out a tea party. There's plenty of sugar and freshly baked shortbread cookies. I pretend to be a grownup lady, drinking tea from pretty China teacups. Jack and Louis eat a handful of cookies then they squirm down from their chairs to go outside to play.

Margaret opens up the piano, and Mary and I sit on a bench where we can watch the boys out the window. Margaret plays a song on the piano and

Mary sings. I soon join in. This is so much fun! The last song is the most fun,

> *Sally go round the moon*
> *Sally go round the stars*
> *Sally go round the moon*
> *On a Sunday afternoon, whoops!*

We sing that song over and over again, ending it with a big Whoops and falling onto the floor with laughter. Suddenly, I stop laughing, knowing I should have been looking after Jack and Louis. I run to the backyard and find Louis playing by his self with his blue ball. "Louis, where's Jack?" Louis points towards the road that leads to the train depot.

I go back inside, and thank the girls for the party, and I ask Mary to look after Louis while I go to bring Jack home from the train depot. I can't wait for Mama. I find Jack at the same spot behind the depot with the boys. Drats! I thought he was done with playing marbles.

"Jack, c'mon, you have to come home. Mama told you not to play with these boys."

"No! Jake and Bobby told me that you cannot tell me what to do. You're not my boss!"

I stomp my foot and grab his arm and drag him down the street to the foot of our stairs. He's crying but he stomps up the stairs to our apartment. I push him into my bedroom, and I lock the door.

I keep busy dusting the parlor, waiting for Mama to come home. Jack finally stops kicking the door and whining, then he is quiet.

I hear Mama coming up the stairs. I tell her what Jack did and she goes downstairs to the yard to cut a switch from the willow tree. She unlocks the door and switches Jack's legs, then she locks him in my room with no supper.

"There, he will stay there 'til morning. Dora, you can sleep with me in my bed tonight."

Mama lets Jack out of the bedroom the next morning for breakfast. I wish I had not told on him, because his legs are still red. I want to cry but I don't say anything because I know Jack has to learn to obey.

After that, Jack behaves again. But Mama has been working longer hours, coming home after dark. She told us that she cooks for banquets at the hotel and sometimes when she comes home, she tells us stories about the people, describing the women in their fancy dresses and hats, and the men who pull out their chairs for them, and tuck napkins in their silk vests. I wonder if I'll ever see such things!

I know it's September because my cousins have gone back to school, but I can't go to school because Mama says I have to mind Jack and Louis. I start to develop a routine, playing with them outside and keeping up with chores around the house. I like being in charge, but I miss school.

It's getting cool now, and colder at night. Mama says I must have caught a cold, but my cough is getting worse. I sound like a dog barking, and it hurts when I cough. I'm cutting up the cabbage for supper one evening, and Doc Donovan hears me coughing so he comes upstairs. He makes me a cup of hot tea sweetened with honey, and he sits at the kitchen table, waiting for Mama to come home.

Mama is cheerful. She had a good day. "Well, Doc, what brings you here?"

"Ella, look at Dora! She has a fever, and I'm certain it's whooping cough. I'll go downstairs to get an elixir, but you are going to have to stay home for a few days to take care of your children."

Mama tries, but she has to go back to work right away. Days turn into weeks. I think I'm getting better, but I can't get my strength back, and then the cough comes back. When I'm finally better, Mama gets a head cold. She's still working, but she's always blowing her nose, using all of her hankies and sometimes the nearest towel. She needs to go to work so we can buy food, and the hotel wants her to cook for a big convention, so she kisses me on the head and says, "Be good," and she goes to work again.

I know she will be too tired to wash hankies when she comes home, so I heat enough water to fill a basin and I wash her hankies in hot water and rinse them in cold water. I find her basket of clothes pins, but I can't reach the clothesline, so I dig through kitchen drawers to find a ball of string to stretch between two kitchen chairs. The string is too fine, so clothes pins won't hold the hankies. I try again, but the clothes pins and hankies fall to the floor.

Mama has a penny jar on the kitchen counter, so I take a penny and put on my coat to walk across the road to the notion store owned by the Larsens.

Mr. Larsen is at the counter when I walk in, and Mrs. Larsen is sitting in a rocking chair at the back of the store.

Mrs. Larsen puts her knitting down and she gets up to greet me, "Well, Dora, what brings you here? I haven't seen you since you moved."

"I have a penny, and I want to buy some pins."

"Of course, but why do you need pins?"

"I've washed my mama's hankies. She has a bad cold, and she is so tired when she comes home from work, so I washed them, but I can't reach the clothesline. If I have some pins, I can pin them to a string to dry."

Mrs. Larsen takes my hand, and she leads me to her chair. There's a tear on her cheek and she pulls me onto her lap. "You are such a wonderful little girl and a real little mother to your brothers." We rock in her chair for a few minutes, but I tell her that I need to get home to Jack and Louis. Mr. Larsen gives me a box of pins and some hard candy, and I run home with the pins, and the penny still in my hand.

When Mama comes home, she really looks sick. "Dora, go downstairs and ask Doc Donovan to come up for a minute. The Donovans come to our apartment and Doc takes Mama to the hospital while Mrs. Donovan stays with us for the next three days.

Then a friend of Mama's from church comes to take Jack, Louis, and me to stay with her in her apartment. I am afraid that Mama might die just like Daddy did, but I don't tell anyone how scared I am. I cry myself to sleep every night until they tell us Mama is coming home the next day.

Mama needs to get her strength back before she can go back to work. We all go to church Sunday morning, and people ask how she is feeling. She tells everyone that she will be going back to work soon.

After church, we're eating a dinner of chicken and noodles with mashed potatoes, when there's a knock on our door. Mama opens the door and there's Doc Donovan and Mrs. Larsen.

"Well, Doc, Mrs. Larsen. This is a nice surprise. Please sit down. We're about done eating. Would you like some tea?"

Doc Donovan explains he is only here to express his concern. "Ella, tell the children to go play in their room."

We go to our room, but I stand by the door, wondering what he wants. I've never heard Doc Donovan be so mean. He says, "Ella, people are concerned about you leaving the children alone. We understand your need to work so you can house and feed your family, but this simply is not working. Mrs. Larsen and I have talked to your brothers-in-law, and they can't give any more. It seems you have run out of options. You need to give the children up so they can be taken in and cared for by other families."

Mrs. Larsen adds, "Dora is taking care of Jack and Louis, cleaning the house and making beds. Most important, she is not going to school. Also, after what happened, why is she boiling water when you're not here? She also told me she had to leave Louis alone more than once. It's very dangerous. What if there was a fire?"

I want my mother to say everything will be all right. That they're wrong. But she just looks down, and says, "I have to work, but Beth is always here."

"Ella, my wife and I have tried to help but we can only look in every now and then. Several people told me that they have seen Jack playing marbles behind the train depot with the town roughnecks. It's a bad situation. You have forced Dora into a role that she is too young to bear."

Mama breaks down with loud sobs, then Mrs. Larsen sees me standing in the doorway. She tries to take me by the hand so she can shut the door of the room, but I pull away and cry out, "I can take of myself and my brothers. We want to be with our Mama!"

Mrs. Larson tries to comfort me, but I hear what she says. "We know you are a good girl, Dora, but you should be in school like other little girls, and looking after two brothers is a big job, too big for a little girl like you."

Mama looks up and catches my eye. "Dora, she's right. Some things have to change."

I run into bed, and cuddle with baby Louis. I don't understand, but I know this is very bad news. As Mrs. Larson closes the door, I hear Mama say, "Will you make the arrangements, Doctor?"

Location of Ullin Village

Illinois Central Train Depot

Train Depot Building; Ullin City Hall and Library, 2020

PART TWO

The Orphan Train

"You'll never find rainbows if you're looking down."

Charlie Chaplin

Englewood

November 12, 1902

A trainman announces, "All aboard, all aboard," and Illinois Central Train No 20 departs St. Louis for the eight-hour trip to Chicago. I cry most of the way and the conductor tries to console me. "Hello there, little girl. What's your name?"

"Dora Belle Kelly."

"Well, Dora Belle Kelly, you are privileged to ride in a brand-new rail car. It's made of steel and look, there are electric lights!"

This is the first time I've seen electric lights. They are bright and the light dances on the white walls of the car. It would be exciting if I wasn't so lonely and dirty and sad.

The bench is hard and uncomfortable but soon the rocking of the train makes me sleepy, and I want to lie down. I try, but the bench is narrow, and it runs in the same direction as the wall of the car, so the rocking motion throws me onto the floor. Like some of the others, I finally crawl into a ball on the floor and drift off to sleep, dreaming about bouncing the blue ball with Jack and Louis in the yard at our cabin.

I wake up to the heat of the setting sun on my face. I climb onto the bench to look out the window. There's a man herding black and white cows towards a red barn next to a pretty white farmhouse. The sun looks like a deflated yellow ball, and the cloudless sky is pink and orange. Is the place where I'm going anything like this farm?

No one's in the mood to laugh or play, but we talk. One boy tells me he boarded a train in New York with other boys, and others came to board the train in St. Louis like I did. They are from places I have not heard of like Kentucky and Indiana. One of the older boys said we're on an Orphan Train, but I don't want them to know that I don't know what an orphan is, so I don't ask.

Several hours later, the door to our car opens and the conductor calls my name. "Dora, we are approaching Chicago. When the train stops, I'll come to get you so gather your belongings. The rest of you, someone will be there to take you to another train, heading west. Don't get lost now! Chicago Central Station next!"

It's dark outside, so all I can see is a dark grey wall of smoke from the locomotive. The engine slows and the smoke clears enough to see the flickering lights of streetlamps on the street above. At first, the only person I can see is a man pushing a baggage cart loaded with trunks and satchels rolling on big metal wheels.

The train rolls to a stop and I notice a young man with a red knitted cap, standing on the platform. The conductor takes me by the hand and walks me over to him. "This is Dora, Jack. Good luck, kid." and he lifts me up onto the train platform.

"Ally – oop! Here we go, Dora. My name is Jack. I'm here to take you to your new home."

I can't believe a man named Jack is here to help me. "Jack, did you say Jack? I have a brother named Jack, but some men took him and Louis away."

I start to cry but the man has a nice, soft voice, "Please don't cry, Dora. I know you must be scared, but you'll see, you are going to live in a nice big house where there are other little girls your age. Look up there! See the new train station? It has a clock tower."

We walk through the warm station to a big reception hall. Out front, horses with carriages are waiting. Jack loads my bag and he lifts me into a carriage. I look out the window of the carriage, trying to figure out where we are. The moon is a silver sliver hanging on the dark sky, and we pass tall buildings that cast dark shadows along our way. Once we leave the center of the city, there are no streetlamps, so the only sources of light are the lanterns on our carriage, and some light from the moon drifting in and out of dark clouds.

We turn off the main street onto a dirt road, and the light from the moon bounces off puddles that splash when we drive through them. I see through the window of one house, and there is a family inside. It looks like the father is telling a story to his children. I start to cry again.

Jack has turned off the road onto a dooryard leading up to an iron gate with a sign that reads Illinois Children's Home and Aid Society. "Stay here, Dora," he says, and he rings the bell at the gate. A man comes to open the gate to a large building. As we approach the front door, I notice a red wagon, some swings, and a sliding board in the yard in the light from a gas lamp.

A lady, with a grey dress and white apron greets us at the door. "Hi Jack. Is this Dora? Dora, welcome to your new home! Have a seat on that pretty pink chair and someone will come in a few minutes to take you to see the head mistress. Don't worry, she's a very nice lady."

Another lady wearing the same clothes comes a few minutes later to take me down long halls with wooden floors, echoing hallways and offices.

The head mistress doesn't say much, and she isn't very kind. "You smell, little girl ! I bet you have lice or fleas!" She says to herself, "Why don't they at least give these children baths? What's your name?"

"Dora."

"How old are you?"

"I'm eight years old, I'll be nine in January."

"My, you are tiny, I would have thought you were only five or six. That's common enough, though. What about school? You should be in the third grade."

"I haven't been going to school, Ma'am. My mama worked so I had to stay home and take care of my brothers. I started first grade..."

"You may call me Miss Patchett. We'll soon take care of you, Dora, and catch you up! I think you will like it here. We have a school, and we'll see if you can start in second grade. But first you'll have a bath, and new clothes, and then you can sleep in a nice clean bed in a room with other girls. We don't tolerate bugs, lice or fleas, so I'll call Mary and she will take you to the bathing room where you will be checked for lice, and she will probably have to disinfect you. Don't cry. It happens to all the girls."

I sniffle but I'm too tired to cry. Good thing! "Also, we have rules here. Your hands, face and hair must be clean and in proper order or you will not be allowed to eat. All meals are in the dining hall, and you cannot bring food to your room. You will be taught the proper care of clothing, and you must make your own bed every morning before coming down for breakfast. You will be polite to the staff, saying Yes Ma'am and No ma'am, and at all times, you will be nice to the other girls and boys that live here. Stop sniffling; you will like it here. This is a nice house in a nice neighborhood with big houses and a church down the street. We will take good care of you. Do you understand?"

Mary comes back – the nice lady was Mary, and Miss Patchett clicks down the hall and disappears. We go down a long hall to a large white room with white walls. She throws all my clothes into a waste bin. She checks me all over, pulling at my hair to make sure I don't have lice.

"No lice, Dora. That's good. Let's get you scrubbed!" She helps me into a warm bath.

I finally speak, "The water feels good. I've never seen such a white bathtub. At home, Mama gives us baths in a wash tub."

Mary smiles but she doesn't talk. She scrubs me all over with a bar of soap rough against my skin, rubbing me until my skin is pink all over. When she's done, she helps me out of the tub, and she wraps a soft towel around me.

Finally, she helps me into a white nightdress, "Have you had anything to eat?"

"No."

"Then we'll stop by the kitchen before you I take you upstairs." She takes me down another long hall to the other end of the house and we turn right into a big kitchen with four cookstoves, and a large worktable. Mary helps me onto a high stool and she gives me some hard biscuits and applesauce. She makes sure I eat everything, then she leads me by the hand up a dark flight of stairs to the top floor with rows of beds, each with a hand sewn quilt. Mary shows me to a bed with a little rag doll with a white dress and matching bonnet, propped up against a pillow.

"This is your bed, Dora, and this is your doll. We'll give you a full set of new clothes – don't worry. In the morning, the girls will show you to the closet, where you will find everything you need. The other girls are downstairs right now for the scripture reading, but they will be up soon to go to bed. You will get up at 5:30 for breakfast at six.

"You must stay on this floor except for suppers, lessons, and prayers. This floor is only for girls. The second floor is only for boys. Boys are not allowed on this floor and girls are not allowed on the second floor. Remember that, Dora. Now climb into bed and wait here. The other girls will be up soon."

Mary leaves me alone and silence creeps across the room. I wonder where Jack and Louis are and what they might be doing. I count thirty beds all the same, with iron frames. There's a stove in the middle of the room for heat and all of the beds look the same, iron beds lined up in two rows like soldiers, with white coverlets and quilts folded on the bottom of each bed. Each bed has a doll dressed in a white pinafore and night cap, propped up on the pillow. I pick up the doll from my bed and hold her in my hand. She does have a nice face, but her dress is plain, and she has ugly brown hair.

"You sure ain't pretty like Maggie Ann, but that's not your fault, so I guess we can be friends. Do you have a name? Maybe Mama or Uncle Jasen will come tomorrow to take me home so they can give you to another little girl. If I decide to stay, I'll think of a name for you tomorrow."

The silence is broken with laughter, which grows louder as the girls and boys climb the stairs. Soon, the room is filled with girls, one giggling so hard she falls on her back onto the bed next to mine. She looks at me, "Hi, I'm Hannah. Who are you?"

Before I can answer, Mary enters the room, clapping her hands to get our attention, "Girls, we have a new friend, and her name is Dora. Make her feel welcome and, Hannah, you can show her the clothes closet in the morning."

Hannah puts on her night dress, and we sit on the edge of our beds, facing one another, whispering until everyone else is sound asleep. "You have pretty curly hair, Dora! Mine is straight and ugly."

"I like your hair; it is shiny and pretty. It's shiny like honey in the moonlight! Hannah and honey, that's funny!" We try to hold back our giggles, not wanting to wake anyone.

"My family lives in Jasper, Indiana but they took me to a man, and we went by carriage to a train in St. Louis. It was smoky but there were lights in the train. How did you get here?"

"I'm from Ullin, Illinois and I came on a train from St. Louis too. One of the boys said it was an Orphan Train. I don't know what that is. "

"Silly, that means our families don't want us. Anyway, that's what Jenny told me"

"I saw my mama crying when I left, so I know she wants me. Some men came into our bedroom while we were sleeping, and they took my brothers and me. They took my brothers away in different carriages. Maybe I can find my brothers here, too.

We yawn because we're tired, but neither one of us want to stop talking. I tell her about Daddy dying, then she tells me that her daddy just went away.

"I had to stay home from school to take care of my little brothers, Jack and Louis. But I didn't mind! One morning I woke up and there were three men in our bedroom. I was so scared! When I started to cry, Jack and Louis woke up. The men just grabbed us, and when we took off, I looked back and Mama was laying on the ground, crying. The man held on to me and he wouldn't let me run back to her. Do you think she knows I'm here?"

Hannah tells her own story, which is even stranger. "One day when I woke up, my sister, Amy, was gone. When I asked where she was, they just said she went away. I cried and cried, but it didn't seem to matter. Then the next day, a woman came to our house and asked me if I would like to go to a candy store. When we left, my mother smiled and waved goodbye, and that's the last I saw her. We went into town where I was put in another carriage, and a man took me to the train in St. Louis. The dirt kicked up by the horses stuck to my face because I was so sweaty. The man was not very nice and after the second day, he really smelled, so I tried to stay away from him as much as I could. But he kept an eye on me until I was on the train."

We lie down in our beds facing one another until we fall asleep talking. I try to stay awake, but the feather pillow is so soft, and it feels so good to be near Hannah, my new best friend.

We wake up in the morning to the ringing of a loud bell. I look over at Hannah and she has pulled her pillow over her head. "C'mon, Hannah, you have to show me where to get my clothes!"

Hannah takes me down the hall to the same white bathroom where I had a bath, and we use the in-door commodes. Then we wash our faces in basins of warm water and go to our room where she shows me two doors that open to a large closet that covers the back wall. One of the thirty drawers has my name on it: Dora Kelly. There's a hairbrush inside the drawer on top of two nightshirts, two pairs of cotton drawers, two pairs of long black socks, a smock, an apron, a play dress and a Sunday dress.

I hold two long tubes of lace in my hand, "What are these for?"

"Those are pantalettes. You wear them on your legs for special occasions."

"Fancy!"

At first, I cry myself to sleep every night but with Hannah nearby to help me, it doesn't take long to get used to the routine of breakfast, school, dinner, playtime, supper and scripture readings before bed. I never stop thinking about Jack and Louis, but I can't tell anyone because one time I asked Miss Patchett if they were here, and she told me never to talk about my past.

Hannah and I share our secrets and sometimes at night we plan ways to get home to our families. "When Uncle Jasen comes to take me home, you can come with me, then we can go to Jasper to see your mama. Then we'll find Amy, Jack and Louis together." It's a good story, but we know it's not going to happen.

The food is always the same, porridge or corn meal mush with tea for breakfast, and soup and sandwiches with a tall glass of milk for dinner and supper. The only dessert is tapioca pudding, which is served every day. I hate it! When I look at the pudding, I gag! To me, it looks like cream with little soap bubbles.

"Hannah, I don't want my pudding. You can have it if you want."

"I don't want it. I hate tapioca pudding!"

A big fat lady with a dirty apron standing in the corner overhears us, "You girls have to eat your pudding and everything that is put in front of you. It's a house rule. Eat everything on your plates!"

In unison, we respond, "Yes Ma'am!

We twirl our spoons in our pudding and take little bites, then we get down from the table, leaving the bowls half full. The next day, we sneak down the tins from the closet, the ones that held our barrettes and ribbons. No one's looking, so we dump the pudding into the tins. We can dispose of the pudding into the commodes after lights out.

Then there's the lines. We have to stand quietly "in formation" before entering the dining hall, school or church. One day, Hannah and I are giggling, and Miss Patchett whacks us with her ruler. We're more careful after that.

They also make us walk in formation to the Methodist church down the street, then back to the home for Sunday dinner. After dinner, we're free to play the rest of the day. I'm starting to like my new doll, so I decide to name her Ella after Mama.

With our dolls, Ella and Leela, Hannah and I become a magic foursome. At bath time, the rule is two girls to a tub, so Hannah and I always team up. We blow the suds from our hands and watch the tiny soap bubbles as they float above our heads until they pop. Sometimes we laugh so hard I can hardly breathe.

We hold hands on the way to formation, we laugh and play together, and when one cries, we both cry. When we go to the dining hall, I always look at the boys to see if I can find Jack and Louis but they're not here. Maybe they are with families, or maybe they went to another orphanage.

Every day at the home is the same. We aren't allowed to talk about the past; we are supposed to only think about today and tomorrow. The seasons are the only way we know time is passing.

It snowed while we were in church and when we return to the home there's Christmas wreaths on the front doors. Everyone's so excited that Christmas is coming, even though I don't think it will be that different. Later that night, I sit on the edge of my bed, hugging Ella, and I start to cry.

Hannah comes to sit next to me, "Dora, why are we crying?"

"I want to be with Jack and Louis for Christmas! What will they be doing Christmas Day? Why aren't they here? Or me, there!"

"I know, Dora, I miss my Mama and Papa, and I wonder where my little sister is. I always remember them in my prayers."

"I miss my family, too. But let's have fun this Christmas, all four of us!"

After supper the next day, we go downstairs for scripture reading, and Miss Patchett announces we're going to have a Christmas pageant on Christmas Eve. She passes out slips of paper with assignments to each girl and boy. Hannah and I are to be angels and we will stand behind Mary and Baby Jesus. Yeah! We can wear pretty costumes and we don't have to memorize a poem.

It's Christmas Eve, and we are first to open the door to go downstairs. We smell the evergreens that drape the stairway railing, and the tree in the main room that's so tall it touches the ceiling. Mary is standing at the foot of the stairs, smiling and proud because she and the other ladies had worked all night to turn our home into a Christmas wonderland.

It's Wednesday so we have the rest of the week off for the holiday, except for church Christmas morning. We play house all day with our dolls until Mary announces, "Girls, boys, go to your rooms and get dressed for supper. C'mon, now, hurry, tonight is special. It's Christmas Eve!"

We open our drawers in the closet, and discover red ribbons for our hair, and matching ribbons to wear as sashes on our dresses, laying on top of our clothes. Since it's a special occasion, we decide to wear our Sunday dresses and pantalettes. Hannah and I brush each other's hair, and we tie the narrow ribbons into bows, pinning them so they trail down the back of our heads, and we put on our fancy sashes, tying bows in the back.

When we see ourselves in the mirror, we are amazed! I grab her hand. "Hannah, we're beautiful! I didn't know we could look this pretty!"

We pretend we are princesses as we walk down the stairs gracefully with pointed toes while holding our heads high as if we are wearing tiaras. We hold onto the stair railing with one hand while sprinkling silver stars with the other.

Heads turn and Mary greets us at the foot of the stairs, "My goodness! Ladies, look at Dora and Hannah. Our little girls have become young ladies. Girls, you may sit on the velvet settee by the tree until you are called for supper."

We sit on the settee, spreading our dresses out. "Hannah, what do you think the other girls will say when they see us? I think they will be surprised because you are such a pretty princess."

"So are you. I can hear them now, Princess Dora Belle Kelly and Princess Hannah Louise Blaney of Englewood."

Soon the main room is filled with girls and boys, laughing and bubbling with excitement. Miss Patchett enters the room from the kitchen, and she claps her hands, "Girls and boys, you may go to the dining room. Our cooks have prepared a special supper for Christmas Eve!"

We enter the dining hall, and we can't believe our eyes! There are tall candelabras on the long wood tables that are draped with white tablecloths, and the tables are decorated with ivy from the front wall of our home, and fruits and candies donated by local shopkeepers.

We have turkey with all of the trimmings, and we can choose our dessert, plum pudding or a special Christmas cake.

"Hannah, I'll take the pudding and you take the cake, then we'll share so we can have both!"

We share the pudding and cake, but the cake is best, a Christmas Lane cake with meringue icing topped with sweet red cherries.

After supper, while they clear the tables and set up chairs, Hannah and I are escorted to the back of a stage so we can put on our angel costumes. When the curtain is pulled, there we are, standing with our hands folded behind Mary, Joseph and Baby Jesus while three wisemen bearing gifts walk slowly towards the manger. I look out at the audience and smile at Jack, still wearing his red knit hat.

Pastor Thomas reads the Christmas story from his Bible, then some of the boys and girls recite poems. They all remember their lines, except the little boy at the end who made a funny mistake:

> *First time I ever said a piece*
> *My knees shook quite a bit,*
> *But maybe if I smell a lot*
> *You'll never notice it!*

Everyone laughs and applauds. Someone shouts, "Smile, not smell!" But no one really minds. Mrs. Wagner from church plays the piano and we all sing *Away in a Manger* as we're escorted back to the main room. There's a big round table in the middle of the room, with glass bowls of oranges next to pillow slips that are neatly folded and tied with green ribbons, one for every boy and girl.

We are all sitting on the floor around the tree when we hear the jingling of bells, then Santa Claus comes through the front door with a gunny sack slung over his shoulder.

"Ho, ho, ho, Merry Christmas!" He stops and he looks down at Hannah and me, "Well, who are you? Are you two sisters?"

I'm so enchanted that I can't talk. Hannah replies, "No, Santa, but Dora is my very best friend."

"Isn't it marvelous to have a best friend? Dora must be a very special little girl. But what is your name?"

"Hannah, Santa. You might remember me from last year. Hannah Blaney. My family lives on a farm in Jasper, Indiana with my mama, papa, and my sister, Amy."

Santa reaches into his sack, and he gives each of us a peppermint candy cane. Then, he passes out candy canes to all of the girls and boys, "My, my, look at you, all dressed up. Don't you look splendid!"

Even Miss Patchett gets a peppermint candy cane before Santa waves and steps into the snow through the front door.

We all turn towards Miss Patchett to see what's next. "Boys and girls, I don't know if you remember Jack. When Jack was a little boy, he came to our home with no family, just like you, and when he turned eighteen, he decided to stay and make this his home. Jack works outside, taking care of the horses and the lawn. Tonight, he has a special gift for us; he is going to play his violin."

There's not even a whisper. At that moment, it's so quiet we can almost hear the snow falling outside. Jack stands next to the tree, still wearing his red knit cap. We watch as he touches his bow to the strings and the magical sound of the violin floats through the air like a dream. From the first note, I can feel the warm embrace of the music that circles the room. Jack's eyes remain closed as his bow dances on the strings to cast mellow notes and chords into the air. I have never imagined anything like it! At the end of his concert, Jack plays a chorus of Silent Night, then a second time so we can sing the carol.

Mary steps to the front of the room, "Children, don't forget your oranges and put a pillow sack at the end of your bed, because Santa will visit us again tonight while we are sleeping."

We climb the stairs to our room and change into our night shirts. We kneel to say our nighttime prayers. I say what I always say.

> *God bless Mama,*
> *God Bless Jack,*
> *and God Bless Baby Louis and Hannah.*
> *Please let them know that I love them,*
> *and please help me to find my brothers.*
> *Amen.*

Hannah and I crawl into our beds as Mary turns off the oil lamps. "Sweet dreams, Hannah."

"Sweet dreams, Dora. I love you."

"I love you too, Hannah."

Mr. Murphy

October 26, 1903

I don't know how much time goes by, but Hannah and I get used to our new life. It's not so bad. Sometimes girls leave, and sometimes we get to say goodbye to them. I'm working on my spelling lesson when Mary enters the classroom. She goes to Miss Eichner, and they talk a few minutes before Miss Eichner says, "Dora, Miss Patchett wants to see you in her office. Mary will take you there."

I know I've followed all of the rules but still, I'm afraid because one of the girls told me about one of the boys who got paddled when he was sent to Miss Patchett's office. She still makes me nervous, always talking about what we are supposed to do, and what will happen if we don't do things right.

Miss Patchett is sitting at her desk, and she stands to walk toward me as we enter the room. "Here, Dora, come sit next to me." We sit on two blue velvet chairs, facing one another. "Dora, a very important man, a politician and an attorney, is here to take in a little girl. I told him about you, and he wants to meet you."

"Miss Patchett, I like living here with my friend Hannah. Why do I have to go away? What's his name?"

"His name is Mr. Murphy. He's Irish like you and I think you will like him. If he wants to take you in, you must go. Besides, Hannah will not be here long, you know that don't you? You'll both find families, so if you stay here, you'll be left alone when she leaves, and you won't have your friend anymore. This isn't your home, Dora. It's an orphanage. Now, be polite."

Miss Patchett takes my hand, and we walk to the parlor. There's a man sitting on the settee, a big man with a white beard and wearing a heavy black suit. I lean away, towards Miss Patchett, but she gently pushes me forward. At first, he looks so stern, but then he starts to talk, and I can see a sparkle in his soft blue eyes.

"Mr. Murphy, this is Dora Kelly, the girl I told you about."

"Well, hello Dora. I am very pleased to meet you."

"Dora, remember your manners and say hello to Mr. Murphy and sit in this chair."

"Hello, Mr. Murphy, it's very nice to meet you."

"Would you like to know where I live?" I nod my head, yes. "I live in a big brick house in Canton. It's a Christian home with servants. You will have a good life if you come home with me. You will have your own bedroom, a carriage and a driver, and Ruby will take you to the seamstress who will sew pretty dresses just for you. Would you like to come home with me to live in Canton?"

"Where is Canton?"

"A long way, due south of Chicago. I came 200 miles just to meet you. Would you like to come home with me?"

"Is Canton in Illinois?"

"Why yes, it is!" Thinking it is still in Illinois, and I might be able to find my brothers, I nod my head, yes.

By now, Mary is standing by, to take me to our room to gather Ella and my clothes. She puts my clothes in a small satchel. "Dora, I'm so happy that you have found a home. You are a good little girl and I know you will be happy with Mr. Murphy. You are very lucky. Mr. Murphy is a very important man. Now, don't cry and remember to bring Ella."

Through the tears and sobs, "Can I say goodbye to Hannah?"

"Hannah is in school but I will take you to her classroom so you can tell her that you are leaving."

When we walk downstairs, Hannah is waiting for me at the bottom of the stairs. We hug each another. "Oh, Hannah, I promise, I will never forget you!"

"I love you too."

Miss Patchett intervenes, "Don't be such babies! The whole point of you coming here was to find you a home. Some girls are not so lucky, some have been taken away only to become servants. Chin up, Dora, Mr. Murphy is a nice man, and you will have a good life. Back to class, Hannah. Mr. Murphy and Dora have to catch a train. Now, say goodbye."

Miss Patchett pulls us apart, and Mary gives me a new red coat. We all walk outside to Jack's carriage. Jack, with his red knit cap, "So, Dora, you are leaving us. Good for you. I know you will be happy."

I look back and see Hannah has followed me. "Oh, Hannah, I want you to have Ella so you will remember me."

Hannah's bottom lip trembles, "Dora, I'll never forget you."

Then Miss Patchett pulls her back into the building, while I get into the carriage.

Joseph L Murphy

RECEIPTS AND DISBURSEMENTS

For year ending May 31, 1904.

Receipts.		Disbursements.	
Cash on hand at beginning of fiscal year	$ 12 35	Cash on hand at end of fiscal year	$ 371 20
From public funds	3,565 00	Office salaries	9,208 94
From donations	33,005 82	Field salaries	12,115 [illegible]
From institutions and friends for care of children	3,200 30	Personal expenses	3,551 68
"Children's Home Finder"	575 21	Traveling expenses	2,511 62
Miscellaneous receipts	450 82	Postage	1,088 00
		Printing and stationery	1,478 08
		Children's Home Finder	1,123 71
		Boarding children	1,313 89
		Middlesworth Home	1,801 80
		Englewood Nursery	2,331 54
		Duquoin Home	45 22
		Routoul Home	2,113 91
		Sundries	3,882 30
		Miscellaneous	10 20
Total receipts	$43,169 20	Total disbursements	$43,169 20

MOVEMENT OF POPULATION

For year ending May 31. 1904.

Children.	Total.	Children.	Total.
Present at beginning of year	73	Placed in homes	394
Committed by Court	130	Placed in institutions, etc	10
Received otherwise	325	Returned to friends	9
		Died	20
		Present at end of year	95
Total	528	Total	528

NOTE—Of the 528 children, 56 were counted more than once, leaving 485 different children.

Children's Home and Aid Society Report, Note 20 Children Died

March 6, 1959

TO WHOM IT MAY CONCERN:

This is to certify that according to the records of
the Illinois Children's Home and Aid Society, Dora Belle Kelley,
now Mrs. Dora Moss, was born January 7, 1894 the daughter of
Cora Ella and Curtis B. Kelley. She came under the care of
this Society on November 12, 1902.

Sincerely yours,

Elizabeth A. Meek

Elizabeth A. Meek
Director
Downstate Division

SUBSCRIBED AND SWORN TO
before me this 6th day of
March, 1959.

Esther B Fell
Notary Public

My Commission Expires Oct. 1, 1961

*Came to Mr. J. L. Murphy's home
at the age of 9 — Oct. 26 1903*

Letter from Orphanage with Dates Dora Entered and Left the Home

PART THREE

Canton

"Hope smiles from the threshold of the year to come,
whispering it will be happier."

Alfred Lord Tennyson

The House on First Street

October 27, 1903, First Street, Canton Illinois

Mr. Murphy tries to console me. "There, there, Dora, you will like Canton. We're going to ride on a special train with a dining car, and we will have a nice dinner." My face is wet from the tears that are falling onto my coat. I try to be quiet, but my nose is running. Mr. Murphy reaches into his breast pocket, and he gives me his hanky.

When we arrive at Union Station, a coachman takes our bags and we immediately board a rail car with a sign, Atchison, Topeka & Santa Fe. Mr. Murphy explains, "Dora we'll have a five hour ride to Pekin, Illinois where R.C. Webster will meet us for a coach ride to Canton. It will be a long day, so let's find the dining car and we'll get something to eat."

The dining car is very nice, with white tablecloths and a small vase of flowers on every table. The car is lit with electric lights, just like the train to Chicago, but nicer. After we are seated, the waiter gives Mr. Murphy a menu so he can order for both of us.

"The young lady will have the creamed chicken and mashed potatoes, along with a glass of milk. Is that all right, dear?"

"Yes, sir."

"Would you like pudding or ice cream for dessert?"

"I would like ice cream." I whisper, "Mr. Murphy, I don't like tapioca pudding."

"Well, I'll see to it that you will never have to eat tapioca pudding!"

Mr. Murphy eats his steak and potato and he shares some of his green beans with me. The food is very good, and the fancy setting makes me feel special.

We return to our seats and before long, I'm sleepy from the rocking of the train, so I lay my head onto Mr. Murphy's lap.

Next thing I know, the trainman wakes me up, announcing, "Pekin. Next stop is Pekin."

Mr. Murphy helps me down the steps and he waves to a man who is sitting on a bench, "R.C., we're here!" The man looks a little like Uncle John in his bib overalls.

"Dora, this is R.C. Webster. He helps around the homestead, and he's a good friend. R.C., this is Dora."

"Hello, Dora. Here, Uncle Joe, let me help you with your bags." R.C. escorts us to a coach with two horses.

Mr. Murphy explains, "it's 24 miles to Canton, so it will take more than four hours. I know you are tired, but this is the last leg of our trip and when we get home, you will be able to sleep on a new bed with a soft mattress on top of coiled springs."

With a crack of the whip, we're on our way. Soon we're on a country road lined by trees. It's very dark outside but the sky is clear so I look out the window to count the stars to pass the time.

Mr. Murphy shows me how to find the North Star. He has a big, deep voice that softens to a whisper. "Look at the two stars that are on the edge of the cup of the big dipper. Do you see the big dipper?"

"Yes, sir."

"Those stars are called pointer stars because when you line them up, they point to the North Star. Can you see it now? Do you see the North Star?"

Smiling, I nod my head, yes. Mr. Murphy was right, I am tired. The road is bumpy, and we are jostled, swaying side to side but I still fall asleep.

I wake up as we enter a long dooryard, leading to a big brick house. The house is so big, and I wonder where Mr. Murphy lives. Maybe he lives on the main floor and other people live upstairs.

After R.C. parks the carriage, he carries me into a kitchen through a side door, and up two flights of stairs to my room. On the way up the stairs, I look back over R.C.'s shoulder and notice a chandelier with crystals that sparkle from the lights.

He pushes the door open with his foot. I am amazed. "R.C., are you sure this is my room? I can't believe this room is just for me!"

"Yup, when Ruby heard you were coming, she fixed this room up just for you! Do you like it?"

Speechless, all I can do is nod my head. There's a four-poster bed with lace curtains tied back with pink ribbons. R,C. helps me up three steps to the high mattress that's covered with a white quilt embroidered with pink roses and piled high with fluffy cotton pillows.

"I'll leave you here, Miss. Ruby will be here soon to help you get settled in."

I jump off the bed and crawl onto the window seat to look out. It's dark out there's the moon and stars. I look for the north star and big dipper but decide they must be on another side of the house. As I look down, I see R.C. pushing the carriage into the coach house, and I watch as he takes the horses to the barn.

A young woman tops the stairs and turns into my room. "Welcome, Dora! We are so happy that you are here. My name is Ruby. Let's get you settled in. There's a basin of warm water here if you want to wash your hands and face."

"Thank you, but I need to go to the privy."

"Well, we don't have an outdoor privy, but there is a nice bathroom with commodes on the second floor."

She takes me down to the second floor, and she shows me how to turn the lock, "You need to lock the door because we only have one bathroom that is used by everyone who lives here, and visitors as well."

After we return to my room, Ruby helps me into a night dress. "Ruby, this house is so big! How many people live here? "

"Uncle Joe, of course. I've lived here a long time so I call him Uncle Joe, but you are to call him Mr. Murphy. Then there's you and me.

"This is a really big house for three people."

"You'll get used to it. I think you will learn to love this house. Now, let me tuck you in."

I crawl onto the middle of the bed. There's no feather ticking to sink into but this bed bounces! I bounce a few times, then I lay on my stomach and lift the linens to peek at the mattress, trying to see the coil springs Mr. Murphy said were there. I've never seen a mattress before.

I feel like this house must be the safest place in the world. Shortly before Ruby turns off the lights, I notice some shelves above the vanity with five China dolls, ladies with long skirts, umbrellas, and hats. I close my eyes, thinking about the house and hoping I'm allowed to explore it all! The house is so quiet. I miss the laughter and excitement of the girls back at the orphanage, and I wish Hannah was here to talk to. I realize that except for the time I was burned, this will be the first time I've slept alone. In the distance, I can hear the ticking of a clock that chimes as I fall asleep, dreaming about Hannah.

"Hannah, let's go look for Amy and my brothers!"

"Dora, hold my hand tight." As soon as I touch her hand, we float up to white clouds, then we fly away!.

"Dora, look down there! There's Amy! She is eating a cookie and she has a new doll! But who's that?" A lady picks Amy up and they disappear.

We continue to fly, barely missing the steeple of the Methodist Church in Ullin. I look down to see if Jack and Louis are there, but our cabin is still empty. However, further down a road, there's Jack with a shovel, cleaning a chicken coop. I call out to him, "Jack, Jack, it's me, Dora. I'm up here!"

Then everything goes dark and I look at Hannah who is surrounded by stars.

Then I wake up.

I smell ham cooking. I slide from the high bed onto the floor and look around. Then I remember the bathroom is on the second floor. Just then, Ruby walks in, and we go downstairs to the bathroom.

"Ruby, should I go upstairs and get dressed?"

"It's okay, Dora, you can come to breakfast in your night dress."

I feel the warmth of the fireplace as we enter the kitchen. There's a large farm table in the middle of the room and a sparkling white floor with little black squares.

"What kind of floor is this? We had wood floors at home, but this floor is so pretty."

Mr. Murphy smiles. "That's called linoleum, Dora. I'm glad that you like it."

Ruby reaches for a bowl on the back of the stove, and she scatters salt on the eggs. "What kind of stove is that? It's not a cookstove."

"No, it's a gas stove, a new invention, and look here, we have what's called a Frigidaire to keep food cold. It's electric, so we don't need the ice man anymore."

"I like the stove, it's so pretty and shiny! Does it get hot, can I touch it?"

Ruby responds, "The only part that gets hot are the burners on top – see? Where the flame is. You can touch the side of the stove, but I wouldn't touch the top in case it's still hot from cooking."

We eat a big breakfast of ham, eggs, and warm biscuits with blackberry jam. I am so hungry! Ruby and Mr. Murphy laugh when I finally take my last sip of tea. He wipes the jam off my face with his napkin. They seem surprised that I could eat so much.

Ruby goes to her room to dress, leaving me alone with Mr. Murphy.

"Ruby has lived with me since she was your age. She delivered milk to me. Her parents are poor, so I took her in. Since she's all grown up now, she's my housekeeper. She'll take care of you, me, and the house. Her name is Ruby O'Grady, but you just call her Ruby."

I'm just finishing getting dressed when Ruby comes to get me. "C'mon, I'll give you a tour of the house, so you know where everything is!"

We go to the parlor where Mr. Murphy's portrait is hanging over the fireplace. He looks stern with his long, white beard but, I think to myself, some people might not notice his kind, blue eyes.

The rooms are big with high ceilings, and lots of pretty furniture. There's a tall piano on the wall next to the door that opens to the staircase. There are patches of sunlight from a big window on the opposite wall and the sun filtering through the curtain splashes nets of gold on the polished wood of the piano.

"Who plays the piano, Ruby?"

"No one. There hasn't been any music in this house for a long time. We were so excited when we learned you were coming. Why did you ask about the piano? Do you play?"

"No, but I would like to learn."

"I'll mention it to Uncle Joe. It will make him happy if you learn to play the piano. Right now, it's nothing more than a dust collector."

We leave the parlor and walk past the stairs. Ruby opens a door to a room behind the kitchen to show me her room. There's a cot with a blue and white quilt, a dresser, and a blue and white ceramic pitcher and bowl next to a small lamp. Blue is my favorite color and the blue and white is pretty. The room is dark, though, 'cuz it's small and there's no window.

The house has a lot of pretty things, and I wonder if I will be allowed in all of the rooms, and what I will be allowed to touch. The stairway walls are lined with polished wood trimmed with what looks like little wooden beads, and there's a crystal chandelier at the foot of the stairs and another in the parlor.

Outside the kitchen door, on the side of the house, there are steps that go down to a path that leads to a carriage house.

Ruby takes me to the back of the house, and we go down some stairs that lead to a cellar. There are shelves of canned food, green, red and purple jars with canned tomatoes, green beans, and beets. So much food for three people to eat! Ruby picks up a broom in the corner and she sweeps the air, knocking down a spider web that's in our way. I jump back, as a little mouse scurries across the floor.

"Follow me, I want to show you something special. There's a chest on the back wall."

As we walk deeper into the cellar, there's no window or light, so it's dark and scary. I stop and Ruby looks back at me, "that's all right, Dora, we don't have to go there now."

We walk back towards the stairs, "Dora, everyone here is nice, so you don't have to be afraid. I know you must be scared now, but you will grow to like it."

We settle back in the kitchen. "You met R.C. He's Uncle Joe's friend and our neighbor across the street. R.C. takes care of the grounds and when we want to go to town, he takes us in a carriage. This is a good time to come because you will meet the neighbors at the bonfire on Halloween. Uncle Joe gave me some money, so this afternoon I will take you to the store to buy some new shoes, a warm coat and hat, and some pretty fabric for new dresses. Think about your favorite colors so we can buy something that you like."

After dinner, R.C. takes us to town in an open carriage. It's cold, but I don' mind 'cuz I'm looking at all of the beautiful houses along the way, with their tall turrets, large windows and porches with swings. We arrive downtown and R.C. parks the carriage in front of a dry goods store. "You ladies take your time. I'll wait right here."

I look up and there's a Dobbins Brothers sign hanging over the front door of the store. A lady with a halo of soft white hair and smiling eyes greets us warmly when we come through the door. "Well, hello, Ruby! I haven't seen you for a while. Who is your friend?"

"It's good to see you. This is Dora Kelly, Mr. Murphy's new ward. Dora, this is Mrs. Lowell. We are here to buy some things for Dora, a coat, hat and shoes, and some fabric for dresses, along with matching accessories for her pretty hair."

"All right, Dora, what is your favorite color?

"Blue, but I also like yellow."

Ruby goes to a table to look through many bolts of fabric that are organized by color. We choose a blue cloth with tiny pink roses, and a yellow print with blue flowers. Ruby asks, "Mrs. Lowell, do you have any velvet fabrics? Dora will need a special dress for the holidays.

"Of course! Dora, come with me so you can see the all the pretty colors. Have you ever touched velvet?"

"I once sat on a velvet chair, but I didn't know you could make a dress from velvet."

"Well, I want you to feel the velvet." I had seen velvet before, but only on the chairs and settee at the orphanage, and those were for special guests only! I brush my hand across the fabric. It is soft and feels like freshly cut grass after a Spring rain. We choose a deep red, the color of cranberries.

"Mrs. Lowell, we'll take three yards each of the prints and two yards of the velvet along with a quarter yard of white linen for a collar.

"That's fine. While I'm cutting the fabric, why don't you take Dora to look for ribbons and barrettes in the corner cupboard?"

We pick a gold barrette with a yellow butterfly and some blue, pink and yellow ribbons that match the fabrics for my new dresses.

"Look, Dora, here's a dark red bow, a perfect match for your Christmas dress. I'll get extra so we can put a bow in your hair!" Ruby winks.

Ruby takes our selections to the counter before walking to the other side of the shop to look at coats and shoes. I try on several coats, and we settle on a grey wool coat with a matching hat. The selection of shoes in my size is limited, but I find some brown boots with laces for every day, and some shiny black slippers to wear with my party dress.

When we come out of the shop, Ruby waves at R.C. as she continues to walk down the street, carrying our packages while I trail behind. We stop in front of a colorful shop with Sweet Shop painted on the window. There are glass shelves with small packages tied with gold and silver ribbons, and glass jars and dishes of candied fruits, truffles, and candied violets. So much more then I could have imagined!

Ruby opens the door, and we are greeted by the sweet aroma of sugar and ginger. I decide I want to be like her because she's pretty, smart, and she seems to be in charge. There's a gingerbread house on a table in the corner, with roof tiles of tiny cookies, piped icing that outlines windows and doors, and a marzipan bird is perched at the top of a chocolate tree.

"Good morning, Ruby. Who did you bring with you today?"

"Good morning to you, Mr. Beck. This is Miss Dora Kelly. Dora is Mr. Murphy's new ward, so she will be living with us."

"Nice to meet you, Miss Kelly. What is your favorite candy?"

Looking at the candy through a window was one thing, but now that I'm inside, there are many candies that I have not seen before. I'm so excited that I can't talk. There's too much to choose from and knowing I can have what I want is like a dream. I point to a tall drinking glass with large lollipops with raspberry swirls.

Ruby laughs, "I think Dora is finding it hard to decide. Just give her one of those lollipops and a small bag of those chocolates, and another with some candied violets."

I clutch the bags of sweets all the way home, hardly believing they're all for me.

The next day, R.C. drives us across town to a small house where Helen lives. Helen is a seamstress, and Ruby says she sews all of her dresses.

"Helen, this is Dora, Mr. Murphy's new ward. She needs some pretty dresses for school, and a special dress for the holidays. Here's some fabrics that we bought at Dobbins Brothers. Blue is Dora's favorite color, so the blue and yellow fabrics will be good for school but, look, at this velvet. I bought two yards. Is that enough to make a dress for the holidays? I thought this white linen would make a pretty collar."

"This will do nicely. The velvet is beautiful. You're a lucky girl, Dora. How about you, Ruby, am I to sew anything for you this time?"

"Not this time. This time is just for Dora."

I can't believe that I'm getting three new dresses all at once. I wish Hannah could see all this. I wonder what she's doing right now. I wonder if she misses me like I miss her.

Mr. Murphy the Pumpkin!

October 31, Halloween

"Happy Halloween!" R.C. opens the side door while we are eating breakfast, holding the biggest pumpkin I have ever seen. Although he is struggling from its weight, he manages to gently place it on the floor by the fireplace. "Uncle Joe, I thought Ruby and Dora might want to carve a pumpkin so you will have a lantern on the porch tonight."

"My goodness, that's a big one! Did it come from my farm?"

"Yes, sir. This is the biggest pumpkin I could find."

"I don't think you could have found a better pumpkin. Ruby, I have to go to the office for a few hours, but I'll be back in plenty of time to see the finished product.

I hurry up to my room to get dressed. By the time I return to the kitchen, Ruby has cleared the dishes and R.C. is lifting the pumpkin onto the table. Ruby retrieves a sharp knife and a big spoon from the cupboard drawer, and she cuts a ring around the stem to form a lid. She pulls the lid back and I can see the guts of the pumpkin inside.

"Yuck!" I back away.

"C'mon, Dora, you get to help." I shake my head, no. "C'mon, this will be fun."

Ruby scoops the fiber loose from the inside of the pumpkin with a large spoon, then she reaches her hand inside and pulls the guts out, putting them on a large platter. "Dora, why don't you pick out the seeds. We'll dry them so you can have your own pumpkin patch next year."

I kneel on a chair, and start picking out seeds, initially trying not to touch the "guts" but I soon realize that the only way to get to all of the seeds is to pull and go through the fibers.

When I'm done, my arms are sticky up to the cuffs of my blouse. Ruby laughs, "Well, look at you, you really got into it! Now go wash your hands and we'll give Mr. Pumpkin a face."

While I'm washing up in the kitchen basin, Ruby asks, "what kind of face shall we give him, Dora, a scary face or a smiley face?"

"I want Mr. Pumpkin to have a happy face!"

"Happy, it is." I watch as Ruby cuts oval eyes, a pointed nose, and a big smile with three teeth. Then she pushes a small yellow box across the table towards me, "Here, Dora, Uncle Joe told me to get these for you. They are the newest thing, and better than a pencil or pen. They call them crayons. Open the box. See, they come in different colors, and if you draw around his eyes and mouth, he will be the best pumpkin in Canton."

I open the box and take a dark grey crayon to draw eyebrows above his eyes, and a red crayon to outline his mouth. Ruby urges me on. "Why don't you give him a black moustache and beard?"

"No, I think he should have a white beard like Mr. Murphy." I check the box and find a white crayon. I have to rub the crayon hard so his white beard will show, but it's worth it.

Now that we are finished and I see what we have made, I'm excited and Ruby and R.C. are laughing. R. C. comments, "We should call him Mr. Murphy, the Pumpkin!".

Just then, Mr. Murphy walks into the kitchen, "What about me?"

I respond, "Look, Mr. Murphy, we carved the pumpkin, and he has a white beard, just like you, so we're naming him Mr. Murphy the Pumpkin!"

I have not seen Mr. Murphy laugh so much before. "Well, Mr. Murphy, the Pumpkin, you will be a spectacular lantern for our front porch this Halloween night!"

Ruby reaches into the pumpkin, and she digs a small hole in the bottom to hold a short candle, then R.C. carries the pumpkin to the front porch.

Mr. Murphy turns to Ruby. "We'll leave for the bonfire at dusk after supper. Make sure everyone's ready." Turning to me with a grin, he asks, "So, Miss Dora, what are you going to be for Halloween?"

Ruby chimes in, "She's going to be Little Bo Peep. We have a full apron to tie over her play dress, she has a new bonnet, and she is going to carry one of your canes for her hook."

"That's marvelous! A perfect costume. Dora, you will be a very pretty Little Bo Peep!"

Ruby has invited R.C. to supper. I'm not hungry and pick at my food because I'm so excited about going to a bonfire. I'm eating too little, but too fast. R.C. is sitting across from me, Mr. Murphy is sitting in the chair he always sits in at the head of the table, and Ruby sits at the other end, closest to the stove so she can serve. "Dora, slow down! You'll get a stomachache."

"I'm sorry, Ruby, but I want to put my costume on so we can leave for the bonfire."

We go out the front door at dusk. The warm glow of the candle flickers and lights up Mr. Murphy the Pumpkin's face. Neighbors passing by, laugh at the pumpkin's white moustache and beard. Mr. Murphy seems proud that we have the best pumpkin in Canton.

We walk around to the side of the house where R.C. is waiting in a carriage. It's only a short distance to the bonfire, which is in an open field across the way. There are buggies and carriages parked near a barn on the other side of the fire, and grownups are sitting on benches to watch their children who are playing and dancing around the fire.

This is the first time I've been to a bonfire. There's a gentle breeze and the flames jump high with the wind. Some of the flames are almost as tall as the barn. A man is sitting on a stump, playing a fiddle, and children are running and dancing around the fire. I look around, but I don't see anyone that I know. Ruby urges me on, "Go ahead, Dora, dance like the other children." I just want to stay close to Ruby.

Mr. Murphy takes me by my hand, and we walk towards a group of people. "Albert, this is Dora, tonight she is Little Bo Peep. Dora, this is Mr. Taff. Mr. Taff is my attorney." Then he turns as a man and woman approach, with two boys in tow. Mr. Murphy has a big smile on his face, "Happy Halloween, Anna, where's your costume? Let me introduce you to Dora, the newest addition to our family. Dora, this is my cousin, Anna Moss and her husband, John. Anna, I see you brought the boys."

"O, yes, the boys wouldn't miss the bonfire. Dora, this is Harold, he's the youngest, and Rex who is closer to your age. Joseph, you must bring Dora to our house for supper sometime so she can get to know the boys."

Harold is dressed like a hobo and Rex is dressed up like a pirate with an eye patch on one eye and black hat. Rex is a lot taller than me, so he must be older. He takes my hand. "C'mon, Dora, let's play around the fire." We run circles around the fire; but with Rex's long legs, I have a hard time keeping up. He stops to look back every now and then, and he waits so I can catch up.

The fiddler is playing happy music. He reminds me of Jack playing his violin on Christmas Eve, except he isn't wearing a red knit hat. I wonder what Hannah is doing tonight. After a while, Rex points towards the barn, "Look, Dora, the cookies are out, c'mon!"

Lanterns are lit inside the barn, and someone has set up a long table; Ruby and other ladies are bringing plates of cookies from their buggies and carriages. Rex and I are first in line and we each grab a handful of cookies before we run back to sit on a log near the fire.

"So, Dora, how old are you?"

"I'm nine, I'm in second grade."

"I'm ten, and I am in the fourth grade. When is your birthday?"

"January 7."

"I have a January birthday too, January 21. How come you're only in second grade?

"My mama had to work after Daddy died. I couldn't go to school 'cuz I had to stay home and take care of my brothers. I started second grade at the orphanage though."

"Gee, I'm sorry. Well, even though you're small, you seem smart enough." I like Rex from the very beginning, and I have a feeling that we will become friends.

We eat all of our cookies. It's getting late and some people are leaving, so we walk over to where Mr. Murphy and Rex's parents are talking.

Mr. Murphy sees us first, "Well, here they are! We were just wondering about you. Did you get some cookies?"

Rex responds, "Yup! She ate a whole handful."

"It looks like everyone is leaving, so we're going to go home. Anna, John, it was a pleasure to see you and, Anna, we will take you up on your offer to come to supper." Rubbing his round belly, "Just remember, I have a big appetite!" Everyone laughs and Mr. Murphy and John shake hands before we go our carriage.

Mr. Murphy, Ruby and I go to the Presbyterian Church the next morning, for Sunday service. After we are settled onto our pew, Mr. Murphy talks in a whisper, to tell me about All Saints Day. He explains that this is a day to celebrate the martyrdom of saints. However, Christians also remember loved ones who have died.

The sun casts a purple beam on the minister as he reads the call to worship. Then organ music fills the room. I think about Daddy being in heaven and for some reason, at that moment, I feel close to him. People start to sing. Mr. Murphy shares his hymnal with me, A Mighty Fortress is Our God.... I like to sing, so I try to keep up, but there's so much to take in and except for Mr. Murphy and Ruby, I'm in a big room with a lot of people that I don't know.

After the service ends, some ladies come to greet Mr. Murphy, "It's so nice to see you, Joseph. Who is the young lady?"

"Dora, Dora Belle Kelly. She is my new ward. Say hello to the ladies, Dora."

I say hello but there are so many people to remember that I just stand, holding tight onto Ruby's hand. I don't like the ladies. They gush and laugh about everything, each trying to be The One to hold Mr. Murphy's attention. One lady's name is Agnes. She's wearing a very nice dark blue dress with a tatted collar and white gloves, but she has a crooked nose, and she talks too loud.

Mr. Murphy is polite, but he soon finds the opportunity to say goodbye, "Well, Thelma, Agnes, Margaret, I enjoyed talking with you, but we must be on our way. Ruby has a chicken cooking on the stove. I hope you enjoy the rest of the day."

On Monday, Mr. Murphy takes me to school.

The principal shows us to my classroom and he introduces me to Miss Lewis, my teacher. "Welcome to Canton Grammar School, Dora. Here we have first, second and third grade, so you can sit at that desk over there in the middle of the room. Children, this is a new student, Dora Kelly. Dora, we are working on arithmetic. Have you done arithmetic before?"

"Yes, Ma'am, I know how to add and subtract."

"Good, that's what we are working on today." She puts a paper with some problems on my desk. "See what you can do with these. Do you need a pencil?"

Mr. Murphy speaks up, "We brought some supplies for her to keep in her desk. Here, Dora, you have your own pencils, some paper, an eraser and crayons. You can put your supplies away in your desk. I'm going to leave you here with Miss Lewis. R.C. will come to take you home when school lets out. Thank you, Miss Lewis, and please let me know if she needs anything else."

Mr. Murphy leaves and, once again, I'm left alone with people I don't know. The other students have their heads down, doing their schoolwork, except the boy who sits in front of me. He turns around and he makes a funny face. I can't tell if he is trying to make me laugh, or if he wants me to be angry. I decide he's just stupid! Miss Lewis looks our way, "Johnny Scott, turn around and pay attention!"

I'm first in line when the school bell rings the next day. A girl runs to catch up with me as we walk towards our classroom. "Hi, Dora. My name is Annie Rose, Annie Rose O'Neal. We just moved here from Peoria, so I'm new too. Maybe we can be friends." I smile and nod my head as we rush to our desks.

I like school because I'm with other girls my own age. My favorite subject is Reading. I like books, and Miss Lewis has a chart on the wall with everyone's name, and she sticks gold stars next to our names every time we finish a book. Before long, I have more gold stars than anyone else.

The best part of school, though, is Annie Rose. Every day when I wake up, I hurry to get dressed and I run to school to meet her. We share secrets and we play together at recess.

I tell Ruby about Annie Rose and soon the two of us are getting together after school and on the weekends to play with our dolls. I show her how I can find four-leafed clovers, and we collect golden maple leaves that fall from the trees to take to school for art projects.

I like my new school, and I have two new friends, including Rex. Annie Rose and I have already promised that she and I will be friends forever, but sometimes when I lie in bed at night, I remind myself that this too could all end, and someone will probably come to take me away.

Blessings!

Thanksgiving, 1903

I stay up late the night before Thanksgiving watching Ruby prepare food for the big feast. R.C. brought us a big tom turkey from the farm, and three bottles of port, Mr. Murphy's favorite! I have never seen such a big bird! She makes cornbread for stuffing, cranberry sauce and four pies, mincemeat, apple, and two pumpkin pies. This time, I am used to the guts, so I help scoop them out so the flesh of the pumpkin can be boiled for pie filling. While the brown bread is baking in the oven, Ruby chops up onions and celery for the main dressing, and we roast chestnuts for the sausage dressing to stuff in the neck of the bird.

I sleep late, waking up to the smell of sage, knowing the turkey and dressings are in the oven. I hurry to the bathroom and splash water on my face, then I go down the stairs to the kitchen. Ruby is at the sink, peeling vegetables, "Well, good morning, sleepy head. Happy Thanksgiving! Do you want some tea and biscuits? Anna, John, and the boys will be here at four, so you can help by setting the table."

I eat my breakfast, worried 'cuz I'm afraid to tell her I don't know how to set a table. But she shows me how after I finish eating.

The dining room table is draped with a white lace tablecloth, and in the center of the table, there's a large platter that is reserved for the bird, with sliver candlesticks with tall white candles on either side.

"First, we set the plates, let me see, we need seven." Ruby goes to the cabinet, and she shows me Mr. Murphy's fancy silverware that is so pretty with the initial M engraved on the handles. "Here, Dora, you can watch me do the first one, then you can do the rest. A knife and two spoons go like this, on the right side of the plate. Then on the left, the dessert fork goes first, next to the plate and the dinner fork goes next to it on the outside. You do that while I get back to fixin' the vegetables. Let me know when you're done, and I'll show you what's next."

I take six more knives from the cabinet, and place one next to each plate, gently touching the engravings, running my finger down to the bottom of the last knife. They are so beautiful. I wonder where they came from. Maybe Mr. Murphy met a queen, and she gave them to him as a gift. I wish my mama was here to see how pretty everything is, and I wonder what Jack and Louis are doing.

"Ruby, I'm done."

"So, you are!"

We work together while Ruby shows me how to set the rest of the table. The wine goblets go to the right of the water goblets at the top of the plates, and teacups at the top of the knives. Then we go to a drawer in the cabinet to count out seven linen napkins with embroidered M's on the corner, and seven porcelain napkin rings with tiny red roses. She shows me how to pull the napkins through the rings, fanning them out so they looked like pretty dresses on the center of each plate. The whole table sparkles as the light from the chandelier glances off the silver and crystal.

"Oh, Ruby, it is so pretty!"

Mr. Murphy walks into the room, "Yes, it is. Ruby always makes a nice Thanksgiving. It's a special day, Dora, and this year we're especially thankful that you are here."

"Yes, we are, Uncle Joe. Dora likes to help. Now Dora, run upstairs and get dressed. Company will be here before you know it."

The clock is chiming four o'clock when I hear the crank of the metal, followed by the ting of the doorbell. I run to open the door and Rex is standing there, cranking the doorbell. Anna comes in first, carrying a plate of cookies, while Rex and Harold trail behind. John is in the dooryard tying up the horse and buggy.

Rex smiles at me, "Hi, Dora, did you do all the cooking?"

"No, silly, Ruby did the cooking, but I helped. I set the table!"

"Nice dress."

I'm not used to receiving compliments from boys, so I'm embarrassed. "Thank you."

Everyone is sitting down and gradually we all stop talking. There's a warm feeling in the room from all the people gathered. The only sound is the crackling of the fire in the fireplace. We all turn towards John who says grace.

Lord, bless this food before us,
The family beside us,
And the love between us
Amen.

There's so much food! I decide to only take one spoonful of everything but I am full and my plate is still full. My favorite is the candied carrots. As we are finishing our pie, Rex broadcasts a loud belch. Everyone laughs except his mama who is embarrassed. "Rex, say excuse me and next time, close your mouth when you belch!"

"Yes, ma'am. Excuse me. Can we play checkers now?"

Mr. Murphy intercedes, "Rex, I think that is a wonderful idea. Let's retire to the parlor while the ladies clear the table. Dora, you can come with us."

Harold runs to the parlor and starts setting up the checkerboard and checkers. He looks up at me, "Dora, do you know how to play checkers?"

I shake my head no. I haven't even seen a checkerboard before.

"Just watch us, you'll learn. It's fun!" He takes the red and black carved discs out of the box and puts them on the board.

Mr. Murphy and John toast with glasses of port while the boys play checkers. Rex wins the first three games, then Harold wins the last one. "Here, Dora, you can play the red checkers, and I'll help you. Hey, Dad, wouldn't it be funny if Rex lost to a girl?" The men laugh.

I play two games and Harold's right, it's fun. Rex takes it easy on me. He knows I don't know how to play checkers, and I suspect he lets me win the last game.

After a while, Anna comes out of the kitchen, "Come, John, let's go home. It's getting late and I know Ruby is tired. Ruby, Joseph, thank you for the lovely dinner. We all had a marvelous time and, Dora, we are so happy that you are part of our family."

Rex smiles at me, and I smile back. I don't know what to make of Rex right now. He doesn't feel like a brother or a cousin, and I've never had a best friend who is a boy before.

We return to school after Thanksgiving. Annie Rose and I walk to school now, but it is so cold! I pull the collar of my coat up towards my face, trying to block out the cold wind. It starts to snow so we look up at the sky to catch the kisses of snowflakes falling on our tongues. Miss Lewis greets us at the door, "Come, girls, come inside where it is warm."

We hang our coats in the closet and we turn to go to our desks, but they've been moved into a circle around the heating stove in the middle of the room. I find my seat and it's so warm that I feel like I could melt to the floor like butter. Of course, I don't.

"Well, class, did everyone have a nice Thanksgiving?"

In unison, we respond with a big, "Yes!"

"So, what comes next?"

"Christmas!"

"That's right! Over the next few weeks, we will finish the lessons in your reading, spelling and arithmetic primers. You will be given new workbooks when you return after the holiday. Also, I will bring a small tree tomorrow so we can decorate our room. Would you like that?"

"Yes!"

"Good! You will do your lessons every morning, then after lunch, we will spend the rest of the day on Christmas projects."

At first, it is really fun! We make paper chain garlands, paper snowflakes, and string popcorn for the tree in our classroom. Miss Lewis says our tree is the best ever! Next, we have an art contest and Miss Lewis tacks all of the pictures on the corkboard on one wall of the room. I color a picture of Mary, Joseph, and Baby Jesus with two angels standing behind (Hannah and me). Amelia's drawing of snowflakes falling down on a Christmas tree wins, but I don't care. Teacher says we can take our pictures home to give to our parents. I wonder if she knows I don't have a mama or daddy, but I decide it's okay – I'll just take mine home to Mr. Murphy.

I'm working on my spelling lesson a week before Christmas, when Miss Lewis claps her hands and announces, "Attention, everyone, first, second and third grade."

She holds up a newspaper with news from the day before. "Class, who will be the first to tell me that we can fly?"

No one speaks up. "How about you, Johnny? Can people fly?"

"No, ma'am."

"Well, in Kitty Hawk, North Carolina, two brothers, Wilbur and Orville Wright flew in an airplane named The Kittyhawk! It was windy so it wasn't easy. Their success came after four years of experiments. I'm sure that some of the experiments during the last four years failed, but when that happened guess what they did! They learned from their failures, and they persevered. The lesson to learn from this is, no matter if other people think your idea is impossible, follow your ideas, and never give up on your dreams."

Johnny Scott raises his hand, "Miss Lewis, I want to fly. Where is North Carolina?"

Miss Lewis pulls down a map of the United States and she points to North Carolina, just as the bell rings for lunch. No one stays at their desk during lunch. In between bites, we form a line to get a closer look at Illinois and North Carolina on the map.

On the last day of school, Miss Lewis gives us construction paper to make Christmas cards for our family. I wish I could make cards for Jack and Louis, but I don't know where they are, so I make cards for Mr. Murphy, Ruby, Annie Rose, Rex, and Harold. I feel really sad, though. I stay after class to talk to Miss Lewis. "Dora, why are you crying? Christmas is coming, you should be happy."

"Miss Lewis, I don't have a family anymore. My daddy died and my mama gave us away. I love my brothers, but I don't know where they are."

"Oh, Dora, I am so sorry. It must be very upsetting when I talk about parents and family. Is that right? I am so sorry!"

She gives me her hanky and I blow my nose while nodding yes.

"Well, I know for a fact that Mr. Murphy is quite taken with you. It's the talk around town. You have a new home now. Mr. Murphy plans to raise you, so this is where you will live. You won't be sent away again, and no one will take you away from here. You are safe. You have a new family now, Mr. Murphy and Ruby."

It's been a long time since a grownup has hugged me. She helps me get into my coat and mittens and holds my hand for a minute when we get outside.

A freezing wind hits my face, so I dry my tears with Miss Lewis' hanky, and I put my head down for the walk home. Home – like Miss Lewis said, I have a new home. Still, it's different.

Noel

Christmas Eve, 1903

I wake up to a door slamming, and I hear people talking downstairs. Then the talk turns to laughter. I jump down from my bed and rush downstairs to see R. C. struggling with the biggest tree I have ever seen. Once upright, it touches the ceiling, and the branches are so full that the bottom sprawls to the middle of the parlor floor.

"R.C., that's a huge tree! My paper chain is too small!!"

Mr. Murphy speaks up, "No, it's not! That green and red paper chain will be perfect on the tree. I know Ruby will find a spot right in the front so everyone will see it."

Ruby comes into the room, carrying a box of ornaments. "Quick, Dora, get dressed while I make breakfast. Then you and I will decorate the tree."

I hurry upstairs to the bathroom. After I wash my face, I go to my room and make my bed. I brush my hair and pull on the white play dress with red roses before going downstairs. Ruby and I spend the rest of that morning, decorating the tree. She shows me how to make a red and white garland, stringing popcorn and cranberries, and she hangs my green and red paper chain, front and center. Ruby adds sprigs of holly and Christmas cards that Mr. Murphy has saved over the years.

Then Ruby opens a box. "Dora, look at Uncle Joe's ornaments. They are very special, so we have to be very careful. He bought some of them on a trip to New York."

We hang them one by one, and then I see that, nestled in the bottom of the first box are six metal shamrocks. "His mother brought them with her when they came to America from Ireland."

Ruby opens another box, and she pulls back the tissue paper that protects delicate white paper snowflakes and stars layered on top of some beautiful glass ornaments from Germany. Most are round balls, except three are egg shaped with designs on the front, one blue, another green, and the third is red.

Ruby was right, the ornaments are special, but my favorite is the ceramic Father Christmas. Ruby says it came from Russia!

Mr. Murphy comes into the room just as we are finished. "Ladies, the tree is just splendid!"

I stand back to look at the tree. Mr. Murphy and I are admiring the tree and I look over at Ruby as she is setting up a carved nativity on the fireplace mantle. She put sprigs of holly here and there and tall silver candlesticks with green candles on each end. Never in a million years, would I have imagined living in a house with so many decorations. It was like the pictures of Christmas shops that you see in picture books.

We snack on tea, biscuits and applesauce while Ruby starts preparations for Christmas Eve dinner. I like to watch her cook. Someday when I grow up, I will be the person in charge of the kitchen. I will go wherever I want to go and do whatever I want to do. Maybe I'll go on a trip and look for Jack and Louis.

I set the table and soon, it's four o'clock. "Dora, you'd better get dressed. Put on your velvet dress and bring your bow to me so I can put it in your pretty, curly hair."

The aroma of mincemeat pies drifts up the stairs as I come down to the kitchen. The holiday officially starts at sunset when John, Anna and the boys drive up the dooryard in their buggy. It's really cold, so they come in through the side door into the kitchen, but everyone goes to the parlor right away to see the tree.

Anna brings her hands to her face, "Oh, my! Joseph, your house is just lovely!"

"Tell Dora and Ruby, they put up the decorations, and look at the paper chain that Dora made in school. I say it's the best paper chain that ever graced a tree!"

Everyone agrees. They step close to look at the decorations, looking for their favorites. John likes the shamrocks, Anna said she loves the white snowflakes and stars, and like me, the boys point to the Father Christmas from Russia as their favorite.

Anna returns to the kitchen, "Ruby, everything smells so good! Can I help?"

"Well, everything is ready, but why don't you get everyone to sit down while I carry the food to the table, and you can pour the cider."

We are all seated, sipping cups of warm cider when Ruby appears with the Christmas goose. We relish the roast goose with apple and potato stuffing, parsnips and scones.

It's quiet for a short while because we are busy eating, then John breaks the silence, "Joseph, did you hear what happened at the rehearsal for tonight's nativity? They decided to include a live baby goat and while Harold and the others were backstage getting their costumes, the goat ate baby Jesus' blanket."

Mr. Murphy's roaring laughter filled the room, "Well, what did they expect? Afterall, the baby goat is just a kid!" Everyone laughs.

Then Harold pipes in, "Yeah, it was funny, and we all laughed, but the preacher's wife kicked the kid out of the Christmas pageant."

Mr. Murphy asks, "So, Harold, you are in this year's pageant?"

Anna responds, "Harold is a shepherd this year, so we will have to leave a little early for church so he can put on his costume and be in his place when everyone arrives. By the way I've been meaning to ask, what do you hear from Louisa and Anne?"

Mr. Murphy shakes his head and looks a little sad. "I've not heard much from my sisters, so I assume they are doing well. I sent letters, inviting them to come for a visit so they can meet Dora, but they have not responded. I know Louisa usually goes to Anne's house to spend holidays with her." Even I know he's changing the subject on purpose when he turns to John. "Did you hear about the two brothers that flew an airplane in North Carolina?"

"I heard someone talking about it at the barbershop."

"Yes, they say it was windy and they nearly crashed several times, but they finally got up in the air and stayed aloft for 120 feet. I wonder what this will mean for our children and grandchildren in the future."

"Hey, Rex, just think of it. We might be able to fly high above the clouds!" Harold grins at the idea.

"Harold, I'll do it if you go with me!" Everyone laughs.

After pie, we all go to the parlor. I feel the warmth of the fireplace, and the candles on the mantel spread a warm glow without making any noise at all. Ruby serves glasses of port to Mr. Murphy and John. The room is quiet while the men sip their wine, then Ruby brings a Bible to Mr. Murphy. Mr. Murphy calls me to his side, "Dora, come sit on my lap while I tell the Christmas story."

He pulls me onto his lap and says, "Thank you, Baby Girl. John, Anna, Dora is a sweet little girl; she's my baby."

He opens the Bible and shows me the part he'll read. "Since the children are here, I'll tell an abbreviated version of Matthew's Gospel. Jesus was born in Bethlehem during the time of Herod the Great. Shepherds watching their flock in a field far away, followed a bright star to the manger. Wisemen from the east came to Herod and asked him where they would find the King of the Jews, because they had also seen his star. Herod sent the Magi to Bethlehem to follow the star and find baby Jesus in a lowly manger, but instead of telling Herod where to find the child, they gave the baby gifts - gold and frankincense and myrrh! The choir of angels sang to celebrate His arrival, and that's why we celebrate Christmas, too."

Anna stands up from the settee, "What a wonderful way to end the evening. Joseph. Everything has been lovely and, Ruby, dinner was delicious. Don't forget, we want you to come for dinner at our house on New Year's Eve!"

"Dora and I are looking forward to it. Ruby won't be there; she has plans with her friends."

"Wait! I almost forgot!" I run to my room and bring down the cards for Harold and Rex. "Here, Merry Christmas. I made these for you."

Harold shoves his card into a pocket, but Rex opens his card, and he smiles, "Thank you Dora. This is real nice. Merry Christmas to you too."

The Moss family put on their coats, hats and scarves, and Mr. Murphy shows them to the door, "We will be there a few minutes before the service starts, so save us seats so we can sit together."

Even Mr. Murphy helps to carry the dishes to the kitchen. After Ruby has the food put away and the dishes are stacked for washing, we put on our coats and hats for the buggy ride to church.

Ruby calls to me, "Dora, wear your nice grey coat. You can wear the hat if you want but if you think it will crush your bow, just this one time, it's all right to only wear mittens."

R.C. is waiting for us in the buggy. Mr. Murphy thanks him for coming out on such a cold night, "Merry Christmas, R.C., what about your family? Are they coming to Christmas Eve service?"

"And a Merry Christmas to you as well, Uncle Joe. Dora, Ruby, Merry Christmas! The wife and kids are already at the church. I dropped them off early so I could come for you. Our young'uns are in the pageant. Dickie is a shepherd, and our little girl is an angel, so they had to be there early."

There's a line of buggies and carriages in front of the church. R.C. lifts me down and Mr. Murphy gives his hand to Ruby as she steps down onto the church step.

When we enter the church, the organ is playing. The golden sparkle of candlelight and the aroma of the evergreens make me feel warm and comfortable. The nativity is in front of the altar. I wave at Annie Rose who is sitting with her parents in another pew. I also wave at Harold but, of course, he can't wave back. It's late and it has been a busy and exciting day, so I'm tired and I lean against Mr. Murphy and start to doze, then everyone stands up for the anthem, *Joy to the World.*

The minister opens the service, "Tonight, we will celebrate the birth of Jesus with songs and prayers. We will sing Christmas carols and after each song, one of our members will lead us in prayer.

Our desire for peace goes back to the first Christmas. All of us have read the story about the angels coming to the shepherds, and the angels ending their announcement by singing, Glory to God in the highest and on earth, peace to those on whom his favor rests. Please be seated while we sing *Away in a Manger* on page 238."

After *Hark the Herald Angels Sing*, a man gives a prayer, thanking God for the love of his family. I guess I have a family now, too. I move closer to Mr. Murphy.

After the last prayer, the organ starts to play, and the soloist leads us while we sing *Silent Night*. Harold and the others in the Nativity leave the stage and we sing the first verse over again and again, until we are all outside in our buggies.

I wake up the next morning, excited about my first Christmas in the house, not knowing what to expect. After I wash, I decide to wear my prettiest school dress that is dark green with a red ribbon bow at the white linen collar. Mr. Murphy is waiting for me on the landing. He holds my hand while we walk down the stairs together, and he steers me away from the parlor towards the kitchen.

We are greeted by the aroma of frying bacon, and Ruby is taking biscuits out of the oven. There's a red tablecloth on the kitchen table, and a bowl of boiled eggs, along with butter and blackberry jam. After we sit down Ruby pours our tea and she brings a basket of biscuits and a pan of fried apples to the table.

We are almost finished eating when Mr. Murphy wipes his mouth with his napkin, "Ruby, that was an outstanding breakfast. The fried apples were a special treat. So, Dora, it's Christmas morning. Do you think Santa might have stopped by our house while we were sleeping?"

"I don't know. I've been a good girl. Maybe."

"Yes, you are a good girl. Let's go look under the tree!"

The light from the candles on the mantle reflect off the gold and silver ribbons on packages that surround the tree, but my eyes are drawn to the center to a doll sitting in front of the packages. She is so beautiful with her China head, and her white dress with a pink ribbon sash. She has lace pantalettes that are perfect against her black China shoes. I carefully pick her up, then I see the dollhouse that has a horse and carriage in front. There's tiny furniture in every room, and figurines of two little girls playing in the parlor.

I am speechless for a minute. This is so much! I wonder if they always have big Christmases, or if this was special because I'm new.

Mr. Murphy breaks the silence, "Look, Dora, the two little girls in the dollhouse are you and your friend, Annie Rose."

"Oh, Mr. Murphy, it is so pretty. Can Annie Rose come over some day so we can play with it together?"

"Of course. Annie Rose is welcome to come here any time."

I lie on my stomach on the floor to look at the dollhouse. The main floor has three rooms, a parlor and kitchen, with a dining room in the middle. The kitchen has a stove and table and chairs, and a figurine of a woman holding a tray of cookies. I decide to name her Ruby.

The dining room table is set with tiny plates, cups and saucers, and there's a fireplace in the parlor with a table and lamp, two velvet chairs and a settee, and there's even a piano on the outer wall.

The second floor has a large bedroom with a bed and dresser, and a bathroom that has a bathtub and commode. There's a bedroom on the third floor with a canopied bed, that looks just like my room.

"You must have been a very good girl to receive such nice presents from Santa! Shall we open the wrapped gifts?"

There are two gifts for Ruby, and a larger gift for Uncle Joe, signed from Albert, Dora and Ruby. Mr. Murphy opens his first, three leather bound books including The Principles of Law. He seems pleased, "Well, thank you. I must thank Albert as well, next time I see him."

Ruby opens her smallest package first, a necklace with a gold pendant. The big package is a new soup pot for her kitchen.

"Dora, are you going to open your presents that Uncle Joe bought for you?"

There are two, both tied with gold ribbon. The first gift is a book that Mr. Murphy says is brand new, *Rebecca of Sunnybrook Farm*. The other package is a wooden box with puzzle blocks that makes a picture of a red bird perched on a holly branch in the snow.

"Oh, thank you, Mr. Murphy. I have never had so many gifts for Christmas. Thank you!"

Ruby picks up the last package, "Here, Dora, this one's from me."

In the box is a tiny China tea set for my new doll. "Thank you, Ruby. I have never had such a Christmas."

I stand up to give Ruby a hug, and I cross the room to sit on Mr. Murphy's lap. "Here, Mr. Murphy, I made this card for you. I hope you like it."

"Is this a reindeer on front? What does it say inside? Merry Christmas! Well, thank you, Dora, this is quite unexpected. Let's find a special place for it on the tree."

"Here, Ruby, I made a card for you too." I hand Ruby her card. She's quite surprised and she says she loves the angel on the front.

For a moment, I wonder what Jack and Louis are doing right now, but I decide not to think about it. I can only hope that they are happy and that they are having a fun Christmas with their new families.

I spend the rest of the morning playing with my dollhouse and I have a pretend tea party with my new doll. I decide to name her Victoria.

Mr. Murphy hears me talking to her, "Victoria, what a great name! What made you think of Victoria for a name?"

"Well, she is so beautiful, and she is very special, so I named her after the Queen. The Queen of England."

"That's wonderful, but I did not realize that you knew about Queen Victoria."

"Sometimes when I have finished my lessons, I listen to Miss Lewis when she teaches third grade. She told the story of Queen Victoria and her son, Edward, who became King."

"Impressive. So, you are not only keeping up with the other students in second grade, but you are also doing some third-grade work. I must talk to Miss Lewis. I'm happy that you are doing so well in school, Dora. "

Ruby calls us from the kitchen, "Dora, Uncle Joe, R.C. and his family are here, and everything is ready for us to sit down and eat."

I run to open the door in time to hear the doorbell. R.C.'s son, Dickie, is first with little Beth trailing behind. Ruby comes to take their coats.

R.C. and Mr. Murphy shake hands, "Merry Christmas, Uncle Joe, and thank you for all that you do for me and my family throughout the year."

"Merry Christmas to you. R.C, and to the Missus as well. I see the good Lord has watched over you because everyone looks happy and healthy."

Ruby calls us to the dining room, "Come, everyone, before the food gets cold."

Christmas dinner is ham, goose fat potatoes with gravy, brussels sprouts, and candied carrots. I decide I'm too full for dessert, but when Ruby comes to the table with a flaming plum pudding, followed by a basket of warm scones, I change my mind and eat everything anyway. I'm so full that I have a stomachache! At last, I'm excused when Mr. Murphy says we can retire to the parlor for warm cider and port.

I love to watch Mr. Murphy when he drinks port. The bottom of his mustache looks like a paint brush with a little purple stain on the edge. This is my new life! There's so much to think about. Still, I know I will never forget my brothers and, someday, I will find them.

I spend the next week reading my new book and playing with my toys. At breakfast on Thursday, Ruby reminds me that it's New Year's Eve, and we are going to the Mosses for dinner. She says I can wear my velvet party dress!

It will be an early night for us, though. "Uncle Joe likes to eat early so he can be home before people start their New Year's Eve parties. Some people become rowdy shooting guns and such."

On the buggy ride over, I look all around for rowdy people, but don't see anyone with guns. Still, it's a relief when we get to Rex's house.

Harold and Rex greet us at the door when we arrive. Their house is much smaller than Mr. Murphy's, but it's nicely furnished. The table is set near a window in the parlor, with pretty china and crystal.

"Anna, your china is so pretty. I like the red roses and the gold edge on the plates."

"It was my mother's China, and I brought it with me on the ship from Ireland. We only use it for special occasions – and family, like you. Come, everyone, find a seat. The food is ready. John sits in that chair at the head of the table. Otherwise, you can sit anywhere you want. Joseph, will you say grace?"

After we are seated, we bow our heads while Mr. Murphy says grace,

> *Lord, thank for all of the blessings*
> *You have given us this year.*
> *We especially thank you for bringing*
> *Dora to us. She is a special joy.*
> *Bless this good food and*
> *Grant us good health and happiness*
> *In the New Year.*
> *Amen.*

Anna is a good cook. We have beef roast with carrots, potatoes and gravy followedby a dessert of baked pears and oatmeal cookies with raisins. Rex is being naughty, kicking me under the table. After taking the last sip of his cider, he broadcasts a loud belch and grins at me. Everyone laughs except Anna, "Rex, I don't want to tell you again, bring your napkin to your mouth if you need to belch. Honestly, Joseph, I try to teach the boys good manners."

"Oh, Anna, we're just family and it's a holiday. Leave him alone this time. I'm sorry to say we must be going, though. We would like to stay longer but we want to get home before the celebrations begin."

Mr. Murphy looks out the window while Harold brings our coats and hats to the door.

"I see R.C. waiting out front with our buggy. Anna, dinner was delicious. Thank you for having us."

We say our goodbyes and we are greeted by a blast of cold wind when Mr. Murphy opens the door. As we walk down the steps, I notice the porch swing is twisting in the wind.

The ride home is quiet, and I look up to see the North Star.

We are all tired when we get home, so we go to bed early. I quickly fall asleep, and I sleep through the end of the year.

Harmony

January 5, 1904

It's too cold to walk, so R.C. drives Dickie and me to school in the buggy We pick Annie Rose up on the way. My birthday is on Thursday, so Ruby asked Annie's mother if she could come to our house after school so I can show her my new dollhouse.

"What kind of cake do you want?"

"Chocolate, with pink icing, or maybe chocolate cupcakes with pink icing."

"I'll see what I can do. Your first birthday with us! It's something to celebrate!"

On Thursday, I assume R.C. will be waiting for Annie, Dickie, and me in front of the school, but Rex and Harold are already on board, and when I step into the buggy they shout, "Surprise!"

Ruby greets us at the kitchen door, "Come this way, it's too cold to walk to the front."

We hurry inside to the warmth from the fireplace. There's a tall cake with pink icing in the middle of the kitchen table with blue and white dessert plates for the six of us. After we are all seated, Ruby gives each of us a steaming cup of hot chocolate.

"There, Dickie, I saved yours for last. All right, it's Dora's birthday, so let's sing Happy Birthday!"

Everyone sings, except Harold can't seem to sit still. "Harold, behave or I'll tell Mother!"

"Oh, he's okay. He's just being a boy. Here, Harold, you can have the first piece with extra icing!"

"Thank you, everyone! Can you believe it? I'm ten years old today!"

Ruby looks surprised, "Ten? I thought you were only nine!"

"Ruby, you're teasing me. You know I'm ten!"

While Ruby is serving more pieces of cake, Rex kicks me under the table while no one's looking. I give him a scrunched face and finally I tell him out loud, "Stop it!"

He laughs, "I'm just giving you ten little kicks because you turned ten today."

When we are done eating, we go to the parlor. Rex and Harold play checkers while Dickie watches. Annie Rose and I play with the dollhouse, pretending that we are small enough to walk inside and climb the stairs for a slide to the bottom.

Ruby comes into the room, and Annie Rose asks, "Is Dora going to open her presents now?"

"Of course. Annie Rose, why don't you help me bring Dora's presents to her? The packages are on the bottom steps of the stairs."

"I have presents, too?" Everyone laughs.

Annie Rose brings a basket with packages wrapped in white paper with red, yellow and blue ribbons. She hands her gift to me first, a tiny package tied with a blue ribbon. Inside the box are some barrettes and ribbons for my hair, and a card she made herself. "I love them, Annie Rose, thank you!"

The present from Harold and Rex is a spinning top, and Dickie's present is a bag of candied violets from the Sweet Shop. "Now, Dora, Mr. Murphy and I have a special gift for you."

I pull the bow and remove the paper to find a carved wooden box. Ruby urges me to open the lid. I open the hinged lid and it plays *Brahms's Lullaby*.

The inside of the box is lined with velvet. "Thank you, everyone, and thank you, Ruby, for the cake and party. We're having so much fun! Harold, show me how this top works."

Harold holds the top up. It is painted like a dancing ballerina. He starts the spin with three fingers, "There you go!"

It's almost like she isn't made of wood. She's holding her hands, one up and the other crossing her waist like a real ballerina, and her skirt seems to flare out as she dances and twirls across the parlor floor.

Our laughter is interrupted by the crank and jingle of the doorbell. I run to open the door, and there's John. "John, you're late for the party. You missed the cake!"

John laughs. "Happy Birthday, Dora. Ruby told us you are ten years old today. You're becoming quite a young lady. You're a twofer now!"

"What's a twofer?"

"You don't know what a twofer is? It's a person who is so old, they need two numbers to tell people how old they are."

"Oh, John, you're teasing me just like Ruby did!"

"Ruby's been teasing you? Well, I guess that's part of having a birthday - cake, surprises, and clowning around."

John walks to the kitchen to find Ruby, "Ruby, I came to pick up the boys and I'll take Annie Rose home on the way."

They all put on their hats and coats, and Ruby calls after them as we see them out the door, "Thanks for coming and come again! Now hurry home so you don't catch a cold."

After everyone is gone, the house is so quiet. "Well, Dora, you had a very nice party. Come help me now, let's pick the paper up off the floor and put things away. Do you want to save the ribbons?"

I nod, yes and gather up the ribbons, making two trips upstairs to put things away. Ruby shouts up the stairs, "Don't tarry, Mr. Murphy will be coming home soon from the office, and he will want to have supper right away."

I soon know every minute of our daily routine. On school days, I wake up at 6:30, wash up in the bathroom and get dressed, then downstairs to breakfast with Mr. Murphy and Ruby, then R.C. is waiting in the buggy outside the kitchen door with Dickie, for the ride to school. School lets out at 4:00, so by the time I get home, it's time to wash up for supper. After supper, we sit in the same chairs in the parlor and Mr. Murphy reads from his Bible.

Saturdays and Sundays are reserved for extra sleep and play. There's no special time for breakfast, I can eat whenever I want. There's always a pot of hot water for tea, and biscuits in a tin, keeping warm on the stove.

I live in a nice house. It's especially nice when it's sunny and I sit in the kitchen feeling the warmth of the sun that bounces off the jars of honey, jams, and jellies on the table. They look like the stained glass in the windows at church.

Still, sometimes when I am alone, I try to be grateful that I have all that I need, even good friends, but sometimes I just sit by the front window and cry. I try not to let Ruby or Mr. Murphy see.

Ruby usually has a pot of soup on the stove for the afternoon and evening meals along with freshly baked bread. However, nothing is scheduled; we simply amble through those days doing whatever comes to mind.

Annie Rose and I take turns going to one another's house on Saturday afternoons. When she comes to our house, we usually play with the dollhouse, and Ruby gives us cookies so we can have pretend tea parties with our dolls and my little tea set. At her house, we like to read in her bedroom. I often bring my book so we can read *Rebecca of Sunnybrook Farm*, even though we've already read it many times. One day after we had just finished reading, we were laying back on Annie Rose's bed with our legs dangling off the side, "Dora, know what? You are just like Rebecca! You left your family and here you are in Canton. I wonder if that is why Mr. Murphy bought the book for you!"

"Oh, Annie Rose, I don't want to think about it just now. I just want to be happy."

"Do you think Rebecca was smart like you and me?"

"Of course, don't you remember..."

Then we recite our favorite line:

I don't expect you to believe it, but I have another idea—
that's two in one day.

And we laugh so hard that we almost fall off the bed.

I wake up late the next Saturday, and when I come downstairs, it seems I'm all alone, 'cuz there's no one else around. As I enter the kitchen, Ruby is coming to the kitchen from her room in the back. "Where's Mr. Murphy?"

"He told me that he had to go into the office this morning. He has a surprise for you! He should be home soon."

After breakfast, I get dressed and when I come downstairs, Mr. Murphy is waiting for me in the parlor. As I cross the room to sit in my favorite chair, there's a knock on the door, followed by the jingle of the doorbell. Ruby opens the door, "Come, come in, Mrs. Smith, Mr. Murphy and Dora are waiting for you."

Ruby takes her coat and Mrs. Smith goes directly to the piano. Mr. Murphy smiles as he takes my hand and leads me to the piano, "Dora, someone told me that you would like to learn to play the piano. Mrs. Smith, here, plays the piano and she's going to give you piano lessons."

I've always wanted to learn to play the piano. At times when playing in the parlor, I've wanted to touch the ivory keys, but I didn't want to get in trouble. Now I can learn and play it whenever I want!

Mrs. Smith pats the cushion on the piano bench, "Here, Dora, you can sit next to me. I'll play a little song for you." Her fingers seem to fly across the black and white keys as she plays, and her operatic voice fills the room with *I'm Called Little Buttercup.*

"I like that song, Mrs. Smith. I haven't heard it before."

"Thank you. I like to play it for my new students. It is from an operetta, *H.M.S. Pinafore.* You will learn to play that song, but that is not how we start. To begin, you will learn the notes and how to read and play scales. Now, it will be important for you to practice every day. What do you do when you come home from school?"

"I play with my doll and dollhouse, and sometimes I Just sit in the kitchen and talk to Ruby."

"Do you think you can practice for 30 minutes every day after school?" I nod, yes. "Do you get good grades in school?"

Mr. Murphy intercedes, "Dora's teacher tells me that she is an excellent student. She is in second grade but doing third grade work. Ruby will make sure that she has time to practice every day."

"Good. Now, Dora, here is your first music book. See inside? There's a picture of the piano keys. This one is called Middle C; can you find Middle C on the piano?"

I stare at the piano, not knowing which key to touch. "Here, let me help you. Just remember when you sit on the bench at the middle of the piano, Middle C is the closest white key to the middle of the piano, next to two black keys and left of this black key - right here. Go ahead, you can touch it."

I touch the key gently and feel the soothing, mellow sound.

"Good. Just remember, if you have trouble finding Middle C when I am not here, when you sit at the middle of the piano, Middle C will be the closest key to your belly button." We all laugh.

"Mr. Murphy, I think she will do fine. Dora, this week I want you to study this book and find the keys on the piano. Once you know how to find Middle C, the rest will come easy. I'll see you next Saturday."

Home Is A Word!

The rest of the school year has flown by, and I have been promoted to third grade! Play times with Annie Rose break the monotony and sometimes Rex comes by to visit. We had a nice Easter with Rex and his family. Rex told me that he is too grown up to believe in the Easter Bunny, so we just enjoy the candy and eggs.

By May, I have memorized all of the scales and chords and I'm playing some songs. My favorite is *The Cat Came Back.*

Annie Rose's birthday is June 2 and her mother invited me and some of the girls from her fourth-grade class for a party. Ruby and I go shopping for a present for the party.

"Do you have something in mind?"

"No, but she likes to jump rope and play hopscotch at school."

"Good ideas. Here's a dollar, so you can buy whatever you want. Now that the weather is nice, maybe you can find something that she can play with outside. What's wrong, why so surprised?"

"You mean I can spend a whole dollar by myself?"

"Of course, she's your friend, so you should be the one to pick the present. Just remember to count the change."

I put on my blue pinafore for the party, and Ruby put a matching bow in my hair. I'm excited for Annie Rose, but Rex and Harold were not invited. She told me this will be an all-girls party, and she invited girls from her class that I don't know.

Annie Rose's mama made a pretty white cake with white icing and a ballerina on top. Some of the other girls gave her necklaces, one gave her a mirror and comb, and she got a coloring book and crayons, but her face lights up and she gives me a big hug when she opens my present, a box with colored chalk, a jump rope, jacks and a ball.

To my surprise, I have a lot of fun. The other girls are nice, and I have made some new friends.

When I return home, Ruby has a supper of chicken and noodles cooking on the stove, but I'm full of cake and candy, and I pick at my food, leaning my head on my hand.

Chicken and noodles are Mr. Murphy's favorite. "What's wrong, Dora? These noodles are very good! Don't you feel like eating?"

"I know, I like Ruby's noodles, but I ate too much cake at Annie Rose's party."

"Did you have a good time? What all did you do?"

"We played games and ran around, then Annie Rose opened her presents. My present was the best one – most of the other presents were just stuff to wear. I gave her colored chalk, a jump rope and a ball and jacks and she said we'd play with them next Saturday! I had a whole dollar to spend. I was a little scared at first because I didn't know the other girls, cuz' they are in Annie Rose's class. I like them and we're the same age, so I think they will be my friends. Mr. Murphy, I'm so much smaller than other girls my age. Sometimes they don't believe me when I tell them I'm ten."

"Well, that will go away in time. Right now, you are new in town, so they are just getting to know you. By the way, a lady from across town came to my office yesterday. She has taken in a boy from the Orphan Train, and we thought the two of you might want to get together."

I want to say "no" because I'm really not interested in meeting boys. I do like Rex and Harold, but some of the boys at school aren't nice, and some are even mean, but he was on the Orphan Train, so maybe he saw Jack or Louis. "That would be nice, Mr. Murphy."

Ruby hears us talking so she comes from the kitchen wiping her hands on a towel, "Uncle Joe, why don't you see if he would like to come to tea on Sunday?"

Sunday, after breakfast, I put on one of my school dresses and I go downstairs. Ruby has already set up a small table in the parlor with a sugar bowl, cups and saucers, and a plate of cookies.

It's five minutes after two when I hear the crank and jingle of the doorbell. I go to the door with Ruby to greet a boy who looks to be about Dickie's age. He has red hair and freckles, and he's wearing a suit with short pants, a white shirt and necktie. I guess it's nice that he dressed up, but he looks like he's about to choke.

"Come on in, Michael. Michael, this is Dora. You can sit over there. There's a plate of cookies and I'll bring you some tea."

Ruby goes to the kitchen, leaving us alone. I didn't know what to say or what to talk about.

"Why are you so dressed up? Is this what you wear on Sundays?"

"No, my mommy made me dress up because she said I was going to Mr. Murphy's house. She said Mr. Murphy is a very important man."

"Oh, I guess we shouldn't go outside to play ball after tea, or you will get dirty."

"Guess not."

"Mr. Murphy told me you rode the Orphan Train. So did I! Some men took my brothers and me away from our mama. Jack is younger than me, and we call Louis, Baby Louis. He really isn't a baby, though; he's almost four now. Do you remember a boy named Jack or Louis from the train?"

"No, but there was mostly boys, only three girls. Your name's Dora?"

I nod my head yes, and Ruby comes into the room with a teapot.

"How old are you?"

"I'm ten. How old are you?"

"Seven. You don't look like you're ten, I'm bigger than you. These are good cookies."

"And you look like you're older than seven." I am not sure what to say, but I'm trying to be polite.

"What do you want to do? I have a book that I like to read, Rebecca of Sunnybrook Farm, but you probably won't like it. It's not a boy's book."

By now, Michael is squirming in his chair. He hasn't touched his tea, but he ate all of the cookies. Neither of us are having fun, and it looks like he might run for the door, at any minute.

"Dora, I have to go home. I need to feed my dog. He'll be waiting for me."

I was right, he runs for the door, and I watch him as he runs up the street towards home. I wonder if he really has a dog.

July 18, 1904.

I roll the ball to Louis, "Here, Louis, catch the red ball!

"It's blue, not red!" I blink my eyes. He's right, the ball turns from red to blue.

Louis kicks the ball towards Jack but the ball rolls down towards the river.
I run down the slope to get the ball, but it's already floating down the river.
"Jack, get it! I can't get it!"

"I don't want to. I'm going to the porch to play marbles."

Louis plops down on the ground and he starts to cry. "See, we lost the ball and you made Baby Louis cry."

Jack runs to Louis. He drops to the ground and hugs him, "Oh, Louis, I'm sorry. I love you!" Jack looks up at me, "Dora, I love you too! Let's go inside and I'll give you some cake."

I wake up and remember that today is Jack's birthday. He's seven today. I wonder if someone will make him a birthday cake. He might not get presents like I do now, but a cake would be nice.

I decide to just lay in bed for a while.

I hear Ruby, walking up the stairs to my room, "Hey, sleepyhead, it's ten o'clock. You don't look like you're sick! Are you just going to lay in bed all day?"

"No, I'm okay. I'll get dressed and come down, but I don't feel like eating."

"All right, but I hope you're not getting sick."

Mr. Murphy is reading in the parlor when I come downstairs, "Well, there's our girl. We were wondering about you. Your eyes are all red, have you been crying?"

I nod my head, yes, and start to cry again.

"Come here, Baby Girl, and sit on my lap. Why are you crying?"

"Today, is Jack's birthday."

"Here, here, don't cry. Who is Jack?"

"He's...he's my brother."

"You have two brothers, right? Which of the two boys is Jack? Is he the oldest?"

I'm crying so hard that I can hardly talk, so I nod my head yes.

"Jack is a good name. How old is he today? Tell me about Jack."

"Seven. Sometimes he was naughty, but I loved him anyway. He would take off to the train depot to play marbles with older boys from across town even though Mama told him not to. I felt bad when Mama switched his legs, 'cuz I told on him. He had red stripes on his legs for a few days once. He said he wouldn't do it again, but he did. I had to lock him in his room."

Mr. Murphy strokes my hair. "He sounds very naughty."

"No, sometimes we had fun, though. We used to take lunch to Daddy at the barbershop, and we played next to the river and fed the ducks on the way."

"Did your mama make a cake for Jack's birthday? What kind of cake did he like?"

"We all like chocolate cake. We spent a week with Aunt Maggie and Uncle John before we moved to the apartment. Everyone came on Sunday for a family picnic and Aunt Maggie made a cake for Jack's birthday. That afternoon Mama took us home with her and we moved to our apartment the next day. We wanted to stay with Aunt Maggie and Uncle John, but Aunt Maggie told me we had to go because Mama missed us."

"Your mother must miss you now."

"Uh huh, when the men came to take us away, she was crying."

"Ruby told me that you like to find four-leafed clovers."

"Know what, Mr. Murphy, some have five leaves! One time when we were all at the park for the 4th of July, I found enough four-leafed clovers to give one to Mama, all my aunts, and all of my cousins. I used to find four-leafed clovers every day in the summer, and Mama always put them in a little glass on the kitchen table."

"I bet Ruby would like to have a glass of four-leafed clovers on the kitchen table. Why don't you bring some to her and see what happens? Baby Girl, you never said – what happened to your father?"

"He got sick. At first, they wouldn't let Jack and me in his room, but right before he died, they let us see him. He was glad to see us, but it was scary. There was blood all over his pillow.""

"That sounds like typhoid fever."

"They sent us to stay with Uncle John and Aunt Maggie, but Doc Donovan came to get us in the middle of the night so we could be with Mama when he died. He was so cold, but Mama told us that it's warm in heaven."

"It must have been hard for her when they took you away, it would be hard for any mother. You said she cried, so she must have loved you."

"You think so?"

"Of course. Did you know that no one has to suffer from typhoid fever anymore? Last year a doctor discovered a vaccine, so no more typhoid!"

"Know what else? One day, Jack accidentally kicked over a pail of hot water and burned my legs. That is why I have these scars. See?"

"That must have really hurt, but I bet Jack felt really bad."

"He did. He cried even though Mama and Doc Donovan told him it was just an accident. But we had to move to an apartment, then Mama got sick. Later, some men came and took us all away. Mama was crying a lot, and I still don't know what happened to my brothers."

"Dora, that's sad, but it's also a remarkable story. You were fortunate to have a loving family, and I know you were such a big help for your mother. You have a lot of spunk, Dora. Ruby and I admire you."

"Mr. Murphy, can you find my brothers? Can we bring my brothers here?"

"Can't say I would even know where to look. Besides, wherever they are, I'm sure the people they are with love them like I love you, and they wouldn't want to give them up. You'll forget them after a while. Why don't we go to the kitchen to see what Ruby is up to, I think she's baking cookies?"

Ruby is rolling out cookie dough when we enter the kitchen. "See, she is baking cookies! Maybe we can convince her to make a cake for Jack's birthday. Ruby, Dora tells me that today is her brother's birthday. I know you are making cookies, but will you have time to make a cake?"

Mr. Murphy's back is turned when Ruby rolls her eyes. She gives a small snort, then she responds with a fake smile, "Not today. It's getting late and I have to cook supper, but we can make a cake tomorrow. Is that okay, Dora?"

I know she doesn't want to do it, but I smile and say, "Yes, thank you!" This has not been a good day. I'll stop crying and just do what I'm asked to, but Mr. Murphy's wrong - I will never forget Jack and Louis!

Ruby shows me how to cut the cookies with a drinking glass dipped in flour, and she put them on baking sheets. I have flour up my arms and all over the front of my dress. We all have a big laugh when I rub some flour on Mr. Murphy's nose.

"That's what we've been missing in this house, laughter! Isn't it wonderful to have Dora around?"

At night when I can't sleep, I sometimes think about Mr. Murphy. I like him but I can't say I love him, like he said to me. I wish he wouldn't call me his Baby, though. So far, he's just a nice man, almost family sometimes, but not always. Soon, I drift off to sleep, and in my dream, I find Louis, hiding in a flour bin or in the barn. What if he's living just down the road and I don't know it?

The night after Jack's birthday, I dream Louis is in my dollhouse! I can't sleep afterwards, so I come downstairs early so I can help Ruby with the cake.

"Here, I'll measure the flour and you can sift the flour. "

After we put the cake tins in the oven, Ruby tells me to walk softly, or the cakes will fall.

That night after supper, we have a chocolate cake with blue icing, and we sing Happy Birthday to Jack! I feel a little better.

Pumpkin and Sage

I'm outgrowing all of my dresses and shoes, and school will be starting soon, so Ruby and I keep busy going to stores to shop for fabric, shoes, and underwear. Then we go to the seamstress Helen's house. She's making me some play dresses and five new dresses for school, one for each day of the week.

On Sunday, before school starts, Harold and Rex stop by with Annie Rose. We decide to play hide and seek, and Harold agrees to be It! Annie Rose takes off towards some bushes and Rex whispers, "Where's a good place to hide?"

"Come with me. I know a good place. He'll never find us."

I lead Rex to the back of the house, down the steps into the cellar. It's dark and we wait. "You're right, Dora, he'll never think of looking for us here. What should we do?"

"Come back here. I want to show you a chest that's on the back wall. Ruby told me it's special."

We walk deeper into the dark cellar, brushing cobwebs out of our way with our hands, laughing while wiping those that we missed, off our faces. Rex finds an oil lamp and some matches so we can see. "Wow, Dora, Ruby's right, this is really neat!"

"When Ruby showed me the cellar, I was scared of the dark, so she told me we would look in the chest, another time. Do you think it's okay to look inside?"

"We'll be careful, so no one will know. Let's see." Rex opens the chest.

There's a musty odor like someone, or something, must have died inside. Rex picks up what looks like a heavy coat, laying on top. "Look, Dora, it's a Union Jack uniform from the War. Look at the brown stain, that's blood!"

I suddenly feel a cold mist move over us, and we watch as it floats towards the door. "Rex, let's go. I don't like it down here!"

Rex puts the uniform back, and he closes the chest. Just as he turns off the lamp, we hear Harold calling for us. "Rex, Dora, where are you? I'm tired of looking for you two! You can come home free."

Rex whispers, "Shh! Don't tell them about our secret hiding place. Don't even tell Annie Rose!"

We can see their legs as they pass the window, and we watch them as they turn the corner towards the other side of the house. Rex takes my hand, and we hurry up the steps. We run to the tree where Harold and Annie are waiting. "Where were you? Look at you, you guys are all dirty. Mother's going to wonder where you've been, Rex. Come on, we better get home for supper!"

I keep the secret. It is our first secret together, and even though I get a shiver thinking of that bloodstain, I know someday, if Rex comes along, I'll feel brave enough to go through the whole chest and see if there's treasure in there.

Mr. Murphy comes with me for the first day of school, and he carries my school supplies in his satchel. Miss Lewis greets us at the door when we enter the classroom, "Mr. Murphy, the principal would like to see you and Dora in his office. It's down the hall on the right."

I try to keep up as Mr. Murphy walks briskly down the hall into the principal's office. "I'm Joseph Murphy, and this is Dora. You wanted to see us? I hope nothing's wrong."

"No, no, nothing's wrong, but I'm glad that you came to school with Dora today. My name is Joseph too, Joseph Feeney. Please have a seat. Miss Lewis tells me that Dora is a good student, and she was doing third grade work last year."

"She told me the same. Dora likes school and she remembers what she learns. She named her doll after Queen Victoria. When I asked her how she knew about the Queen, she told me Miss Lewis had told the third-grade class a story about the Queen and her son, Edward, who became King of England."

"Well, the reason I wanted to see you is we think Dora is ready to move up to fourth grade. She's ten, so she will still be one year behind, but she is small so she will fit in just fine. Besides, we want her to continue to like school and Miss Lewis told me that Dora has already done a lot of the work she would be doing this year in third grade."

"Thank you, Mr. Feeney, this is quite a surprise. Well, Dora, what do you think? Would you like to move up to fourth grade?"

"Oh, yes, then I will be in the same class as Annie Rose!"

"Annie Rose? Who is Annie Rose?" the principal asks.

"Annie Rose O'Neal, she's my best friend. We play and read books together."

"Oh yes! She's a good student, too. If it is all right with you, Mr. Murphy, I will walk with you to Dora's new classroom."

When we get to the classroom, Mr. Murphy and I stand by the door while Mr. Feeney talks to the teacher. Annie Rose sees us, and she waves, looking a little surprised.

"Dora, this is your new teacher, Mrs. Hart. Mrs. Hart will take over now. I know you will do well in fourth grade."

"Dora, the fourth grade is on this side of the room, so you can have this desk."

Mr. Murphy helps me to put my school supplies in my desk; when I lift the lid of the desk, my schoolbooks are inside. Mr. Murphy and Mr. Feeney wave goodbye and leave.

I like school and I'm making good grades. I'm so glad that I'm in the same class with Annie Rose. That means we will have the same recess every day, and we will have the same friends. After school we meet up with Rex and he walks us home, even though he lives the other way down Main.

A few weeks later, Annie Rose comes home with me after school, and Ruby asks if we will rake the leaves. Rex does most of the raking, making three big piles. He's nearly done when Annie Rose and I jump onto the biggest pile. We roll in the leaves, and a breeze scatters the leaves across the lawn. Annie Rose and I laugh; Rex doesn't say anything, but we can hear him talking to himself while he rakes the leaves, again, into new piles.

"Whoops, Dora, I don't think Rex thought that was funny!"

Halloween is coming and Annie Rose and I spend an afternoon deciding on costumes to wear to the bonfire. We decide to be Jack and Jill so we can fill the pail with candy and cookies. Annie Rose is going to be Jill, and I ask Dickie if I can borrow some of his clothes so I can dress like Jack. He also gives me a bucket from his sandbox for Jack's pail of water.

The Saturday before Halloween, R.C. takes the four of us to the farm for a hayride. He comes out of the barn with a wagon with a bed of hay, hitched to a brown and white horse. Rex is the first to climb up into the wagon. R.C. lifts Annie Rose and me so we can grab Rex's hand and he pulls us up to land on the hay.

Harold asks, "R.C., can I ride with you up front?"

"I don't see why not. I'll even let you take the reins. The horse's name is Jennie and she's friendly. You can give it a try."

Harold climbs onto the seat next to R.C. R.C. shakes the reins on her back, "Gee, Jennie, let's go!"

The wagon lurches as we take off toward a path between the soybeans and a cornfield. Suddenly, a fox runs out from one of the rows of corn and Jennie spooks, rearing up and whinnying. The front of the wagon tips enough to the right to throw Harold to the ground in front of the wheels of the wagon. The wagon is still rolling, and Harold tries to roll out of the way. The wagon stops when it hits Jennie's rump, but not in time to miss Harold's right arm.

Harold is wailing. Rex and R.C. jump down from the wagon, running to help him to his feet. "What's wrong, son, are you okay?"

Harold continues to howl, holding his arm, now hanging at an odd angle.

"Girls, come on down, be careful, but jump down from the wagon. We need to get Harold to the doctor."

We leave Jennie and the wagon in the field and all of us board the carriage. I look back and Jennie is pulling the wagon on her own, slowly plodding her way towards the barn.

Annie Rose, Rex and I sit on the porch at the doctor's office while Harold is inside with the doctor. After a while, the yelling stops and it's so quiet that we wonder if Harold might have died. We sit there a long while. It's almost dark when Harold comes out with a big plaster cast on his arm.

"Get on the wagon, Harold first, so I can take you all home. We'll drop Harold and Rex off first, so he can lie down and I'll try to explain this to his mother."

Monday night is Halloween and the bonfire. Mr. Murphy, The Pumpkin, is now a tradition. People smile and point to Annie Rose and me, the perfect Jack and Jill team. We play around the bonfire, and Harold just sits on a log, holding his arm. We fill my pail with candy and cookies from the table in the barn.

"Annie Rose, let's take some cookies to Harold."

"Okay, I'll just eat one. You'd better have one too. He can have the rest."

When Harold sees us walking his way, he tries to smile, but we can tell he's not feeling good.

"Hi, Harold. How's your arm? It must've really hurt."

Harold tries to appear tough, "Oh, it was nothing. Doc says I will have the cast off by Christmas."

Rex comes strutting up as Annie Rose hands the pail, brimming with cookies. "Harold, we brought these for you!"

"Thanks, girls, that's nice of you. I'll eat all of them."

"What? You're not going to share them with your only brother, the one who has to do his own chores and all of yours until you get rid of that cast?"

We all laugh, even Harold. Harold holds out the pail, "Here, you guys, have a cookie. Just one, Rex!"

"Only one?"

"Hey, you guys didn't break your arm!"

The fiddler stops playing and the Mayor announces from a flat bed, "Ladies and Gentlemen, thank you for coming tonight. We've all been looking forward to our annual bonfire! Let's give a round of applause for the ladies from the Presbyterian Church for organizing this event, and to our fiddler, Elmer Coleman. Without Elmer, it wouldn't be half as much fun."

Everyone applauds.

"Also, don't forget to visit the barn for cookies and cider. Now, what everyone has been waiting for. This year's prize for best costume goes to Jack and Jill, Dora Kelly and Annie Rose O'Neal! Girls, come up and get your prize."

Annie Rose and I are surprised. When we reach the wagon, a man lifts us up and the Mayor hands envelopes to us. We say thank you and jump down to run to the chairs where Mr. Murphy and Ruby are sitting next to Annie Rose's parents. Her mother looks in Annie Rose's envelope and she laughs. "Annie, you won a haircut at Louis' Barbershop. I guess they thought a boy would win!"

Just then a lady walks up with two envelopes in her hand, "Annie Rose, Dora, we are so sorry – your prizes aren't good for girls. Take these, I think they will suit you better."

Mr. Murphy opens my envelope, and he smiles, "Much better, I think you girls will like this. Open yours, Annie Rose. Dora's envelope has a letter so she can buy a dollar's worth of candy at the Sweet Shoppe!"

We are eating breakfast when the door opens, and a cold blast of air follows R.C. into the kitchen. "Morning, Uncle Joe! I talked to Hoffman and he's getting the horse to the farm. It's a good thing you didn't pay much because she's really a nag. Still, we can use her for plowing."

"I didn't expect much when they quoted their price, but they said they were going to shoot her if I didn't want her. She'll work out. I see here in the paper that Teddy Roosevelt won reelection. I doubt Parker will have a place in history; he was a weak candidate."

"That's good. I voted for Teddy. Cain't talk much politics around the house, though. The missus gets all worked up 'cuz she can't vote."

"I agree with her. It's the women who kept up the farms and tended the wounded during the war. In fact, it was a woman who sewed the first American flag, yet she didn't have the right to vote. I know some men who could not have done what women have done for our country! You'll have to tell Mary what I said when you see her. Maybe it will make her feel better."

"How many are coming for Thanksgiving? I have my eye on a couple birds for you. One is a big Tom, and the other is a good-sized hen."

"It will just be Anna and her family so, let's see, that's seven, but go ahead and kill the Tom. We like to have turkey left over for sandwiches and soup over the weekend."

I'm excited for this Thanksgiving, because Ruby told me that this year, I'm old enough to help her with cooking dinner. R.C. brought the turkey early this morning and after it is stuffed, it will be so heavy that Mr. Murphy will have to help Ruby lift the turkey in and out of the oven.

Thanksgiving is like no other day. The aroma of roasting turkey drifts through the house and all the way up the stairs to my room on the third floor. There are two open bottles of wine on the kitchen table, Sherry for the sausage and chestnut stuffing and Port for the cranberry sauce with dried cherries. The smell is a combination of roasting turkey basted with butter and sage, and the stuffed dressings, sausage and chestnut stuffing for the neck and cornbread stuffing for the other end.

Even though this is my first time to help with cooking, Ruby and I soon develop a rhythm, each working on a different dish. This time, I learn to make Candied Carrots, and I'm going to make Orange Butter for the Boston Brown Bread. The table is set, so I can go upstairs to get dressed.

I look out the front window and John has just turned his buggy onto the dooryard that leads to our carriage house. Rex jumps down before it comes to a complete stop, and he runs to the front door. Harold is not far behind. I open the door before he even has time to crank the doorbell. "Hurry,

Harold, we want to shut the door. It's cold!" Harold comes in and Rex slams the door shut.

Anna and John must have come in the side door because I can hear them talking to Ruby in the kitchen. Mr. Murphy comes downstairs when he hears the door slam, and we all linger, enjoying the warmth of the kitchen while Ruby finishes making gravy. "Dora, boys, find your seats at the dining room table. Uncle Joe will bring the turkey. Anna, would you please bring the side dishes?"

"Of course." She gives Rex a stern look. "And Rex, no kicking under the table this time. You sit next to me, and Dora will sit at the other end."

Rex looks at me and he shrugs. I smile back even though I wish we could sit closer so we could talk.

The turkey is in the center of the table, plump with a golden-brown coat, and I close my eyes for John to give the blessing, I breathe in the aroma of the sage from the dressings, mixed with smell of the melting candles and the sweetness of the candied carrots.

"Let us bow our heads in prayer."

> *Lord God, we are grateful for this*
> *wonderful meal and for all of the*
> *blessings of life that you give to us.*
> *Thank you for this food but most of all,*
> *thank you for the love of family.*
> *In Jesus' name we pray.*
> *Amen.*

Mr. Murphy looks up at John, "Thank you John. Now, everybody, let's eat! I prefer the dark meat myself."

We eat so much! After we are done, Rex and Harold go to the parlor to find the checkerboard, but I'm so full that all I want to do is to lay down. Rex calls me over, "C'mon, Dora, we'll have a checker tournament. You can have the red checkers and play against Harold, then I will play the winner."

"I can't, I'm too full! Besides, you know Harold will win!"

"C'mon, it will be fun. You won one game last year."

Of course, Harold wins, then it's Rex against Harold. It's an exciting game.

Harold gets excited and it seems he forgets about his arm. Laughing, he jumps three of Rex's checkers. "I always want to win! If you beat me, it will bother me. I just like to win!"

As Harold captures the last red checker, Mr. Murphy puts his wine glass on the table. "All right, Harold, so you like to win. Let's see how really good you are. See if you can beat me!"

I can't believe it! Mr. Murphy gets down on the floor. He props himself up with his elbow as he lays on his side. Soon he has a King and he's jumping Harold's checkers in all directions. Finally, it's Harold's turn, but no matter which way he moves, the game is over.

"Now, John, you get down here and play against me!"

The tournament is on! Mr. Murphy beats John, then it's Rex's turn to win, catching Mr. Murphy by surprise. "Rex, that was a brilliant move! Now let's see if you can beat your father."

Silence fills the room, and it looks like this will be a serious game. I curl up in a chair, as the father against son game commences. Both are slow to make moves, neither wanting to make a mistake. John captures the last red checker. "You win, Father. I didn't know you were so good at checkers. We will have to play at home."

Mr. Murphy gets up to sit in his chair, "Okay it's down to the final game. Harold, it's your turn to try to beat your father."

Again, the room is quiet as the players carefully plan their moves. Harold is the first to capture his opponent's checker. Then he does a double jump leaving nine black to twelve red checkers. As Harold becomes more confident, he makes a quick move, and two of his checkers are in jeopardy.

"Not a good move, Son. You know the rules, I have to jump you!"

Now the game is tied, nine to nine, but John's checker has made it to Kings Row, so he is crowned King. John takes full advantage and before long, Harold's remaining checkers are boxed in. "Gee, Dad, you're good. I want to try again."

Anna is standing in the doorway to the kitchen, watching the tournament. "Another game, another day. It's time for us to go home. Look at Dora, she's sound asleep. Too much food!"

"I'm not asleep!" I shake myself – maybe I am sleepy. I feel Ruby shaking me a little.

"Wake up, Dora, our guests are leaving."

"Did I miss something? Who's the champion?"

"No, my father won. He's the champion this time but wait until next time!"

Mr. Murphy pulls me onto his lap as Ruby sees our guests out the door. After they are gone, he asks, "Well , Baby Girl, I know you fell asleep, but did you have a good time?"

Ruby smiles, "I think she had a good time – she ate a lot of turkey and chestnut stuffing. Then she ate apple pie. Too much for such a little girl. Come on, Dora, I'll take you to your room and help you into your nightdress."

I slip off of Mr. Murphy's lap and go up the stairs, ready for bed.

The First Street Threesome

Christmas is as wonderful this year as it was last year. It turns out Santa and Mr. Murphy are just as generous, even though I'm not new anymore, and dinner is perfect. I can't wait to play with Annie Rose, and this year she comes by before New Year's Eve.

"Annie Rose, what did you get for Christmas?"

"I got my very own sewing box with needles and thread, and Mommy is going to teach me to sew. Then Santa brought me a sled and a new baby doll in a cradle. How about you?"

"I got some dresses for my doll. Ruby gave me some paper dolls and Mr. Murphy gave me a globe so I can learn more about geography."

Annie Rose still believes in Santa Claus, and I don't want to tell her that Johnny Scott told me there's no Santa, so I made up the last part, "and Santa brought me a musical carousel with pretty white horses that move up and down as the carousel goes round and round. When some horses are up, others are down, just like a real merry-go-round."

We're invited to Rex's house again for dinner on New Year's Eve. After dinner, John and Mr. Murphy celebrate with a glass of port, while Anna and Ruby wash the dishes. Harold's cast was removed yesterday, but he's just sitting on a chair in the parlor, holding his arm.

"Harold, does your arm still hurt?"

"No, it just feels funny now that the cast is off. Besides, Rex is doing all the chores so why hurry? Kidding!" He smiles when Rex gives him a dirty look.

Rex shows me a toy chest, next to the sideboard in the dining room. He raises his voice so everyone can hear, "Here, Dora, you can choose whatever you want to play with." Then he whispers, "Have you gone back to the cellar to look in the chest?"

"No, I'm too scared to go down there alone. I've been waiting for you. Are you coming to our house next Saturday for my birthday?"

"Sure. I will definitely be there, and Harold will probably come 'cuz he's tired of sitting around the house. What do you want for your birthday?"

"Just cake and a party."

January 7 comes so quickly! I wake up on my birthday wondering what Ruby has planned for today. The best part of having a birthday are the surprises.

Annie Rose, Rex, and Harold arrive around two o'clock, and some of the girls I met at Annie Rose's party come a little later. Ruby serves my favorite chocolate cake with pink icing, and she has bags of candy for everyone from the Sweet Shoppe. There are lots of presents, even more than last year. My favorite present is the one from Annie Rose, a bracelet with blue stones and a book, *Alice's Adventures in Wonderland*, that we will read together. There's a book from Ruby too, *A Cookbook for Little Girls*. Mr. Murphy gives me a small table and chairs for tea parties with Annie and my doll, so his present isn't wrapped. Harold gives me some Old Maid cards, and Rex's gift is a puzzle with a picture of a little girl in a blue dress, playing a piano.

After everyone leaves, I go to the kitchen to talk to Ruby, "Ruby, thank you for the party. Everyone liked the cake!"

Just then Mr. Murphy calls from his chair in the parlor, "Dora, why don't you come sit with me while Ruby cleans up?"

Mr. Murphy pats his knee with his hand. I hang back a little. "Mr. Murphy, I was just wondering. Don't you think I'm getting too old to be your Baby and to sit on your lap?"

"I thought you liked sitting on my lap."

"I did when I was little, but I'm eleven years old now. I'm not a baby anymore, and my legs are getting longer. I can sit with you, but not on your lap."

"I guess I'll always think of you as my Baby Girl, but maybe you can just sit here next to me from now on when we want to talk."

I climb onto the hassock in front of his chair, relieved and happy.

Anna invites us for supper for Rex's birthday. She tells Mr. Murphy that she isn't going to have a party, except for supper with us. Rex never dresses warm enough for the ride to school, so I decide to give him a soft woolen muffler. He really likes it!

It snows, then it snows some more into February, making it difficult to get to school. Mr. Murphy says we are having record snowfall. On days when the streets are closed our school is closed, so we stay home close to the fire. I practice my piano and play with my dollhouse and doll, but it's not as much fun, playing alone.

In March there's still snow on the ground, but we can finally get to school. I look for Annie Rose, but she's not there. Teacher tells me that Annie Rose has chicken pox, so she will miss school for a while. It's too cold to go outside for recess, so we play games in the lunchroom. When I tell Rex about Annie Rose, he gets really nervous.

"Oh no, Dora, I have some spots on my stomach and they itch. What if I have chicken pox?"

He goes back to his classroom to tell his teacher. She lifts his shirt up to look at his stomach, and she tells him to go home.

Finally, on the very day that Annie Rose and Rex will be back in school, I come down with the pox, too. Ruby notices a spot on my cheek. Then she looks closer, and I have another on my neck.

"Dora, it looks like you're coming down with chicken pox. You'll have to stay home. Go on up to your room."

Ruby follows me up the stairs to my room with my mittens. "Here, let me help you into your nightdress, and you'll have to wear these mittens, so you won't scratch. If you scratch, it will leave scars."

The next ten days are boring and what I remember most is, I ITCH! I can't go to school and the blisters have increased more and more, especially on my face. I cry when I look in the mirror, so I decide to stop looking in the mirror until it's all over. I have a headache, and I hate the feeling, itching, itching, itching, all over my head, tummy, arms and legs. I so much want to scratch!

Mr. Murphy has been up to see me a couple times. One day, he brought the newspaper with pictures of President Roosevelt's inauguration, and the other time, be brought chocolates from the Sweet Shoppe.

Finally, the blisters scab over, so Ruby tells me I can go to school. I want to go back to school but I know I look terrible. "Ruby, I'm not ready to go back to school. Not yet."

"Aren't you feeling better?"

"Well, yes."

"Is it because you don't want your friends to see the scabs on your face and arms?"

I nod.

"Well, don't worry, half the school caught the chicken pox so there will be others who look just like you."

Ruby was right, Johnny and Martha in my class have scabs on their face and arms. Ruby has been putting body cream on me everywhere so, gradually, I look a little better. Before long I'm back to normal except for two scars where I scratched my forehead.

It's finally warm enough that we can go outside for recess. Rex and Annie Rose find me on the playground. Harold is the only one who didn't catch the pox. We're glad for him. We decide it wouldn't be fair for Harold to get the pox after breaking his arm.

Easter is late this year. Now that I'm older, I don't believe in Santa or the Easter Bunny, but Miss Lewis shows us how to weave Easter baskets with strips of construction paper, so that's fun. I take mine home and Ruby put it in the center of the kitchen table to hold our colored eggs on Easter Sunday.

School ends in May so the older boys who live on farms can help with Spring planting. Mr. Murphy has been helping me to catch up on my schoolwork, because I've fallen behind, and I want to be promoted to fifth grade!

Harold plays with kids his own age, so I don't see him much, but Annie Rose, Rex and I are together every day, sometimes at their houses, but most of the time they come to my house. We play outside as often as we can, except when it rains. Every night at dusk, we played Kick the Can with other boys and girls in the neighborhood.

Rex and I haven't returned to the cellar. We've talked about it a couple times but decide to wait and go later. I still remember the cold feeling of the mist floating through me towards the cellar door. Rex hasn't talked about it and he tries to be tough, but I think he was scared that day, just like me.

Summer, 1905.

I'm spending most of my time with Annie Rose and Rex. We call ourselves The First Street Threesome! Sometimes Harold stops by for a game of hide and seek, but he spends most of his time with his friends.

Annie likes to play hopscotch, but it's hot.

Rex stands up, "Hey, girls, I have an idea! Why don't we use the chalk for sidewalk art?" "Great idea!"

I go into the house to get my colored chalk, and Annie Rose starts by drawing a rainbow. Rex and I draw stick pictures of ourselves holding different colored balloons. Then while Annie is signing "Annie Rose" on the bottom corner, I add some four-leafed clovers next to our names.

We are admiring our work and Rex says, "Gee, I think it looks great, but I think now that we've done one, that the next one will be even better!"

Annie Rose and I chime in at the same time, "Yeah, let's do another one!"

It's close to supper time, so Rex and Annie Rose have to go home. The next day, they come after breakfast with their chalk, and we move to the next section of the sidewalk. People walking by start to notice our project, and some even stop to talk to us, offering suggestions. One lady says, "My, isn't this lovely. Can you draw something in front of my house?"

On the third day, our idea really takes off and other kids in the neighborhood draw sidewalk art in front of their houses. It doesn't rain, so by the end of the week, all of the sidewalks on First Street are decorated with drawings of the sun, rainbows, houses, barns, people and flowers.

Thursday afternoon Mr. Murphy comes home from the office and Ruby has invited Rex and Annie Rose to stay for supper.

"Ruby tells me that she had to go to the store to get more chalk. It seems that you three have started quite an art project. I want to see it as soon as we finish eating."

Rex replies, "We'd like to show it to you! It's all over First Street. Once we got started, kids our age joined in, then some older kids bought chalk and did some more artwork. It's really neat – you'll see!"

Anna, John, and Harold stop in, just as Mr. Murphy is leaving for his art walk. "I suppose you came to get Rex, but why don't you come with me on a walk up the street? It seems our children started a neighborhood project."

We all go outside to walk up and down both sides of First Street, Mr. Murphy, John, Harold, Ruby, Rex, Annie Rose and me. Mr. Murphy stops now and then to admire some of the better drawings. Some of the neighbors come out of their houses to walk with us, and before long there's a parade of men, women, children, and dogs walking up the street to look at the sidewalk art.

Mr. Murphy said he is going to contact the Canton Weekly Register to tell them about our project, but it rains that night, and our art is washed away. But I will never forget the fun we had.

Early evenings after supper, kids in our neighborhood all meet at our house for a game of hide-and-seek or kick-the-can. Rex and I haven't returned to our secret hiding place in the cellar, but we found a new place to hide, under a bush behind the carriage house. After hiding for what seemed like a long time, we decide it's time to chance running to tag "home."

Johnny Scott is It. "Where were you guys? We looked everywhere!"

Harold comes walking up the drive, "You'll never find them. They have a secret place, and they won't even tell me where it is."

Johnny frowns, "That's not fair, they will never be "It"!"

"I'll tell you what, Johnny, Dora and I will take turns being It for the first games the next two nights, and I bet we will find you and everyone else!"

"No, you won't. I know how to hide so you can't find me."

"We'll see!"

It's getting dark so everyone heads for home, but the plan is set for the next two nights.

Rex is It the next night. I hide in a different place, in the hayloft, and I'm the last to be found, but Rex finds everyone, including Johnny who thought he could get by, hiding behind a tree so he could run "home" when it wasn't protected. "Ha, caught ya!"

I'm It on the second night. Thinking I know where she is, I decide to look for Annie Rose first, so I go looking for her, leaving home unprotected. As soon as I go around the corner of the house, I hear Johnny call out, "Olly oxen free!" Everyone runs from their hiding place for the next game. I'm It for all of the games tonight.

Rex is the only one who isn't laughing at me. "Sorry, Dora, I shouldn't have volunteered you. You're good at hiding, but you're a lousy It! Still friends?"

"Still best friends!"

Summer is fun, but the one person we do not miss is Dickie Webster! Dickie is okay. He tries to keep up, but he's too young to hang out with the First Street Threesome and our friends. Most days, we go all day without seeing Dickie. Rex said he's seen him playing by himself in the barn, and in the yard out back. But every day, as soon as Mr. Murphy comes home, there's Dickie, knocking on the kitchen door.

I've been thinking a lot about Jack and Louis, so I decide to be nice to Dickie, "Hey, Dickie, have you ever played marbles?"

"No. I don't know how."

"My brother liked to play marbles, so I bought some the other day. I'll go get them and I'll show you how to shoot marbles right here, on the kitchen floor."

Dickie has a big grin, showing the gap from two missing teeth.

I come back, holding marbles in both hands. "Here, Dickie, I'll give you six and I'll keep six. I don't know all the rules like my brother Jack did, but we can have fun shooting the marbles."

We kneel on the floor, and I show Dickie how to line up his marbles facing my line of marbles. "See, just flick a marble with your fingers and try to hit one of my marbles."

Before long, marbles are shooting in all directions across the linoleum when Mr. Murphy comes downstairs and enters the kitchen. "What's this?"

"I was just showing Dickie how to shoot marbles."

"Now, Dora, Dickie has things to do with me, here and on the farm. You just go play with your dollhouse and dolls. I know Ruby is planning to bake a cake. You can help her – that's what girls do. Pick up all the marbles and put them away now."

Mr. Murphy likes Dickie, so I guess it doesn't bother him when Dickie follows him around. They are together all of the time, including when Mr. Murphy has to go to the farm and, sometimes he takes him to his office.

On Monday at breakfast, Mr. Murphy tells Ruby, "I need to go to Quincy on business and I'm thinking about taking Dickie with me. We'll be gone about a week, so I'll leave some money with you so you can buy groceries, or you can just charge what you need to my account. Maybe you and Dora will want to go shopping. I'll tell R.C. to keep an eye out for you."

I know Mr. Murphy likes Dickie, but he hasn't asked me to go with him on a business trip. Rex said Mr. Murphy told his mother that I'm like a daughter, and Dickie is just a kid from across the street. Why didn't he ask me to go?

Mr. Murphy and Dickie leave the next day in a carriage driven by one of the farmhands. R.C. and Ruby are in charge at home.

Annie Rose's mama gives her some money so she can come shopping with Ruby and me. We visit all of the good shops. We go to the toy store first where Annie Rose and I buy some paper dolls. Then we go to Dobbins Brothers. Ruby buys some fabric and ribbon to take to Helen to sew dresses for her and for me. Annie Rose's mama is teaching her to sew, so she buys some fabric to sew a dress for her doll.

We have a lot of packages, so we take them to R.C. who is waiting in the carriage before we walk to the Sweet Shoppe. Mr. Beck greets us as soon as we walk through the door, "Why, hello Miss Kelly, and Annie Rose! I didn't know you two were friends. What would you like? Ruby, what did you have in mind?"

"Well, we are going to the Tea Room for tea and cookies, so just let the girls pick out what they want to take home."

"I don't know, it's hard to choose. What do you like, Annie Rose?"

"I usually get the same, I'll have some butter drops, four green mint patties, and a milk chocolate bar."

"I'll have the same!"

Mr. Beck fills our sacks, and he ties them with red ribbons. "How about you, Ruby? I know you like candy."

"Just some of those red cinnamon candies – oh, and I'll try some of the butter drops."

We walk up the street from the Sweet Shoppe to the Tea Room, where we have tea in fancy china cups, sweet biscuits, and ginger cookies. In between sips, we sneak some of the candies from our sacks. By the time we are done with our tea, we are full.

"My goodness, girls, I think we spoiled our suppers!"

We all laugh. "Ruby and me can skip dinner because Mr. Murphy is gone, but how about you, Annie Rose? What will you say to your mama?"

"It's okay, I just won't eat. It's not like I do this all the time."

Mr. Murphy comes home just before supper on Saturday; he has invited Albert Taff for supper to talk business.

"Bring us some coffee, Ruby," Taff says, not even greeting her. He shakes Mr. Murphy's hand and they sit at the table, already set with Mr. Murphy's favorites.

"I had a productive trip to Quincy. Dickie and I explored the countryside, and we ate supper at my sister's house every night. Of course, you know the man that owned the farm next to mine died. If I buy his farm, we can increase crop production, and I can buy more livestock. They know I plan to talk to you, so I want you to contact their attorney and draw up the papers. His son just wants to get rid of it, so I negotiated a good price."

Coffee slops on the table when Ruby slams the cup of coffee down. Taff doesn't look up or say anything. "You took Dickie Webster with you to Quincy?"

"Yes, he's a lot like you were, Albert. He likes to follow me around. and I think he is going to become a fine young man. R.C. is always working so he has little time to pay attention to the boy. He likes school, so I plan to offer guidance regarding his schooling."

"No formal commitment?"

"No formal commitment. Right now, I'm raising Dora. She's like a daughter to me, so she comes first. Like you did, all those years I was raising you."

"What about Ruby? She's a good housekeeper and a decent cook, but I keep wondering how long she'll be around. I remember when she was just a dirty-faced kid from the other side of town delivering milk. You invited her in, and she never left. Strange, her parents still live in the same house across town."

"Ruby can stay here as long as she works and earns her keep."

I'm not finished eating, but I put my fork down to run upstairs to my room.

Ruby follows me up the stairs to my room, "Dora? Are you okay?"

"I'm okay. I'm just tired."

Mr. Murphy must have meant it when he said they're my family now. That he loves me. This is the first time since that man took me away from Mama, that I thought for sure someone wanted to take care of me. I guess it's good to know that he won't be sending me away, but I'm having trouble understanding how this should make me feel. I need to think about it but, at least, I know I really have a home. I need to tell Rex.

I run between the raindrops to the mailbox. There's a fancy, ivory colored envelope addressed to Mr. Murphy and me, Dora Kelly! I take the mail inside for Mr. Murphy to open.

"Well, what do you know! Look here, Dora, you and I are invited to a wedding! Says here Albert Taff is marrying Neva Michaels on October 25. Odd, he didn't mention it the other day when he was here."

"I've not been to a wedding before. Is Ruby going?"

"No, unless her invitation will come later, I guess she's not invited. I want you to go to Dobbins to get a pretty fabric so Helen can make you a special dress. The wedding's coming up, so you should have R.C. take you downtown in the morning."

"I can hardly wait! Maybe a taffeta or a velvet since it's fall. Then I can wear it for the holidays."

"Good thinking. Whatever you choose, I know you will be lovely."

Hayride!

Annie Rose and I are starting fifth grade; Rex is in sixth grade, so his desk is on the other side of the room. Mrs. Hart passes out our books, "While I am getting our fourth-grade students started with their spelling lesson, you fifth grade students can read the first chapter in your reading primer. Sixth grade students, I want you to open your history books and start on page 37, the Revolutionary War. While you are reading, make a list of the names of generals from that war."

I open my book to the first story, *The Goose Who Tried to Keep the Summer*. Johnny Scott is sitting behind me and he tugs the collar of my shirt, whispering, "Dora, this is stupid! Why do we have to read it? A goose can't talk!"

Mrs. Hart looks in our direction. "'Cuz teacher said to. Just read it. It's a funny story."

I finish reading the story just as the Mrs. Hart finishes teaching spelling to the fourth- grade class.

"Johnny Scott, stand up and tell the class what this story is about."

Johnny stands up, looking down at his feet. "Of course, you read the story, it's not a long one."

"I didn't finish it, teacher."

"Well, can you tell us about the main character, the Goose?"

"He was a Wild Goose that was the leader of a flock of geese."

"Good. Annie Rose, can you tell us about the story?"

Annie Rose stands up. "He didn't want to fly south, so he wanted summer to stay forever."

"That's right, and what can we learn from this story?" Everyone raises their hand except Johnny. "Dora?"

"There are some things we can't change, like winter, and even if we don't feel like it, we have to do what's right!"

"Very good, Dora, very good insight!"

Johnny raises his hand, "Teacher, what's insight?"

Some of the girls giggle. "Shh, it's not nice to laugh when someone asks a question. Johnny asked a good question. Insight is how we understand a person or a thing. Dora had good insight – she understood the moral of the story. Now, start working on the math assignment in the first four pages of your math book, while I move on to sixth grade."

That is how Mrs. Hart teaches three grades in one room. She's a good teacher. We are used to the rhythm of her teaching and to our learning, and I like learning in the same room with Annie Rose and Rex.

Boys from all three grades are crowding around the bulletin board. I'm shorter than anyone else, so I can't see what they are doing. Rex takes me by the shoulder, and he gently pushes me to the front of the crowd. Mrs. Hart has tacked a newspaper article and picture of the Wright Brothers standing in front of an airplane. This plane flew 39 minutes, the first that has flown more than 30 minutes!

"Really neat don't you think? Harold says we're going to fly someday."

"How are you going to do that? You don't have a plane. Besides, even if you do, what if the plane falls down?"

"We'll see. We're young, Dora. They will keep building better planes."

Mrs. Hart walks into the room, clapping her hands, "Children, go to your desks. We'll start with fifth grade today."

As usual, Rex walks me home from school.

"Dora, what's with you? Even Mother noticed. You're bubbling all over the place, what's happened? Why are you so happy?"

"Didn't I tell you? Albert Taff is getting married, and Mr. Murphy and I are invited to the wedding!"

"Really! Was Ruby invited?"

"No, just Mr. Murphy and me."

"Guess that says a lot about what he thinks of her. They sort of grew up together. Wonder why she's not invited."

"I don't know, but when he comes to the house, he just ignores her. In fact, there are times he's not so nice to Ruby. He went to college and he's a lawyer. Ruby stayed behind, and she stopped going to school to cook and clean. I want to go to school and make something of myself. At first, I wanted to be like Ruby, but I've changed my mind."

"Mr. Murphy tells everyone how much he cares for you. Look at all of the books he buys for you."

"I know, but there are times when he scolds me that certain work is for girls, like cooking and dolls."

"Just enjoy the wedding, Dora. Deep inside, he cares for you."

October 25, 1905.

Mr. Murphy is calling for me at the bottom of the stairs. "Hurry, Dora, R.C. is waiting. We must not be late for the wedding."

I come down the stairs, wearing my new dress, a powder blue taffeta skirt with a matching velvet top.

"Well, look at you! That color matches your pretty blue eyes, and the lace anklets show off your dainty black slippers. I'm stepping out tonight with a beautiful young lady! Let's go, miss. I want to show you off!"

The organ is playing when we enter the church. Bows made from ivory ribbon hang at the end of every pew. The sanctuary is filled with candlelight, and there are four large bouquets of white flowers on the altar.

The room becomes quiet, then the organist plays a song while three bridesmaids, wearing emerald green velvet dresses, and carrying bouquets of white chrysanthemums stroll gracefully down the aisle.

Mr. Murphy leans over to whisper in my ear, "The music is Brahms. A lovely selection."

Next the organ swells, playing the wedding march. We all stand while Miss Michaels' father walks her down the aisle. She is so pretty in her ball gown trimmed in lace. Her lace veil and long, black curls frame her face. Her eyes sparkle from the candlelight. I look at Albert. He seems so proud.

I can't believe the actual ceremony only takes a few minutes. Everyone lines up to greet the bridal party and the bride and groom.

"Uncle Joe, I want you to be here for me in the reception line. You are the only family that I have."

"Well, I didn't expect this, but I'd be honored. Excuse me, Dora."

I wait for Mr. Murphy until the reception line is over, and we go to the church parlor for the reception, where maids in black dresses and white aprons serve punch and wedding cake. The only people I know are Albert and Mr. Murphy, so I find a chair so I can eat my cake.

A lady comes up to me. "You must be Dora. Albert told us about you. I'm Neva's mother. I'm so glad you came. What a pretty dress."

"Thank you!"

When I look across the room, Mr. Murphy is handing an envelope to Albert. They seem to be talking, so I just stay in my chair and wait for Mr. Murphy to let me know when he wants to go home.

I come home from school the next day, and we talk about the wedding over supper. Ruby seems interested but she doesn't say much. Mr. Murphy changes the subject and asks about Halloween. It's hard to believe another year has gone by!

"Dora, have you decided on a costume for the bonfire? What would you like to do for Halloween?"

"I need to talk to Annie Rose. Mr. Murphy, I think this might be the last year I will dress up for Halloween. Next year, I'll be twelve and the older kids don't wear costumes. Rex isn't wearing a costume this year."

"I thought you might be thinking that way. You are growing up and so are your friends. I was wondering if you would like to do something special with your friends this Halloween."

"Everyone's coming to the bonfire, and they will be there with their parents, so I can't think of anything else to do."

"Well, Halloween is on Tuesday, so what if I write a letter to your teacher, inviting everyone in your classroom to come to the farm on Sunday for a hayride? Let's see, that will be fourth, fifth and sixth grades, right? How many children would that be?"

"There's six in fourth grade, seven in my class, and five in sixth grade including Rex! Can Harold come too?"

"Of course! Ruby, can you bake some cookies and bring some cider? After the ride, everyone can go into the barn for refreshments."

"I'll make oatmeal raisin cookies. Dora, we can bake them on Saturday, would you like to help?"

I'm so excited! This will be special – no one has ever had a party for all three grades and hayrides are really fun!

I deliver Mr. Murphy's letter to Mrs. Hart. She reads it, raises her eyebrows and she smiles as she reads the letter to the classes,

> "Mrs. Hart, this letter is to be read to everyone in your fourth, fifth
> and sixth grade classes: Dora Kelly and I would like to invite you to
> my farm at three o'clock on Sunday, October 28, for a hayride. Talk
> to your parents and tell Mrs. Hart if you plan to come so we have a
> count for cookies and cider after. We hope you all will come!
>
> Signed, Joseph L. Murphy."

All of the kids come up to me during recess to let me know that they want to come, "Do we have to wear costumes?"

"No, just come in play clothes 'cuz we'll be sitting on piles of hay."

"Mr. Murphy isn't going to be there, is he?"

"I don't think so, but he might come with Ruby when she brings the cookies and cider!"

During the rest of the month leading up to the Sunday hayride, the kids become more and more excited and it seems like they all want to be my best friend. Even Johnny Scott is nice to me.

Counting Harold, sixteen board the wagon for the hayride. Harold, Rex, Annie and I are already on the wagon when they arrive, sitting close to the front. R.C. turns around, asking, "is everyone on and sitting down?"

A loud unison response, "Yes!"

R.C. has two horses hitched to the wagon. "Okay, giddy-up, Jennie."

Jennie starts walking and the other horse follows, pulling the wagon slowly forward and soon, we are rolling along. Everyone is talking and laughing. R.C. takes us around a big cornfield and past a soybean field. The sky is yellow, and the sun is falling like a big orange ball. Everyone stops talking and soon it is just too quiet.

Rex gets up to sit high on a bale of hay, "I know, how about I tell you a ghost story?" He makes a mysterious face, and tells the story in a spooky voice.

The Mystery of Widow Hayes

There was a woman who lived in Greenville, KY, widow Priscilla Hayes. She took in travelers and over the years, and people started to notice that people came to visit Priscilla, yet none went away – that is all anyone knew.

Bishop Miller, an Amish minister, was driving over a bridge near Priscilla's farm one night; there was a bit of a moon above a layer of mist that lay along the ground. Bishop Miller was whistling a tune as he crossed the bridge. He saw a man standing by the gate at Priscilla's house. The man was holding a lantern and he carried a heavy stick. Bishop Miller thought the man might be lost, he didn't seem to know where he was, and it was almost like he was walking in his sleep.

'Ho, if you're going my way, I'll give you a ride.' The man raised his head and looked him squarely in the face, but he didn't move. The bishop repeated his invitation. The man threw out is right hand and pointed towards Priscilla's barn, then he disappeared!

The horse gave a brief snort of terror and started to run away. The bishop got control of the horse, and came to a stop, shaking a little. When he looked back, he sees the man again, still with the lantern in his hand.

When he got home, he told his family about what he had seen, and the next day he went to Priscilla's house with two deacons, Joseph Lapp and Walter Beiler. They knocked on her door and called her name, but there was no answer. Joseph walked to the back of the house and called out, 'No answer here. Let's go see if she's in the barn.'

In the barn, they found Priscilla hanging by the neck from one of the beams. An unlit lantern was on the floor under her feet. When Bishop Millerreached down to move the lantern out of the way so they could cut her down, the lantern started to glow a bright red and it was so hot it burned his hand. He ran outside to the horse trough and plunged his hand into the water.

The three men were terrified, and decided they would leave her there and let the sheriff deal with it! On the way out, they paused to look at the ground where the man the minister had seen was standing. There was no grass and the ground had been dampened by the mist, but there were no footprints. The only footprints were those of Bishop Miller's horse!"

"Oooh. That was scary!" A few girls cling together or sit lower into the hay.

Johnny Scott barks a laugh, "Rex, you made that up. It really didn't happen, did it?"

"There was a man at the barbershop, said he was from Greenville, passing through. He told Father and me this story, and he swore it's true."

The wagon comes to a halt and Mr. Murphy is there to greet us, "Jump down, boys. Girls, let me help you down. Ruby has cookies and cider in the barn."

The red and gold leaves crunch beneath our feet as we walk towards the barn. My friends swarm the table, smelling the warm cider. R.C. lumbers through the door, "Boys, girls, remember your manners. Form a line."

Everyone falls in line, girls first, except me, because I'm the hostess, and we all eat cookies while we stand in line, waiting for the cider. Mr. Murphy, The Pumpkin is perched on top of a bucket next to a pitchfork, and there are other, uncarved pumpkins everywhere. Our seats are bales of hay. Rex and I are last in line, "Wow! This cider hits the spot! Everyone is having a good time, Dora."

I put the cup to my lips and fill my mouth with the warm cider. I close my eyes and slowly swallow it as it trickles down the back of my throat.

Rex touches my arm, "Dora, your friends are starting to leave!"

Jenny Parsons runs up as I open my eyes, "Dora, thank you for inviting me. It was really fun! That pumpkin with a white beard is really funny. He looks like Mr. Murphy!"

"He's supposed to. He's Mr. Murphy, The Pumpkin. We make him every Halloween; it's a tradition."

"Funny!"

We go outside. It's dark, but there's a half-moon, so I can see buggies and carriages parked in the shadows by the barn. Mr. Murphy and R.C, are talking to a group of parents. For a brief moment, I see a boy who looks like my brother, Jack, standing by one of the horses, but I shake my head and he disappears.

As we approach, Mr. Murphy is talking, ".... Yes, Dora's a true delight. I love her like a daughter. Thank you for bringing Johnny. I think they all had a good time. Someone told me my cousin's boy, Rex, told a ghost story!"

Everyone's talking at once, telling their parents about the hayride. I'm happy that everyone had a good time. One by one, my friends thank me before they leave with their parents. Mr. Murphy, R.C., Harold, Rex, and I help Ruby to pack up for the ride home.

"Mr. Murphy, thank you. That was so much fun!"

"Baby Girl, I had fun too. You know, I was watching when you and your friends were lined up for cider in the barn. Ruby didn't need her lantern; you could light up the world with your smile! Well, I guess everything is loaded and Ruby and R.C. are ready, so we should all go."

Being Me!

Rex is waiting for Annie Rose and me when we get out of school, "C'mon, Dora, I'll walk you and Annie Rose home. What are you guys goin' to be this year for the bonfire? Do you really want to wear costumes? That's for little kids. I'm not wearing one. It'll be fun to just hang out with you guys and listen to the music. Then, there's the cookies."

I hang my head and think for a minute, "I really like to dress up but, you're right, Rex, we're growing up, so dressing up should probably be left to the little kids. I know what! What if we organize a pumpkin carving contest? I'll talk to Ruby and Mr. Murphy."

"That's a good idea, but I don't think girls should be allowed to use knives, you might cut yourself."

"C'mon, Rex, this year I helped to carve Mr. Murphy The Pumpkin!"

Mr. Murphy walks up, "What's this about girls and knives?"

Annie Rose tells him about our idea. "That's a great idea! We'll have an adult there to supervise the pumpkin cutting. And Rex, I know some boys who shouldn't be allowed around knives!"

Rex blushes a little. "Yeah, you're right.

Mr. Murphy agrees to talk to the organizers and promises to donate the pumpkins. He and Ruby will take charge of the arrangements.

It's Halloween night and Rex and Harold stop by our house to carry Mr. Murphy, The Pumpkin to the bonfire. Ruby is in the barn, setting up a table lined with newspapers for a carving station, with plenty of pumpkins from Mr. Murphy's farm. There's a bale of hay next to the table – a perfect spot to set our celebrity pumpkin. Mr. Murphy made a sign with an age limit for the carving activity, 12 years old or older.

Ruby hands each of us a knife while Annie Rose picks the smallest pumpkin. "I want to carve a pumpkin, Ruby. Do we have to wait? How should I start?

Should I make a happy face or a scary pumpkin?"

"It's not hard, just messy. The best way to start is to draw a face on the pumpkin with a Crayola, so you can follow the lines when you carve. See, I've already started mine."

Harold says he wants the biggest pumpkin. "You can tell your pumpkin was done by a girl, Dora. Annie Rose, you should make something scary!"

Rex comes to my rescue. "Harold, don't make fun of Dora's pumpkin. She is a girl! I know, why don't we make our pumpkins the 'First Street Threesome'? Dora has a good start; her happy pumpkin has a Dora smile. Annie Rose, try to make your pumpkin look like you, and I will make a funny pumpkin with a big nose, that looks like me!"

Annie Rose uses a blue crayon to draw her face, and I show her how to cut a lid on top. "You might not like the next part, but you have to do it! Ruby, where do we put the guts?"

"There's a stack of buckets behind the barn door, and you can wash your hands in the horse trough when you're done."

Annie Rose watches Rex as he starts to pull the guts from his pumpkin. "Ewww! That's disgusting! I'm not going to do that!"

"That's what I thought the first year we carved Mr. Murphy, The Pumpkin, but you get used to it. Just dive in and pull everything out. Then you scrape the inside with a big spoon. See, Ruby brought spoons for us to use."

We set our pumpkins up next to Mr. Murphy, The Pumpkin. and Rex finds a piece of paper to make a sign, "The First Street Threesome." Rex's pumpkin is the funniest with a big pointy nose. Harold can't stop laughing. "He looks like a clown, with that nose! Just like you, bloke!"

We don't win first prize, but everyone who lives on First Street knows what the sign means, so we get a lot of laughs.

After the pumpkin carving contest is over, we help Ruby to pack and load everything onto R.C.'s wagon. People are starting to leave, but we are lagging behind.

Mr. Murphy calls me over. "Dora, do you want to leave, or would you and your friends like to stay for a while?"

All of us, Rex, Harold and their parents, Annie Rose and her parents, Ruby,

Mr. Murphy and I decide to stay and sit around the fire. Some people that I don't know pull up chairs and sit behind us. The men start swapping jokes and for a while, there's a lot of laughter, but then it gets quiet. The only sound is the crackling of the wood burning. I'm watching the beauty of the flames and I feel warm and comfortable, and sleepy!

"It's quiet, too quiet."

Mr. Murphy asks, "What are you suggesting, Dora?"

"I don't know, it just got quiet, and I started to get sleepy. I know – I can sing a song that my daddy taught me. Sometimes I sing when I'm alone, so don't look at me, I'll just sing like no one's watching!" I close my eyes and my voice fills the circle.

> *I'll tell me ma when I go home,*
> *The boys won't leave the girls alone,*
> *They pull my hair they stole my comb,*
> *And that's all right till I go home.*
> *Albert Mooney says he loves her,*
> *All the boys are fighting for her,*
> *They rap at the door and ring the bell,*
> *Saying, Oh my true love, are you well.*
> *Wind and the rain and the hail blow high,*
> *And the snow comes shoving from the sky,*
> *She's as nice as apple pie,*
> *And she'll get her own lad by and by!*

Rex is the first to applaud and everyone joins in, "Gee, Dora, I didn't know you can sing."

"My daddy was Curtis Kelly, and he used to teach us Irish songs."

"But people say you're shy – you're really not shy, are you?

"No, I'm not. If I have something to say, I let people know, and if I decide I want to sing, then I sing."

A lady sitting behind us comments, "Seems to me you should sing more often!"

Mr. Murphy stands up, "I agree. Well, it's getting late, and I think we should go home. Good night, everyone, it's been a pleasure!"

"Good night and God speed!"

Mr. Murphy takes my hand as we walk towards our carriage. I wave goodbye to Rex and his family.

"Dora, you are full of surprises. You are a joy and you have brought new life into my home. Ruby and I are so glad that you came to live with us."

I look over at Ruby, just in time to see her roll her eyes. I wonder for a minute what that was all about, but I don't really care. She had a good time talking to her friends, just like I did. I pull my hand away and run the rest of the way to R.C. and Dickie who are waiting by the carriage.

The Farmer and the Carpenter

R.C. is sitting at the kitchen table drinking coffee when I come down for breakfast. "Since Anna and the boys are coming, I'll just kill the biggest hen for your Thanksgiving dinner."

"That'll be fine. Ruby always makes a wonderful dinner. Dora sets the table and this year, she's going to help Ruby with the cooking!"

I have a sore throat and runny nose, so I don't feel like talking but, whatever. I guess Ruby will tell me what she wants me to do. The hot tea feels good as it trickles down the back of my throat, so I'm able to eat some rice and raisins with warm milk. "Excuse me, I'm going back to bed." I wait until I'm away from the kitchen, climbing the stairs before I blow my nose into my hanky.

It seems that once Halloween is over, that it's one holiday after another. School lets out early on Wednesday before Thanksgiving. Mr. Murphy has caught my cold and he passed it on to Ruby. Knowing she doesn't feel well, I hurry home to help her with baking for tomorrow's dinner.

"Ruby, I'm home! What do you want me to do?"

"Why don't you make cornbread for the stuffing - here's the recipe. You know where everything is." She sniffs as she wipes her nose with the back of her hand.

Making cornbread is easy. Ruby has boiled the chestnuts so after I put the cornbread in the oven, I shell the chestnuts – not so easy, so it takes a while, but we have time to talk.

"Ruby, you know when Albert Taff was here the other day for dinner?"

"Yes."

"I don't think he's so nice." Lowering my voice to imitate Taff, "Ruby, bring me a cup of coffee!" "And he didn't even thank you, and Mr. Murphy didn't say anything."

"Dora, Albert Taff has always been Uncle Joe's favorite. He took Albert in when his parents died when he was three years old. He raised him and gave him a good education. He even put him through law school and had him clerk at his law firm. I was fourteen when our housekeeper left, and Mr. Murphy told me that I had to quit school so I could take care of the house."

"That's not fair!"

"What do you think he has in mind for you? He says he loves you like a daughter now, but you're just like me, you're a girl. Someday, you will have to stop going to school. You're no better than me, and if you know what's good for you, you will do what's expected of you just like I did."

We hear Mr. Murphy's footsteps on the top stair. Ruby has the pies in the oven when he enters the kitchen. "The house smells good. It smells like Thanksgiving! What are you ladies up to?"

"Well, the breads are finished baking, and the pies are in the oven. All that's left to do this evening is the cranberry sauce. Dora has been a big help. It's a good thing 'cuz I'm miserable with this cold."

"We'll try not to make tomorrow a late night. I'm sure Anna will be happy to help you and Dora with the dishes."

"I'll get up early to set the table, then I can help Ruby with the cooking."

"Most of the cooking will be done today. Once the turkey is in the oven, there's not much to do."

"I'll make you tea, and you can just sit and tell me what to do."

When I come downstairs the next morning, Ruby has already done everything. The turkey is in the oven and the vegetables are in kettles of water, waiting to be boiled, and she has tea, scones, boiled eggs, and fried apples waiting on the table for breakfast.

After breakfast, Mr. Murphy goes to his chair in the parlor, and he plays opera records on his phonograph. His favorite is Lillian Nordca, which he plays again and again. Still in my night dress, I curl up in a chair to read my book.

Before I even know it, I find myself dancing along with Dorothy down the yellow brick road to find the wonderful wizard. The sparkle of Dorothy's silver slippers lights the way and we meet friends to come with us to the Emerald City. The Tin Woodsman clanks as he walks stiff legged, and the Cowardly Lion has finally stopped crying. As we come around a bend in the road, we see a scarecrow standing in a field.

I wake up to a crash in the kitchen.

Mr. Murphy and I run to the kitchen to find Ruby in tears. "What happened?"

"The pan was hot, and I dropped the sweet potatoes!"

"Can they be salvaged? Don't cry. What do you want us to do?"

"No, they splattered all over the floor."

"So, we just won't have sweet potatoes. Not a tragedy. I know you're tired and don't feel well with that cold, so just sit down and Dora will make you a cup of tea. Dora and I will clean up the spill. Is there anything else that needs to be done right now?"

Ruby honks when she blows her nose, "Nnnooo! I'll just sit here for a few minutes. Thank you, Dora, for the tea. You'd better go get dressed, Anna and the family will be arriving soon."

It seems like every Thanksgiving that dinner is better than the year before. Even Ruby smiles and we all applaud when John carries the turkey to the table. All of the sides are steaming, the turkey is a golden brown, and the aroma of sage fills the room.

"Ohhhh!"

Mr. Murphy expresses concern, "What's wrong, Dora?"

"I ate too much. I think my stomach's about to burst!"

Harold laughs, "We all ate too much. That's what Thanksgiving is all about!"

Rex scoffs. "No it isn't, you dummy. Thanksgiving is a day to give thanks!"

"Don't call your brother a dummy. We all know what he meant. Ruby, I'll help with the dishes. The men can go to the parlor for their port, and I'm sure they will have another checkers tournament."

Ruby, Anna and I carry the dishes to the kitchen, and I put food away while they wash and dry the dishes.

"Ruby, I'm sorry you have a cold, especially on Thanksgiving, but I hear you may have good news, that you are dating a young man named Jim. Who is he?"

Even though her eyes are red, and her nose is running, Ruby breaks into a smile and she blushes when she talks about Jim, "Jim Kucharek, he's a farmer that I met at church. He's very nice. I care a lot about him. But I haven't told Uncle Joe. Where did you hear about us?"

"I think one of the ladies at the quilting bee mentioned it. Dora, you must not say anything about this to Mr. Murphy. Ruby is the one who needs to tell him. But you should tell him soon, dear."

As soon as we finish the dishes, Anna gathers up her family, they thank Ruby and leave for home. We are all tired and Ruby doesn't feel well, so we all head for our rooms to go to bed. I pull up the quilt as I lay back on my pillows wondering what Mr. Murphy and I will do if Ruby decides to leave and get married. Maybe Ruby will come to clean house and cook if Mr. Murphy pays her, or maybe she and her husband can move in so she can keep house and cook, and he can take over for R.C. No, Mr. Murphy wouldn't go along with that, R.C. is his best friend. He wouldn't let me bring my brothers here, so why would he let Ruby and her husband move in?

Actually, I don't think Ruby likes me. I think that's why she rolls her eyes when Mr. Murphy says nice things to me. She and Albert call him Uncle Joe, but she told me I have to call him Mr. Murphy. I bet Ruby can't wait to move out and she probably won't want to come back. Besides, what would he do about his farm? It doesn't matter, though. If I can't get Mr. Murphy to help me, I'll stay here until I find my brothers, and we'll get our own farm.

We're going to need help if she leaves, though. I make my own bed and keep my room clean, and sometimes I help Ruby, but I can't take care of the whole house alone! It's not like keeping house while Mama worked. I was smaller then, but the cabin was small, too. This is really a big house! I don't mind taking care of Mr. Murphy, but I just can't do everything! I'll talk to Mr. Murphy. I'll tell him that I want to keep going to school, no matter what. Ruby told me she had to quit school; I don't want to quit school. I'll tell Mr. Murphy that we need help. I'm sure he'll understand. After all, he calls me his Baby, so why would he expect me to do so much?

I fall asleep and dream about Agnes, the lady with the crooked nose at church who likes Mr. Murphy.

> Agnes swoops into the room wearing a black dress with a white apron, carrying a broom, "Of course, Joseph, I'll be happy to take over. That's fine with you, isn't it dear?"

> I shake my head yes and look down, not wanting to tell her that I don't like her, that she looks like the wicked witch. Maybe if I close my eyes a house will fall on her.

> Suddenly, I'm flying towards the kitchen door, it blows open and there's a loud crash!

> I'm standing on the ground next to the carriage house, and there's Agnes, sprawled under a house and flat as a piece of paper, except for the toes of her pointy shoes that curl back. I turn around and walk towards our house, and it hasn't been touched by the storm.

It takes me a few minutes after I wake up to realize it was just a dream. I look around the room to make sure nothing is broken. The five china dolls are still there on the shelf above my vanity and Victoria is where I left her, sitting on the rocking chair. The dollhouse is on its table, and the tiny furniture is untouched except the little rocking chair in the parlor is rocking.

I jump out of bed and run downstairs to the kitchen. Mr. Murphy and Ruby are drinking tea and talking. No Agnes.

"Is something wrong, dear? Did something scare you?"

"No, I just had a bad dream. I'm fine. Ruby, you look better, your eyes aren't so red. Is your cold better?"

"I'm better, but I think I'll rest today. We have the rest of the weekend to put the tree up. What do you want to do today?"

"If it's all right with you, I'd like to get together with Rex and Annie Rose."

"That's fine, but if you plan to walk across town, wear a warm coat, hat, and mittens. Why don't you wear your new winter coat and hat that we bought? It's cold outside. Are you hungry? We have tea and Boston Brown Bread and Orange Butter left over from dinner."

"There's some left? My favorite! I'll have that."

I wolf down my breakfast, get dressed, and hurry out the door. I know Anna told me not to say anything to Mr. Murphy, but I have to tell Annie Rose and Rex about Ruby's secret romance. I especially need to talk to Rex. Maybe his Mama and Daddy have talked about Ruby, and what we might do if she leaves. Maybe Rex knows what's going to happen.

I'm still worried that Ruby might leave, but I've been busy helping Ruby to get the house ready for Christmas. But it looks like Christmas will not be the same this year. Even though he hasn't said anything, I don't think Mr. Murphy feels well. When he walks up the stairs to his room, he walks real slow taking one step at a time, and I think he's having a hard time breathing.

Rex and his family stop by with a plate of cookies on Christmas Eve before church, but they don't even take their coats off.

Anna crosses the room to talk to Mr. Murphy, "Joseph, I'm sorry you're not feeling well."

"Oh, Anna, I'm not sick, I'm just tired all of the time. Don't worry about me, I'll be fine if I can just get some rest. Thank you for the cookies and thank you for taking Dora to Christmas Eve service. You know, Dora is singing a solo this year, *Away in a Manger.* I wish I could be there, but I'm just not up to it. You go on now. Dora, I know you will make us proud."

There's nothing more beautiful than candlelight service on Christmas Eve. I love the live nativity, the music, and the sanctuary that is wrapped in a golden glow from the candles, almost like God's gift to everyone there.

I go to my appointed spot next to the nativity, the organ starts, and I sing Away in a Manger. I look for Rex and his family. Anna is smiling and Rex waves. I guess I did good - I didn't forget any of the words, but I wish Mr. Murphy was here.

There aren't as many presents the next morning because Mr. Murphy hasn't felt like getting out to shop. Still, he made sure there were some presents for me. All of the gifts are wrapped. The first gift I open is a white silk blouse. I'm surprised by such a grownup present, "Oh, Mr. Murphy, Ruby, it's beautiful! Maybe I can wear it when I go to Anna and John's house for New Year's Eve!"

"That's what Ruby said. Open the next one." The next present is a dark green taffeta skirt.

"You'll be quite the young lady on New Year's Eve."

"Well, she'll have to try them on, but they should fit. I know the blouse is her size and Helen knows her size, so the skirt should fit."

"Ruby, will you go out with your friends again this year?"

"Yes. Since you're staying home, I'll go after I fix your supper."

When I come downstairs, Ruby is waiting by the kitchen door for her ride wearing a red velvet dress with puffed sleeves, embroidered with silver thread.

"Ruby, your dress is beautiful! Did you buy it, or did Helen make it?"

"No, I went to the store to buy fabric and told them I wanted something very special, so they ordered my dress from a fashion center in New York. Don't say anything to Uncle Joe - it was very expensive!"

I look out the window in time to see R.C. pulling up in his carriage. Mr. Murphy calls me to the parlor, "Dora, let me see you in your new outfit."

I take my coat off and go to the parlor. "Dora, you are becoming a beautiful young lady! Tell everyone that I said hello!"

"Thank you, Mr. Murphy. I promise not to be late. I feel bad that you will be here alone."

"Oh, pshaw! It won't be the first time and probably not the last. Now, go on. R.C. is waiting."

Rex and Harold greet me at the door, "Hurry, come in, it's cold!"

Harold takes my coat and Rex takes me by my hand to show his mother my new outfit, "Look, Mother, Dora's all dressed up!"

"So, she is! Dora, that's a beautiful blouse, and look at the skirt! Were they Christmas presents?"

"Yes. Ruby said Mr. Murphy had the idea, then she bought the blouse and fabric for the skirt. I really like them, my first grown up outfit!"

Let's sit down and eat. We're having my traditional roast beef tonight."

"Anna, the table is very pretty. You got your crystal out this year!"

"I was cleaning the china closet the other day and the crystal was dusty. When I was cleaning the goblets, I held one up to the sunlight. It sparkled when the sun reflected off the glass, and it cast blue and lavender diamonds on the wall. I decided I should be using these beautiful things, so I brought them out this year for our celebration."

After the blessing, John stands up and he takes each dish around the table to serve. There's roast beef, mashed potatoes and gravy, green beans and candied carrots. Usually, it gets quiet while everyone's eating, but Harold and Rex keep the conversation going.

"Hey, Rex, did you tell Dora what Santa gave you for Christmas?"

Rex gives Harold a dirty look, "Why did you bring that up? It's not funny!"

"How can a Christmas gift be funny? Tell her what you got!"

"Two years ago, Mother found Great Grandpa's shaving mug, stored in a chest in the attic. She put it in the china closet. This year, they gave me Great Grandpa's mug. I'm not shaving yet, but I'll have it to use when I do."

"Maybe you shouldn't use them. They must be very old and very special."

"You're right, Dora. Did you know, John's father was a carpenter in Denver, Colorado? He built a number of houses. He talked about one house, a mansion he built while working for an architect named Lang."

Harold is taking a sip of water and he is so surprised that he chokes, taking a bite out of the fragile crystal goblet. "Mother, I'm sorry. I didn't mean to break the glass."

"Are you all right? Did you cut yourself?"

"No, but did you say he built a mansion?"

John replied, "Yes, he did. He said they wanted stone on the outside, so he had big stones brought down from mountain streams by train, then they were transported to the construction site by truck. He told me he had to do three inspections of the loading operation. He said he liked to go up the night before so he could be there early morning because the cook made donuts and he liked the taste of coffee cooked on an open fire.

"What was amazing was how they got the rocks from the water to the train. He said the stones were waterlogged and very heavy, but they had a crew of muscled men who would pass the stones to the last man who would lift then onto wagons. He said it was amazing to watch the motion as they would swing the heavy stones, to pass to the next in line while chanting, Heave 'er up and away we go, away Santiana! It was hard work and they had reason to complain but he said they seemed happy to be working, and their singing echoed off the mountains.

"Once the wagons were loaded, the horses had to pull them up a hill to the train. Dad was there with twelve wagons to meet the train. Each wagon had to make three trips to transport the stones to the job site, where they were stored on the ground. You would think they were just rocks, but he told me they had to protect them until they were cut.

"Stonecutters tooled the stones by hand to build walls. They cut grooves into the surface of the stones, making sure each stone would fit, then the walls were lifted into place in sections, using wooden derricks and geared winches. It was a major feat."

"Wow! Can you imagine that? I wish I could've been there. Maybe I'll try to find that house someday."

"If you do, the couple that originally built the house, sold it later to a wealthy mining engineer, J. J. Brown. I still remember his wife's name, Ruby, but they called her Molly. She was high society in Denver."

"Like our Ruby!" I said, "But richer."

I stand up to help Anna carry dishes to the kitchen. "That's okay, Dora, I'll get it. I have a surprise for dessert, so I want everyone to stay seated."

Anna sets china dessert plates in the center of the table. She goes back to the kitchen and returns with a flaming plum pudding. We all applaud. Harold and Rex reach for plates but Anna insists on serving John and me first.

"Anna, I told R.C. to come for me at eight. I know that's early, but I don't like to leave Mr. Murphy alone too long. It's a holiday, and he's not steady when he goes up stairs. We should have time to finish the dishes before he gets here."

"I don't want you to splash food or water on your new outfit, but it will be nice if you just sit and talk to me while I clean up the kitchen. I think Rex has planned another checkers tournament with Harold and his father."

We go to the kitchen and I pick up a dish towel, but Anna insists that I just sit so we can talk. Anna asks, almost whispering, "Has Ruby said anything to Joseph about her farmer?"

"I don't think so. I think she's afraid she might upset him."

"Perhaps, but the whole town is talking about it. She will have to tell him soon or he'll find out from someone else. Just don't let it be you!"

"Yes, Ma'am. Anna, what will we do if Ruby gets married and leaves? Ruby told me the other day that I'll have to quit school and take over her job, but I can't do everything. I want to go to school."

"I don't know. John and I talked about it. You will certainly need help."

Rex comes into the kitchen with my coat, "Here, Dora, R.C.'s waiting out front."

"Thank you, Anna. I had a good time, but I need to get home."

Mr. Murphy is waiting for me in the parlor. "Dora, hurry! Catch R.C. before he leaves. Ask him to come in for a few minutes."

R.C. is taking his boots off at the kitchen door when Mr. Murphy calls out, "R.C., I need you to help me up the stairs to my room. I'm tired."

After Mr. Murphy is settled in, I thank R.C.

"You're welcome, Miss. He's not doing so good, is he?"

"No, he's not. He's not really sick. He just walks slow, and he has to catch his breath."

"Just let me know if you need anything. Good night, and Happy New Year!"

"Happy New Year to you, too. Good night."

I close the door behind R.C. and decide to change out of my new clothes. I put on a night dress, wondering if I should wait up for Ruby. I don't know when she plans to come home and I'm tired, so I just go to bed, and I fall asleep right away.

January 1, 1906.

The sun wakes me up. I listen for a few minutes, but the house is quiet. No sound of Ruby fixing breakfast in the kitchen.

I go downstairs and Mr. Murphy is sitting in his robe in the parlor, but there's no sign of Ruby.

"Where's Ruby?"

"I'm not sure. I didn't hear her come in last night. Go check her room to see if she's all right."

I go to Ruby's room and slowly open the door to peek in. She's not there and there's no sign that she slept in her bed.

"Mr. Murphy, she's not there and her bed hasn't been slept in."

Just then, the kitchen door opens, and I watch as Ruby tiptoes towards her room, thinking we're still in bed.

Mr. Murphy stops her, "Ruby O'Grady, get in here and explain yourself. Where have you been and who were you with?"

Ruby mumbles and she looks down at the floor.

Mr. Murphy's voice gets louder, "Where were you, Ruby? Decent young ladies don't stay out all night! Who were you with, and what have you been doing?"

"No cause for concern, I was with my friends, and it was so late we decided it would be better to wait for daylight to be on the road."

"You know, of course, that the town gossips are having a heyday talking about you. Is what they're saying true? Are you lovin' it up with some farmer? I didn't want to believe them, but now I am beginning to wonder!"

"Yes, he was there, but I spent most of the night talking to Jennie and Margaret."

"I know you went there to be with your farmer, so tell me the truth! You are to stop seeing him! I'll find you a better husband when the time is right. You need a man to take care of you, not some boy, and if you want to live a good life like you have now, a man that has more than two cents to rub together!"

"He's not a boy, he's a man, and you can't stop me from marrying him. We're going to be married!"

"I can't, hey? You've brought shame to this house. I only hope no one saw you coming home this morning. All you are thinking about is running off with that farm boy. You need to be here to run this house. If you think you can just pick up and leave after all I've done for you, think again! The whole town knows you are indebted to me."

"Maybe some people saw us when he brought me home, but I don't care. His name is Jim Kucharek, and I care for him."

"Well, you can't get married. I won't allow it! Not yet anyway. Besides, if you are that serious, why haven't I met him? You should have come to me. Why didn't you tell me? "

"We've been trying to keep it a secret until we have a plan."

"Well, since you have the whole town talking, that makes little sense. Aren't you worried about your reputation? I've worked hard to bring you up in a Christian home. Take my advice, drop that boy. You are beholden to me after all I have done for you."

"Just when will it be okay for me to get married? I'm entitled to have a life. Besides, I'm tired of taking care of this big house, I want a place of my own. Also, I'm tired of taking care of your little princess. I hear you telling people about how much Dora means to you, but you never mention me even though I do all of the work. Dora and Dickie get all the attention. You really don't care about me, so why should I worry about you?"

"I saved you from living in poverty, or did you forget that? You might think that Dora is a princess because she has a better life living here than she had at the orphanage. She has nice clothes, and we take care of her at Christmas, but she is grateful and cheerful and humble. She accepts my gifts and thanks me for them. She is here because I brought her here; she didn't come begging. You know you'll be taken care of, Ruby. I will find you the right kind of husband. For now, you just need to worry about caring for this house and me. Now, get yourself together and make us breakfast!"

Ruby lowers her head, and she goes about her cooking in the kitchen. No one talks the rest of the day, not even when we eat breakfast. I take advantage of the quiet, to curl up with a book in my chair in the parlor while Mr. Murphy reads one of his law books.

Ruby has dinner ready at noon. Mr. Murphy says the blessing and he asks God to forgive Ruby for her sins, and to lead her in the right direction. After dinner, she goes to her room where she stays the rest of the day, so I have to make supper for Mr. Murphy and me.

After cleaning up the kitchen, I help him up the stairs and we both retire early. I'm tired, but I'm wide awake, thinking about Ruby and wondering what to expect.

I've never seen Mr. Murphy get angry and yell like he did. I don't know if I should be scared of him, or if I should just worry about what Ruby might do. I'll just have to be good, so he doesn't get angry with me.

Ruby's Secret

Ruby is busy making breakfast when I come down the next morning. "Where's Mr. Murphy?"

"He hasn't been down yet. He's probably sleeping late. Hurry, eat your breakfast and get dressed or you'll be late for school."

I almost forgot that we go back to school today. Honestly, it's a good excuse to get out of the house, away from the arguing. When I come downstairs, R.C. has the carriage waiting outside the kitchen door. Dickie is his normal happy self, and for a change, I enjoy being with him. He's full of excitement, telling me about his Christmas and the toys from Santa.

When I get home from school, Mr. Murphy is gone, and Ruby is waiting to talk to me.

"Dora, I was wondering. What if we just have Rex, Harold and Annie Rose for cake for your birthday this year instead of a party? Uncle Joe isn't feeling well, and it looks like we're in for a winter storm, so maybe everyone will want to stay inside."

"That's all right, Ruby. You and Uncle Joe, oops, I mean Mr. Murphy, have done a lot for me. I don't need a party every year."

My birthday is on Sunday. I decide not to go to church so I can fold laundry and help Ruby in the kitchen. Annie Rose, Rex and Harold arrive promptly at two o o'clock. Rex is cranking the doorbell when I open the door, "Hey, girl, Happy Birthday! We're here for cake!"

We all go to the kitchen where Ruby has my favorite on the middle of the table, a chocolate cake with pink icing.

"Ruby, you make the best cakes," says Harold.

"I'm goin' to tell Mother you said that."

"Don't you care! If you do, I have a thing or two I could tell her about you! So, let me think, how old does this make you?"

"I'm twelve."

Annie Rose chimes in, "Yeah, she's twelve going on fifteen. She's the smartest one in her class."

Rex asks, "How's Mr. Murphy? Is he going to be here when you open your presents?"

Ruby responds, "He said he would be back before you all leave. He had to go to the office for a short while."

"Should we wait, or can she open her presents?"

"No reason to wait, let's go to the parlor where we can be comfortable."

I open the gift from Annie Rose first, a book, *The Cornflower and Other Poems.*

"Thank you, Annie Rose, you know how much I like books. Now we have another book to read together. We'll memorize some of the poems."

Rex hands his gift to me, "Here, Dora, open mine next!"

I can tell it's another book, but I'm surprised that it's a diary with a lace handkerchief on top. "Thank you, Rex, I'll start writing in it right away, starting with our little party."

"Just be careful what you say about me. Only good things!"

"I can't think of anything bad to say about you, or about Harold and Annie Rose! You are my best friends!"

Harold is fidgeting with the checkerboard on his lap, so I hurry to open the rest of the gifts, a tin of Butterscotch Daisies from Harold, a white Bible from Mr. Murphy, and Ruby gave me a four-leafed clover pin for my coat.

Mr. Murphy comes home as we are picking up the wrapping paper and ribbons, "Well, here's the First Street Gang! How are you all doing? Did you get enough cake?"

"The cake was great! Rex and I were just going to play a game of checkers. Do you want to play?"

"Not today. I'll just sit in my chair and watch."

I go to sit on the hassock next to Mr. Murphy, "Thank you for the Bible. I've never seen a white Bible before, it's so pretty."

Harold and Rex play two games and it's already dusk when John is at the front door, waiting to take everyone home. After they leave, we eat a light supper of milk toast. I take my things to my room, and I put on my nightdress, then settle in to write in my diary.

Let's see, where should I start? How about my birthday?

January 7, 1906 — Dear Diary, I turned twelve today and Rex gave me this diary. It was just Annie Rose, Rex, and Harold, but we had a good time. Ruby made my favorite cake. I got a new book from Annie Rose; Harold gave me a tin of butterscotch daisies (my favorite.) Mr. Murphy gave me a pretty, white Bible and Ruby's gift was a pin, a 4 - leafed clover. Of course, I know she really didn't buy it, she just charges everything to Mr. Murphy's account. They're still not talking. Mr. Murphy was really upset. I don't think he feels good. He walks slow, sometimes with his shoes untied because his feet are so swollen. Maybe tomorrow will be better! Signed, Dora

I finish writing and I listen – the house is very quiet so Mr. Murphy must be reading, or he went to bed. I sneak downstairs but he's not there, so I guess he was tired. I check the kitchen, but Ruby must be in her room. I hope they start talking again so we can get back to normal. Sometimes people say hurtful things they really don't mean. I hope Ruby didn't really mean what she said about me.

January 21

Rex is thirteen today. R.C. is waiting in the carriage by the church steps to take Annie Rose and me to Rex's house for Sunday dinner. Of course, Anna will have a cake and John told me that he's making ice cream.

Annie Rose climbs into the carriage behind me. "Dora, what did you get Rex for his birthday? It's so hard to buy for boys."

"He's been tinkering. He likes to make things out of wood, so Mr. Murphy went to the Carpenter Shop and asked them to make a wooden toolbox. I think he'll be surprised."

"That's great! My gift will be boring. I'm giving him some mittens. He told me he's always losing one, so he's been wearing mittens that don't match."

"I don't think that's a boring present."

As soon as we step on the porch, Harold opens the door. "Come, come in out of the cold." He yells, "Rex, Dora and Annie Rose are here!"

Harold takes our coats and Annie Rose puts her gift on a table next to a lamp, and I set mine on the floor. We follow the aroma of chicken and noodles into the kitchen. Anna is dishing them up into a tureen. "Hello, girls, thank you for coming. I hope you like chicken and noodles!"

Annie Rose says, "It's my favorite! I've not been to your house before. You have a lot of pretty things. My mama only takes our lace tablecloth and China plates out for special occasions. Boys don't notice those things, but Rex is very lucky. Thank you for letting me come."

"'Tis nothing. Let's sit down and eat. Dora, why don't you take that bowl of peas."

After dinner, Rex opens his presents and of course, he likes the mittens. He decides to open the present from Mr. Murphy and me last, he says because it's the biggest. His present from his parents is a white shirt and bow tie, and Harold got him a Little Nemo comic book. I've not heard of Little Nemo before, but Rex really likes it.

Finally, he opens our gift. He lifts the lid and there's a tray inside, "Wow, Dora, my very own toolbox. Thank you!"

"Look, Son, rub your hand across the wood. It's made from oak. This is a very special gift!"

"Thanks again, Dora. Tell Mr. Murphy that I said thank you, and that I really like it!"

Anna calls us back to the table for cake and ice cream. There's a candle on the cake and we sing Happy Birthday. Rex's voice has been changing, so I try to imitate him, issuing several croaks in the middle of the song. Everyone laughs, including Rex.

On the way home, Annie Rose talks all the way home, about what a good time she had and how much she likes Rex's parents.

"Annie Rose, Rex and his family are so special to me. They're really not my family, but Anna is Mr. Murphy's cousin, so they feel like family to me."

I hate winter! There's really nothing to do. Everyone's staying home because of the weather, so the only time I go outside is to go to school.

Things are getting better at home. Mr. Murphy and Ruby are talking again but not as much as before the argument. Since the holidays are over, they don't have as much to talk about. Most of the time we just sit around and I read my books.

February 22, 1906.

I wake up because someone is running up the stairs. I get up and peek around my bedroom door; no one's there so I go to the bathroom. Ruby is on her knees with her head in the commode, throwing up.

"Ruby, what's wrong? You're sick! What can I do for you?"

"Just get out of here and go downstairs! See if Uncle Joe is here and if he is, ask him to call Doc Nelson."

When I go downstairs, I can smell vomit. I walk back through the kitchen to Ruby's room, and there's vomit on the floor, so I get a bucket of hot water and some rags, and I clean up the mess. The room still smells, and I notice that there's some vomit on her bed linens, so I get linens from the closet and change her bed.

I'm walking with the dirty linens towards the kitchen when Mr. Murphy comes down the stairs in his robe. "What's going on? I tried to go to the bathroom, but the door is locked. Where's Ruby?"

"Ruby's sick. She said you should call Doc Nelson." Mr. Murphy goes to the phone and rings up Doc Nelson. I'm almost gagging from the smell, "Let me put these out back." I drop the dirty linens in the back room where Ruby keeps the wringer washer, and hurry back to the kitchen and start to fix breakfast.

"W.D., you need to get over here. Something's wrong with Ruby."

Mr. Murphy and I are eating oatmeal when Ruby walks through the kitchen towards her room. "I changed your bed, Ruby, so you can lay down."

"Doc Nelson's on his way. She probably has a case of influenza."

Since the doctor is coming, I decide to get dressed before I clean up the kitchen. When I come downstairs, Mr. Murphy is talking to the doctor in the parlor.

"I don't know, she was fine last night, then I got up and Dora told me that she had vomited in her room, and she was sick again in the bathroom."

I show Doc Nelson to Ruby's room, he closes the door behind him.

He stays with Ruby for a long time; finally, he opens the door, and he nods to Mr. Murphy. Ruby stays in her room, but I can hear her crying. Mr. Murphy and the doctor go to the parlor. I start to follow, but Mr. Murphy tells me to go to my room.

I hear the door close when Doc Nelson leaves, and Mr. Murphy calls Ruby from her room, "Ruby, get out here. We need to talk." I need to know what's happened, so I listen just out of sight.

"What do you have to say for yourself?"

"Nothing. I have nothing to say."

"Well, what are you going to do? Are you going to tell that Kucharek fella that you are with child? And if you do, will he marry you, or just abandon you? You're in a mess, girl."

"I don't want to get married just yet. If you will let me, I would like to stay here in this house."

"I can see why you want to. You have a good life here and who knows what it will be like if you go to his farm. Can he care for you at all? Right now, you're sick and you need doctoring. But, Ruby, this is outrageous! What you have done is shameful and this not only affects you and me, but Dora as well. I need to think about it, and we will have to talk to Dora. I just don't know right now. I am hurt and disappointed. What would you do if you were me?"

"I don't know, Uncle Joe. Please give me a chance. I need your help."

I duck back into my room before she comes upstairs. Of course, I will do what I'm told, but I wonder what's going to happen. I stay in my room until Mr. Murphy calls me to come downstairs. Mr. Murphy is sitting in his chair in the parlor, silent, and the room is dark. I don't want him to yell at me, so I decide to just go to the kitchen and start supper.

I go to Ruby's door and peek into the room, "Ruby, I'll make supper. What should I fix?"

"There's some leftover stew, just heat that up."

"O.K. Maybe I'll make some cornbread to go with it. Do you feel like eating?"

"No, but the doctor told me I will feel better if I eat, so I'll try to eat a little. What's Uncle Joe doing? I know he's upset with me."

"Nothing. He's sitting in the parlor. I'll call you when supper is ready."

Mr. Murphy comes to the kitchen, just as I'm taking the cornbread out of the oven. The stew is ready, and the table is set. Mr. Murphy likes butter, so I put a bowl of freshly churned butter on the table.

"Well, this is nice. Everything smells good. I'm hungry! There are three plates. Is Ruby eating?"

"She said Doc Nelson told her to eat." I call to Ruby's room, "Ruby, it's ready. Come eat!"

We all sit down. Mr. Murphy butters a square of cornbread, and he dives into the stew. It's quiet at first, but he breaks the silence, "Ruby, you do make good stew."

She says, "Thank you," while continuing to look down, picking at her dinner.

After I finish, I start to leave the table to clear the dishes.

"Dora, thank you for supper. I suppose you heard us talking after Doc Nelson left. Sit down, Ruby has something to tell you."

Ruby looks startled and she gives Mr. Murphy a dirty look, but she turns toward me and explains, "Dora, the reason I don't feel well is I am going to have a baby."

"I don't understand. How could that happen? I thought the only way a woman can get pregnant is to be married."

Mr. Murphy shakes his head. "It's not your concern as to how it happened. We just need to decide if we want Ruby to stay here in this house until the baby is born. Right now, Ruby is sick so she won't be much help, which will burden you. However, if we make her leave, then we will not have any help until I can find another housekeeper, so there will be even more for you to do."

"Do you want her to stay?"

"I don't know. I've cared for Ruby since she was a little girl, but a lot depends on you. If she does stay, what's happened must be kept a secret. No one outside this house is to know what's happened to Ruby. She will not be allowed to go outside this house and that farmer will not be allowed in this house. I know Dora can keep a secret, but can you live with those terms, Ruby?"

"I want to be able to see Jim."

"Those are my terms. If you don't like it, then go back to your father's house! See if they want to take care of you. Dora, will this be all right with you? You will have chores, there won't be any piano lessons, and your friends, Annie Rose and Rex, will not be able to visit here until this is over."

"If Annie Rose and Rex can't come here, can I go see them?"

"You can do that, but you probably won't have much time for friends this year. Being forced into seclusion will make a lonely life for all of us."

"If you want me to help, I will." I try to smile, but I feel worried.

He turns to Ruby, "It seems Dora is agreeable, but can you live with my terms?"

Ruby breaks down and she starts to cry, "I have nowhere else to go, so I have no choice."

"Fine. I assume the two of you will get together and agree on what has to be done, what you think you can handle, Ruby, and what Dora is to do. W.D. said you will start feeling better in a couple months, so we will just have to adjust as things change."

Ruby goes to her room and Mr. Murphy decides to retire early. After I clean up the kitchen, I go upstairs to my room. I'm going to have to talk to Mr. Murphy when Ruby isn't around. I know he wants this to be a secret, but from everyone? R.C. is here every day and he always walks in without knocking. Then, there's Anna and John; they are family. Will he tell them? How can I explain to Annie Rose and Rex that they can't come here? Maybe not inside, but maybe we can still play games outside during the summer.

Now I'm back to worrying about what we will do if Ruby leaves. Even though she will probably stay for now, where will she go after the baby is born? Mr. Murphy did say he would have to find a housekeeper. This gives us time, so maybe I don't have to worry.

When I come downstairs the next morning, Mr. Murphy is waiting for me in the kitchen.

"Good morning, Sunshine! You're up bright and early!"

"I have to eat breakfast and get ready for school."

"Sorry, Dora. You won't be going to school for a while. You'll have to stay home to take care of the house and Ruby. I know you want to go, but you can't - it's just until Ruby feels better."

I don't know what to say! I can't believe he expects me to miss school, and he's telling me this before I even have a chance to talk to Ruby.

"Mr. Murphy, I'll stay home today but let me talk to Ruby so she can tell me what she wants me to do. I know you want me to stay home until Ruby feels better, but if I miss too much school, I'll fall back a grade."

"I don't think you'll have time for school. There's too much to do."

I make breakfast, porridge and tea. Mr. Murphy and I try to eat while we hear Ruby vomiting. R.C. is waiting outside the kitchen door so Mr. Murphy leaves for the office, I clean up the kitchen and go upstairs to get dressed. When I come downstairs, Ruby is sitting at the kitchen table drinking tea, with her head in her hand.

"I had to stay home from school to help you and keep the house. Maybe we can figure out how I can go back, though. Maybe you won't feel so sick soon." I try to get Ruby to help me, but she only looks a little smug.

"I told you that someday he would tell you to stop going to school."

"He told me that I'll have to stay home only until you're feeling better."

"Whenever that will be. Right now, I just want to die! Well, I'm glad you'll be here working. There's a lot that has to be done. Tell me what you think you can do."

"I can do the cooking and I can clean and change beds, but this is a big house. I can't do everything."

"Well, the rest of the house will not need cleaning every day. One day you can clean and dust the main floor, another day you can clean the bathroom and Mr. Murphy's room and change his linens, then you can clean your room on a third day. Basically, cleaning every other day."

"What about laundry? I can't carry the water and I can't reach the clothesline. Another thing, no one has showed me how to iron. I know Mr. Murphy wants his shirts starched and ironed."

"I can do the ironing if you just get the clothes washed. R.C. can carry the water for you and he will probably help you with getting the clothes on and off the clothesline. You'll see, though, you'll be busy and Mr. Murphy's right, you won't have time for school at all. Now, can you make me something to eat?"

I leave the kitchen, crying as I hurry upstairs to my room. Ruby can make her own breakfast. I know she can at least make a cup of tea. It's not fair, but I can't tell anyone about Ruby's condition, so I have no one to turn to. At least R.C. will be around to help. Somehow, I need to find a way to talk to Rex.

Just as I thought, I'm spending most of my time cooking and cleaning.

My Waterfall!

Sunday, March 4, 1906 —Dear Diary. I'm doing a good job, keeping house. Mr. Murphy told Ruby to help; I told him I can't do everything, but I am. I clean on Monday, Wednesday, and Friday, and R.C. and I wash clothes on Saturday if the sun is shining. Otherwise, dirty clothes wait until Tuesday. I haven't seen Annie Rose or Rex, and I've been so busy that I haven't had time to miss school. Ruby is sick every morning, then she gets better as the day goes on, but she's no help. She just lays around. I'm really tired but looking forward to tomorrow because Mary is supposed to stop by. I assume she knows - she probably heard it from R.C. Signed, Dora

Mid-morning, the kitchen door opens, and R.C. holds the door for Mary who is carrying a baking dish with steam floating off the top.

She puts the dish on the stove, "Dora, I made a double batch of chicken pot pie, one for you and another for us. There should be enough for you to have leftovers."

"Oh, thank you, Mary. Mr. Murphy will be home soon for dinner. It smells good – I'm sure we will like it. Thanks, again, you saved me from having to cook."

"Happy to do it. How are you doing? R.C. says you are doing a good job, keeping up the place. Is there anything else I can do to help?"

"Can't think of anything right now, but if you don't mind, it would be nice if you would stop in every now and then. I don't get out of the house and Mr. Murphy doesn't want outsiders in the house, so it would be nice to have someone to talk to."

"I would like that too. R.C., you go on. Dora and I are going to have a cup of tea."

We are still drinking tea and chatting when Mr. Murphy comes home. He doesn't look happy, but he has a warm welcome for Mary, "Why, hello, Mary.

What brings you here?"

"Just wanted to drop off a chicken pot pie. R.C. brought a couple chickens home, so I decided to make two pies. Dora and I were just having a cup of tea, but I have to get home. Dickie's probably wondering where I am."

Mr. Murphy sees her out the door, then he turns to me, "I thought I told you, no one is to be in this house until this Ruby situation is over."

"But she came with R.C. As usual, he just walked in without knocking. Besides, what would I say if he did knock? Should I tell him he can't come in? I thought you might have said something and that's why she brought the pie."

"No, I haven't decided what to say to R.C. It doesn't make sense to tell him to stay away. He hasn't done anything wrong, and he'll wonder what's going on. I'll just tell Ruby that she will have to go to her room and stay out of sight whenever R.C. is here. It's all right, Dora. Now I understand; you did nothing wrong. We will just have to figure everything out, you and I."

"Ruby's been in her room all day, so she didn't come out while Mary was here. It was nice of Mary to bring the pie. It smells good! I'll see if Ruby wants to eat."

I set the table with three plates and utensils, then I knock on Ruby's door, "Ruby, it's me, Dora. Mary brought a chicken pot pie. Do you want some dinner?"

Ruby comes out of her room, and she goes directly to her seat at the table without talking. We bow our heads and say silent prayers, then we dig in. Mary has tucked creamy chicken and vegetables under a buttery crust.

"Yum! This is really good!"

"Agree. That Mary is a good cook. Aren't you goin' to try it, Ruby?"

"I don't know. It does smell good, but I'm afraid to eat. I've been throwing up so much, my stomach hurts."

"You can't not eat. You don't look good. You're pale and it looks like you've lost weight. Dora, scoop a spoonful and put it on her plate."

Ruby picks up her fork and she takes a few bites. Then she starts to pick at her food. Suddenly, she jumps up, knocking her chair over, and she runs to her room. We can hear her being sick.

"Poor Ruby."

"Don't feel too sorry for her. She's the one that got herself in this mess!"

"Mr. Murphy, I was wondering. Since it's Sunday, can I go to Annie Rose's house for a little while? I'll be back in time to make supper."

"Go ahead. You've been working hard. I have some reading to do, and it looks like Ruby will just stay in her room, so she shouldn't need anything. You might want to empty her bucket before you leave."

I go to Ruby's room and carry the bucket, turning my head sideways to avoid the smell, and I flush the vomit down the commode. I wonder if I will ever get the smell out of my nose. If this is what women have to go through to have babies, then I don't want any.

I return the bucket to Ruby's room. She has a bottle of rose water on her dresser. She's sleeping so I sneak a few drops, rubbing it on my hands and face to get rid of the smell.

I put on my coat and bring my hands to my face. They smell like roses, not vomit, so I leave. The first time I've been out of the house since Ruby got sick.

Annie Rose squeals with excitement when she opens the door, "Mama, Dora's here!"

Annie Rose's mama comes from the kitchen, "So she is. Did you come for a visit? I hope you can stay for a while. Annie Rose has really missed you."

"I can stay for a little while. I just need to be home in time to make supper."

"You have to make supper? What about Ruby? Did she go somewhere for a visit?"

I don't know what to say, so I take Annie Rose's hand, "Can we go to your room? I brought a new book that Anna gave me for Christmas."

"What's the name of the book?"

"It's called *The Little White Bird*. I've been saving it so we can read it together."

We giggle as we walk up the stairs to her room. We run and plop on her bed. Annie Rose opens the book. We take turns reading paragraphs out loud, and in no time at all, we are in London, walking through Kensington Gardens.

After a while, I hear the rattle of pots and pans and realize that I'm back in Canton.

"Golly, gosh, your mama must be making supper. I need to get home!"

Annie Rose starts to cry, "I wish you didn't have to leave. How come you don't come to school anymore?"

"I can't tell you right now, but I'll only miss school for a few more months. Mr. Murphy says I have to stay home for now."

"I'll come to your house to see you, then."

At first, I don't know what to say, but she can't come to our house. "That's okay, Annie Rose, I'll come to your house, but right now, I can't have visitors."

I don't want Annie Rose to see me crying, so I hurry out the door and run all the way home.

Mr. Murphy opens the door, "I was watching for you and saw you running. You're crying. What's wrong? Did you have a nice visit with Annie Rose?"

He gives me his hanky, and I dry my tears. "I really had a good time. Thank you for letting me go. We started to read the book that Anna gave me for Christmas, but we didn't finish. Annie Rose was crying when I left. She misses me just like I miss her."

"I understand. I know what! If nothing comes up, let's just plan on you taking time to see your friends on Sunday afternoons. I assume you might want to see Rex as well. Maybe the three of you can get together. Let me know what you want to do, and maybe I can make some arrangements."

Sunday, March 11 — Dear Diary. I've been keeping up with my chores. Ruby isn't any better. Doc Nelson was here on Wednesday, but he just goes to Ruby's room to see her, then he leaves without saying anything to me. I wish he would talk to me. Ruby says he wants her to start moving around. I'd like to tell him the truth about her laying around all the time. I didn't get to see Annie Rose or Rex today because I had to look after Ruby. I miss my friends. All I do is work and go to bed. Signed, Dora

I cleaned the main floor yesterday, but we forgot to plan cleaning of the stairwell and it's getting dirty! The walls don't need much, but the dark wood of the stairs is dusty, so that will be my task for the day.

I go to the kitchen to heat a pot of water. They don't look so bad, but the stairs are really dirty from our shoes and boots, and from carrying Ruby's bucket up the stairs. I heat the water until it is just warm, then I pour it into a bucket and carry it up to start at the top of the stairs. I wash each stair with an old towel and get down to the first landing. I look back and water is dripping down the stairs, so I get another towel to dry them off.

I turn to start on the next section of stairs, catching the pail with my knee. The bucket tips over and water is running down the stairs like a waterfall. Darn it! I run to get more towels and start drying, bottom stairs up, but the water keeps running. I'm soaked, my dress and apron are wet, and I hear the kitchen door open.

Mr. Murphy takes one look at me and he laughs, "What are you trying to do? Whatever it is, you've created quite a mess!"

"I'm sorry, Mr. Murphy. I was trying to wash the stairs."

"Well, it looks like you did. But did you need this much water?"

Still laughing, he helps me up, "Hand me some of those towels so I can help you. You need to stop the water that's running down, so you go up and dry the top stairs, and I'll work my way up from the bottom. My goodness!"

We manage to sop the water up and after the steps are dry, the wood on the stairs is clean, and when I look up to admire what I've done, the sun creeps through the window on the landing, so it looks like the wood is polished with gold.

I go upstairs to change into dry clothes, and I come downstairs to make dinner.

"Since you've been so busy, why don't we have a light dinner, then you can make a nice supper? Ruby always feels better later in the day anyway."

There's enough leftover pot pie for the three of us. Ruby joins us and she manages to finish her plate without getting sick. We all sit back in our chairs to finish our tea.

"Ruby, our girl has been working hard. She's doing a good job keeping everything clean, but I don't think she will want to clean the stairs for a while."

I'm embarrassed, but happy that Mr. Murphy is not angry with me. "Guess what I did? My knee knocked a bucket of water over and we had a waterfall down the stairs!"

While it wasn't funny to me at the time, it is funny now, so we all laugh.

"I realize that I stay in my room a lot. I'll try to spend more time with you, but you can come to me if you have questions."

The next morning, Mr. Murphy goes to the office, and I am cleaning up the breakfast dishes when Ruby comes to the kitchen table.

"Mornin', Ruby. Feel like eating?"

"Maybe some toast. I think I need to start eating and moving around. Maybe I'll feel better."

"Tea too? I'll have a cup of tea with you."

Ruby spreads jam on her toast. She drinks tea between small bites, but she is eating all of her toast. She doesn't look as pale today.

"So, what are you and Uncle Joe up to? Has he told anyone about me?"

"I don't know. I got in trouble the other day when Mary brought the chicken pot pie. We were drinking a cup of tea when Mr. Murphy came home. I just assumed since R.C. is in and out that R.C. and Mary would know, but he yelled at me, no one is to be in this house. I don't know how he's going to stop it since R.C. is in and out and he just walks in without knocking."

"Doc Nelson says the baby will be born in November. That's a long time to keep a secret from people close to him."

"I know. I don't say anything, I just do my work. I really miss school. I've seen Annie Rose a couple times, but I haven't seen Rex or anyone else."

"What are you doing today?"

"Fridays are easy, I just clean my room. I was trying to figure out what to make for dinner. Maybe I'll just make a pan of cornbread and fry up some sausages with apples."

"Uncle Joe will like that. Bring the apples to me. I'll peel them while you make the cornbread. Dora, I was wondering if you would do me a favor. I need to get a note to Jim, so I was wondering if you will sneak it into the mailbox. You can't tell Uncle Joe. It will be our secret."

"Oh, my! Oh, me! I don't know. What if he finds out?"

"You are my only hope. I can't risk going outside. The mailman comes in the afternoon, so if you put it in the mailbox before Uncle Joe comes back for dinner, he will never know."

She gives the letter to me. I look out the front window and none of the neighbors are outside, so I run and shove the letter into the mailbox, then hurry back to the house. When I get back to the kitchen, Ruby's not there. The house is quiet and the door to Ruby's room is closed.

I don't clean on Saturday and it's raining, so I can't do laundry. I decide to bake cookies. Dickie Webster is rapping on the kitchen door, but I just pretend I don't hear him, then Mr. Murphy comes downstairs.

"What's that knocking?"

"Knocking? I don't hear anything."

Mr. Murphy looks out the kitchen window. "It's Dickie. You didn't hear him knocking on the kitchen door?" He opens the door a crack. "Shhh, Dickie. People are sleeping. I'll come for you after breakfast, and you can go with me to the farm. You'll get to see the new baby chicks that hatched this week. Wear your boots, it's muddy."

He shuts the door and Dickie takes off running home. After we finish our tea and biscuits, Mr. Murphy puts on his work coat and boots, and he leaves, walking towards R.C.'s house to get Dickie.

I finish all the dishes and go to the cupboard, hoping I can find Ruby's recipe for sugar cookies. She just throws her recipes in a drawer, so I have to sort through all of them on the kitchen table. I almost give up, but there it is, the last piece of paper in the bottom of the drawer!

I put the first batch of cookies in the oven and roll out more dough while they are baking. Shoot! Why did I put the sugar away? I get the sugar can out of the cupboard and carefully sprinkle the tops of the cookies. I decide to wash the mixing bowl and rolling pin while the first batch is baking. The sink is filling with warm sudsy water and when I look out the window. I see a robin. The first robin of spring!

Suddenly, I hear footsteps and Ruby's door opens, "Dora, what's burning?"

I turn towards Ruby and realize the kitchen is filled with smoke! "The cookies! Oh, Ruby, I burned the cookies!"

Ruby grabs a towel to lift the baking sheet out of the oven, and when she opens the oven door, there's even more smoke! I open the kitchen door and windows and we fan the smoke with towels. I sit down on a chair and start to cry. Ruby sits but she's laughing!

"Ruby, it isn't funny!"

"Oh, Dora, you'll laugh about it someday. Don't let anyone tell you they've never burned cookies. We've all done it. If this is your first cooking catastrophe, you're lucky but, believe me, it won't be the last. We just need to get the place aired out before Uncle Joe comes home."

I take the burned cookies to the waste bin behind the barn, so Mr. Murphy won't see them. Ruby helps me to clean the baking sheets. I put the second batch in the oven and sit, not taking my eyes off the oven door, while they bake. One of the cookies is broken, so Ruby and I do a taste test. They're perfect – the color of straw with sprinkles of white sugar. I put the rest of the cookies on a plate, in the center of the table. Mr. Murphy will be surprised when he comes home!

March 17, 1906 — Dear Diary. I made perfect sugar cookies today! Mr. Murphy told me I'm a good cook, but he should have been there when I burned the first batch! I didn't know they were burning 'til Ruby came out of her room yelling 'cuz she smelled the smoke. We opened the windows and door and she teased me while we cleared the smoke. I'm not going to tell Mr. Murphy 'cuz I'm scared he will yell at me for wasting food. Ruby's not throwing up as much. She looks better and I think she must feel better, but she still lets me do all the work. When I talk about missing school, she just walks away and says, "I told you so!" She doesn't know. Like Mr. Murphy said, I will go back to school when she gets better. I'm going to Anna and John's tomorrow afternoon. I like them, and it will be fun to see Rex and Harold. Signed, Dora

Rex is sitting on the porch swing, waiting for me. "Dora, what's going on? Where have you been? Why haven't you been in school?"

"I'm not sure. I don't know. I just do what Mr. Murphy tells me to do."

I look up and Anna is standing inside the door; she must have overheard us talking. "But, Dora, that doesn't explain why you have to miss school. Are you staying home to help Ruby? That makes no sense. What can be so important that you have to miss school?"

"I can't say, Anna. I'm not supposed to tell. I don't want to talk about it."

Anna goes back inside. I hear her talking to John, but I can't hear what she is saying. Rex nudges me with his elbow. "Hey, kid, what do you want to do today?"

"I don't know. I just wanted to get out of the house so I could see you. I guess we could just sit here and talk, or maybe we can play checkers. I'm not very good, but I want to learn."

We just talk, the swing going back and forth while Rex tells me about what's going on at school.

"Father says eighth grade is an important year 'cuz next year is high school. I'm getting good grades, but History is tough. We have to memorize a lot of dates. I won't be able to see you as much when I go to high school but guess what? I can sign up for wood shop!"

"Mr. Murphy says I'll just have to miss school for a while, but I'm afraid I'll be held back a grade. But maybe in November I can go back."

Anna calls us inside for tea and cookies. Harold has already set up the checkerboard.

"Hi, John, Harold. What kind of cookies are these? They're so pretty!"

"They're just sugar cookies with icing instead of sugar."

"Wow! I make sugar cookies, but this is the first time I've seen sugar cookies with icing!"

Nothing more is said about me missing school. I play one game, then I watch Rex and Harold play checkers the rest of the afternoon. Before I know it, R.C. is waiting outside to take me home.

Anna comes out of the kitchen with a plate of cookies for me to take home. "Dora, are you going home because you have to make supper?"

"Yes, Ma'am."

"Are you doing all of the cooking now?"

"Yes."

"Tell Joseph I'll be by sometime this week. I'll bring a meatloaf for one of your dinners."

"Thank you. That would be real nice. I have to keep up with the cleaning so I'm pretty busy. I'll tell Mr. Murphy; he might want to talk to you before you come."

I climb onto R.C.'s carriage and we eat cookies while he takes me home. Mr. Murphy is waiting for me at the kitchen table.

"Did you have a good time? How are Anna, John and the boys?"

"They're fine. They wanted to know why I'm not in school, but I didn't say anything. Anna said to let you know she will be coming by sometime this week to drop off a meatloaf."

"Did you tell her that you can't have company? What did you tell her?"

"I didn't say anything. I just said I didn't want to talk about school."

"Did you say anything to your friends?"

I don't know what to say.

"Dora, look at me! What did you tell Annie Rose and Rex?"

"Nothing. I just told them I have to miss school for a while."

"Well, I hope that's all you said. If it is, you did good. I think you should stay here and stop visiting your friends for a while. You won't be allowed to go to see them, and they can't come here. There's too much at stake. Just for a while, until this whole thing is over. Now stop crying!"

"Please, Mr. Murphy! Please let me see my friends. I haven't told anyone about Ruby. I won't say anything, I promise!"

He pulls me close to comfort me, "Now, now, it won't be that bad. It's just for a little while. And I will tell Anna and John what's going on, so they can help you a little now and then. They can keep a secret."

☙❧

It's Monday, so I'm cleaning the kitchen floor on my hands and knees when someone raps on the kitchen door. I look up and it's Dickie Webster! I'm not going to bother getting up for Dickie! He keeps knocking and I wave at him to go away. I look up again, and he has his thumbs in his ears, his eyes crossed, and he's sticking his tongue out at me. I just look down and go back to my cleaning. He finally goes away.

The kitchen is clean, so I'll finish making dinner, then I can finish the main floor after we eat. The stew meat is tender, so I add the vegetables, set the table, and sit down to wait for Mr. Murphy to come home.

As soon as he walks in the door, Ruby comes out of her room. I suppose Mr. Murphy doesn't know she hides in her room, that he thinks she at least helps a little.

"What smells so good? Is that beef stew? Ruby's beef stew is one of my favorites."

"This is Dora's stew. It's the first time she's made it, so I helped her."

"No, you didn't! I made it all by myself. You don't do anything; you just stay in your bed all day."

"Ruby, you need to get out of that bed and help her. You are clearly feeling better. Dora is just a little girl. If you don't start helping, I'll let her go back to school, then you'll have to do everything!"

I mix some water into a spoonful of flour, and add it to the stew, making a rich brown gravy. Mr. Murphy doesn't talk, but he eats all of his stew. Ruby picks at hers, eating all of the vegetables.

"Ruby, don't you like the beef?"

"Oh, Dora, it's fine. You made a good stew. I just don't feel like eating meat right now. Maybe tomorrow. Stew always tastes better the second day."

Mr. Murphy sees Anna at the kitchen door, and he gets up to let her in.

"Come on in, Anna. We were just finishing dinner – Dora made stew. Would you like some?"

"Oh, no, I already ate, but it smells good. I just wanted to stop in for a few minutes to see how you all are doing. No special reason. I'm going to the grocers. Is there anything that you need?"

I speak up, "I need lots of things, but I haven't made a list. I know we need flour and lard."

"Why don't you make your list, and I'll come by tomorrow and take you to the store. Is it all right with you, Joseph, if she goes to the store with me?"

"I suppose that'll be all right."

March 31, 1906 — Dear Diary, the wind must have caught the kitchen door, 'cuz I woke up when I heard it slam shut. I'm not sure what time it was, but it was middle of the night, or maybe early morning. I looked out the front window and Ruby was sneaking a letter to the mailbox. I know she's getting better. She's still sick in the morning when she gets up but after breakfast, she throws up then she's fine the rest of the day. She still stays in her room, though, except for meals and when she goes to the bathroom. I don't think she wants me to know she's better. Mr. Murphy doesn't know she's still laying around, doing nothing. If she doesn't start helping soon, I'm goin' to tell him. I'm getting used to cooking and cleaning. I like polishing the piano and the table in the parlor. They shine and when the sun comes through the window, golden sunlight bounces off the wood. Anna stops in most days and sometimes she takes me to the store. I like her and it's good to get out of the house. Tomorrow's Sunday and Mr. Murphy said I can go to see Annie Rose. I hope she doesn't start asking questions that I can't answer. I just want to have fun. Signed, Dora

Annie Rose's mama has a tea party ready on the parlor table. She set three chairs at the table with her fine China cups, and a silver tray with a matching tea service.

"Take your seats, ladies while I get the scones."

The three of us eat scones and drink tea, holding our pinky fingers out like we're high society. Annie Rose's mama is funny. She tells one of her great stories.

"When I was a young girl, I had a best friend, Jenny Hall. We used to pretend we were brides, using old lace curtains for veils. One day, we decided to make pies. We used sand from the sandbox and mixed it with water and we set the tins in the sun to dry, and they formed hard crusts. Then we caught grasshoppers. When we had enough, we smashed them for the filling, so we made grasshopper pies!"

"Yuck! Mama, you never told me that! You didn't eat them!"

"Of course not, we just pretended they were for supper."

We are laughing so hard, I almost fall off my chair. We spend the rest of the day, taking turns to read a story to our dolls.

"Dora, when can you come again, and when will you be back in school?"

"I already told you, I don't know. I want to see Rex too. Maybe if it's all right with your mama, he can come here. I can't talk about school, though. When we talk about it, it makes me feel worse. Ruby's doing better but she still makes me do all of the work!"

Annie Rose knows I can't say more, so she just holds my hand, and gets out a book so we can read together.

When it gets close to supper time, I go to the kitchen to thank Mrs. O'Neal for the tea party. "It was so much fun, and I really liked the scones!"

My Circumstance

Thursday, April 18, 1906

Mr. Murphy is reading the newspaper when I come downstairs to fix breakfast. "Says here that they had a big earthquake in San Francisco, California yesterday. The ground shook and split wide open. The whole town was destroyed. Lots of people dead and those that survived lost everything. People are sleeping on the ground or in tents on a hill. Dora, we must pray for those poor people."

I can't get those suffering people out of my mind, people with babies sleeping on the ground! When we go to church on Sunday, I pray for the people in San Francisco.

The opening hymn is ***A Mighty Fortress is Our God***, then Pastor leads us in a silent prayer. The church is so quiet. I pray especially for the children without homes, and some who have lost their families. A baby starts to cry, breaking the silence.

Rev. Denham is a good preacher. "We must have faith, faith in God. Some things are hard to explain, but we must remember when tragedy strikes, that it is God's will."

I stop listening and my mind wanders. He's pastor, so I guess he knows, but I wonder why God would cause such a tragedy. Just like Aunt Dora said, that it was God's will to take my daddy to heaven. Some things are hard to understand.

"Today's collection will be sent to the American Red Cross to help those poor people in San Francisco."

Mr. Murphy gave me a nickel for the collection plate. The plate is passed, and I drop my coin into the plate, feeling proud that I can help.

I run home after church. Ruby surprises me by making dinner. This is the first time she has done anything for a long time.

"Ruby, you must be feeling better!"

"Yes, I do. Doc Nelson told me I should start moving around. I don't think I'll want to clean, but I can start to help with the cooking."

It's a start! I have to clean up the dishes, but Mr. Murphy lets me go to see Annie Rose and Rex after dinner.

We have fun, the three of us. It's like old times except Rex is really getting tall. Rex and Annie Rose see one another at school, and Rex says they spend most of the time, talking about me, what's going on, and when I will be returning to school.

"Mr. Murphy said it would only be for a while, but I have given up on school, at least until next year."

"But you'll be held back a grade. That's not fair! I'm going to talk to my mother and father."

"No. Please don't say anything. Right now, your mother is coming to our house every day or so. I look forward to her visits and she helps me keep groceries in the house. If you say something, Mr. Murphy might not let her come over, or he might not let me visit you. Let's talk about something else."

"But, Dora, look at yourself! All you do is cry when we try to talk to you."

"Yeah, and my mama says you are too young to be burdened with housework. Why do you have to do everything? I don't want you to lose a grade. I want you to be in my class!"

"Please, I'm not allowed to say anything. I hate Ruby, and I hate her for making me miss school. She has started to help with the cooking, though, so I hope this will all be over soon."

"What's wrong with her? What if she doesn't get better?"

"Yeah, she's been sick a long time. Doesn't she care that she's making you miss school? Time's flying. Next year, I'll be in high school, so we won't see each other as much."

"I'll get in trouble if I tell you anything and, no, if you must know, I don't think Ruby cares about anyone except herself. I need to get home now in case she doesn't want to make supper. It's always what she wants or doesn't want. She really doesn't care about me. I miss seeing you guys. If I can get out, can we do this again next Sunday?"

"If it's okay with Annie Rose, I'll be here."

"You know it's okay."

"Good, then I'll ask Mr. Murphy to let me come again next week. But next week, let's not talk about Ruby or school. Let's just have fun!"

Rex walks me home. We talk about all that has happened recently, then he doesn't say anything for several blocks.

"Dora, I know about Ruby. I was standing inside the doorway when Mr. Murphy talked to my mother."

"Oh, no! You didn't say anything to your mother, did you?"

"No, of course not!"

"You can't tell anyone, not even Harold or Annie Rose. I could get in trouble with Mr. Murphy. He might even stop me from seeing you, and I don't want to take a chance that he would tell Anna that she's no longer welcome. You haven't done anything wrong, and neither did she, but sometimes he says things when he's upset."

"Don't worry, it will be our secret. I had already decided not to tell anyone except you. I worry about you, though. If you like, I'll come by on Saturdays to help you with some of the heavy work. I'll start with outside work, so I don't have to come inside."

As we reach the front steps, he comments, "Looks like the windows need washing."

❧

Friday, May 4, 1906.

I decide to sneak into the kitchen early to bake a cake for Ruby's birthday tomorrow. Maybe if I make her a cake, she'll be nice to me. After the cake is in the oven, I wash the bowls and spoon so there's no evidence of my surprise. Ruby says she is still queasy in the morning, so she never comes to breakfast.

Mr. Murphy comes down for breakfast before he leaves for the office. "What's in the oven? It smells like a cake."

"Shhh! It's a surprise! I'm making a cake for Ruby's birthday. If I can just get the cake made, I'll hide it in my room and ice it in the morning."

"A cake for Ruby? Why would you make a cake for her when you have so much to do? Don't do this again. You're not here to satisfy her. You have enough to do as it is. Where is she anyway?"

"She's in her room. She still stays in her room all day."

"Every day? She's not helping you? I see R.C. is waiting for me, so I'll hurry and eat so I can go. I'll talk to her when I get home."

I don't want the cake to burn, so I can't go upstairs to clean my room until the cake is done. I know, I'll go up and get my book to read while I wait. Then I see something strange. Who's that? A man is outside the kitchen door, looking in the window. He's kind of scary. His face is hidden by the shadow of his hat, and he's wearing old work clothes and boots. He's holding a red rose in his hand.

I open the door a crack so I can peek out, "Who are you? What do you want?"

"I'm Jim Kucharek. I'm here to see Ruby. Tomorrow's her birthday and I decided to come today while Murphy is gone."

"You can't come in here. I'll get in trouble! Mr. Murphy told us that you aren't allowed to come into our house!"

"Dora? You are Dora, aren't you? I know you took Ruby's letter for me to the mailbox, so you must care how she feels, even just a little bit. She's been locked up in this house, sick and lonely. Please, just let me come in. I won't stay long."

"Wait here."

I close the door and go to Ruby's room. "Ruby, Jim is outside. He wants to see you!"

Ruby runs her hands through her hair, "Goodness, I'm a mess! Tell him I'll be right out."

"You know he can't come in the house. There will be trouble if Mr. Murphy catches him. He's standing on the steps outside the door."

"Oh, Dora, I do love him, and I want to see him. Please, just for a few minutes."

"I'm going upstairs to clean my room. If you decide to see him, I don't want to know about it."

I hurry to the kitchen to take the cake out of the oven. I put the pans on a wooden tray and take them to my room. Then I sneak down to the landing to listen. I need to know what they're planning.

I hear the kitchen door close. "Come over to the table. We don't want the neighbors to see you standing there. You shouldn't be here!"

I hear Jim laugh. "You're my girl, and you're carrying my child. Has he kicked yet? I've tried to do the right thing and stay away, but ever since that night, I knew I wanted to be with you. Look, I brought you a rose for your birthday."

Ruby giggles a little. "Thank you, I love the smell of a rose. Silly, stop touching my belly! It's too early to feel him kicking. Good news is, I'm feeling better. I was pretty sick. Uncle Joe told the Princess that she had to take over. She tries but still, she is just a young girl. But that's not my concern. She wants to go back to school. She doesn't know this is going to be her job for a long time."

"Don't be so hard on her. She mailed your letter, and she turned her back just now so I could see you."

"I suppose. Well, I don't care. Let her do the work. She gets all of the attention. I'm just going to take it easy. But, Jim, you have to go now before someone sees you."

I hear the door open and a thump, which sounds like Jim pushing Ruby against it. "Oh, Jim!" Ruby says, with a breathless giggle.

In a husky voice, Jim says, "I love you, Babe." I step into the kitchen to interrupt and they are locked in a lingering kiss.

Ruby looks shocked to see me, but I just feel disgusted. "You're still here? I told you not to come into the house! Ruby! You know what Mr. Murphy said. We'll both be in trouble if he finds out."

"It's all right, I was about ready to leave." Jim heads for the door and looks back, "I love you, Ruby. Don't give up! We'll get through this. Then I will make you my wife."

When he leaves, Ruby tries to go upstairs but I stand in the doorway. "Ruby, how could you? Maybe it was worth it for you, but I don't want any trouble."

"I didn't know!"

"I don't believe you! Somehow you must have got word to him. How did he know when Mr. Murphy wouldn't be here?"

She doesn't answer. She just hangs her head, and then I move out of the way and she heads up to her room.

I hate her! She's a liar! I'm not going to help her anymore. If she wants to mail a letter to Jim, then she'll have to go to the mailbox herself. If someone sees her, then she'll be the one who's in trouble with Mr. Murphy, not me!

Just like I thought, she doesn't care about me, even though I clean up her vomit! I wish I hadn't bothered to make a cake. I feel like throwing it in the trash, but Mr. Murphy doesn't want us to waste food.

Ruby stays in her room the rest of the day.

When Mr. Murphy comes home, I pretend everything is all right, but he asks, "What's wrong with Ruby? She's not goin' to eat supper?"

I go to her room and knock on her door, "Ruby, supper is ready." No answer.

I return to the kitchen. "She must be sleeping."

May 5, 1906: Ruby's Birthday

I get up early so I can ice the cake before Ruby wakes up. Since Mr. Murphy knows I baked it, I have to finish it. She doesn't come out of her room until she hears Mr. Murphy leave. The cake is set in the middle of the table.

"Happy Birthday, Ruby. I fried up some ham, and there's biscuits and tea for breakfast. Help yourself."

"Thanks, but you know I can't eat first thing in the morning. You baked a cake? Uncle Joe will like that."

"It's your birthday cake. I made it yesterday before Jim came."

"Thank you. I wish I was hungry. You know, you've had a cake every year on your birthday since you've been here. The last time I had a birthday cake was on my tenth birthday. I guess I should say I'm sorry about yesterday, but I'm really not. I'm not sorry that he came. I needed to see him."

"Just don't do it again. If you do, I'll go get R.C. He'll make him leave, and then he'll tell Mr. Murphy, and then you will be in big trouble. By the way, Anna is coming by tomorrow. She has some clothes for you."

"Maternity clothes? Good, my clothes are starting to get tight."

"You won't be able to keep them. Anyway, you aren't goin' anywhere, and you wear night dresses most of the time, so I told her you won't need much. She'll want them back after you have the baby, so take good care of them."

"Now that I'm starting to feel better, I plan to get up and do more around the house."

"You keep saying that, but you don't do anything. I don't believe you."

"You believe what you want. I really don't care what you think. You're nothing but a spoiled brat! I'll decide what I need to wear and who I want to see, and if you tell Uncle Joe that Jim was here, I'll tell him that I heard you telling Annie Rose about me."

"But I didn't!"

"That doesn't stop me from saying you did, does it?"

May 5, 1906 — Dear Diary, I can't do anything right! I thought I would be nice and bake a birthday cake for Ruby. I felt sorry for her being cooped up in the house. Then, Mr. Murphy yelled at me. He said I shouldn't have baked her a cake 'cuz I have too much work to do. He told me not to do it again. What does that really mean? Then Ruby let Jim in the kitchen. I can stop being nice to Ruby now! She's really mean! As for the cake, she was thankless. Reminded me that she can't eat in the morning. So what? Who said we had to eat the cake for breakfast? Then she really made me feel bad for making it, calling me names. She said I've had more birthday cakes than she has, like that's my fault! Also, I told her Anna is bringing some clothes for her to wear, and she told me to mind my own business. Also, it's obvious that she plans to see that farmer whenever she can. I can't tell Mr. Murphy 'cuz if I do, she said she will lie and tell him I told Annie Rose about her being pregnant. Of course, I didn't. I've kept the secret just like Mr. Murphy told me to. I feel trapped in this house. I can talk to Anna, but I can't tell her about this. Maybe someday, I'll tell her. Signed, Dora

The Curse!

June 2, 1906

It's Saturday, and I get to go to Annie Rose's birthday party! I'm sitting on the front steps with my head in my hands, trying to figure out what to do 'cuz I haven't had time to go downtown shopping for a present.

Johnny calls out as he rides by on his bicycle, "Hey, Dora!"

I watch him as he rides down the street, and then I notice the peony bush at the corner of the house is in full bloom. I walk over to look at one of the blooms nodding in the breeze. Sugary pink, it's as big as a dinner plate.

I go to the kitchen to get a knife and a glass of water. I cut the stem long enough so the flower will stand up in the glass. Perfect! While walking back to the kitchen to put the peony on the table, I decide to get a second bouquet of four-leafed clovers.

I go outside and sit in the grass. Good thing R.C. doesn't mow until Monday. I quickly find one, then another, and a third with five leaves. She's really going to be surprised. Six is enough – I take them inside to put them in a small glass, then I go upstairs to get dressed for the party.

At first, I try to put on my blue dress with pink flowers, but I must have grown 'cuz I can't button it. I try on two more dresses and finally settle on my yellow play dress. Somehow, I need to get some new dresses. I put a blue ribbon in my hair that matches the tiny blue flowers in my dress. There! I'm ready!

Mr. Murphy comes out of his room, just as I'm going downstairs. "Well, look at you! All pretty and dressed up! What's the occasion?"

"Remember, it's Annie Rose's birthday. You said I could go to her party."

"So, I did. Do you have a present for her?"

"Oh, yes, and I think she will really like it. Let me show you!"

We go to the kitchen and he sees the peony standing up in the glass, looking like a giant pink rose. "That's the biggest peony I've ever seen. Did that come from our bush out front?"

"Mm hmm. I didn't get downtown to shop, but that's okay. I know she will love the flower, and I am also bringing a bouquet of clovers to bring her good luck."

"Well, I wish you had told me you needed to go shopping, but I think this is an even better gift. Believe me, all young ladies like flowers. Now you go on and have a good time. Stay as long as you like. Ruby and I will get along just fine. I'll ask R.C. to take you since you have to carry two glasses."

It's a warm sunny day, so Annie Rose's mama has spread three blankets on the lawn in the backyard, like a picnic. It's the same group of girls I met before. When I come out the back door, I hear Annie Rose say, "My mother will bring the cake out as soon as Dora gets here – Oh! Here she is!"

She runs up to greet me. "Here, Annie Rose, I brought these for you. The big flower is a peony, and here's a bouquet of four-leafed clovers for good luck. Happy Birthday!"

"They're beautiful! Look, girls, look at the peony that Dora brought. I've never seen a flower this big before!"

They smile, but I can tell they're wondering why I didn't bring a wrapped present. I don't care, as long as Annie Rose likes it.

Annie Rose's mama goes to the kitchen to get the cake and she sets it on a wood table by the back porch. She turns to go back inside to get plates and forks, but Annie Rose catches up with her to show her my presents.

"Dora, what a beautiful flower, and such a thoughtful present! How did you find so many four-leafed clovers?"

"There's one that even has five leaves."

"Mama, you wouldn't believe how easy it is for Dora to find four-leafed clovers. Sometimes we sit in the grass, and I look and look while she just picks a bouquet. You would think they just raised their heads, but no. None of us can find them but Dora picks them like she would if she was picking daisies in a field. Rex says it's because she's Irish!"

"Well, let's set them on the table next to the cake. I'll be back in a minute with a knife and forks."

The cake is scrumptious, an angel cake with strawberries and pink icing! Annie Rose opens her other presents after we finish eating cake. She gets more of the same old thing, barrettes for her hair, three necklaces, and two boxes of sidewalk chalk.

"Thanks everyone! I know, let's play hopscotch!"

We all run to the sidewalk in front, and Annie Rose passes chalk around so we can draw the squares. Her mama comes out of the house to give us a silver dollar for the game. It's Annie Rose's birthday, so she goes first. She tosses the coin, and it lands on number 6. She takes off on her right foot, hops to land with two feet on 4 and 5, then she jumps onto 6 standing on one leg with her right foot. She weaves and waits for a minute trying not to fall when she bends over to pick up the coin, but when she bends over, she loses her balance, and she falls to the ground.

She gets up laughing. "All right, see if you can do it! Martha, want to go next?"

Everyone takes their turn. Some are able to pick the coin up, but most of us fall over.

The sun is getting lower in the sky. I know Mr. Murphy said I could stay as long as I like, but I want to go home, so he'll let me come again.

"Annie Rose, I need to go home. I really had fun! Thank you for inviting me, and Happy Birthday!

Thursday, June 14, 1906 — Dear Diary, Ruby is finally helping out. She's been washing her clothes and she helps with cleaning as long as she doesn't have to bend over. Doc Nelson was here today. I heard him tell Ruby he would see her in November when the baby comes. Rex has been coming by to help me with some of the heavy work. He washed the windows outside, and he sweeps the front porch whenever he stops by. The chandeliers need cleaning, so I'm going to ask Mr. Murphy if Rex can come inside, 'cuz I can't reach them. I'll tell Ruby to stay in her room while he helps. She doesn't care but I guess it wouldn't make any difference if she did. Mr. Murphy said I can invite Annie Rose for a visit on Sunday. He told Ruby to stay out of sight while she's here. She was mad, but I don't care. School is over for the year, so I'll have to repeat sixth grade. I'm still stuck in this house because I have to clean and cook our meals. Signed, Dora

Sunday, June 17, 1906

Rex and Annie Rose are staying home with their families today, 'cuz it's Father's Day. They're having nice dinners. I know he's not my father, but Mr. Murphy does take care of me, so I want to do something to make him feel better today.

I don't know what's happening, but he looks really bad. His feet are swollen, and he walks real slow with his shoes untied. You would think he'd be happy 'cuz Ruby isn't sick anymore, but he just ignores her now that her belly is getting big. It's been a while since he smiled.

I go outside to get him a bouquet of four-leafed clovers for Father's Day. I come back into the house and Mr. Murphy is sitting at the kitchen table, waiting for his breakfast.

"Good morning, Mr. Murphy! Happy Father's Day! I picked these for you!"

"Four leafed clovers? You found all of these just for me? Goodness! You know, I'm Irish! Thank you, Dora, but you should be the one getting presents for all of the work you've been doing. Shall we put them in water?"

"I'll get a little glass. My mama always had a bouquet of four-leafed clovers on our kitchen table. Now that it's summer if you like, I'll keep fresh ones on the table. We're both Irish! I like being Irish!"

"It's good to be proud of our heritage. Dora, you have brought so much joy into this house. I don't know what I would have done the last few months, if you weren't here. I know I get angry at times, but I've never been angry with you. Come here and give me a hug – for Father's Day."

I love summertime more than anything else in the whole wide world! In the morning, the world smells like fresh cut grass, and every night except when it rains, we play hide and seek or kick the can. Annie Rose and Rex show up after supper. Sometimes Harold tags along, but not tonight.

By the time we get outside, friends from the neighborhood are waiting for us by the sycamore tree.

"Hey, they're here! We've been waiting. Dale said he'll be It first tonight. I brought a can."

He hands the can to Dale, and we all run out to the street. Dale puts the can in the middle right in line with our porch steps, so it will be easy to find. Dale covers his eyes with his hands and starts counting to 100, and everyone runs to their favorite hiding place. Rex and I head for the barn and Annie Rose takes off in a different direction.

"100! Here I come! Dickie Webster, I see you trying to hide under the porch. Come on out!"

Dale walks Dickie to the jail area, then he takes off, looking everywhere, and one-by-one he pulls others out from under bushes and walks them to jail. His search is taking him further and further from the can.

"Look Dora! He went around the corner of the house. He can't see the can!"

Rex takes off running, but Dale sees him. They speed up and race, but Rex is taller, and his legs are longer, so he wins. He gives the can a big kick, freeing everyone in jail! Dale covers his eyes with his hands, "1, 2, 3, 4, 5, 6......."

I'm laughing so hard I fall to the ground. Rex reaches his hand to help me up, "C'mon, Dora, we have to hurry!" We go back to our hiding place behind the barn.

Dale is It all night. Kick the Can is fun if you're not It. Twelve kids hiding are hard to find without taking your eye off the can. Besides, the barn is behind the house, so he can't see us from the street.

Rex frees everyone again, including Annie Rose. Annie Rose runs toward me, "Dora, I had fun, but I have to go home. It's getting late and I'm tired. Do you think Rex will walk me home since it's dark?"

"Let's catch him before he hides. Rex....!"

Rex and Annie Rose leave, and the others take off for home. Tired and happy, I run for the kitchen door, then up the stairs to the bathroom. My drawers are wet – I must have sat on something.

I pull my play dress up and hurry to sit down and pee. I look down and there's blood on my drawers. What happened? I don't remember seeing blood outside anywhere. I wipe with a paper sheet and stand up to see if there's any blood on my dress, but I look down into the commode, there was blood on the paper sheet and the water is brown. I reach my hand down between my legs, I'm bleeding!

I SCREAM! Ruby comes running up the stairs and she bursts into the bathroom, out of breath, holding her belly.

"What's wrong? Did you hurt yourself? Stop crying and tell me what's wrong!"

"I'm dying! Look, I'm bleeding!"

"You're bleeding? Where?"

I show her my drawers.

"O, that! You're such a pain! Stop wailing, and I'll tell you what to do. I guess I should have told you. There's no one else around to tell you these things."

"No one's told me what? That I'm going to die?"

"You're not dying, silly! You just started your monthlies. It's just part of growing up. This isn't all about you. Everyone gets them. I'll get a towel and show you how to take care of yourself."

"Everyone? Will I bleed all the time now?"

"No! Only women get it, and you only get it once a month and only for a few days. They call it the curse. You'll just have to learn how to deal with it."

"I think I'll just hide in my room 'til it's over."

"I know it's a shock, but you'll get used to it. Now, go to bed. I'll put out some fresh towels for you in the morning. And don't use this as an excuse not to do your work. You have to do laundry tomorrow."

I stay in my room. Ruby calls me down for popcorn, but I don't answer, hoping they will think I'm sleeping.

When I go to the bathroom the next morning, I get another towel and wash up. I go to the kitchen to make breakfast. Mr. Murphy is drinking tea and reading the newspaper.

"Well, there she is. How are you? Are you feeling okay? You look a little peaked."

"I'm fine. I was just tired from playing outside. What do you want for breakfast?"

"I don't know, whatever you want to make. Something light. I'm not very hungry."

I get the butter dish (he really likes butter), along with a loaf of bread, a jar of grape jelly, and some stewed prunes from the refrigerator.

"Anna made the bread. She dropped it off yesterday."

"This is fine. Why don't you make yourself a cup of tea and eat breakfast with me?"

I get a sharp knife from the drawer and pour my tea while Mr. Murphy slices the bread. It's crusty but soft on the inside.

"That Anna. She's a good cook – John's a lucky man. Want some butter?" He takes a big bite from his slice, with its thick layer of butter.

"That's okay, I'll just have jelly. Are you feeling better?"

He turns his head, and he has a coughing spell. Lately, he breathes heavy, and he coughs all the time. Finally, he catches his breath. "I'm all right, Dora. I assure you I know how to take care of myself. Don't you worry about me."

I wonder but decide to talk about something else. "I think Anna is coming by this afternoon. She always asks about you."

"You tell her that I'm just fine."

"Mr. Murphy, do you think Ruby likes me? I don't think she likes me."

"Why? Did something happen?"

"Just wondering."

"You know you can come to me if there's anything wrong. Do you want me to talk to her?"

"No. I was just asking."

We finish eating and I put everything away and wipe the table off. I go upstairs to get dressed while Mr. Murphy reads his paper.

Dinner smells good today, ham and potatoes, but I don't feel much like eating. I start the dishes, and R.C. knocks to take Mr. Murphy to the office. He almost trips on his shoelaces on one of the steps outside the kitchen door, but R.C. catches him.

I'm putting the plates away when Anna knocks on the kitchen door.

"Hi, Anna. Come in!"

"I brought some morels. John went mushroom hunting and I have more than I can use."

"Thank you, but you'll have to tell me what to do with them."

"Just wash them and fry them up in some butter. They are really good as a side dish with beef. Joseph likes them."

"Good. We'll have them tomorrow with dinner. Anna, I was hoping you would come today. I need to talk to you."

"Why? Is something wrong?"

"Not really. Well, I guess." I whisper, "I started my monthlies, and when I saw the blood, I was really scared. I thought I was dying! Ruby just laughed at me."

"Oh, you poor child. And no one told you."

"I don't want Mr. Murphy to find out 'cuz he'll be angry with me for bringing shame on the house."

"Dora, you haven't done anything wrong. What's happening to you is a beautiful thing. All it means is that you're a woman now. God planned it that way."

"Sometimes I don't like God. Every time something bad happens, it's God's will or God's plan. My daddy died and went to heaven, and a lot of people died in that earthquake. I don't believe God can be that mean."

"God does good things too. He makes the sun and the flowers, and when it rains, a rainbow. Then there's you. Do you realize how special you are? God bought you to live in this house. While Ruby has caused some tension, your life here has been good, and you've brought happiness here. Before you came, this house was quiet, and no one laughed. I remember how happy Joseph was when you first came. He tells all of us how much he cares for you, and his eyes light up when he sees you. Your monthlies aren't the end of the world, Dora. It's just part of life."

"Maybe. But Anna, I don't think Ruby likes me. Sometimes she's not nice, and she makes me do all the work, even though I know she's feeling better."

"I sensed that."

"Besides, I don't understand why Ruby being sick has to be such a big secret."

"It's because she isn't married. Getting pregnant when you aren't married is scandalous. Joseph is a good man and he takes pride that he has a Christian home. He is highly respected in Fulton County and in the State of Illinois. This is a small town, and everyone knows everybody else's business. There's a group of women who are notorious gossips. If they find out about Ruby, word will spread throughout Fulton County. Joseph is concerned about his reputation."

"That Ruby. She did a bad thing."

"Yes, she did, but the reason we don't tell anyone is out of concern for Joseph, not Ruby."

Thursday, June 21, 1906 — Dear Diary, I haven't talked to you the last few days 'cuz I've been upset. I've had a terrible time. I had my first monthly. No one told me all girls have to go through this. I've stopped bleeding, finally, just like Ruby said I would. I know Ruby doesn't like me. She laughed at me and she called me "Silly." She was so mean I didn't believe her, so I talked to Anna. She is so nice. She made me feel better. She said it's just part of God's plan like the sun and rainbows. Ruby is not a nice person, but I can't tell my friends how mean she is because it will hurt Mr. Murphy's reputation. At least I can talk to

Anna sometimes. I can't wait to see Annie Rose, so I can tell her that I started my monthlies. It seems like it's always something. Does growing up mean having no time to have fun? I just want to be happy! Now I know how Mama felt after Daddy died. Annie Rose is coming early on Sunday, so we'll have time together before the others get here for hide and seek. I have a lot to tell her. Signed, Dora

It's Friday, so the only thing I have to do is change my bed and clean my room. Mr. Murphy comes downstairs just as I'm putting a pitcher of milk on the table for porridge.

"Good morning, Mr. Murphy. I made porridge for breakfast. Want some?"

"That would be good. Please fetch the honey from the cupboard. I'll have that instead of sugar. I'm thinking sugar may be the reason my legs are swelling."

"What did the doctor say? Did he tell you to stop eating sugar?"

"No, no, just my idea. He thinks it's something else."

I don't want to pry. Maybe I shouldn't have asked.

"Porridge and tea hit the spot this morning. You did good, but then you always make good meals."

"Thank you. There's something I've been wanting to ask."

"You can ask me anything. You shouldn't be afraid to ask by now."

"I was wondering if I can go back to school in September. I can still do chores after school."

"I don't see why not. By then, Ruby will really be big so we might not get much out of her. Still, that's not your fault. We'll see when it gets closer to time, but for now, just plan on going back to school."

"Well, the reason I'm asking now is I'm going to need some new dresses if I'm going to school. The other day when I got dressed for Annie Rose's party, I tried on four dresses before I found one that fit. I guess I've been growing."

"Next time Anna comes by, tell her you need to go downtown to buy cloth, then she'll take you to Helen's to get fitted for some new dresses."

"Annie Rose is coming over Sunday afternoon before hide and seek. We'll go upstairs to my room if she comes inside."

"I'll tell Ruby to stay in her room. It's getting hot outside so you might want to stay downstairs or outside. I'll tell her, though. You deserve to have some fun."

I've just finished dishes from dinner when Annie Rose is at the front door.

Mr. Murphy opens the door. "Come on in, Annie Rose. Dora's in the kitchen."

She comes into the kitchen as I am hanging my apron on the back of a chair to dry. "Annie Rose, it's hot upstairs, so let's go outside. I'll get a quilt so we can sit in the shade. Come with me and help carry some things outside."

We go upstairs; she takes our latest book and a book of paper dolls, and I take a quilt from the chest. When we come downstairs, I notice she's looking over the bannister, back towards the kitchen.

"What are you looking for?"

"Oh, nothing. I was just thinking, it's been a long time since I've seen Ruby."

"She stays in her room most of the time. Let's go out the kitchen door. It's closer to the sycamore tree."

I spread the quilt on the ground, and Annie Rose puts the books down.

"Annie Rose, I have a secret to tell you. You're not going to believe it!"

"What, now?"

"Did you know that girls have monthlies, that we bleed?"

"Oh, that! My mama told me. I haven't started yet, but she told me what to do when I do."

"Well, no one told me, and I was really scared when I started. You're lucky to have a mama."

"You had a monthly?"

"Yup. Ruby heard me scream, and she ran upstairs to the bathroom to help me. She told me what was happening. It only lasted three days, but it's yucky! I just wanted to hide out in my room until it was over, but we had laundry to do the next day."

"Dora, did you have to cook Sunday dinner?"

"Yes, I did. Why?"

"What's wrong with Ruby? She's been sick a long time! Does she stay in bed all day?"

"I can't talk about it."

"Why not? We're best friends. I know how to keep a secret."

"I know you do but promise you'll stop asking! I can't tell you."

"Another thing, why is it that Rex is always around? You even hide with him instead of me when we play kick the can. I like Rex, but sometimes it would be fun to just spend time with you. Either you have to cook or clean, or it's all three of us."

"Annie Rose O'Neal, what's wrong with you? I thought you liked me, and I thought you were my best friend, so you would understand. I'm really tired but I thought we would have fun this afternoon. What I do is really none of your business, so maybe you should just go home!"

Sunday, June 24, 1906 — Dear Diary. Annie Rose and I had a fight. She was crying when she left. We were sitting in the shade by the sycamore, and I just laid back on the quilt for a while until I stopped crying. Why doesn't she understand that I can't tell her what's going on? And what difference does it make if Rex likes to hang out with us? I thought Annie Rose was my best friend, but now I have no one to talk to. Mr. Murphy is sick, and I'm tied to this house, and I don't think Ruby is ever going to do her chores again. I feel so alone. Another thing, no one has said what we're going to do with a baby. And it seems to me when a baby comes, everyone will know Ruby's secret anyway. I suppose if she has a baby to take care of, that will be another excuse not to work. I wonder if she even knows how to take care of a baby. I used to take care of Louis, but I don't want to take care of her baby and the house! I want to go back to school in September. Mr. Murphy said, we'll see. Anna and I are going to go shopping for cloth so Helen can sew some dresses for me to wear to school. Just in case I get to go. But I bet nothing much will change in the Fall, except that I'll have even more work here to do. Signed, Dora

Goodbye Annie Rose!

School starts next week, and Ruby is feeling better. She can at least get around until I get home, so Mr. Murphy said I can go back to school!

Annie Rose is starting middle school, but I have to do sixth grade again. Maybe it doesn't matter since I haven't seen or talked to her since our argument. I really miss her, but I'm still angry. I see her walking up the steps at the other end of the building. She sees me and waves. I wave back and look down, and go straight to my classroom. There's a new teacher.

"All right, class, find your seats."

I open the lid of my desk and take my books out, then I wait for class to start. I am so excited to get back to school, but today is not what I expected. It's not the same. I don't know anyone in my class because they were a grade behind me. A grade behind – that's me!

"Hello, class. Welcome to sixth grade! My name is Miss Lewis. Tell me who you are, and what is your favorite game? Let's start with you, on the front row."

A boy sitting in the first desk starts talking. "Stand up and face the class. I don't think they can hear you, so speak up."

He stands and turns to face us, "I'm Billy Swank. I like to play tug-of-war, 'cuz I'm really strong."

"Well, that's a good start. Thank you, Billy! Next?"

One-by-one everyone takes their turn, the girl who sits in front of me sits down. I take my turn, "My name is Dora Kelly and I like to play hopscotch."

A boy across the room speaks up, "Yeah, she was in sixth grade last year, but she's okay. Her papa has a really neat farm. One time, he invited us for a hayride!"

I forgot about that, so maybe I will remember some of the other girls. This might not be too bad, going back a grade.

Rex is standing outside the door, waiting to walk me home from school. "I was thinking, Dora. I'll just meet you here every day, then I'll walk you home from school so we can talk. That is, if you'd like."

"I'd like that." I feel excited and upset at the same time. "I don't remember anyone but they remember the hayride. I hate being held back. I feel sad 'cuz I'm going back a grade, but the teacher is nice. Maybe some of the girls will want to be my friend. 'cuz I'm going back a grade. I'll get used to it, but I wish I was in class with Annie Rose."

Rex slips his hand into mine. "You'll do fine. You always fit in, no matter where you are. Everyone likes you."

"I don't think so. Annie Rose and I had a fight and it's been a long time since I've seen or talked to her."

"But you guys are best friends! I'll talk to her. Whatever happened can't be that bad."

The next day, as promised, he's in the same spot, leaning against the building. I'm so excited to see him that I can't stop smiling.

"Hi! Here, give me your books. I talked to Annie Rose, and I have bad news."

"She doesn't want to see me!"

"No, I mean yes, she does. But her father has been transferred so they are moving to Wisconsin. Her last day at school will be at the end of the month."

I wipe the tears from my eyes, "Does she really want to see me?"

"Uh huh."

"When we get to my house, I'll write a note so you can take it to her. What should I say?"

"Just tell her that you want to see her. Maybe we can all meet tomorrow after school."

September 27, 1906 — Dear Diary, Rex has been walking Annie Rose and me home every day after school. It's almost like old times except the thought that she will be leaving Canton is hanging over our heads. Tomorrow is her last day at school, so Rex is taking us to the drugstore after school for ice cream sodas. I am trying not to be sad because Annie Rose is a little scared. But I should have expected this. Everyone leaves me. I don't know how to find Jack and Louis, and I had to leave Hannah behind at the orphanage. Oh, well, she probably has a new family somewhere. Whatever, I'll be alone again. At least there's Rex, until he graduates. He always seems to understand how I feel. Signed, Dora Kelly

Annie Rose and Rex are waiting for me after school. The drugstore is packed, so Rex tells us to find a table while he orders the sodas. Chocolate, of course!

"Look, Dora, there's Harold! What's he doing here?"

"Maybe he came to see you because he heard it's your last day."

"I doubt it. He's too young to be part of this crowd."

We find a booth and Rex and Harold are weaving through the crowd with four ice cream sodas.

"Hi, Annie Rose! I heard you are moving so I came to say goodbye. Besides, Rex told me he'd buy me an ice cream soda!"

Girls start gathering around our table. It's hard to tell if they want to talk to Annie Rose, or if they're hoping they can talk to Rex.

"Annie Rose, we heard you're moving."

"To Milwaukee. My father got a big job with Allis Chalmers. My mom says we're moving to a bigger house and Milwaukee is a big town. My mother's excited."

Rex asks, "That's your mother, but how about you?"

"We've moved around before for my father's work. I hate to leave friends behind. I'm going to miss you all. I don't know, I guess I'll get used to it." She takes a big spoonful of ice cream.

"I know how you feel. My daddy died, so he left us, then Mama gave us away, and I don't know where my brothers are. I had a good friend at the orphanage, Hannah, but Mr. Murphy came to take me in. It's terrible when you leave someone behind. You never get used to it."

Harold sucks the air out of the bottom of his glass, "Yeah, and look how lucky you are - you have us, Dora! Besides, even though she's moving away, you can always write letters."

"C'mon, Harold, when Annie Rose leaves, Dora will be stuck with you and me!"

We're laughing and having a good time. The girls must have decided Rex wasn't going to talk to them 'cuz they left.

The four of us walk across town to take Annie Rose home. We stop by her front gate. We hug, crying, not wanting to let go.

"I can't believe you are leaving! I love you!"

"I love you too, Dora. I promise, I'll write."

"When are you leaving?"

"After church on Sunday."

"Can you come over on Saturday to spend the day? We haven't finished our book."

"I'll ask my mother, maybe."

Annie Rose didn't come this morning, and it's almost lunchtime, so I'm afraid I won't see her again. Then the doorbell clanks. Is that her? I run to the front door to let her in.

"You came!"

"I wanted to come sooner, but my mother made me pack my bedroom. I have to be home for supper."

"That's okay. I'm just glad that you could come."

"Hey, I watched you and Rex when you left my house, holding hands. Do you like him?"

"Yes, we're friends. You know that."

"I do, but holding hands is getting serious. C'mon, admit it. You don't just like him, you really, really like Rex. I always knew you two would end up together."

"Oh, come on! Holding hands is not that serious. He's just easy to talk to and he treats me nice."

"Rex is nice to everyone, but he's nicest to you! I can tell he really likes you."

"Annie Rose, you're being silly! Let's go finish that book!"

We are reading ***The Tale of Mrs. Tiggy-Winkle,*** and it's Annie Rose's turn to read.

"The laundered clothing is tied up in bundles and Lucie's handkerchiefs are neatly folded into her clean pinafore. They set off together down the path to return the fresh laundry to the little animals and birds in the neighborhood. At the bottom of the hill, Lucie mounts the stile and turns to thank Mrs. Tiggy-Winkle.

Your turn!"

"But what a very odd thing! Mrs. Tiggy-Winkle is running, running, running up the hill. Her cap, shawl, and print gown are nowhere to be seen. How small and brown she has grown – and covered with prickles! Why! Mrs. Tiggy-Winkle is nothing but a HEDGEHOG!"

"It's your turn, you finish it!"

"It says here that some people thought Lucie might have fallen asleep and this was just a dream, but if so, then how could she have three clean handkerchiefs and a laundered pinafore?

Besides, I have seen that door into the back of the hill called Cat Bells – and besides, I am very well acquainted with dear Miss Tiggy-Winkle!"

We fall back on the bed laughing. Annie Rose sits up, "Dora, why do you suppose she decided to write a book about a hedgehog, for heaven's sake? Hedgehogs are kind of ugly."

"I don't think so. Mrs. Tiggy-Winkle is round and kind of cute. Really funny name, though."

"Yeah, Tiggy Winkle! Wonder where she got that. I'm going to miss you, Dora. I like reading books with you."

Annie Rose jumps down from the bed, and she crosses the room to the dollhouse, "Your room is so nice. What are you going to do with your dolls and the dollhouse? They are so pretty, but they are for little girls, not grownup girls like you and me."

"I want to keep them forever! The dollhouse is the first present Mr. Murphy gave me. Besides, like you said, it's pretty. I'll just keep them here to decorate when I don't want to play with them as much."

Annie Rose suddenly hugs me. "Oh, Dora, I have to be home for supper. I have to go!"

"You're not leaving so soon, are you?"

"I have to. Also, you got me thinking. My mother told me to put my dolls in a basket to be given away. I want to hurry before she does, so I can take them with me."

I walk Annie Rose to the front door. We hug one another real tight.

"Send me a letter and let me know where you are, so I can send one back. I promise, I'll write back. I've already lost my brothers, so I don't want to lose you."

Mr. Murphy is coming down the stairs and he shuffles to his chair in the parlor.

"Hello, Annie Rose, nice to see you! What's all the tears about?"

"Annie Rose is moving away. She's moving to Wisconsin!"

"Wisconsin is pretty far. It's nice, though, so you'll probably like it."

"My father has a new job. I have a feeling we'll see one another again. I hope we move back here! Dora, I promise, I'll write. Give me one more hug 'cuz I have to go."

Laughing through my tears, I bid Annie Rose goodbye, "Besides, you have to hurry so you can rescue your dolls!"

September 29, 1906 — Dear Diary, I said goodbye to Annie Rose today. She is moving a long ways away, to Wisconsin. We read Mrs. Tiggy-Wiggle in my room. Ruby stayed in her room like Mr. Murphy told her to. Annie Rose left earlier than I expected 'cuz she had to save her dolls from being given away. I can't believe Annie Rose would even think about letting them go! I'll start watching the mailbox every day on Monday. I tried to read myself to sleep, but without her, it wasn't as much fun. The house is so quiet, and I feel so lonely. I love my room, but even here, I feel cooped up because it's part of this house, and pretty soon, with the baby coming, I'm probably going to have to drop out of school. It's a good thing I have Rex and Harold, they always make me laugh. Rex told me he will never move away, and we will always be best friends. Signed, Dora

The Hitless Wonders!

Sunday, October 7, 1906

Mr. Murphy is in a good mood today. "Ladies, once again, that was a great dinner! Where did you get the apples for the pie? From the orchard or from the grocer?"

"Dora told me that R.C. dropped them off, so I assume he got them from the orchard."

"Good. By the way, Dora, have you heard anything from Annie Rose?"

"I got a letter on Friday. I already wrote back. Anna gave me some stamps, so I put it in the mailbox yesterday."

"I'm glad. That's good. Friends are important. Matter of fact, I've invited some of my friends to come to the house this week so we can follow some ball games. You probably don't follow baseball, but the World Series starts on Tuesday and it's the Chicago White Sox against the Chicago Cubs. This the first time a World Series has been played between two teams in the same city, and it's happening right here in Illinois, in Chicago! Thought we could pop some corn and have cider and port for drinks. Maybe we can have some apple pies to serve on the last day of the series? Some of the games are during the day, so Dora will be at school. Of course, Ruby, you'll have to stay in your room whenever they're here."

"That's fine. The bigger I get, the harder it is for me to get around."

"I think that will be fun! I made the pie today, so I can make the pies. Is there a game every day? How many days?"

"The winner is the team that wins four games out seven, so if it takes seven games, it could go into the following Monday, but it could happen sooner."

"Who's coming, so I know how many pies to make?"

"Let's see, there's R.C., Albert, John, and George Miller. I don't think you've met him, he's my partner and a good friend. It will be five of us, so make a couple pies."

Monday, October 8, 1906 — Dear Diary, I'm popping popcorn for Mr. Murphy and his friends tomorrow. He's going to track the winners of the World Series. The game starts at 1:45 so I told him I'd make some bowls of popcorn before I go to school, but he said he'd pop the corn. I'm going to surprise him tomorrow and do it before I go to school. The game makes little difference to me, but it's been a long time since I've seen Mr. Murphy excited about anything, so I'm happy about that. I don't know how he is going to know what's going on in Chicago. Maybe he'll get a telegram? Mr. Murphy told me that he's a Sox fan, so I hope they win. Signed Dora Kelly

Tuesday, October 9, 1906, Opening Day, Cubs West Side Grounds

"C'mon in, George. Everyone else is here. There's port and cider on the kitchen table, so help yourself. The game started a few minutes ago, so the phone should ring fairly soon.

George goes to the kitchen and Albert gives him a glass of cider. "Hey, George, I'm taking bets on today's game and on the series. It's two bits a game, and four bits on the series."

"It seems like a safe bet. The series opener is on the west side, so the Cubs have home field advantage. Everyone knows the Cubs are going to beat the Hitless Wonders, so I'm betting on the Cubs!"

Murphy is drinking port, leaning against the kitchen sink, "Glad to hear that, George, because I'm going to enjoy taking everyone's money. I am the only one betting on the Sox, so I guess you are betting against me. This is going to be fun!"

John joins the conversation, "so how are we going to keep up with the scores?"

"Well, when I went to Chicago to get Dora, there was a young man, Jack, who worked at the orphanage. I contacted him and sent him money to buy tickets for the series. He's going to call at the end of each inning with updates on the progress of the games. I think Albert has set up some tables in the parlor for checkers and Pinocle. Watch out for John, though, he's a champion at checkers!"

Jack calls at the end of each inning. There was no score in the first inning. Sox batted first. Hahn and Isbell struck out. Jones flied to center. The first three batters for the Cubs had groundouts. No score!

In the bottom of the 4th, the Cubs had a strikeout and groundout, then Schulte singled. He was caught stealing second, but Evans dropped the ball, so Schulte was safe. Jack said the crowd went wild when Schulte was called safe. Chance grounded out. Still no score!

Rohe tripled to lead off the 5th, Donahue struck out, then Patsy Dougherty singled, scoring Rohe! The Cubs went down, 1, 2, 3 in the bottom half. 1 – 0 Sox!

Jack calls again at the end of the 6th inning. Mr. Murphy answers the phone, "Slow down, Jack! Talk slower. I know you're excited! Mhmm, mhmm. What's wrong with Altrock? Is he getting tired?"

Murphy hangs up the phone, "Lots of action, 2 -1 Sox after six!"

I get home from school, and it's funny to see Albert getting excited, "What happened?"

"Here's the play by play according to Jack. Altrock lead off and he walked. Hahn sacrificed, Altrock to second. Jones singled to center. Altrock was thrown out at the plate trying to score. Jones to second. Jones advanced to third on a passed ball. Isbell singled to left field and Jones scored! Isbell made it to second, but Rohe grounded out.

Kling walked, leading off the bottom half. Brown singled and Kling advanced to 2nd. Then Hofman sacrificed, Kling to 3rd and Brown to 2nd. Sheckard popped out and Schulte grounded out. 2 - 1 Sox!

Jack continues to call in at the end of every inning. There were more than 12,000 fans in attendance. Sox win 2 – 1!

The men reconvene for every game and Jack continues to call with inning updates. Games alternate between the Sox southside park and the Cubs park on the west side. Except for the last game on the southside, neither team wins at home.

The second game was on the south side. Cubs pitcher Ed Reulbach pitched the first one – hitter in World Series history. 7 – 1 Cubs.

Back to the west side for the third game. After Schulte hit a first inning double, Walsh retired 25 of 27 Cubs batters. 3 - 0 Sox!

Fourth game, south side, three - fingered Mordecai Brown pitched five innings of no - hit ball and settled for a two hitter to even the series. The game lasted only 96 minutes.

Game five on the west side was wild! Total 18 hits, 10 walks, 6 errors, and 3 wild pitches. "Big" Ed Walsh earned his second win of the series with the help of a relief pitcher, Doc White. Score 12 - 6, Sox!

Sunday, October 14, 1906.

Today will probably be the last game, so I baked two apple pies last night. I don't know anything about baseball, but Mr. Murphy has been so excited, and he gave us game updates every night at supper. He is very patient with me, explaining all of the terms, so I can understand what happened. I'm excited, and I really want the Sox to win.

The game is at Sox Park and the Hitless Wonders really pulled it off! Every time the phone rings, I jump. Mr. Murphy says Jack was breathless when he called at the end of the game. In the bottom of the ninth, the Cubs scored a run with bases loaded, then Schulte had a ground out for the final out of the series. Final score, 14 - 7, Sox!

I can't believe it! Mr. Murphy is cutting the pies, 'cuz I'm just jumping up and down. I'm so glad the final game is on Sunday so I could be here! I finally stop jumping up and down in time to cut the second pie. "So, Jack must be having a great time. Did he thank you for the tickets, and did he ask about me?"

"He did thank me and said it was an experience that he will never forget. No, he didn't ask about you, but to no surprise. There was so much noise from the crowd that it was hard to hear. I'm sure we will talk again."

Mr. Murphy shakes the popcorn, so it won't burn. "You know, Dora, he was so happy that I called. When I came to Chicago to get you, I liked him immediately. I think he must have been a good friend to you. And he did just what we needed him to do - he called us after every inning to let us know the score, and how our team was doing. And we won! A great day for the White Sox!"

We serve the pies, and everyone is cheering even though they bet on the Cubs. I guess being a sports fan is hungry work!

Mr. Murphy calls for a toast, and I get a glass of cider and join in. "To three-fingered Mordecai Brown, Big Ed Walsh, and all the Sox players! They turned the Cubs into Hitless Wonders! Now gentlemen, time to settle up your bets!"

John speaks first, "This is one bet I don't mind paying. It was a good series."

George gave his money over to Mr. Murphy with a grin. "I've enjoyed everyone's company. Joseph, thank you for doing this, but next time, let's get tickets and go to Chicago!"

"If it happens again, I'll buy the tickets for everyone. Now, let's eat more of Dora's magnificent pies! Who wants more port?"

I grab a handful of popcorn and turn my head so they don't see me blushing. I'm so glad everyone is so happy, and Mr. Murphy said my pies were a home run!

Monday, October 15, 1906

It's pretty early in the morning, and I'm making applesauce with the apples from the bottom of the bushel because they're a little bruised, and Mr. Murphy comes in for his coffee.

"Well, you got started early, Dora! Thank you. You do my heart good! Is there coffee?"

He looks a little pale, but I think he's coughing less. I pour him a cup, and he goes to the phone in the parlor to sit in his chair. As I'm stirring the pot, I overhear his phone call.

"George, I was just checking in. How are the cases going? No, no, I should be back at work soon. My legs and feet are just swollen, so I walk slow and when I go up the stairs, I have to take my time. But I always get there! W.D. insists I should retire, that my heart is giving out, but that's nonsense! What would I do with myself?!"

There's a long pause, and Mr. Murphy says almost so quietly I can't hear, "Yes, that's a good point, George. I do want Dora to be cared for. I've spoken with Albert. I know I need a new will, and I would like you to prepare it for me. I should sign it soon, you're right. I'll make notes and get them to you so you can draw it all up."

Then he snorts a little, laughing or not, I can't tell. Well, Ruby, she's been a disappointment. In complete confidence, she got herself in a bad way, if you know what I mean, with that dirt farmer; you've probably heard the rumors. Yes, well, I've tried to reason with her, but she doesn't care what shame she brings to this household! At any rate, she'll probably marry that Kucharek fellow when the baby comes, so I think she's made her choice. The main thing is to make sure Dora is all right if I pass. She has brought nothing but joy to me, George, nothing but joy! Do you know she gave me a bouquet of four-leaf clovers for Father's Day? I intend to honor the contract with the orphanage and assure her a comfortable life, whatever happens. Yes, yes. Thank you, George. You're more than a partner – you're a true friend."

I breathe a sigh of relief and get busy with the applesauce. I decide I'll make it extra special, and try the applesauce cake recipe I found in the drawer.

Thursday, November 1, 1906

It's six o'clock, still dark, but time to get ready for school. When I come out of the bathroom, I hear unfamiliar voices downstairs. Ruby is crying, then she lets out a loud scream!

I run downstairs. Doc Nelson is in Ruby's room and there's a colored lady in the kitchen. I turn towards Ruby's room to see what's wrong, but she's yelling at the doctor, so I follow the nurse into Ruby's room. She's laying on her back with her legs apart, and there's blood all over her bedding. I lean against the wall, trying to be invisible. I feel a little sick, but I want to be there.

"Just get it out of me! You didn't tell me how much it would hurt!"

The nurse is wiping the blood off her legs with wet cloths, "That baby's gonna come out the same way it went in."

The doctor is talking to Mr. Murphy in the parlor. "Joseph, she's in trouble. The baby's in breach position. We will try to turn it, but it's not going to be easy and she's not going to like it."

"Is she in any danger?"

"Other than being uncomfortable, no. However, if the butt comes first, her pelvis may not be big enough to deliver the head, so right now, the baby is at risk."

I run up the stairs to my room. I crawl onto my bed and cover my head with my pillow.

God, please let this be over soon. Please help Ruby and let the baby be okay.

After a while, I realize I must have fallen asleep, because I look out the window and the sky is pink and orange, and the sun is low. I haven't had breakfast or dinner, so I'm hungry. The house is quiet, so I guess it's over. I go downstairs and Mr. Murphy is sitting in the parlor with his head in his hands.

I whisper, "Is Ruby all right? I don't hear anything."

"It's over, Baby Girl. W.D. gave her some laudanum, so she's sleeping. They had to pull the baby out, but they couldn't get to him in time."

"In time for what?"

"Dora, the baby died. W.D. is taking him to the funeral home to be disposed of. Ruby's sleeping so she doesn't know yet. She probably won't care. She just kept screaming at the nurse to get 'it' out. That's something. A mother calling her baby 'it'."

"Is Ruby going to be okay?"

"She lost a lot of blood, so she'll be bedridden for a while, but Doc says she'll recover."

"So, she didn't even get to see him? Who's going to tell her?"

"The doctor says it's best this way. It was difficult to get the baby out, so it's best she didn't see him. W.D. said she should sleep through tonight and he'll be here early tomorrow to talk to her."

"That's so sad. I guess it's good that it's over. Are you alright? Have you had anything to eat?"

"No. Goodness, I guess we haven't eaten all day. Would you fix us something? Ask that nurse if she's hungry. She's had her hands full with Ruby. Most likely she will want to eat."

November 1, 1906 — Dear Diary, Ruby had a baby boy today but he got stuck and died. Her screams woke me up this morning, and I wanted to see but it was so scary. Doc Nelson and a nurse were taking care of her, and they told me to just stay out of the way. I guess there was nothing I could do anyway. I went to my room and hid under my pillow. I said a prayer for Ruby and the baby. She hasn't been nice to me, but that doesn't mean it didn't bother me to hear her crying and screaming. I feel really sad. I didn't realize how much I was looking forward to taking care of a baby. I made biscuits and soup and Mr. Murphy and the nurse and I ate everything, we were so hungry. Mr. Murphy said the funeral home is "disposing' of him." I don't know what that means, and I didn't ask 'cuz I really don't want to know. He doesn't even have a name. I wonder if Louis would mind if we borrowed his name. I'm glad that I have school tomorrow, so I won't be here when the doctor tells Ruby about the baby. Another little person taken away. Another secret in this great big house. Signed, Dora Kelly

I don't know what to expect when I get home, but I hurry home from school in case they need me to help. It's a good thing that it's Friday so I will have the weekend to get things done.

The house is quiet when I enter the kitchen door. Mr. Murphy is in his chair in the parlor, reading his Bible. I turn to go check on Ruby but there's a man sitting on a chair next to her bed. They are whispering and I can't hear what they are saying but he turns his head as I walk towards Ruby's room, and I realize it's Jim! I go back to the parlor.

"Mr. Murphy, that's Jim. What's he doing here? Did you send for him?"

"I asked R.C. to send for him. I still do not approve but W.D. is probably right, it doesn't matter what I think and whether I approve or not, it will not change the way she feels. Besides, he's the baby's father and they lost their baby. We decided yesterday that seeing the baby would just upset her. It was a difficult birth, as you know."

"The nurse is gone. What are we supposed to do?"

"W.D. said she will be in bed about ten days, then she will gradually get her strength back. I'm hoping things will be back to normal by Thanksgiving. We'll give her some drops for the pain until she feels better. She'll be very sad, and I just hope that farmer can step up and help her. Although between you and me, I'm not sure he's to be trusted. Please keep an eye out, Dora, when you're here, and make sure Ruby gets what she needs. Do you think you can keep up around here while going to school?"

"Mr. Murphy, if you let me stay in school, I'll hurry home every day so I can do chores before supper, and I'll have all day on Saturday and Sunday to get things done. I'll work on a schedule. The only problem is meals. Breakfast and supper will not be a problem, but I won't be here to fix your dinner."

"So, just make soups and stews and we'll eat leftovers. It will only be a few weeks. We can get by."

I am so relieved! I'll make sure everything is done, as long as I can stay in school. It looks like Jim is getting ready to leave, so I'll see him out the door.

I stick my head inside her bedroom door. "Ruby, can I bring you anything?"

"No, but you can empty my chamber pot. I didn't want to ask the men to do it."

Ugh! Not what I meant, but I understand. I take the chamber pot upstairs to the bathroom. I turn my head and dump pee mixed with blood down the commode. It should be washed because it smells awful! I decide to take it downstairs to the back, and after a good washing, it's good as new.

She's sleeping when I return it to her room, so she doesn't thank me. Not that she probably would, anyway. Still, I feel good that I could do something for her, and she will wake up to a clean pot.

Heartache!

November 17, 1906

Ruby is up and around, and I've kept up enough with the cleaning and cooking to stay in school. She's still tired, but maybe we can get back to normal.

"Dora, that was a good breakfast. You're getting good at making biscuits. And I love ham and eggs! It's good to eat and not feel sick all the time."

I clear off the table. "While Mr. Murphy is upstairs getting dressed, I wondered if you want to talk about Thanksgiving."

"I really don't care. I don't feel very grateful right now, not after losing a baby. But I guess Uncle Joe is probably expecting us to do something."

"Anna invited us to come to her house, but I don't think Mr. Murphy feels like going out. I was thinking we should do something small this year. I can make a dinner just for the three of us. What do you think?"

"That's a good idea, but let's see what Uncle Joe wants."

We hear him shuffling from the stairs towards the kitchen. I stand up and pull out his chair. "Thank you, Dora. I'll just rest here for a little while."

"Mr. Murphy, we were just trying to plan what to do about Thanksgiving."

He thinks for a minute before responding, "You know Anna invited us to her house, but I doubt you feel like going anywhere. Ruby and I thought it might be too much to do a big celebration here."

Ruby nods, "That's what we thought. Dora has a good idea. What would you think if we just make a nice dinner for the three of us?"

"I agree. We don't need any more stress. I'll ask R.C. to kill a hen instead of a Tom, and I will enjoy the company of two beautiful ladies!"

"Good. Ruby and I will plan the menu and I'll make a list for the grocer."

Tuesday, November 20, 1906 — Dear Diary. Thursday is Thanksgiving. We are cooking turkey and dressing and mashed potatoes and some simple vegetables. School will let out early tomorrow, so I'll bake the pie and make the cranberry sauce tomorrow night. I'll miss spending Thanksgiving with Rex and his family, but it's best that we stay in this year. One good thing about Thanksgiving, Ruby and I have been getting along, planning a nice dinner for Mr. Murphy. Still, I don't trust her. She was mean before, so I expect she will lie again if it suits her. For now, I'm just trying to be nice to everyone because I don't want to upset Mr. Murphy. He is such a nice person. He made sure I stayed in school while Ruby recovered. I think he cares for me, and I really care for him. Still, I worry. He still walks around with his shoes untied all the time because of the swelling in his feet. He moves so slowly, and his cough isn't any better. If anything, he seems worse. I pray for him every day. Signed, Dora Kelly.

Thanksgiving Day, 1906

R.C brought a nice twelve-pound hen, and it's in the oven. I made a pumpkin pie and the cranberry sauce last night. Ruby said she will peel the potatoes and rutabagas.

"Ruby, where should we eat? Should we set the dining room table, or should we just eat in the kitchen?"

"Let's eat in the dining room so we don't have to look at dirty pots and pans."

I set the table as usual, except there are only three settings. Mr. Murphy will sit at the head of the table, so I put settings for Ruby and me on either side. Mary Brewster dropped off a mum plant and a loaf of homemade bread. Centered on the table, everything looks nice. Time to baste the turkey!

I return to the kitchen and get a swab from the cupboard. Butter has been melting on the back of the stove, from the warmth of the oven. With a hot pad in my right hand, I open the oven and I remove the lid from the roasting pan toward me, and steam erupts from the pan, burning my left hand. I cry out and drop the lid and run to the sink so I can dip my hand in the pan of cold water with potatoes.

Ruby comes running from her room, "What happened?"

Blisters are already forming, and it hurts! Mr. Murphy calls from his chair in the parlor. "Ruby, what's wrong? What happened?"

I can't control my tears, and by now I guess I'm shrieking because Ruby covers her ears! Mr. Murphy comes to the kitchen, and he takes one look at my hand, "I'll call W.D. Thanksgiving or not, we need him here."

The doctor comes right away. He puts a salve on my blisters, and he wraps my hand in a white cloth. Ruby finishes the cooking.

Everything is on the table, and it looks good, but I don't feel like eating. No one is talking.

Mr. Murphy breaks the silence, "I guess I should say grace to thank God for this good meal and all of our blessings."

We don't say anything. Ruby and I just look down and bow our heads.

> *Dear God, We thank you for this good food,*
> *and we thank you for all that you have given us.*

But, God, we have been going through
difficult times. We thank you for restoring
Ruby's health, and hope you will
take the pain away from Dora's hand.
Bless this food to our bodies,
and bring joy and gladness to our home.
Amen.

Everything looks good, but I pick at my food. I can't do anything to help, so I go to my room as soon as we finish eating. Just like when my legs were burned, I just want to sleep, except now I know it will take a little while for the pain to be gone.

I'm sitting on the porch step next to a bucket of hot water. Mama leaves to go inside to the kitchen when the bucket takes off, flying through the air.

The water splashes out both sides of the bucket, like wings flapping to lift it higher. Jack and Louis are crying, and I look down. My legs are red. Jack cries, "Look at Dora, she has big blisters! Dora, does it hurt?"

Someone is screaming. I realize it's me. I want to sleep. I don't want to wake up. Daddy, help me!

I wake up and run to the bathroom in search of some cool water. Mr. Murphy meets me on the landing. "I heard you shout. Are you all right? Does it hurt?"

"I just had a bad dream. I want some cool water for my hand."

"Let's go to the kitchen. W.D. gave Ruby a salve to put on your hand, and he told her to keep it covered. We don't want you to get an infection."

"Mr. Murphy, I can't sleep! It's just like my legs. I've been burned before. It really hurts. I'll be down as soon as I go to the bathroom."

I go to the bathroom and look around the room for something, anything, that might help to ease the pain, but decide it's better to do what the doctor says. As I'm leaving the bathroom, I hear Mr. Murphy, coming up the stairs.

"I'm coming down! I want to put on the salve like the doctor said."

"Oh, I wasn't coming up to check on you. I'm just tired, so I'm going to lie down for a while. Ruby's waiting for you in the kitchen."

Ruby puts the salve on and she's re-wrapping my hand, but I can tell, something's bothering her.

"There. Well, Princess, once again you've managed to grab all the attention."

"What? What are you talking about?"

"You know what I'm talking about. I should be getting everyone's sympathy and attention right now. Instead, all Uncle Joe is concerned about is Dora's hand!"

"Do you really think I burned my hand on purpose, just to get attention?"

"Well, you are the Princess here. This is nothing compared to what I'm feeling."

"Look, Ruby, I'm sorry that you lost your baby. Truth is, I was looking forward to having a baby in the house. Right now what we should be worried about is Mr. Murphy. He's failing. You and I will never be close, but Christmas is coming, so can we work together and plan a nice Christmas for Mr. Murphy? He's done a lot for us. I don't know about you, but he means a lot to me."

"I used to feel the way you do now. I suppose there are hurt feelings on both sides. It did make me feel good when he sent R.C. to get Jim, after I lost the baby. But why didn't they let me see my baby? Uncle Joe just took it upon himself to have him taken away! I didn't get to say goodbye. Princess, I really don't care much about Christmas this year."

"You need to talk with the doctor. They did what they thought was right. All I am asking you to do is to put on a good front and work with me to try to have a happy Christmas. For Mr. Murphy."

"It seems I have no choice. You can't cook or clean with that hand, so everything will be on me as usual."

"What? Are you kidding? I did everything around here for eight months while you were pregnant. I missed school, even when you were getting better. All you did was lay around!"

"Well, Princess, get used to it. What did you think was going to happen? Can't you see what's going on? You are being trained to take over for me when I leave! It's time for you to grow up!"

"Don't say that! I know that's not true!"

"Well, we'll see after I marry Jim and get out of here. I don't feel sorry for you at all, but I bet you're going to feel plenty sorry for yourself when you're in my shoes. For now, Dora, I will work with you, for Uncle Joe's sake. We'll decorate the house like we normally do, and we will see to it that we have a nice Christmas. Just don't expect too much. I'll be the one buying all the presents."

Tuesday, December 15, 1906.

My hand is a little better, and Ruby has me doing chores again when Mr. Murphy isn't looking. After Christmas, I'll talk with him, and I hope things get back to normal. I'm dressed and ready for school, Mr. Murphy is putting his coat on when I come to the kitchen for breakfast.

"Good morning, Mr. Murphy. You're going out? Why so early?"

"Good morning to you as well. R.C. is waiting outside. We're going to the farm. They put a new roof on the barn, so I want to see it before winter sets in. It will be good to get out. I'll be home in time for dinner."

"Your shoes are untied. Do you want me to tie them for you?"

"No, I'm more comfortable this way. Thank you, though. Well, he's waiting. I'd better go."

It's good to see Mr. Murphy get out. He's in good spirits considering he hasn't been feeling well. A visit to the farm will do him good.

"Ruby, I'll just have a biscuit and apple butter. I want to get to school early. We're working on crafts for Christmas." I leave for school with the feeling that today will be a good day.

I had a fun day at school. When I get home, R.C. and Ruby are sitting at the table looking very serious. Is something wrong?

R.C. tells me Mr. Murphy got very confused and weak today, and he's asleep upstairs. Apparently, Mr. Murphy was looking up at the new roof he wanted to inspect, but he wasn't steady on his feet, and then he just had to sit down near the stove. Then he didn't even recognize Jeremy, who has been running the farm for years! And he wanted to go into the farmhouse and go to bed, because he thought he still lived there, and he was too tired to stay outside and work.

R.C. looks upset when he says, "I told him, he lives in a big house in town, and I live across the street. He hasn't lived in the farmhouse for years and years! He just looked at me, and shook his head a little. When I told him he lives in a house with you two, he seemed to remember, and said he hoped he'd see Albert too. I just brought him home and put him to bed. You girls need to take special care of Uncle Joe. The good news is, eventually, he came back to himself, but he is still very weak. That, and his breathing is not good. I'm worried about him. He's upstairs in bed but you ladies need to make sure you look in on him. You should call Doc Nelson, too. I'll call Albert to let him know what happened."

As soon as R.C, leaves, I tip toe into Mr. Murphy's room. He's sleeping so I return to the kitchen.

"Do you think we should call the doctor?" I ask Ruby.

"Not if he's sleeping. Just let him be. It's nothing new. He gets confused sometimes. It's been happening a lot. You just haven't noticed. You can check on him if you want, but Jim is coming for a visit, so I don't have time for any doctor."

"Did Mr. Murphy say it's okay for Jim to come here? What if he finds out? It will upset him."

"I don't care. I'm entitled to have a life. It's not your concern. You're to mind your own business, Princess!"

"It is my concern. We can both get in trouble if he finds out and, besides, I don't want anything to upset him. He's not well. Don't you care?"

"I used to. Just let him rest, Dora. R.C. is worried over nothing."

I heat up some leftover stew for supper. It's ready, so I go upstairs to see if Mr. Murphy is awake and hungry. He's still sleeping, so I eat my supper and go to my room after doing the dishes. I don't want to be downstairs when Jim is there. The house is quiet, and I hope Ruby is right, that he just needs to rest. Eventually, I fall asleep.

I wake up in the morning to hear footsteps and a door slam. I go to Mr. Murphy's room. He's awake, but still in bed.

"Good morning, Mr. Murphy. Did I hear you get up?"

"Good morning, Dora. I just went to the bathroom. I'm just going to rest today."

"Do you want me to bring breakfast to you? I can fix a nice tray."

"That will be nice, but don't bring too much. Maybe I'll just have tea.'

I go to the kitchen and get our nice wooden tray from the pantry. He didn't have supper, so he needs to eat. I go to the cellar for a jar of peaches, and make him a tray of biscuits, tea and a small bowl of peaches.

"Thank you dear. That looks good. I'll try to eat a little."

I leave him alone and go to the kitchen to get my breakfast. "Ruby, should I stay home from school?"

Ruby is making her tea. "Why would you stay home from school?"

"Someone needs to look after Mr. Murphy. Will you look in on him while I'm gone? I gave him breakfast, but you will need to make him a tray for dinner. He said he just wants to rest today."

"I can take care of things. Don't worry."

Wednesday, December 16, 1906 — Dear Diary, Mr. Murphy is not doing so good. R.C. took him to the farm yesterday and he said he was confused and he had trouble breathing. He told Ruby and me to look after him. He also said we should call the doctor, but Ruby wouldn't let me call because Jim was coming for a visit. Halfway to school, I almost turned around to come home, but Ruby did say she would look after him, so I kept going. I should have stayed home because I couldn't concentrate, and he's no better tonight. I hope he is better tomorrow. If not, I'll stay home and call Doc Nelson. Ruby seems more interested in spending time with Jim than doing anything around the house, and with Mr. Murphy in bed, she's doing whatever she wants. I will make sure Mr. Murphy gets nice suppers and breakfasts, no matter what. But if he doesn't get better I'm calling Doc Nelson. Signed, Dora Kelly

It's early, but I get dressed and hurry to Mr. Murphy's room to make sure he's all right, and to see if he needs anything. He's awake, but his voice is weak.

"Dora, I need to get up. Can you help me with my slippers, and bring my robe from the closet?"

I bring his slippers and robe but wonder if that was the right thing to do. "Do you feel like getting out of bed? Shouldn't you rest today? I'm going to call Doc Nelson."

"Oh, those doctors! If they have their way, I'd be resting all the time. I have things to do. Planning my trip, you know."

"Are you still going? I thought you would want to wait 'til you're feeling better."

"That would be nice but at my age, this is probably as good as I'm going to get. Let's go downstairs and you can fix me breakfast. Wait, it's Thursday. Don't you have school?"

I don't want to tell him that I decided to miss school because I'm worried about him. "No, there's no school today or tomorrow."

Since he didn't have any supper last night, I decide to make a big breakfast. After I put biscuits in the oven and start frying some ham, I pour tea. I call out to Ruby, "Yoo hoo, Ruby, we're eating breakfast. Do you want to eat with us?"

Ruby comes out of her room. She's wearing a pretty velvet robe that's the color of a pink rose. I think it's new, but I don't say anything.

"Good morning, Ruby. Dora's making breakfast."

"Good day, Uncle Joe. You look a little better. How do you feel?"

"Oh, I'll be all right. Like I told Dora, I just need to get up and move around. Planning my trip, you know."

"You're still going to California? You really must be feeling better!"

"I'm not getting any younger and I'm looking forward to seeing my sister, so I'm going."

We eat breakfast, but Mr. Murphy doesn't eat very much. He makes himself a small sandwich with a biscuit and ham to eat with his tea.

I try to get him to eat more. "You didn't eat very much. I thought you'd be hungry since you didn't have supper."

"Don't worry about me. With this weight, I can stand to miss a meal or two. I'm going up to my room. I think I'll rest for a while before I go to the office."

Ruby and I start to help him up the stairs.

"I told you not to worry about me. You just go about your business. I know you have things to do."

He walks up the stairs to his room, but he walks slow, resting between steps. It's hard not to run to the stairs so I can at least walk behind him. I want to help him, but I don't know what I would do if he falls backward. So, I go back to cleaning up the dishes and Ruby goes back to her room. I guess she's not concerned.

I clean the second floor on Thursdays, so I go through a regular day, cleaning the bathroom and guest room, but I'll have to do Mr. Murphy's room later after he gets up from his nap. When I go downstairs, Ruby is making dinner, finally helping!

"Oh, there you are. Did you finish your chores?"

"I cleaned all of the rooms except Mr. Murphy's room, so I guess I'm done for today."

"Dinner's almost ready. Why don't you set the table, then you can go upstairs to see if Uncle Joe wants to eat."

I set the table for the three of us and as I turn to go to the cabinet in the dining room for napkins, we hear a loud crash from upstairs. I look at Ruby. Like me, I think she's alarmed, but she doesn't move. I run up the stairs as fast as I can, and I go into Mr. Murphy's room without knocking. He's lying on the floor with the lamp from his bedside table in his hand. The lamp is broken, and the paper shade is crushed by his weight.

I scream as loud as I can, "Ruby! Mr. Murphy fell, and his face is turning gray!

Ruby's coming up the stairs, "Is he awake?"

"No, and I can't get him up." He's laying with his head on the floor and one leg is still on the bed.

Ruby comes to his side. "Uncle Joe, wake up! You have to get up. Oh, Dora, something's really wrong. Go get R.C."

I run down the stairs and out the door, not taking time to put on my coat. I open R.C.'s kitchen door without knocking.

Mary calls out, "R.C., come quick. Something's happened. Dora, what's wrong?"

I'm crying so hard I can hardly talk. All I can say is, "It's Mr. Murphy!"

R.C. runs out the door towards our house. Mary and I run, trying to keep up. R.C. bounds up the stairs, taking two steps at a time.

"Ruby, go downstairs and call Doc Nelson. Tell him Uncle Joe has had a heart attack!"

"How do you know it's a heart attack?"

"I just know. Don't ask questions, just get downstairs and call the doctor!"

R.C. gently lifts Mr. Murphy's leg from the bed so he can lie flat on the floor. Mary, bring a pillow and blanket from the bed so we can make him comfortable. I don't think we should move him!"

I decide to sit on the porch step and wait for Doc Nelson. I want him to hurry. It seems like hours, but it must have only been a few minutes.

"They're upstairs in Mr. Murphy's room. He's on the floor!"

The doctor has a black bag, and he goes upstairs to Mr. Murphy's room. R.C. and Ruby come to the kitchen.

She rolls her eyes when she sees how hard I'm crying. "Dora, it's all right. He'll be fine now that the doctor is here."

"You don't know that, Ruby. This is serious. It's my fault! He should have stayed in bed this morning. I shouldn't have let him get up."

Mary pulls me to her and she hugs me close. "Dora, this is not your fault. Uncle Joe's not been well for some time. R.C., you'd better go upstairs to see if the doctor needs help getting him to bed."

R.C. is upstairs for what seems like a long time. Doc Nelson comes down the stairs and he goes to the telephone. "Mattie! Yes, Mattie, it's Doctor Nelson. Joseph Murphy's had a heart attack. He's going to need a nurse for a few days. How soon can you get here?"

Pause.

"Yes. Yes. That's fine. I'll stay with him until you get here."

The nurse arrives and Ruby shows her to Mr. Murphy's room. I go upstairs to see him. I'm glad the nurse is here – I was afraid he had died!

I enter the room and Mr. Murphy is in his bed. I whisper, "Doctor, is he going to be okay? He just looks like he's sleeping."

"Oh, Dora. R.C. told me that you were really scared. I know you were very helpful. Heart attacks are scary, but he's fine for now. I gave him some medicine and Miss Havermale will look after him until I come back in the morning. We'll know more tomorrow."

After Doc Nelson leaves. R.C., Ruby and I sit at the kitchen table, drinking tea, but not talking, not knowing what to say.

"R.C., do you think I should call Anna?"

"I hadn't thought of that. I would if I were you. She's the only family he has in Canton. She should at least know what happened."

I go to the telephone to call Anna. She answers but I start crying again, so I can hardly talk. R.C. takes the phone, "Anna. It's R.C., Uncle Joe had a heart attack. Doc Nelson called in a nurse, and he's resting now, but we thought you would want to know. Yes, that was Dora. She's all right, too, just scared."

After a long talk, R.C. hangs up. "She'll come by tomorrow morning when the doctor is back, Dora. Why don't you come to our house, tonight? Mary will take care of you, and I'll stay here to keep watch over Uncle Joe. I'll call right away if there's any change."

He dials another number. "Albert, R.C. here. Look, there's nothing to do right now, but Uncle Joe had a heart attack. Thought you would want to know…. Yes, come tomorrow morning. We are taking good care of him tonight."

Mary and I go upstairs to my room to get my nightdress and some clothes for tomorrow. When we come downstairs, R.C. and Ruby are talking.

"If all he's going to do is sleep, there's really no need for you to stay here."

"I'm staying. Maybe you don't realize how serious this is. Besides, if he needs something, you won't hear him from your room. I'll catch some sleep in the chair beside his bed so I will hear him if he needs anything, or if something happens. Mary, you should go home with Dora, now. I'll take care of Uncle Joe."

When we get to R.C.'s house, Dickie is entertaining his little sister, playing with his toy trucks. "Dickie! You're such a good big brother!"

"Mama, did Uncle Joe die?"

"No, but he's very sick. The doctor came and Daddy is staying with him tonight. But Dora is spending the night at our house. How about that?"

I can only imagine what Dickie is thinking, although it seems he's trying to be nice.

"Mary, I'm really tired. Where do you want me to sleep?"

"We only have two bedrooms, but there's a comfortable cot in the corner of the kitchen for overnight guests. Goodness, Ruby told me you haven't had dinner or supper. You need to eat something."

"I'm not very hungry, but maybe I could eat a few bites."

Mary takes a baked ham out of the icebox. "I baked bread this morning, so we can make sandwiches."

The aroma of the coffee percolating on the stove, fills the room. I've not had coffee before, but if it tastes as good as it smells, then I want a cup.

Mary pours coffee into a cup, "Do you normally drink coffee?"

"No, this is the first time I've had it."

"Then you should add milk and sugar." She pours the coffee in my cup, half full. Then she stirs in sugar, and she adds milk, filling the cup.

Mary slices the ham and she cuts thick slices of the bread. "I know I said I wasn't hungry, but this ham sandwich and coffee is the best ever!"

"Good. I'm glad you like it. If you don't mind watching Dickie and Beth, I think I'll take some to R.C. and Ruby."

I don't know why she asked me to watch Dickie. They did fine before, when they were alone. I walk around the house and find a room with a door, so I can change into my nightdress.

"Dickie, where's the bathroom."

"Out back. Do you want me to take you there?"

"No, I'll find it."

I go to the backdoor and Dickie is waiting for me with a broom in his hand. "Here, you can use this."

"What do I need a broom for?"

"The geese. They chase you and peck at your feet. You just swing the broom like this..."

The broom hits a pitcher full of water that's sitting on the corner of the table. The water spills and the pitcher shatters across the kitchen floor just as Mary opens the door.

"Dickie Webster! What are you doing? Look what you've done!"

"Mary, please don't yell at Dickie. It was my fault. He was just trying to help me. Here, Dickie, hand me the broom and I'll help your mama with the mess after I go to the privy."

I hurry to the privy so I can help Mary but when I return, she already has the water and broken pitcher cleaned up.

"Mary, I was going to help you with that."

"No bother. Why don't we go sit in the parlor? I'll light a fire in the fireplace, and we can just relax. Sound good?"

"Sounds good!"

I lay on the floor in front of the fireplace while Mary reads a story to Dickie and Beth. I'm tired, and the warmth of the fire makes me sleepy. Mary covers me with a quilt, and I finally relax.

It must be Christmas Eve because we are sleeping on the floor near the tree and the fireplace. The fire and the candles on the tree are the only light in the room. Baby Louis has snuggled up next to me. He and Jack have already fallen asleep. There's a giant Santa floating through the air, along the ceiling. He looks down at me and my sleeping brothers. "Have your brothers been good?"

"Yes, Santa."

"And do you take good care of your brothers?"

"I want to, but I can't, Santa. They took us away, and I don't know how to find them."

"Look, they are here. They are right next to you!"

Santa drops three candy canes, and they drift down slowly into my hand, then with a swoosh, Santa rises up the chimney and he's gone!

Someone is shaking me. I push their hand away, "No, leave me alone."

"Dora, it's Mary. You fell asleep on the floor. Let me help you up so you can sleep comfortably on the cot."

Caring!

Saturday, December 22, 1906

It's early but I hear voices in the kitchen. I leave my bed to go to the bathroom and not knowing who is downstairs, I put on a play dress and I go to the kitchen. Mr. Murphy is already dressed; he's eating breakfast and talking to Ruby.

"I can't stay in bed. I have things to do. You can call Albert or whomever you want, but I'm not going to change my mind. George is expecting me, I need to finalize plans for my trip."

Ruby looks at me, "He says he's going to the office."

"But you've been sick, and this is the first time you have come downstairs. Maybe George can come here so you can talk to him."

"No, there's some business matters that I need to settle. I have to go to the office."

"Have you talked to the doctor about your trip?"

"Not since last week. He said I can go, just to take it easy".

"Yeah, but that was before...."

"Don't worry, Baby Girl. I'll be fine. My sister needs my help. I will leave after the holidays, and stay for a few weeks. You all are worrying far too much about me, ladies. I know you mean well, but I am still the master of this house."

Ruby and I simply nod our heads. I decide I will just get R.C. to try to change his mind, and pray for the best. I'll make a special supper, and maybe we can talk him into resting instead of traveling.

It's early evening when he comes home, looking so tired! I try to be cheerful. "Mr. Murphy, you're home! Ruby and I are just getting ready to eat dinner. Want some?"

"Thank you. I'll eat a bite or two, but I'm tired. I just want to lie down. What do you have? Soup? That's good."

Ruby dishes up the soup while I get the bread and butter. I'm ready to sit down and notice that Mr. Murphy is sitting with his eyes closed. I wonder if we should wake him up.

I whisper, "Mr. Murphy." No response. A little louder, "Mr. Murphy!"

His eyes open and he looks at Ruby, "When did you get here?"

"What? You dozed off so you're confused. I was here when you came home. I never left."

"Oh, that's right. You live here. Let me eat some soup, then I think I'll lie down."

Ruby and I look at one another. No one talks while we eat. Mr. Murphy's bowl is still half full when he puts his spoon down.

"I'm going upstairs. Thank you for dinner. That was good."

I follow him up the stairs to his room. He gets in bed, still with his clothes on.

"Is there anything you want me to do? Do you want me to turn off the lamp?"

He's already snoring.

I return to the kitchen to help Ruby with dishes. Earlier, I had planned on asking if I could go see Anna and Rex, but now I think I need to stay here. I go upstairs to get my pencil and paper so I can write a letter to Annie Rose. I just sit down to the secretary when the doorbell clanks and rings. Ruby answers the door.

"Doctor, come on in."

"Where is he? How's he doing?"

"He seemed a little better this morning, but he went to the office. Said he had to settle some business affairs and plan for a trip. He was confused and did not look as good when he got home. He went to bed early."

Doc Nelson goes upstairs to Mr. Murphy's room for what seems to be a long time. Finally, we hear the door close and he comes to the kitchen.

"Well, as you no doubt already know, he's not really better. He over-extended himself."

I feel a little panicked. What if he insists on traveling? "He's still making plans to go to California!"

"Dora, he needs to stay here. I'll talk to him. Here's some drops. Over the next few days, put a couple drops in his tea. It will make him sleepy so he will just rest."

Ruby shows the doctor out the door, "Thank you doctor. We didn't know what to do. It's hard on Dora and me. We don't know how to stop him when he decides to go somewhere. Maybe the drops will help."

"Talk to R.C. Tell him I said not to take him anywhere. Tell him to just say he's busy. If need be, he can call me."

The next morning, when I come downstairs, Mr. Murphy is sitting at the table waiting for breakfast.

"Dora, I've been waiting for you. I'm hungry!"

"You should have called me. I would have come down sooner. I was going to make oatmeal. Is that okay?"

"Oatmeal's fine. Maybe a boiled egg or two."

He seems fine – almost like old times, talking and laughing.

"So, how are you doing in school?"

"I'm doing fine. I get A's and B's on my papers, but school is out for Christmas."

"Oh, yes. Christmas. What day is today?"

"It's Sunday. Christmas is day after tomorrow. I was going to ask you, but you've been sick. I bought a few presents. I hope that's okay."

"Of course, it's okay. I'm glad that you went ahead."

"Mr. Murphy, what do you want to do for Christmas? Anna was asking. Would you like them to come for a little while? We can have cookies and tea, and you and John can have your Port."

"That sounds nice. I like Anna and John. Maybe in the morning before I get tired."

"They invited me to go with them to church tomorrow night. That is, if it's all right with you."

"Christmas Eve service? Of course, you must go. Just make sure Ruby will be here until you get home. Now, I think I'll sit up in my chair and read for a while."

Ruby comes out of her room just in time to help him to his chair in the parlor. I bring him his tea with a few drops of the medicine in it, and before long he leans his head back and he falls asleep.

"Ruby, what should we do?"

"I don't know. I guess we didn't think about getting him up the stairs."

"I know, I'll go get R.C. He'll know what to do."

I put on my coat and go across the street to R.C.'s house. He opens the door, "What's wrong? Is it Uncle Joe again?"

"He's okay. We just need help getting him up the stairs."

R.C. takes off running. "R.C., R.C.! He's okay. He's just sleeping."

When we get to the kitchen, R.C. is out of breath, "Where...is he?"

We go to the parlor and R.C. shakes him to wake him up. "Uncle Joe. You fell asleep in your chair. Let's get you upstairs to your bed."

Mr. Murphy looks up at R.C. "All right."

Even R.C., as strong as he is, has trouble getting him up the stairs. Mr. Murphy is a big man but he's very weak and unable to help himself. After a series of grunts, and one step at a time, they make it to the landing in front of his room.

R.C. returns to the kitchen. "Does Doc Nelson know he's like this? He was wide awake last time I talked to him."

"I think it's the tea I gave him."

"What do you mean?"

Ruby intercedes, "Uncle Joe went to the office yesterday and Doc Nelson said he overdid it. He gave us some drops to put in his tea so he will stay home and rest. Dora made him tea after breakfast."

I can't stop my tears, "I didn't mean to put him to sleep. I used the dropper and put two drops in his tea, then another slipped out by mistake."

"You mean you gave him three drops? He only gets two!"

"Oh, come on, Ruby. It was a mistake. No harm done, it's like he's drunk. He'll sleep it off. Funny, though. Uncle Joe always wants to be proper, but Dora got him drunk with one little drop!"

R.C. laughs, then we all laugh.

"Does he know? Does he know about the drops?"

"No, and if he did, he might not drink the tea. We just didn't expect him to fall asleep!"

"That's a good one! Wait 'til I tell Mary. Let's not tell anyone else, though. Not even the doctor!"

Christmas Eve comes and we're settled into our pew. I'm comfortable sitting between Harold and Rex. Anna nods to a woman across the aisle. She's the one who always flirts with Mr. Murphy! She's probably wondering why he isn't here.

I lean back and look up at the candlelight bouncing off the ceiling. I close my eyes and the smell of the evergreens makes me feel safe. No matter what happens, they will not change. The pine trees will always be there, green and rising up like soldiers along roads covered with snow. Like Rex and Anna, I know they will always be there.

Rex leans towards me to whisper in my ear, "We have gifts for you at the house. We're taking you there after church for cookies and punch."

I shake my head no and start to tell him I need to go home, but the organ breaks through the quiet and we all stand to sing Joy to the World! My mind wanders back home while the pastor says a prayer, wondering if Mr. Murphy is going to be okay. I add a special request to my own prayer. I miss him being there with us.

John comes to the front steps of the church in his buggy. Harold picks me up at my waist to lift me up, "Here, I'll help you so you can get inside and stay warm. You know, Dora, Rex is right. You really are teeny tiny!"

I smile and thank him thinking, I'm not small, I'm growing up. Like Mr. Murphy said, I'm becoming a young lady.

It's a short ride to their house on Main. John takes the horse and buggy to the carriage house, and Harold runs ahead to light a fire in the fireplace. Rex takes my coat and I follow Anna to the kitchen. I turn around when I hear the whoosh of the freshly lit fire; the yellow and orange flames rise to warm the room.

I carry the Christmas cake to the parlor, where Anna has a table set with fancy plates and a spoon jar, and there's a crystal bowl with punch and matching cups.

"Dora, you go first. You are our guest tonight."

I take a small slice of cake and a cup of punch and sit on a high-backed wooden chair, away from the fire.

"No, Dora, Mother wants you to sit here. Like Father said, you're the guest of honor!" Rex carries my plate and cup, showing me to a blue velvet chair near the fire.

I feel special. I think this is the first time I've been allowed the first taste and the best seat. At the orphan home, I was always last in line, and at Mr. Murphy's, he always gets the first plate unless there are important guests visiting.

"Church was pretty boring tonight."

"Walter Rex Moss, the service was lovely."

"Oh, Mother, he didn't mean anything by it. He was just anxious to get home so we can give Dora her gifts."

John pipes in, "Speaking of which, young lady, there are quite a few gifts for you under the tree. Rex, go get them and bring them to her."

Rex puts four packages on the floor at my feet, wrapped in white paper and tied with red ribbons.

The first gift is from Anna, a pink sweater. "It's so pretty! Did you knit this?"

Harold interrupts, "You know she did. She started working on it in July and she threatened Rex and me with no cookies or cake for a month if we told you about it."

I'm surprised to see, there's a gift from John. I pull the ribbon to unwrap the box – inside is a wooden box. I open the lid, and the inside is lined with rose-colored velvet.

Rex explained, "Dad made that too."

"Oh, thank you. You and Anna make me feel so special. I don't know what to say!"

"Dora, you are special. You are special to us and to Joseph. You have made him happy, and you take care of him. That's a lot for a young girl your age to take on, but you never complain. Don't think people haven't noticed."

"You should have opened the gifts that Rex and I bought first. They aren't as nice as the sweater and jewelry box but, here, open mine next."

I know before I open it. Harold always gives me candy from the Sweet Shoppe. This year, it's two cloth bags, one with ribbon candy and the other with raspberry Christmas candy.

"Harold, how did you know? Raspberry candy is one of my favorites! Thank you."

"I like them too. I bought some for me, too."

Rex kneels on the floor in front of me, and he hands the last gift to me. "Here, Dora, this one's from me."

I open the tiny box – inside is a gold necklace with a heart. I blush – it's a little embarrassing. Surely, his mother knew what he was giving me. "Thank you, Rex, it's very nice."

I hurry to put the lid back on the box and I get my bag from the closet. "I have gifts for you too."

Anna is happy with her embroidered hanky, and John is really surprised with the bookmark I made for him that has a green shamrock and green silk ribbons.

"This is so detailed! Did you make this?"

"Yes. I thought you could use it for your Bible."

"Well, thank you. I'm flabbergasted!"

Harold opens his gift, a keychain with an image of the Kittyhawk.

"Look, Father, an airplane. Every time I use my key, I'll remember we're going to fly someday!"

Rex snorts, "I'll fly when the planes stop falling to the ground."

"You'll see. Someday it will be ordinary and very safe! It's part of our future."

"Harold's right, our world is changing. Did you hear, John Ingram from across town is getting one of those automobiles? He told me he's ordered one of those Runabouts."

"Rex, this last one's for you. I hope you like it."

I hand him his package. Inside is a long, wood box, with a new ruler and a compass.

"Gee, Dora."

"Mr. Murphy said you will need them for drawing plans to build things."

"I will. I really like them. For now, I'll keep them in the toolbox you gave me."

Anna stands up, "Well, we all received nice presents. I'm going to the kitchen. Does anyone want anything? Tea, or more cake and punch?"

"No, thank you. I really need to go home. I've been gone too long already. I want to see how Mr. Murphy is doing."

Anna and Harold stay at the house while John and Rex drive me home.

"Here, Rex, take this blanket to keep your legs warm."

We board the buggy and Rex spreads the blanket. It is cold, so I pull the blanket up over my arms. Rex slips his hand under the blanket, and he takes mine. I look into his eyes and smile. He is such a special friend. I wish we could spend more time together, but I am so busy that all we can do is walk home from school together. With John so near, I can't ask him what he meant by his present. Maybe it's enough just to be friends like we are, with things so strange at home.

John pulls the buggy up, next to our side door. "Here you are, Miss Kelly. Thank you for spending Christmas Eve with us and tell Joseph that I sent my regards."

Christmas Day, December 25, 1906.

I wake up listing everything I have to do today, all the cooking and organizing. We've decorated the house, but there's still so much to do to make this the perfect Christmas!

I put the presents that I bought for Mr. Murphy and Ruby under the tree. Mr. Murphy is sitting at the kitchen table, and I can hear his labored breathing all the way into the parlor.

"Merry Christmas, Mr. Murphy! How do you feel?"

"Oh, I'm all right, Baby Girl. Merry Christmas to you as well! Are those surprises that you just put under the tree?"

"Yes, sir, one for you and the other one is for Ruby."

"That's kind of you. I've noticed, you're always nice to her, but I know she hasn't always been nice to you."

I decide it's best, not to talk about Ruby. I'm glad I didn't say anything 'cuz I hear the door to her room open and she comes to the kitchen, still in her nightdress.

"Merry Christmas, everyone! What can I make you for breakfast? We're having roast beef for dinner, so do you want a big breakfast, or should we just have biscuits and stewed prunes?"

Mr. Murphy talks between breaths, "I don't feel so well today. I'll just have my tea."

I look at Ruby and she just rolls her eyes.

"Mr. Murphy, Doctor Nelson told us that you have to eat something when you drink tea."

"Is that so? I don't feel like arguing so just give me one biscuit and a couple prunes, and I'll try to get them down."

He eats the prunes and part of his biscuit, then he stands up, holding onto the table, "Dora, you can bring my tea to the parlor." We watch as he shuffles to his chair in the parlor, and I give him his tea.

"Mr. Murphy, do you want to sit here, or do you want to go to your room since you don't feel well?"

"I want to sit here with you. I brought a book from a shelf upstairs that I want to share with you. It's about our homeland, Ireland. I thought you would like to look at it with me. It's there on the lamp table. Bring it to me."

The book is heavy. The dark green leather is embossed with little shamrocks.

"Mr. Murphy, this is a beautiful book."

"And you haven't even looked inside. See the title is in gold, Ireland in Pictures and there are four family crests. This one at the top is the Murphy crest."

His tea gets cold while we page through the book, looking at the pictures but it doesn't matter. He seems content and I love spending this time with him.

He closes the book when we are about halfway through the book, "Dora, I think I'll go lie down. Come get me when dinner is ready."

I follow him up the stairs and help him to his bed. When I get downstairs, I find dirty dishes from breakfast. Ruby is in her room, singing! I finish washing the dishes and she comes out of her room, all dressed up like she's going to a party.

"You look nice. Is that a new dress?"

"Yes. I ordered it from a store in Chicago. Do you like it?" It's a rose-colored velvet with a lace collar. I'm sure it was expensive.

"It's very pretty. Are you going somewhere?"

"I'll be here for dinner, then I'm going out, and you don't need to be telling Uncle Joe where I got my new dress."

While our simple dinner, roast beef, potatoes and carrots, is in the oven, Anna and John come for a visit.

"Here, Dora, I made you a sponge cake."

"Thank you, Anna. I can hardly wait to taste it. You always make good cakes!"

John asks, "Where's Joseph? Is he lying down?"

Ruby answers with a shrug, "He went upstairs a while ago. He came down for breakfast and read a book with Dora, but decided he would take a nap before dinner. We can see if he wants to come down now."

"I'll see." I go to his room and open the door a crack. He's resting but he's awake.

"Mr. Murphy, Anna and John are here to see you. Do you want to come downstairs?"

He doesn't say anything, but he turns to put his feet on the floor, and he shuffles to the landing. John comes up the stairs to help him down. Mr. Murphy walks very slowly down the twelve steps, one step at a time. We go to the parlor, and he falls into his chair.

Anna is talking to Ruby in the kitchen, and it sounds like they're having an argument. But she comes to the parlor with a big smile for Mr. Murphy.

"Well, there he is! It's so good to see you. Merry Christmas, Joseph!"

"Merry Christmas to you as well, and thank you, John for helping me. Those stairs are a worry. I don't want to fall, so I take my time."

"Helping you is a privilege. It's an honor to be part of your family. We can't stay long. The boys are home, waiting to open presents, and we don't want to tire you out."

Anna nods, "Besides, their dinner is about ready, so we should go. We just wanted to wish you a Merry Christmas, and bring a sponge cake for your dinner."

"Thank you and give the boys my kindest regards."

We decide to open our gifts while Mr. Murphy is sitting in the parlor. Ruby gives him some wool socks, but he really likes the present from me, a needlepointed bookmark with a cross in gold thread.

"Thank you, Baby Girl. This is very special because I know you made it just for me. Come give me a hug." I kneel on the ottoman and give him a hug. I don't mind anymore that he uses that nickname. I can feel how cold his hands are through my sweater.

Ruby opens her gift from me. "Did you embroider this?"

"Yes."

"It's a very pretty handkerchief. I'm going to save it for something special. Now open your presents, Dora."

This is the first time there are no big presents from Santa, but that's okay. It's been a long time since I believed in him. But I guess Ruby was right when she told me not to expect much. There are only two presents for me.

I open the gift from Ruby first, two plain nightdresses. I thank her politely, "I really need these."

The gift from Mr. Murphy is in a large box that's professionally wrapped. I pull back the tissue to find a blue wool coat with matching hat and mittens. "Oh, thank you! It's so pretty, and it's my favorite color!"

"Uncle Joe told me what to get. He knew exactly what he wanted to give you this year."

Ruby opens the last gift, signed "Uncle Joe," a pair of ruby earrings. I can tell they are very expensive but all she says is, "Thank you." Also, she didn't have a gift for Mr. Murphy, even though she could have charged it to his account. Sometimes she's just plain mean.

"It smells like the roast is ready. Mr. Murphy, would you like a glass of Port with your dinner?"

"That's a splendid idea! I usually have Port after dinner, but I'll probably be too tired to stay up, so a glass with dinner will be fine."

Dinner is good; the roast is perfect, and Mr. Murphy is enjoying the meal. He doesn't eat all his food, but he enjoys his Port. He takes the last sip and announces that he's ready to go back to bed.

I walk behind him up the stairs. He's short of breath, so we have to take our time. When I finally return to the kitchen, Ruby is standing by the door with her coat on.

"You're leaving now?"

"I told you I'd leave after dinner. Jim is waiting outside."

I feel like saying, what about me? But I know she really doesn't care about leaving me alone for Christmas, so I don't say anything.

I cry the entire time I'm doing the dishes. This Christmas hasn't been much fun. I like the coat and hat from Mr. Murphy, and I enjoyed looking at the picture book with him, but it seems all I do is take care of him and clean up.

I start to go upstairs to my room when the door to Mr. Murphy's room opens.

"Oh, you're up. I was just going upstairs to my room but since you are up, I'll go to the parlor with you."

He's breathing heavy as he starts to shuffle down the stairs.

"Careful. Don't trip on your shoelaces."

"Dora, where's Ruby? I don't feel so well. Go get Ruby so the two of you can help me down the stairs."

"Ruby left."

I start to go down the stairs ahead of him. It sounds like he just took a big sigh, but I look back just in time to see him fall to the floor of the landing. I run up the stairs and kneel beside him, cradling his head in my hands. I want to ask him if he is all right, but his eyes are closed, so I know he can't hear me. I don't want to leave him alone, but I have no choice. I hurry to the closet to get my coat, and I take off running to get R.C.

I'm frantic and keep knocking until R.C. opens the door. "R.C., it's Mr. Murphy. He fell on the stairs! I can't get him up and I don't know what to do!"

R.C. puts on his coat and we run back to our house. I run ahead, "He's up here!"

Mr. Murphy can't seem to catch his breath, and his face is grey. R.C. takes charge. "Dora, you stay here with him. I'll call Doc Nelson."

I pull a blanket and pillow off of his bed to make him comfortable until the doctor gets here. R.C. actually makes two phone calls. When he hangs up the phone from the first call, he shouts up the stairs, "He's on his way."

Then I hear him making a second call, "Albert, R.C. here. It's Uncle Joe. He fell. I called the doctor and he's on his way, but you need to get here right away!"

It seems like a long time, but finally Doc Nelson arrives. Albert is right behind him, and they rush up the stairs.

I move out of the way and go down the stairs and stand next to R.C. He puts his arm across my shoulder to comfort me, "You did good, Dora. I'm glad that you came for me."

Doc Nelson examines Mr. Murphy. He's still not awake. I can't stand to watch, so I go to sit in the kitchen.

After the doctor finishes his examination, he comes downstairs to talk to Albert and R.C. He's almost whispering, so I move closer to listen from the door to the hallway.

"Well, it seems he's had another attack, but this one's much more serious. We need to move him to his bed, then I'll call in a nurse. He's going to need 24-hour care."

Albert asks, "Is he going to recover?"

"I don't know. This was a bad one. All we can do is to help him rest so he doesn't have another one. If he does, I don't know how much more his heart can take. He might recover, but it doesn't look good."

Crying, I run up the stairs to be with Mr. Murphy. I lay my head on his chest. It seems like a long time between each breath. The doctor makes a few phone calls, then the three men come up the stairs to move him into his bedroom.

"There, there, Dora. R.C. told me you were with him and that you got help right away. That's all anyone could do. I'm just sorry that you had to see this, a young girl like you."

"Oh, Albert, I really care for Mr. Murphy. He's all I have."

"I know. Why don't you go downstairs and make us a pot of tea?"

I hear them talking and grunting as they move him, "He's a big man. The nurse can get him in night clothes to make him comfortable."

The four of us are drinking tea when the doorbell cranks. I run to the door - it's a lady wearing a nurse's cap. I take her coat.

Doc Nelson introduces her to Albert and me. "Dora, this is Miss. Havermale. Maude will be Murphy's night nurse and her sister, Mattie Havermale will be the day nurse. You've met her before. Maude, this is Dora. She lives here." He turns to me, "Where is Ruby?"

"She went out with her friends."

"You mean you were here alone with Murphy?"

"Yes, sir."

"When will she be back?"

"I don't know. Sometimes she doesn't come home 'til the next morning."

"W.D., I'm just across the street, but I'll stay here tonight in case I'm needed."

"That's good, R.C. I'll be back in the morning. I'm going to call in Coleman and Schoeles for consultation. They're heart specialists. I don't know if they will come with me in the morning, or if they will come later this evening. You should help Dora notify the rest of his family. Call me if you need me. Day or night."

I make up a bed for R.C. in the room down the hall next to Mr. Murphy's room, and then I go downstairs to call Anna. When Harold answers the phone, I start to cry and can't get words out, so R.C. takes over.

"Who is this?" Harold asks, uncertain what to do.

"Oh, Harold, is your father there?" When John comes to the phone, R.C. tells him about Mr. Murphy. I sniffle next to him. "Yes, Dora is all right, but she's very upset.... No, it doesn't look good, I'm afraid. He's resting now."

"Will John and Anna come over?" I can't help myself. I need to see them.

"Yes, Dora! They're coming tomorrow morning!" He hugs my shoulders and turns back to the phone. "She's fine, John. Yes, she's all right. I'll stay with her until Ruby gets home. We'll see you tomorrow."

R.C. and I try to wait up for Ruby, but at midnight we give up and I go to bed.

Christmas Day, December 25, 1906 — Dear Diary, I was here alone with Mr. Murphy when he had another attack. I was so scared. Doc Nelson said this one is much worse than the one last week. I can't believe Ruby went out with her friends on Christmas Day when he is so sick! I should have stood up to her. Mr. Murphy may not make it. He is so big, and when he fell, I couldn't get him up. I had to leave him alone and run to R.C. for help. This is my life. It's awful! I never knew I could work so hard or feel so bad, living in a nice, big house, with my own room and nice clothes, but it's really not my house, it's Mr. Murphy's house. What will happen to me if he dies? I don't want to go back to the orphanage; I want to stay here near Rex! I put on the heart necklace he gave me yesterday. It's so pretty! I'll wear it always - even when I'm cleaning! But all the other girls like him, too, and I am probably going to have to leave school. Oh, I don't know! But it felt good when Rex held my hand under the lap blanket. His hand was warm, and it made me feel safe. I wish I was a normal girl, like the ones in Rex's class. Anna and John are coming here in the morning. I hope they bring Rex with them. If not, I'll go see him. We need to talk. Signed, Dora Kelly

I close my diary and decide to lay back on my pillows just for a minute before I put on my nightdress. The next thing I know, the sun is shining in my face. I smile and stretch, then I remember what happened last night.

I put on a play dress and hurry to the bathroom. I'm hungry and I want to see if Ruby came home. Her bed hasn't been slept in, so she didn't come home last night.

I go downstairs and stir up some biscuits and while they are baking, I fry up some ham and boil some eggs. It feels good to keep busy.

R.C. comes down the stairs, "I could use some coffee. Is that ham I'm smelling?"

We hear a woman's footsteps; Miss Havermale has her bag, and she comes to the kitchen.

"Miss Havermale, I made breakfast. Would you like to join us?"

"No, thank you. Mattie will be here in a few minutes, then I will go home so I can get some sleep. I left some notes for the doctor on the table beside Mr. Murphy's bed. I gave him the drops the doctor ordered, so he's resting."

The doorbell cranks and rings. Miss Havermale goes to the front door to let her sister in. They talk in whispers for a few minutes, then Nurse Mattie comes in.

She pokes her head into the kitchen. "I'll just go upstairs. I know where to hang my coat."

R.C. and I look at one another. "I guess they're professional, just not too friendly."

I shrug my shoulders. "Wonder where Ruby is."

"Does she do this a lot?"

"More and more. Sometimes her boyfriend, Jim, comes here during the day, too, when Mr. Murphy isn't here."

R.C. shakes his head, but says nothing.

We are just finishing breakfast when the doorbell cranks and rings again. I go to the front door, but John and Anna have already let themselves in. I run to Anna, and she holds me close.

"Oh, Dora, I'm sorry you had to go through all this. What can we do? How is he?"

R.C. pats my head. "The nurse gave him some drops that the doctor ordered. He's still asleep. The doctors should be here soon. Dora made coffee. Can I pour you a cup?"

"That would be nice, R.C. I take mine with cream and sugar. John likes his black. I'll just go upstairs for a minute to look in on Joseph."

Anna goes upstairs and we hear her talking to the nurse, but she quickly comes back downstairs to the kitchen.

"She said the doctor told her, no visitors. I told her I'm not a visitor, that I'm his cousin, but she still turned me away. I'll talk to the doctor about that!"

R.C. sits down at the kitchen table to drink his third cup of coffee. "I understand why you're upset but sit down and try to relax. We'll get this straightened out when W.D. gets here."

Anna takes a sip, and she looks around, "Where's Ruby?"

R.C. glances at me, "She didn't come home last night."

"She left Dora alone with a sick man?"

I can tell that Anna is angry, but I just keep quiet and drink my coffee. I say quietly, "Looks like I should put on another pot."

"Good idea. It's probably going to be a long day."

I fill the coffeepot and excuse myself to go to the bathroom. When I come out, I hear loud voices, so I sneak down the stairs to see what it's all about.

Ruby, Anna, John and R.C. are in the kitchen talking and yelling all at the same time. Ruby is still in her party dress. She probably thought she could sneak into her room, and no one would notice.

I've never heard John raise his voice before, "Where the hell have you been?"

Anna steps in. "That, and what kind of person are you, leaving a young girl alone on Christmas Day with a sick man?"

Ruby looks surprised. "I just went to a party! What happened?"

I watch as R.C. explains, all over again, about Mr. Murphy's attack. "You went to a party even though you knew he was very ill. And you stayed out all night? I wish he was well enough to reprimand you, and I know he would!"

"I'm sorry he had another attack, but I was out with my friends. I'm entitled to have my own life."

John looks disgusted. "You should be ashamed of yourself. You and that farmer have already made one baby. I suppose you're working on another. Either you didn't learn from your mistake, or you just don't care what anyone thinks of you."

"I'm a grown woman, I don't have to answer to you or anyone else."

"Is that what your friends tell you? You can't shirk your responsibilities, Ruby. As long as you live here, you need to be sure that Dora and Joseph are well cared for. Dora is a young girl. She was alone with Joseph when he fell ill. Doesn't that bother you?"

"I'm not going to be locked up in this house like a slave."

Anna intercedes, "Oh, come on, Ruby. We know everything. Dora missed school because she had to take care of you and Joseph. She did your work even though you had recovered."

"Who told you that?"

"No one told me, I saw it with my own eyes when I came by to bring food and help Dora. Joseph told me how much you shamed him. Don't you care how your behavior made him feel, after all he has done for you?"

"My pregnancy was my business."

R.C. ends the argument, "You're wrong, Ruby. You made it everyone's business. Like Anna said, Dora had to miss school and she went back a grade, and all of us were involved in keeping your secret, making sure you did not cast a shadow on Uncle Joe and this house. It was very painful for Uncle Joe."

I finally find the courage to speak. "Ruby, you should go to your room and change."

"I will. I assume the doctor will be here sometime this morning."

Anna still looks angry. "W.D. called in two other doctors for consultation. It's that serious. John and I came early so we can be here when they come. Oh, by the way, there's a nurse upstairs and she won't let anyone in his room to see him. Take off that party dress, and make yourself presentable. Maybe you should clean up the kitchen before the doctors get here, and make more coffee."

Ruby slips into her room without saying anything, but I can see that she is just pretending to agree.

Doc Nelson arrives with the two specialists, and they go directly upstairs to Mr. Murphy's room. R.C. says they went into the room and closed the door so he couldn't see in.

The doctors come downstairs and start to leave without saying anything, but Anna stops Dr. Nelson. "Doctor, what can you tell us? I'm Anna Moss, Joseph's cousin, and you know my husband, John."

"There's not much to tell. We want him to rest because we don't want him to have another attack. He opened his eyes, but he isn't talking. I've prescribed some drops, so he will sleep most of the time."

"When can we see him? Why won't the nurse let us visit him?"

Doc Nelson looks stern. "I consulted with Dr. Coleman, and he confirmed my instructions to the nurse, not to allow visitors."

John tries to intercede, "But this is family and we are the people who care about him. Why are nurses, strangers, the only ones allowed in? It's hard to understand why those closest to him can't see him, if only for a few minutes."

"Those are my instructions, and all three of us agree."

The doctors leave and R.C. goes home as well. He looks tired.

John walks R.C. to the door. "Thank you for being a good neighbor and a good friend. We will talk to Albert to see what he can do."

When Albert arrives, he goes directly to Mr. Murphy's room. He's been up there a long time, so the nurse must have let him in. Maybe he will have some good news when he comes downstairs.

We hear the bedroom door close. Albert comes down the stairs with his coat on. He doesn't stop to talk to us, he just keeps walking, looking down at the floor, and he slams the front door on his way out.

Anna snorts, "Well! How do you like that? If he thinks he can get past me, he's wrong. We'll just go to his office. Dora, we're going to leave now that Ruby's here. I want to see if we can find Albert. He needs to tell us what's going on."

I go to my room, leaving Ruby in the kitchen to do the dishes.

Two O'Clock in the Morning

January 7, 1907.

I wake up to doors opening and closing on the second floor. Yesterday was crazy, with people in and out. Neighbors and even some of Mr. Murphy's clients stopped by to see him. Some brought flowers and one man brought a bottle of Port, but Nurse Havermale turned everyone away. I wanted to get up before sunrise this morning so I could get the house in order before more people stopped by, but I must have been more tired than I thought.

Then I realize, today's the seventh! My birthday! I'm 13! No one's said anything. That's okay, I wouldn't want a party anyway. It would be nice to see Rex, though. Mr. Murphy would want me to have a birthday. It's my birthday, so I'm going to do what I want. I'm going to see Mr. Murphy.

I decide to wear the blue play dress (Mr. Murphy's favorite) and white stockings – no shoes. I sit in the shadows on the top stair outside my room and wait. After a while I get bored, so I start to get up to find a book, when I hear the door open. I lean down just enough to see Nurse Havermale leave his room. She's a big lady and she wears ugly shoes, probably with hollow heels, because her footsteps clunk when she walks to the bathroom.

When she closes the door, I sneak down the stairs into Mr. Murphy's room. The blue/green shade of the Tiffany lamp on his bedside table make Mr. Murphy's face and white beard look green, making him look like he's dead, except his chest is moving so I know he's breathing. His eyes are closed so I lean down and whisper in his ear, "Mr. Murphy, it's me, Dora. I've missed you. I came to see you."

I jump back, surprised, when his eyes open. He tries to talk, but he's too weak. "It's okay, you don't have to talk. I'll just sit with you and hold your hand. I might have to leave, though, 'cuz I'm not supposed to be here."

I pull a chair next to his bed, and I take his hand. It's so cold! I try to warm his hand, holding it between my hands, but my hands are too small to make a difference. He starts to smile, then he is startled, trying to call out when the nurse grabs me by my shoulders, yanking me out of the chair.

She's yelling, "You were warned. You can't come in here!"

"I just wanted to see him for a few minutes. I care for Mr. Murphy. You're just a nurse!"

She slaps me so hard that I fall to the floor.

"Now, get out of here, and don't try to come back. I'm going to tell Taff that you're not to be trusted. You're a sneak!"

Between my sobs, "I'd rather be a sneak than a mean old witch! You go ahead and tell Albert. I'm going to tell everyone how you treated me!"

I go downstairs to the kitchen. I stop by the mirror in the hallway and see my face is starting to swell where she hit me. Maybe I'll get a black eye. If I do, maybe they will fire her.

Ruby is making breakfast and she looks at my face, but she doesn't say anything when I go to my chair. "Thank you for making breakfast, Ruby. I'll just have tea and biscuits this morning."

"I decided to make breakfast since it's your birthday."

"I didn't think anyone remembered."

"I remembered, but there's not much to celebrate around here." I eat my breakfast in silence.

Ruby is cleaning the biscuit flour from the end of the table, and I'm just about done washing dishes, when the doorbell cranks and rings. I dry my hands and go to the door expecting Doc Nelson, but Rex standing outside the door, shifting from one foot to another because it's so cold. I open the door to let him in and Anna is right behind him on the porch.

"Happy Birthday, Dora, I brought you a present."

I thank him and put the gift on the ottoman, so I can take their coats.

"Dora Belle! What happened to you?"

I put my hand up to my face, and I look down, embarrassed.

"Who did that to you? Look, Rex, her face is swollen!"

I start to cry, and I tell them what happened. "It's my fault. I should have listened, but I wanted to see Mr. Murphy. She called me a sneak. But I had to sneak to see him."

Rex laughs, "Good for you!"

Anna charges into the kitchen to confront Ruby. "Did she tell you what happened?"

"No. I figured it wasn't my concern."

"You can't be serious! She's just a girl. She wanted to see Joseph because she cares about him. Is it wrong to care about someone who's taken care of you? You need to stick up for her and look after her."

"I heard some yelling, so I figured something happened, but I was in the middle of cutting biscuits."

"Ruby, you're an adult. Don't let that nurse or anyone else be mean to her, and don't you dare be mean to her. Any more incidents and you'll have to deal with me. Do you understand?"

"But...."

"No buts, and no excuses. Do you understand?"

"Yes, ma'am."

"I'll have some tea. I'll be here for a while."

Anna sits down at the kitchen table and Ruby pours a cup of tea. Rex and I sit on the sofa in the parlor. I open his gift, knowing it will be the only one I'll receive today.

"It's not much. Mother always says big things come in small packages.

That's why I like you, Dora. You're small but special."

There's a bracelet locket inside a tiny box, with a single charm, a gold four-leafed clover.

"Oh, Rex, it's so pretty. You know I like four-leafed clovers."

He helps me put the bracelet on.

"I know. You can find them like no one else. Maybe this one will bring good luck. Dora, your face is really swelling. Does it hurt?"

"A little."

"Let's ask Mother if there's anything you can do to stop it from getting worse."

We go to the kitchen I assume to talk to Anna. I stop by her chair, but Rex continues to walk through the door leading to the stairs.

"Walter Rex Moss! Where do you think you are going! Get back here."

"I was just going to the bathroom."

"You stay down here! We'll wait for the doctor, so I can talk to him. He's the one to set the nurses straight. I'll show him what she did to Dora."

We sit in silence at the kitchen table, waiting. The only sound is the ticking of the grandfather clock that chimes on the hour and half hour. Finally, at half past three the doorbell cranks and rings. Anna goes to the door to let three doctors in. Anna stops Dr. Nelson at the foot of the stairs. I can only hear parts of what she is saying, but she's shaking her finger in his face, and I can tell she's talking very fast.

"Now, now, Mrs. Moss. I see she's getting a black eye, but I'm sure Nurse Havermale has a reasonable explanation. Let me talk to her."

He joins the other doctors upstairs. After a while, Dr. Coleman comes to the head of the stairs, "Miss O'Grady, would you please come up here?"

Ruby goes upstairs. I look up and they are standing on the landing, talking, then they go to Mr. Murphy's room, and they shut the door.

Anna is standing behind me, "Well, what do you think of that?"

There's nothing to say so I just go back to the kitchen. They are up there a long time. Eventually, they come down and the doctors start to leave. Anna catches Doc Nelson by the arm. He stops long enough to tell her that Ruby will talk to us.

We all gather around the kitchen table.

"Well, they've left me in charge. I'm to decide who can or cannot see Uncle Joe, but just so you know, Dr. Coleman gave me instructions not to let anyone in his room."

"That's shocking! Who are you to be in charge?"

John intercedes, "Anna, let me handle this. Ruby, you know that Anna is Joseph's closest family member, so I'm sure she will be allowed daily visits if only for a few minutes."

"No. No one will be allowed in. You know it wouldn't make any difference, don't you? They are giving him drops so he sleeps most of the time. If I do let you in, he won't even know you're there."

"That's not true! He opened his eyes when he heard my voice. After she slapped me, I looked back and there was a tear running down his face, so he knew what was going on."

"Did they say anything to the nurse about Dora?"

"They just said I'm in charge. I'll make sure Dora stays out, so he won't be disturbed."

It's so confusing. "But that's not fair. I can't believe you are in charge. Mr. Murphy knows how you treat me, so he wouldn't pick you to be in charge. Anna is family, she should be in charge."

"Obviously, I'm the adult living here, so I'm the best person to be in charge. You're just another kid he took in, nothing special, so what makes you think he would be concerned about you?"

"Dora, she's wrong! Joseph loved you. You made such a difference in his life."

"Really? Did he say that?" Ruby scoffs. "I never heard him say that."

"Anna, get your coat. We're going home. Dora, we will see you tomorrow. Call us if you need us and, Ruby, you make sure that Dora is safe. It's your job to take care of her."

I go outside to get Rex, and he says, "I'm so sorry, Dora." And he kisses me on my cheek. "Happy Birthday!"

January 7, 1907 – Dear Diary, I turned 13 today but no one remembered, except Rex. Ruby didn't do anything special. Rex gave me a charm bracelet with a four-leafed clover. And he kissed me on the cheek! I really like him, and he likes me too. Except for that it was a terrible day. I sneaked into Mr. Murphy's room this morning. He woke up, so he knew I was there. Nurse Havermale slapped me so hard I fell down. No one has ever hit me like that! Anna was really angry when she saw my face. But no one did anything, and they put Ruby in charge instead of Anna, so there's nothing anyone can do. Miss Fancy Pants said she will keep everyone out of his room. Poor Anna. Ruby doesn't care about anyone except herself. Happy Birthday to me! It's such a pretty bracelet, though. I hope I can see Rex again soon. Signed, Dora Kelly.

January 8, 1907

Nurse Havermale yells down the stairs, "Ruby, Ruby! Call the doctor!"

I jump down from my bed and run down the stairs to the nurse who is standing on the landing. "Nurse, what's wrong?"

"I don't know. Go downstairs and make sure she heard me."

Ruby is already on the phone when I reach the kitchen. "I don't know. She just said to call you. I think she wants you to come."

She hangs up the phone and we both head up the stairs. The nurse is wiping Mr. Murphy's face with a damp cloth. His eyes are closed and he's hardly breathing. When he does breathe, we can count the seconds between each breath.

"Doc Nelson is on his way. What do you want us to do?"

"Nothing for now. You should get dressed as people will be coming, doctors and such."

"I'm going to call Anna."

"Oh, Dora, not now. The last thing I need is for Mrs. Busy Body to stick her nose in."

"But she's family. I don't care, I'm going to call her."

John answers the phone, and promises they will get dressed and be here as soon as they can, so I go to my room to get dressed.

The doctors arrive and they go directly upstairs. When I come down from my room, I can see them leaning over Mr. Murphy. They come out of the room and stand on the landing to talk in whispers to Ruby. I can only hear bits and pieces, "Taff..." "sisters...." "it's time..."

The doctors go back to Mr. Murphy's room to talk to the nurse, and Ruby comes downstairs. She goes to the phone to call Albert.

After she hangs up the phone, "He wasn't too happy. I guess I woke him up. Too bad!"

When Albert arrives, again, all I hear are whispers. Anna and John are at the kitchen door. I run to let them in. Anna gives me a hug.

"You seem to be all right. What's happened?"

Ruby answers, "They say he's slipped into a coma, that he probably won't come out. I think it's those drops."

"What drops?"

"They give him laudanum so he will rest. That started right after his first attack, but there's been no sense talking to him the last few days. They told me to call Albert. You need to call Louisa."

"Yes. I guess it's that bad. I'll call his sisters. It will take them a few days to get here. Can I see him?"

"No. they want him to rest."

"I won't disturb him. Besides, if he's in a coma....." Anna starts up the stairs, determined.

"No! They told me no visitors!"

We hear footsteps and look up to see Jim coming out of Ruby's room. "Ruby, if I can just have a cup of coffee, I'll be on my way."

John's mouth drops, "Well I'll be! Ruby, was he here with you all night?"

"That's not your business."

"It sure as hell is! Of course, we are concerned about Joseph, but we are also concerned about Dora, her safety and the sanctity of this home. Joseph would be outraged!"

Anna agrees, "This is still the Murphy house. It's not your house."

"But I'm in charge, so I guess I can do what I want. There's nothing you can do about it."

Albert is standing at the kitchen door, "She's right. Ruby's in charge. Dora's old enough to take care of herself. Unless the nurse calls sooner, we will be back this evening."

It's Sunday night, and there's been no time to rest the last few days. People have been in and out, neighbors stopping by some with food. Everyone seems to know that Mr. Murphy is dying.

Albert and the doctors come every night at eight. Jim is here every night, too, gradually taking over. He stays the night, and Ruby fixes him a big breakfast every morning before he leaves.

I try to talk to the doctors, but I only come out of my room now when Anna is here. I cry a lot. When the doctors come, I listen at my door. Tonight, I hear Doc Coleman telling the nurse not to give Mr. Murphy his drops, so they can talk to him. Then around 10, I wake up when Albert calls Ruby to the upstairs guest room for a meeting with the doctors.

I try to sneak closer to listen, but Doc Coleman yells at me. I hide in the linen closet in the hall, though, and hear them all going in around midnight. "Well, boys, I have him all set up and ready to go!" says Doc Coleman. I don't know what that means. I'm sleepy, but I stay awake anyway.

2:00 a.m., Monday, January 14, 1907

After an hour, I go to sit on the top step, where I can hear better. They leave the door ajar, and don't realize it. Mr. Murphy wakes up and says, "Who's there?"

"It's me, Uncle Joe, Albert."

Murphy talks in a whisper, "Oh, it's you. Who are all these people?"

"You know who they are. See, Nurse Havermale, and Ruby and your doctors are here."

"Oh." He closes his eyes.

Albert shakes him, "Wake up, Uncle Joe, just for a few minutes. You need to sign this for me. "

"What is it?"

"You know, we talked about it."

"We did?"

"Just sign here and I'll take care of everything. You can just sleep and get well."

Murphy takes the paper and he scribbles something on the bottom. I wonder what it is. I run to hide quickly. Dr. Coleman nods to the nurse and they all leave the room. Outside the door, on the landing, they seem happy, laughing and talking as they walk down the stairs.

"Nurse, Ruby, again, no visitors, especially now. Good night, everyone, I'm going home to get some sleep."

Tuesday, January 15.

Ruby and Jim are eating breakfast when I come downstairs. "Help yourself, Dora. We already ate. You have to clean the house today. Uncle Joe's sister is coming."

I thought I'd go to school. I'm getting behind."

"No school today. I need you here."

"Oh, I get it. You need me when there's work to do. I'll do it for Mr. Murphy and his sister, but I won't do anything for you."

"Just shut up and clean the house and make up the guest room for Louisa. You know where to find the linens."

January 15, 1907 — Dear Diary, It took me two days to clean the house and get it ready for Mr. Murphy's sister. She's coming tomorrow. Ruby did nothing except sit around with Jim and order me around. She just flits around the doctors like she's a queen. I haven't been to school since Mr. Murphy fell ill, so I'm getting further and further behind. That farmer, Jim Kucharek, is here every night and most of the days now. Sometimes I see them smooching when they think I'm not looking. Anna says they're on their way to making another baby. I didn't know you can get pregnant with a kiss on the lips. I won't let Rex kiss me again. Anyway, it looks like I'll never get back to school, and maybe never see him again, because Mr. Murphy is dying. Everyone is sneaking around, and no one has told me what will happen to me. Most likely they will send me back to the orphanage. I don't want to leave Canton. I want to live near Rex. As bad as life is, I feel safe when he's around. Maybe I can talk to Louisa. Maybe she'll help me. Anna said she will talk to her, too. Maybe Louisa will kick Ruby out and move in. Maybe I can go back to school. I am so tired! Signed, Dora Kelly

Mr. Murphy's sister comes, and she looks a little like him. But she doesn't have the twinkle in her eye that he used to have. I wear my best play dress to make a good impression.

"Hello, Dora. Joseph told us all about you. I can see why he loves you so much. You are a sweet little girl."

"Nice to meet you, Miss Murphy."

"Oh, call me Louisa. After all, we're family. Now, I think I'll put my things in my room, then I'll check in on my brother."

I go with her to show her to her room, then I watch as she crosses towards Mr. Murphy's bedroom. Ruby is standing in front of the door. "Miss Murphy, he's not allowed visitors."

"Ruby, get out of my way. You'll not keep me from seeing my brother. I don't know who left you in charge, but now that I'm here, I'm the mistress of this house. Now go to the kitchen and start supper. It's been a long trip, and I'm hungry."

Louisa pushes Ruby aside and she charges into the room to see her brother. Nurse Havermale is leaning over Mr. Murphy and she looks startled when the door flies open. "Who are you? He can't have visitors."

"And who are you? I assume you're his nurse, but what's your name?"

"My name is Mattie Havermale. My sister, Maude, is the nurse at night."

"Well, Mattie, you can have the rest of the day off. I'll be here when your sister comes."

"Are you a trained nurse?"

"No, I'm his sister, but I can take care of him for a few hours."

Louisa goes to Mr. Murphy. His eyes are closed, "Oh, Joseph, what are they doing to you?"

His eyes open, but they are glassy. It seems he doesn't recognize her. Louisa leaves the room to talk to the nurse.

"What medications are you giving him?"

"You will have to ask the doctor. I just give him drops so he can rest."

"He's not resting. He's drugged! I'm his sister and he doesn't even know who I am!"

The nurse goes back to Mr. Murphy's room, and Louisa goes down to the kitchen to talk to Ruby. Ruby and Jim are so wrapped up in one another, they don't hear her coming.

"You stop that! I will not stand for you carrying on in my brother's house! There's a young girl living here. Have you no shame? You, what's your name? You get out of here. You're not welcome anymore."

I hear Ruby talking. "Jim, you'd better go for now."

"Not just for now," Louisa says. "Ruby, start supper and you best make enough for both Dora and me. Now, Dora," she turns to me. "I haven't seen your room. Why don't you show me?"

We climb the stairs, talking on the way.

"Anna has told me all about you, that Ruby mistreats you, and how you have taken care of Joseph and the house. Such a big job for such a little girl."

"I didn't mind. Mr. Murphy's been good to me. The only bad part is I missed school so I had to go back a grade. Ruby leaves the work for to me, so I can't go to school."

I push the door open to my room. "Dora, such a pretty room and you keep it so nice. I love the canopied bed, and everything is arranged perfectly. Tell me all about your dolls and the dollhouse."

"Mr. Murphy gave me everything. I had nothing when I came. Well, the China dolls were here when I came."

"I remember them. They belonged to our mother. I'm glad you are taking such good care of them. Dora, I know you have been through a lot. Tell me everything."

We spend the next two hours talking. I tell her about my brothers and how the men charged into our bedroom while we were sleeping to take us away. I tell her about the fun I've had with Rex and Harold, and about my best friend, Annie Rose, moving away, and I tell her how much I care for Anna and John. Then I tell her about the baby and how Ruby treats me.

"Anna told me that the nurse slapped you and Ruby said nothing."

"Yes, Ma'am."

"Well, there will be some changes around here. I'm going to check on Joseph, then I'll ask R.C. if he will take me to Anna's house. I'll be back in time for supper. I want to be here when the doctors come."

Louisa returns and we have a quiet supper without the farmer, and one I didn't have to cook, for a change. Louisa greets the three doctors at the door when they arrive promptly at eight. They don't seem to object when she follows them to Mr. Murphy's room.

She returns to the kitchen with W.D. "W.D., it's nice to see you again, but we have to protect Joseph and Dora, now. Dora, the nurse that slapped you. Was that Mattie Havermale, the day nurse?"

"Yes, ma'am."

"W.D., she is to be dismissed. Also, I don't believe it is proper to have a woman as night nurse. If you decide to keep Maude, you can switch her to days, but I want a male nurse at night."

Doc Nelson looks surprised. "Oh, Louisa, I don't believe that is necessary. We had a nice talk with Mattie."

"It's not negotiable. She's not to be trusted. Also, what medications are you giving him? He didn't even know me."

"After his first attack, he went to the office and exhausted himself, so we have been sedating him so he will rest."

"I wouldn't call it resting. He's drugged out of his mind! Another thing, why are you keeping Anna and Dora from seeing him?"

"Louisa, he needs to rest."

"You will no longer shield him from his family! I want a male nurse to start immediately."

"Tonight?"

"Tonight!"

We are in our night clothes when the doorbell cranks and rings. I follow Louisa to the door.

"Hello, I'm William Ferguson, the new night nurse. Can you show me to the patient's room?"

Louisa escorts him to Mr. Murphy's bedroom. I can hear them talking, then Maude Havermale leaves, looking angry. I am so happy to see her go!

Fallen Hero

January 23, 1907 — Dear Diary. I haven't had time to talk to you, it's been crazy around here. Louisa only stayed three days. She only stirred things up, though. Anna and I went with her to Mr. Murphy's room before she left. It was so sad - we just cried and hugged one another. I really like her. She stood up for me, but now that she's gone, it's the same old thing. Dora, do this, Dora, do that! Ruby and Jim ate all of the leftovers that I had planned for supper last night and they didn't save any for me, so I had to find something else to eat. I couldn't believe it! All I do is cook and clean. Now, Ruby's in her room with Jim again. He's been staying all night and I have to make breakfast for him in the morning before he goes out to his farm, or wherever he goes during the day. One time, when Ruby and the nurses were distracted, I sneaked into Mr. Murphy's room again. He didn't open his eyes this time. I stayed a few minutes, counting his breaths. At times, it was so long between them I wondered if he was dead. Nurse Ferguson caught me, but he's nicer than the Havermale sisters. He said he was sorry, but the doctors want Mr. Murphy to rest. Seems that's all he does! Anna came by today and she promised she would come for me every day to go to their house for dinner, then we will come back here in time to see Albert and the doctors. That will be good. I feel comfortable at their house, and I will get to see Rex. Signed, Dora.

January 24, 1907.

I make breakfast and clean up the kitchen, then I go up to my room to get ready to go to Anna's. When I get downstairs at nine, R.C. is already waiting for me in his carriage. I take my coat off the coat hook in the hallway on the way to the kitchen door.

Ruby comes out of her room in her dressing gown. "Just where do you think you're going?

"Not that it's any of your business, I'm going to Anna's."

"Have you looked around the house? It needs to be cleaned!"

"I keep my room clean, and I cleaned the bathroom. You can do the rest."

Ruby follows me out the kitchen door. She grabs my arm.

"Take your hands off me! I hate you!" I pull away, R.C. stands between Ruby and me.

"R.C., let's go!"

Rex is waiting for me at their door. I start to cry when I see him. I tell him about the argument with Ruby, "She just wanted me to stay because the house needs cleaning. She let me go when R.C. stood up to her. What am I going to do? I don't know what will happen to me if Mr. Murphy dies. I feel like running away but I don't want to leave Canton. I want to be near you and your family. "

"Don't worry. I'm sure my mother will take you in. Dora, I will always take care of you."

"How can you do that? You're just a kid, like me! Besides, you don't have a job."

"Don't cry, kid. I hate it when you cry." Rex takes my head between his hands, and he kisses me on the forehead. He gives me a big hug. He is so gentle, and I feel so safe when I am with him. Anyway, I know they'll send me away soon. I will just enjoy whatever time I have with him and Anna and John and Harold. After all, we're just kids, and I know I can only stay for a little while.

But for a minute, I feel better, and Rex gives me a wink and we just hold hands and look at one another. Harold comes from the kitchen, "Hey, you two, better not let Mother and Father see you doing that!"

January 24, 1907 — Dear Diary, I had a chance to talk to Rex today. I told him everything. I don't know what will happen to me if Mr. Murphy dies. I can't stay here if that Jim Kucharek moves in, but I have nowhere else to go. I want to stay in Canton, but what if they send me away without telling Anna. I wish Annie Rose was here. Her mama is nice. She would probably help. Anyway, I can't count on Annie Rose, she's in Wisconsin. Maybe, if Mr. Murphy dies, I'll look for Jack. He might be living with some rich people who will take me in. Then we can look for Louis. I wonder if we could live on Mr. Murphy's farm. I've been taking care of this house. I'll get a job. I know how to cook and clean. We'll find Louis and we will be together again. We'll get by just like we did before. We would have to live on the farm, though. I don't want to leave Rex behind. I pretend that everything will be all right. I pray that Mr. Murphy will wake up tomorrow, and everything will go back to normal. Signed, Dora Kelly

January 25, 1907

It must be morning, but it's dark. I lift my head and realize I must have crawled under the covers to the bottom of my bed. I fight my way out from under the covers. It's a dreary day. The rain mixed with snow sounds like tiny pebbles are hitting my window. Everyone must be sleeping because the house is quiet. I slip out of my bed to go to the bathroom. The house is cold, so I run to the toilet.

I start down the hall to return to my room in time to see the shadow of a large man in a flowing gown, Mr. Murphy is standing on the landing. Maybe my prayers have come true! Nurse Ferguson comes out of the bedroom and takes him by the hand, "Come, Mr. Murphy, let's get you back to bed." He turns to me, "Sorry, Miss, I must have dozed off."

I take Mr. Murphy's other hand to lead him back to bed, "Mr. Murphy, how did you get out of bed by yourself?"

"Looking for Catherine. Need to find Catherine."

I shrug my shoulders at the nurse. I don't know any Catherine. As I come out of the room, a chill sweeps across my shoulders and down my back, and I have a sense of hopelessness that is hard to explain. Someone is watching me! I look up and there's a barn owl perched on a limb outside the window. It has a ghastly pale face, and it casts a shadow on the outside wall of the house. It doesn't make a sound.

I'd better call Anna to let her know he's awake!

Ruby hears me when I go to the phone. "Anna, you won't believe it! He's awake. He was standing on the landing. We put him back to bed."

"Okay, I'll call the doctor. Have tea and coffee ready."

I hang up and Ruby makes a call, "Albert, you'd better get over here. Something's happening. He's awake and walking around."

Jim comes out of the bedroom, "What now?"

"Uncle Joe is awake, and he got out of bed. Anna and Albert are on their way."

"Doc Nelson, too. Anna is going to call him."

R.C. is walking into the kitchen in time to hear Jim yelling, "I'm sick and tired of people coming in and out of here all times of the day and night. We're entitled to some privacy. Why doesn't he just die?"

R.C. explodes, "You're not entitled to anything! This is not your house. What a terrible thing to say. Ruby, is this the person you want to marry? Really?"

Ruby just holds on to Jim's arm and looks at the floor.

The doorbell clangs and rings. I go to the door to let Maude Havermale in; Doc Nelson and Albert are right behind. The two nurses talk a few minutes in the parlor before Nurse Ferguson leaves.

Nurse Havermale goes upstairs to attend to her duties. Her cries echo off the wood walls of the stairway, "Oh, No! Doctor! Doctor, come quick!"

Manky!

I stay in my room until they take Mr. Murphy away right before noon. When I come downstairs, the dooryard is already full of carriages and buggies. People have been in and out of the house all day, some I know but many I've never met.

Anna and John come right away, and Rex comes right after school. Some people are bringing food, so Anna made it my job to put it all away. I have to move things around to make room for a big ham in the Frigidaire, and Rex takes three loaves of warm bread from his mother, and he puts them in the pantry.

"I'm so glad your mother is here to take charge 'cuz Ruby is just standing around. I think she's forgotten how to be helpful."

"Mother will set her straight. I'm hungry. Let's see if we can find something to eat."

Anna is standing in the parlor talking to some ladies. She sees us waiting to get her attention.

"Yes, dear, do you need something?"

I stand on my tiptoes to whisper in her ear, "We're getting hungry."

"Of course, it's almost supper time. Ruby, pull yourself together! Make some sandwiches and coffee for our supper."

Ruby talks to herself while she is slicing the ham on a cutting board. I try to help her with the sandwiches, but she shoo's me away. "Get away from me, Princess."

"I was just trying to help."

"I don't need your help. You just run along and talk to your boyfriend."

I look at Rex and shrug my shoulders. He takes a sandwich off the plate, and we go sit on the stairs to share it.

"How you doin', kid? Lots of people here. Ruby seems to be her cheerful self."

"Ruby is Ruby. The only time she's happy is when the farmer is here. Now that Mr. Murphy is gone, I bet he'll just move in."

Anna comes to the stairs and asks me to follow her to Mr. Murphy's room. Unlike the other night when I was here, the room feels warm and it smells fresh and clean. Maude must have changed the bed linens before she left. There's a sky-blue quilt on the bed. I recognize some of the squares, made from Mr. Murphy's old dress shirts, and white flannel nightshirts. I touch the hem of the quilt, and for a brief moment, I remember the time I sat next to him, and he showed me the picture book of Ireland.

"Poor Dora. I know you will miss him. Goodness, it's getting dark and gloomy in here. Let's turn on the lamp to shed some light."

"I like his room. Look, at the quilt, it's so pretty and look at the blue and green circles of light on the wall from the lamp shade. Anna, they wouldn't let me come to his room to see him. One time, when I was in this room, I had sneaked in to see him and I got in trouble. It was dark and gloomy then. His eyes were open, but he looked like he was dead. Isn't it strange that it's the same lamp that made Mr. Murphy look so dark and scary when he was dying, but today the light from the same lamp makes the room look pretty?"

"You're right, it is a nice room. I know he liked the color blue, like you do. Come now, I need your help. We need to gather some of his clothes so Albert can take them to the funeral home. Help me to choose one of his favorite shirts. Do you think he would want to wear a blue shirt?"

We open the door to his armoire, there's a small suitcase on the shelf. Anna opens a dresser drawer, and she finds some underwear and socks. We agree that he would want to wear his black suit and a pale blue dress shirt.

"One more important thing."

She opens all of the drawers until she finds what she's looking for. She carefully lays a black and gold Masonic bowtie, a lambskin Masonic apron and collar, and a box with a gold pin on top of the clothes, then she closes the suitcase. "There, just like he'd want it! I'll take these things to Albert. You know, in all the confusion, we forgot to call Louisa. I'll ask John to call her."

We go downstairs, and run into Rex on the landing, "Hey. I've been looking for you."

"We're done up here for now. We had to get some clothes together for Albert to take to the funeral home. Here – why don't you take the suitcase down to Albert?"

"Okay, but R.C. brought the Canton paper. There's an article about Mr. Murphy. Thought you'd want to know."

Rex walks down the stairs ahead of us. "I found them. They were upstairs."

R.C. has a newspaper spread on the kitchen table. Look at this, Dora, it's in the newspaper already with his picture and everything.

Canton Daily Register Evening News, Friday, January 25, 1907

Joseph L. Murphy, Another Old and Prominent Citizen, Finished Life's Journey This Morning

Twice elected mayor, more than 40 years a member of the Fulton County Bar, born Mount Rock, Queen's County Ireland. Age 76. Mr. Murphy came to America with his parents when he was two years old...

"Wow, Albert, you never told me that he was mayor."

"Not only that. Uncle Joe was a very important man. He's well known throughout the state. He once ran for State's Attorney, and he only lost by a slim margin."

Ruby stands up and rolls her eyes. "I'm tired, so I'm going to bed. I hope people will stay away and leave us alone tomorrow."

Anna shakes her head. "What a mean-spirited thing to say. The reason they came is out of respect for Joseph. You should be proud that so many people care. Maybe you should go to bed. That way you can get up early to clean and get the house ready in case people do stop by."

"Don't think you can tell me what to do, Anna Moss. You've been ordering me around all day. I can think for myself."

"Of course, you can, but you don't do it very well. Your way of thinking got you in trouble, didn't it?"

John tries to intercede, "Now ladies, it's been a difficult day. There's no need to let emotions take over. This is not what Joseph would have wanted. Anna, Rex, it is getting late. Let's go home. R.C. thank you for everything. We'll be back tomorrow."

Albert stands. "I'm going as well. I have an appointment early tomorrow at the funeral home. Like John said, it's been a difficult day. Let's just try to get along."

Monday, January 28, 1907.

Louisa and her cousin, Margaret, have been staying in the guest room since they arrived on Saturday. We are all waiting with our coats on, for the coaches to take us to the church for the funeral. It's the first time I've seen R.C. all dressed up; he and Mary have Dickie and Beth in tow. Ruby hired Mattie Havermale to go with her to the funeral, because she says she's not feeling well. Her father and sister, who she says is our new maid even though I still do all the work, are supposed to meet us at the church. At least Jim has been staying away.

The church is packed with people standing in the back and on the side walls. An usher shows us to a pew in the front. We take our seats and settle in, Louisa, Margaret, Anna, Ruby, Albert, and I'm sitting right next to the aisle. John and the boys are sitting behind us, next to Albert's wife, R.C. and his family. Rex wiggles his fingers to wave at me, and I smile a little.

I miss Mr. Murphy. The house is not the same without him, and I was used to leaning against him when we went to church. Anna hands me a program. Mr. Murphy's photo is on the front; inside is the order of service. Anna was right, this is going to be a long one.

Pastor announces a call to worship, the organ swells and everyone stands. *Nearer My God to Thee....* I feel warm and I'm having a hard time breathing. I cover my face with the front of my dress to muffle my sobs. The song ends. I look up and Albert is walking to the front to give the eulogy. I put my head back down on my lap, just wanting this to be over.

Albert steps down and Pastor gives his sermon. I lean forward to look at Ruby. Her head is turned, like she's looking for someone. It could only be the farmer. Who else would she be looking for?

I put my head back down, but Anna takes my arm, pulling me to my feet. I look down so people can't see me crying. I can hear people singing, but I can't find my voice. Anna pulls me close which is some comfort. The music ends and there's the shuffling sound of everyone sitting down.

The organ is playing beautiful music. It sounds like Mozart. The program says it's Mozart's Masonic Funeral Music. I didn't know Mr. Murphy was a Mason until Anna and I gathered his things for the undertaker. I look at Mr. Murphy, looking so elegant in his picture with his Masonic collar and pin. My mind wanders so I'm not paying attention to what's being said. I decide to follow the rest of the program, so I know who's talking and what's happening.

The Worshipful Master recites the Sacred Roll, followed by a very long prayer.

"So mote it be."

The Master speaks in monotone as he recites the ritual. I cover my ears and put my head down in my lap when he mentions the messenger of death. I try to think of happy things. I wonder if Rex and Harold are as bored as I am. We'll talk later when we get back to the house.

Anna nudges my arm and whispers, "Sit up and look, Dora, this is an interesting part."

They are putting a lambskin on Mr. Murphy's casket. It says here, the lambskin is an emblem of innocence and the badge of a Freemason. Then they add an evergreen.

My favorite part is towards the end when the Master continues,

".....May the earliest buds of spring unfold their beauties over his resting place, and, in the bright morning of the world's resurrection, may his soul spring into newness of life and expand into immortal beauty in realms beyond the skies. Until then, dear friend and brother, until then – Farewell."

Mr. Murphy would like all this. Heaven must be a pretty place. I'm going to save the program, so I have this last passage. Anna and John have their eyes closed while the Chaplain is saying a closing prayer. The service ends.

"So mote it be."

It's finally over! I just want to go home. We are ushered out first. Ruby walks ahead of us supported by her father and Hattie Havermale. Then a lady cries out. Ruby has fallen to the floor. Hattie is fanning Ruby's face with her program. Anna whispers, "She looks like she's out cold!"

John says under his breath, "She's just putting on a show for the newsmen."

The rest of the congregation is leaving but everyone has to walk around the newspaper journalists who rush to Ruby's side with their notebooks. Mr.

O'Grady tells them that she will be fine, that she just needs sleep. Ruby is revived and she leaves in a carriage with Mattie, her father, and sister.

Anna had arranged for two carriages to take us back to our house. I'm glad that I'm riding with Anna and Rex. Louisa and her cousin, Margaret, are in the second carriage with Albert and his wife. R.C. brought his own coach.

Earlier, Ruby and I made a plate of sandwiches and some salads. I don't feel like eating, I just want to go to my room. Truth is, I don't feel like being nice and talking to everyone. Ruby puts on quite a show. She is telling everyone that she hired a maid, but she means her sister. I assume "the maid" will serve lunch but, no, she just plunks her butt in a chair at the table waiting to be served. Ruby is in her room talking to Jim, so Anna helps me to put out the food and pitchers of lemonade and tea. I fix my plate and sit on the bottom step with Rex and Harold.

I bump Rex's shoulder, "What did you think of the funeral?".

"Nice, but I agree with Harold, it was too long."

"Me too, but it would have meant a lot to Mr. Murphy, so I think it was worth it."

People are standing around eating and Louisa comes looking for me. "I can't say it enough, Dora, thank you for everything you have done for Joseph and for me. Margaret and I have appreciated your hospitality the last two days, but now that the funeral is over, it's obvious that Ruby plans to take over so I'm no longer comfortable staying here. We're going to gather our belongings and stay with the Conklins until we leave tomorrow evening. We'll see you in the morning, though, at the reading of the will." She gives me a big hug. "Dora, you are a sweet young girl and I'm sorry to leave you alone in this house with those two, but there's little I can do. I guess we'll know more after tomorrow."

Anna joins in, "Louisa, we understand. We'll be leaving too, as soon as everyone else leaves. Do you have transportation to get to the Conklins?"

"I asked R.C. to take us. If you don't mind, maybe you and John can pick us up in the morning so the only thing R.C. will need to worry about is getting Dora and himself to Albert's office."

"We don't mind. We'll pick you up at 8:45."

Louisa and R.C.'s departure signals the others, and soon everyone is gone. Ruby and I look at one another but neither of us has anything to say, so I go to my room. I'd planned to write in my diary tonight, but I'm too tired. Maybe tomorrow.

January 29, 1907

We are all gathered around a large table in Albert's office for the reading of the will. Albert has spectacles perched on the end of his nose, and he stands at the head of the table with a large stack of papers. His secretary is recording all of our names: Louisa Murphy, Anna Moss, John Moss, Margaret Murphy, Ruby O'Grady, Dora Kelly, R.C. Webster, Dr. Coleman and Dr. Nelson. Anna makes sure she is seated next to me. She leans over and whispers to Louisa, "Wonder why the doctors are here...."

"Ladies, gentlemen, I will be reading two documents to you this morning. A word of caution, I do not want any emotional outbursts. After the documents have been read, I will be happy to answer any questions that you might have.

The first document is the last will and testament of Joseph Leopold Murphy, dated January 14, 1907...."

I had planned to pay attention, but I start to wonder what Mr. Murphy would think about all this, the funeral and now, today, who will get his house, the farm, and his money.

Anna takes my hand and whispers in my ear, "Dora, it's important that you pay attention."

"Second – I hereby give, devise and bequeath to Dora Kelly, the girl now living with me, the sum of three thousand ($3,000) dollars, and I further recommend her to the care of Ruby O'Grady. Said amount to be held and used for her, the said Dora Kelly's benefit, as shall to my executor, hereinafter named seem meet...."

Oh, no! I have to live with Ruby? I look up at Anna and she nods her head in Albert's direction, reminding me to pay attention.

"We'll talk later."

"Fourth – I hereby give, devise and bequeath for the purpose of erecting and endowing of a hospital in the city of Canton, the sum of forty thousand

($40,000) dollars, the amount to be expended in the erection of a building, to be decided by the Physician's Club of the City of Canton. The difference between the said forty thousand ($40,000) dollars and the cost of the building to be used as an endowment fund to be handled under the supervision of the state.

Fifth – I hereby give, devise and bequeath to A. E. Taff the sum of nine thousand ($9,000) dollars in money together with a section of land now owned by me and situated in the state of Iowa, together with all of the houses and lots I now own in the township of Canton, and from which I receive rent.

Sixth - I hereby give, devise and bequeath to Ruby O'Grady the house and premises, where I now reside, together with all of its contents, and further devise of nine thousand ($9,000) dollars in money. As to the residue of my estate, whether real or personal, I give, devise and bequeath to Ruby O'Grady, this bequest in addition to the bequest previously mentioned in this will.

Louisa gasps. I stand up to go to her, thinking something's wrong, but Anna pulls me back to my chair. John is saying something to Louisa.

There's no other reaction. Anna breaks the silence, "Albert, we need to take a break."

"That's fine. The bathroom is down the hall to the left. Let's re-convene in ten minutes."

I follow Anna, John, and Louisa to the hallway. John is gently leading Louisa to the opposite end of the hall from the bathroom.

"Louisa, Anna and I know you must be upset. It's certainly understandable."

"Of course, I'm upset. I don't take issue with the monies left to build the hospital. Joseph has always thought Canton needs a hospital, but you and I both know, Joseph would not have left the bulk of his estate to that woman. I have been suspicious all along, about the will being signed in the middle of the night."

Louisa breaks down, "Poor Joseph! I don't know what to do!"

"Just stay calm. Don't let on. You don't want them to know how you feel. Come to our house when this is over. I'll help you to make some calls. You need to retain an attorney. Now, wipe your tears. Just don't let them know you're upset. We need time to sort things out."

We go back to Albert's office. Albert has already started to explain the contract with the orphanage. "When Uncle Joe went to Chicago, before he brought Dora home, he signed a contract with the orphanage, the Illinois Children's Home and Aid Society. Dora's mother is still alive so she cannot be adopted, so the purpose of the contract was to commit Dora to Uncle Joe's care. The contract is important from the standpoint it legally binds Joseph L. Murphy to provide for Dora beyond his death."

"Here's what it says:

> Whereby said Murphy agrees to take said Dora Kelly, to rear and Murphy is to furnish her, the said Dora Kelly, with all the necessaries of life, including her board and clothing, and to send her to school.
> That said J. L. Murphy shall devise and bequest to said Dora Kelly in said will of J. L. Murphy is in lieu of and to carry out this contract to which said Murphy has entered in his life-time, the same as if he were still living.

"In summary, Ruby will be responsible for Dora's care, and she will be legally bound to the terms of the contract until Dora reaches the age of majority.

Ruby's mouth drops and she raises her hand. "Question, Ruby?"

"How long? What's the age of majority?"

"Until she's 21 years old. Any other questions?"

I have to ask. "You mean I have to live with Ruby until I'm 21?"

"I guess you don't have to, but it seems to be your best option. Also, monies from the estate will cover your needs."

"Will I be able to go to school?"

"The contract specifically states you will be sent to school."

Anna and John stand to leave. "Dora, we can talk when we get to our house. Come with us. Put your coat on, we're leaving."

January 29, 1907 — Dear Diary, A lot happened today. Mr. Murphy left the house and the farm and most of his estate to Ruby. His sisters were not even mentioned in the will. Louisa is very upset. We went to Anna's, and John helped her. She finally decided to hire a law firm in Quincy. She's going to contest the will – good for her! We had dinner at Anna's then Louisa left for home. Mr. Murphy left $3,000 for me in his will, but I have to live with Ruby and, probably, Jim Kucharek until I'm an adult. I am supposed to go to school. I hope so. I didn't know there was a contract with the orphanage. I bet they took care of it while I was upstairs packing my clothes. Maybe Ruby will have her sister do the cooking and cleaning. Ruby told Louisa that her sister is our new maid but so far, I haven't seen her do any work. Let's face it, Ruby doesn't like me, and I don't like her. She wasn't happy when she found out she has to take care of me. I think she just thought she would get everything free and clear, that she and Jim could get married, and live on Mr. Murphy's money. The only way this will possibly work is if I can go to school and get out of the house every day. I can visit Rex and my friends during the day in the summer. At least I don't have to go back to the orphanage. I have a place to live, and I can stay near Rex in Canton. Another good thing, eventually I will have money to hire someone to help me find Jack and Louis. Eight years is a long time, though, to live with someone you don't like. I'm so tired. I have no more tears. I'm just going to sleep, and I'll just take one day at a time. Signed, Dora Kelly.

January 30, 1907

When I get to the kitchen to make breakfast, R.C. is sitting at the table with a pile of newspapers. "Morning Dora! I've been waiting for you. Coffee's good."

"I usually drink tea but thank you. What's all this?"

"Headlines, all about Uncle Joe's family and the will. The first one is Monday issue of the Quincy Daily Herald, the day of the funeral, headline, "Leaves $40,000 for Hospital" – says here, the Graham sisters proposed to erect a hospital to cost $20,000, and the endowment of an equal sum was to be raised to ensure its perpetuity, but that sum was never raised. Also, Uncle Joe's will and the funeral made the front page of yesterday's Register. Anna called Louisa right away. They are both surprised that they published the full text of the will on the front page of the newspaper."

"But how did they find out?"

"I guess it's a matter of public record, although the will still has to be admitted. Unless someone talked."

Ruby doesn't say anything, she just goes to her room.

"You said they mentioned the funeral. I thought it was nice. What did they say?"

"Nothing that means much. Said Ruby was accompanied by her father, Dora Kelly, a nurse and a maid, that she collapsed due to worry and lack of sleep. I don't know if she passed out or put on a show. She sure choked on the smelling salts!"

"This is manky!"

"What? What was that you said?"

"Manky! My papa used to say it when something was dirty. Sometimes he cursed in Gaelic when he was angry, too. Look, I don't want my name in the newspaper. I just want to go to school and have friends without worrying about what their parents might be telling them about me. I don't even know what this all means to me. One thing for sure, I don't trust Ruby. Albert said I can come to him if I need help, but I want to talk to Anna first."

> January 30, 1907.
>
> Dear Annie Rose, You probably already know, Mr. Murphy died on Friday. It's been in all of the newspapers. Mr. Murphy's will gives the house and farm to Ruby and it directs her to take care of me until I am 21 years old. Mr. Murphy's sister believes he was drugged and didn't know what he was signing, so she is contesting his will. It's a mess. I don't know what will happen to me if the will is set aside. Who will own the homestead and who will take care of me? I took care of Mr. Murphy and Ruby, so I can take care of myself, but I don't have money or a place to live. Anna told me not to worry, but I can't stop thinking about it.
>
> Love, Dora.

Lewistown

We read the papers every day. Taff is authorized to pay all outstanding bills, and apparently therre many requests for payment, and no one is asked for proof. He said he has paid more than $30,000! Can you imagine? R.C. and I are amazed. Also, Anna says Ruby gets money every month for me, and all I get is a budget for food and supplies. She has bought so many dresses, and keeps asking Albert for more money. I decide to keep my mouth shut until I figure out what I'm going to do.

Albert is at the door, and he looks upset! Ruby is moving her things to Mr. Murphy's room. When I call, she comes down the stairs, and she puts a box of men's clothing on the floor by the kitchen door, then proceeds to the parlor, looking for Albert. I take my book to the kitchen table, close enough to overhear but looking innocent. I can't believe I have to sneak around like this. But it's the only way I know anything.

"Ah, Ruby. Dora said you are moving to the upstairs bedroom."

"Yes. It gives me more room and we can use the room behind the kitchen for naps or a housekeeper, if I get one. I was going to call you. I need a check for $600. Just show it on legacy."

"$600? Your last draw was only two days ago for $100. In fact, this is what I came to talk to you about. You have been drawing hundreds of dollars every week. What are you doing with all the money I've given you? I've been paying all your bills, and you can't possibly be spending money that fast."

"It's none of your business. Besides, it's my money, Uncle Joe left it to me."

"It's not your money until the court says so. The will has been contested and there's no guarantee of the outcome. I've been paying thousands of dollars to you and other claimants. If you keep spending money at this rate, we will have to sell off some real estate which could include the homestead. What are you doing? Taking all that you can get in case it doesn't go your way? What if you have to pay the money back? Think about it, do you really need $600 now?"

"I have expenses. Just send me a check."

Albert puts on his coat and leaves without saying goodbye to me or Ruby. Ruby sees me sitting at the kitchen table, so she knows I overheard the conversation. But I take my book and walk towards the stairs, "I'm going to see Rex for a while. I'll be home in time for supper."

"I need you here to help me move my things, and I want you to change the bed linens."

"That's okay. You can do it, and I don't think I should be making up your bed. Besides, I don't know where to put your things. I'm going."

I run all the way to Rex's house. He's in his father's workshop, painting a birdhouse. I tell him about the argument between Ruby and Albert while he's cleaning his paint brush.

"Come with me. Let's find Mother."

Anna is in the kitchen kneading break dough. "Mother, Albert and Ruby had an argument. Albert told her to stop taking so much money out of the estate, that he might have to sell the homestead if the money runs out. Dora's worried that her money might not be there when she turns 21."

"Legally, he has to keep your money in a separate account so it should be there for you, Dora. I think we can trust Albert to do that, but if he doesn't, I honestly don't know what we can do. But it does no good to worry!"

I can't help but worry, though. "Anna, I've been thinking, if Mr. Murphy's will is set aside, what will happen to me? Will I have a place to live? Where will I go? I don't want to go back to the orphan home. I want to stay in Canton so I can be near you and Rex."

Anna gives me a sad smile. "Dora, come sit next to me so I can hug you. We don't know what's going to happen. I need you to trust you will be all right. I talked to Albert, and he said you should be protected by the contract Joseph signed with the orphanage. The court will decide who will be responsible for your care if it isn't Ruby's job. And obviously, Joseph wanted you to continue to live in the house. Louisa is going to talk to Boyer. We love you, Dora. We won't let anything bad happen to you."

"But what should I do if someone comes to take me away? I can run, but they will probably catch me."

"You just stand your ground and you tell them to talk to your attorney, Albert Taff. He's executor, so he's in charge for now, then you get to a phone and call me right away. Unless Ruby tries to kick you out, I don't believe anyone will try to send you away. Just remember, if the will is set aside, there is no guarantee that Ruby will have a place to live. But you will be all right."

"What about the money Mr. Murphy left for me. $3,000 is a lot of money! I can take care of myself, and I could get a job taking care of children or an older person who needs help. I saw some women haying last fall. There's work, I'd just have to make my way."

"Haying is just a few weeks in the fall. People know you and they like you, so you could probably get a job, but just wait a little while. You don't want to jeopardize your inheritance, and you won't get that money until you turn 21, because that's the age of majority in Illinois. It's up to you, though. I think it's worth the wait."

"I didn't know that. I thought I would get the money right away, once this is settled. If something happens and I don't have a place to go, can I stay with you?"

"We would love to have you, but we just don't have the room. We only have two bedrooms and there's no place for another bed."

"When I lived with my mama and daddy, my brother and I slept on cots in the kitchen. There's room over there for a cot. I wouldn't mind."

"No, Dora, that wouldn't work. You were a little girl when you lived with your mother and father. You are a young lady now, so you need privacy. If need be, I'll talk to Louisa. We could send you to Quincy and you could live with her. She lives alone and she has lots of space."

When I get home, Ruby is sitting in the kitchen, drinking a glass of Fort. I hate it when Ruby is waiting to talk to me when I come home. She's never happy and usually it means she has work for me to do.

I'm in no mood to deal with her right now, so I'll just go to my room so I can be alone with my thoughts. From now on, I'm going to try to ignore her as much as possible so I can try to be happy.

January 7, 1908.

Like every other school day, Rex is waiting out front to walk me home from school.

"Happy Birthday, Kid! I thought I'd take you to the drug store for an ice cream soda."

"That will be fun. I forgot my birthday. Wow, I'm 14!"

We spend the rest of the afternoon holding hands. Rex buys a chocolate soda with two straws for us to share. Some of the afterschool crowd are looking at us, but Rex doesn't seem to notice.

"Look, Rex, I think they're talking about me."

"So what? Just ignore them. Just look at me and drink the soda before it's all gone."

"You've been drinking it? It's my birthday! You said we'd share."

Rex has kind blue eyes that sparkle when he laughs, "C'mon, Kid, it's really good. I'll share the rest."

We finish the soda and I slurp so hard I almost get a headache. Neither one of us want to quit, so we just keep on slurping and laughing. When I'm with Rex, I always think things will work out fine.

We stroll home and take our time. Albert is sitting at the kitchen table when we get to the house.

"Dora, Happy Birthday! I brought you some flowers. My wife Neva reminded me that flowers is an appropriate gift for a young lady. I'm glad to see you're adjusting so well."

"Thank you, and tell Neva I said thank you."

While I'm putting the flowers in a canning jar, Albert continues to talk. "Also, I wanted to let you know there's going to be a trial at the courthouse in Lewistown. Because you are named as a defendant in the case, you will have to go. Louisa has hired an attorney, Boyer. He plans to call you to testify. You needn't worry. He's a nice man, so you don't have to be afraid. Mr. Chipperfield said he would talk to you beforehand so you will know what to expect. You'll stay with a nice widow lady in Lewiston, close to the courthouse. Have Helen make you some new dresses - you should look nice during the trial."

"Who else is going? Will I be there all alone?"

"I'll be there every day. Of course, Ruby will be there too. R.C. and Anna are planning to be there. Louisa will be there but Anne, her sister, is too feeble to travel, so Louisa will represent her interests. I know you like her, but please don't talk to Louisa until the trial is over, since she's on the opposing side."

"I do like her, and she told me she doesn't have any problem with the money left to R.C. and me. I'll follow your advice, though. Albert, what will happen to me if the will is set aside? Will I still have a place to live?"

"Anna told me you asked about that. Like she said, you are protected by the contract Uncle Joe signed with the orphan home, but I'll be honest with you, if the will is set aside, we don't know what will happen to the house. The judge could order it sold and the money could go to the estate. Obviously, Uncle Joe wanted you to be able to live in the house, so we can only hope that the judge will take that into consideration. Try not to worry. I will do everything in my power to make sure you are cared for."

"Can they send me back to the orphanage? I don't want to leave Canton."

"I suppose they might try, but you have a lot of people here who care for you, so I don't think that will happen. Now I must go. Call me if you have any questions, and don't worry."

Sunday, January 26, 1908 — Dear Diary, John and Rex brought me a chest so I can pack my belongings for an extended stay in Lewistown. Helen sewed five pretty dresses for me to wear at the trial, one for each day of the week. I think I remembered everything, night dresses, dress boots, stockings, bloomers, and the coat, the hat and mittens that I wear to church. I'm taking Victoria with me and some books to read. I think I should take some extra towels in case I have my monthly. I don't know what it will be like to live with someone I don't know. And I don't know how to testify at a trial. It's easy for Albert to say I shouldn't worry! I just hope they don't ask what happened when I put the drops in Mr. Murphy's tea. I didn't mean to do anything wrong! But that started all the problems, so what if I lose everything because of it? I wish I could talk to Anna about it, but it's something I don't want anyone ever to know! Signed, Dora Kelly

I go to Ruby's room to say goodbye while R.C. is taking my chest to the carriage. "I'll see you in Lewistown, Ruby."

"Mind your manners while you are there. Just remember, you have to live with me or you won't get your money when you turn 21, so don't go blabbing our personal business on the witness stand. I know you heard me talking to Albert. Don't you dare tell the judge that I've been taking money on legacy. Legally, I have to take care of you but don't go gettin' big ideas. I'm in charge and I am the only one who can decide if you are to go to school. I didn't get schoolin' and I'm just fine, and you're no better than me."

"But the orphanage contract says I will always go to school. If you won't let me, I am going to tell Louisa that you've been getting checks from Albert."

"Huh! Just keep in mind, you have nowhere else to go because no one else wants you. Besides, if you cause trouble, I will tell everyone about the time you gave Uncle Joe too much medicine, and how you made him sick. He never recovered, you know, and he never left his bed after you doped him up."

My heart drops. "But, that was an accident!"

"Maybe. But no one will care how it happened. You will get in trouble. Now, go on. R.C.'s waiting, and you have a long ride to Lewistown."

It's 15 miles to Lewistown but it doesn't take as long as I expected. R.C. takes me to Mrs. Blackahy's house and he helps me to settle in. She seems nice enough, and she has a pretty house.

"Welcome, Dora. I'll enjoy your company. The room you're sleeping in was my daughter's room before she left to take a job in Peoria. Where are you staying, Mr. Webster?"

"Oh, I rented a room at the boarding house downtown. The trial starts at one tomorrow, Dora, so I'll come by to get you about 12:30. Thank you again, Mrs. Blackahy."

R.C. leaves and I already miss Rex, but it's not so bad here. I just want this to be over so I will know where I belong.

John Grafton Moss and Anna Moss

The Murphy Homestead on First Street

Main Street, Canton, Illinois

PART FOUR

The Trial

*"Remember, rainbows have never been attracted to
Cloudless days. They only follow the storms."*

Richelle E. Goodrich, Being Bold

The Courthouse

Tuesday, January 28, 1908, The Memphis Commercial Appeal

The first day of the trial is grim, taking place in an unsightly paintless building with cracked masonry. They say the old brick building on Adams Street, between Main and Second, is a shelter for prisoners who work on rock piles. It's a cold and cloudy day. Still the courtroom is packed with spectators hoping to see the Attorney General and former Illinois Governor Yates who have been called to testify at the trial.

R.C. comes by, so we can walk together to the courthouse. It's a gloomy winter day with no sun. I'm glad I'm wearing boots because the street is snowy and icy. We had hoped to get there early to avoid the crowd, but the courtroom is already packed. Anna waves at us. She saved a seat for me next to her on the front row. R.C. finds a seat in the back.

The seats are hard, long wooden benches in three sections separated by dark red runners that cover a highly polished wood floor. This room is depressing. The wallpaper has a dirty grey floral design, and the judge's platform and the witness box are the same wood as the benches. Our seats are in the center section, next to the journalists to our right.

Albert is sitting at a table with Mr. Chipperfield, Ruby's lawyer and Louisa is sitting at another table with three men, I assume her attorneys. One, wearing a brown suit and bow tie, stands up. He turns and faces us while he looks at his pocket watch. John looks at his watch; it's one o'clock.

The room becomes silent, and then I hear the heavy footsteps entering the courtroom. The jury, all men wearing suits except one wearing bib overalls, files in and they take seats in the jury box. We all stand when Judge Thompson enters the courtroom.

The judge brings down his gavel to open the proceedings "Ladies and gentlemen, please be seated. Mr. Boyer, you wish to make an opening motion?"

"Yes, your honor. We respectfully request that the Canton Physicians Club, including Doctors Coleman, Nelson, and Schoeles, the three doctors who witnessed the signing of the will, be added as defendants in the case."

"Motion denied. It would not be proper to make witnesses to the will parties in the suit. However, two other housekeeping items. You requested a change of venue to Galesburg, Illinois. I've learned that the local judge is tied up with sessions in appellate court, so he could not try the case until December. In the interest of moving this along, I am denying your request for a change of venue. Secondly, in response to your earlier request to add William H. Stead, Attorney General of the State of Illinois as a defendant, I will rule in favor of that motion. Would the stenographer please make that change and read the new suit entitled Louisa M. Murphy and Anna E. Hopkins vs. A. E. Taff, et. al.?"

The stenographer is pretty. She turns to face the audience with a paper in her hand. She must be nervous because her voice is shaking, "Louisa M. Murphy and Anna E. Hopkins vs, A. E. Taff, and A.E. Taff, executor of the last will and testament of J.L. Murphy, deceased; Ruby O'Grady; Dora Kelly; R.C. Webster; J.E. Coleman, M.D.; W. D. Nelson, M.D.; P.S. Scholes, M.D.; the Physicians Club of Canton; and William H. Stead as Attorney General of the State of Illinois."

"Thank you, Miss Jones. Is counsel ready to present an opening statement?"

Louisa's attorney, Mr. Boyer, stands up, "We're ready, your honor."

Mr. Boyer stands, and he faces the jury, while he reviews the case. He's not a large man, but he is very confident. He struts back and forth in front of the jury box telling them that he is simply presenting the facts, that Mr. Murphy was suffering from a severe illness when the will was supposedly executed, that his mind and memory were affected, impaired, and weakened by drugs and medicines which had been administered to him under the direction of Doctors Coleman, Nelson, and Scholes; and Ruby O'Grady.

The jurors all turn to look at Ruby. She just looks down and squirms in her seat. Funny. My mind begins to wander as I look at the judge. I think he's trying to look stern in his black robe, but I think his eyes look kind, and like Mr. Murphy, he has a white beard. I bet he knew Mr. Murphy.

Attorney Boyer talks for close to an hour, and then he wraps up his argument. "......As an attorney and as a friend of the court, all I am asking you to do is to acknowledge the truth, that the will is fraudulent, therefore, should be set aside."

Two journalists stand up and run out of the room. Judge Thompson calls a ten-minute recess and the other journalists run out the door of the courtroom.

I turn towards Anna, "Yes, dear, what is it?"

"I don't understand, everything he said is true. Why am I on their side? What are they going to say that I did wrong? Is it because I sneaked into his room when I wasn't supposed to?"

"No, you haven't done anything wrong. Louisa and Anne are just objecting to the way the estate has been divided. Louisa is not objecting to the monies left to you and R.C. No one is going to accuse you of doing anything wrong."

Ruby's lawyer, Chipperfield waives opening comments, so they start testimony right away.

Boyer stands and he walks towards the judge, "Your honor, I call the plaintiff, Louisa M. Murphy, to the stand."

Louisa is sitting on the other side of John. She hurries towards the witness box, but then she slows down, and she walks gracefully, her clunky heels of her boots clicking as they strike the wood floor. She looks very smart sitting there in the witness box in her purple ankle length coat with fur trim and matching jeweled toque. The room is quiet. Some of the people in the gallery are leaning forward, not wanting to miss a single word.

"First of all, Miss Murphy, we are all saddened by the loss of your brother. You are here representing yourself and your sister, Anne E. Hopkins, is that right?"

"Yes. My sister is aged and feeble so she is not able to travel."

"Please tell us about your relationship with Joseph Murphy."

"He was my twin brother, so we have always been very close. We were small when we came to America. The ship was dark and dirty and many of the people were sick. Even though we were very young, I'll never forget the smell. Joseph looked after me like a big brother and he protected me while we slept. After I moved to Quincy, we each had our own lives, but we exchanged letters. He owns properties in the Quincy area, so he would come for visits in the summer. I always made a rhubarb pie when he came for a visit, that was his favorite."

"When did you learn that your brother had fallen ill?

"My cousin's husband, John Moss, called me early on December 26. He said Joseph had another attack, that the doctor said it looked bad. I called my sister, Anne, and made arrangements to go to Canton."

"Please tell the court about your visit to Canton."

"Dora Kelly, Joseph's ward, had the guest room made up for me, so I felt quite welcome until I walked down the hall towards his chamber. The housekeeper, Ruby O'Grady, insisted I was not allowed to see him. I just pushed her aside. There was no way I was going to allow a servant to keep me from seeing my brother!"

"Was he conscious when you entered his room?

"His eyes were open, but they were glassy. I asked the nurse about his condition and medications, but she said I would have to talk to the doctor. I tried to talk to my brother, but he didn't recognize me. I just stayed a few minutes. As I was leaving, the nurse was putting drops into his mouth. It was obvious that they were drugging him, which is the reason he was in a confused state. That was the last time I saw Joseph. I was not allowed entry to his chamber after that."

"You issued instructions to change nurses. Why was that?"

"Well first of all, the day nurse, Mattie Havermale, slapped Dora so hard she had a black eye when she caught her in my brother's room. That was shocking. She's an adult. If she can't control her emotions with a 12-year-old girl, then how can she be trusted? Also, I didn't believe it to be proper for my brother to be alone at night with a female nurse. I talked to Albert Taff and the solution was obvious. We switched the night nurse to days so we could hire a male nurse for nights."

"But you stayed a few days to visit your cousin, is that right?"

"Yes. When I came to Canton, I assumed I would have to take charge of the house and his care, but Mr. Taff put Ruby O'Grady in charge, so I spent time with Anna and her family at their house. She told me everything that had been going on. She said a new will had been signed in the middle of the night only a few days before. She was also upset about the way Ruby had been treating Dora Kelly. It's clear that Ruby has changed. She doesn't seem to be the decent young lady that my brother raised. During the two days I stayed at the house, I had to turn her beau away several times. It's apparent that he has free rein of the house because he would just come in without knocking. One time I found him sitting at the kitchen table, and as it turned out, he was waiting for his supper. Then one morning when I came downstairs, he was coming out of Ruby's room. Joseph would be outraged if he knew."

"How was Ruby disrespectful to Dora?"

"Ruby has been turning Dora into a scullery maid, and they argue a lot. Dora is an innocent young girl, and she is entitled to an education by contract with the orphanage, but Ruby ordered her to stay home from school so she could cook and clean. In one of their arguments, I heard Ruby tell Dora she 'doesn't need schoolin' to cook and clean.'"

"Miss Murphy, you returned to Canton for the funeral and for the reading of the will. Of course, you were aware that your brother had previously made a will, were you not?"

"Yes, he told me about a will that he made in the summer, after Dora came to live with him. He came for his annual trip to Quincy that summer. He was very fond of Dora and said he wanted to make sure she would be provided for if something happened to him. I was shocked when they told me he had signed another will in the middle of the night, shortly before his death. I became even more upset at the reading of the will."

"What made you decide to contest the will?"

"When I learned he had supposedly bequeathed the homestead and other properties to Ruby O'Grady and Albert Taff. In our discussions regarding our estates, it was understood that my sister, Anne, and I would be the primary benefactors of his estate. Joseph would never have signed that will. Also, it was written in someone else's handwriting and the signature is scribbled, and unreadable. It is not my brother's signature."

Ruby's lawyer stood abruptly. "Objection. Miss Murphy is not a handwriting expert."

"I'll allow it. They exchanged letters over the years, so she should be able to tell if it was his handwriting."

"Please continue, Louisa."

"The fact that it was supposedly signed in the dead of night is suspect in itself. He often talked about the need for a hospital in Canton, so my sister and I are not taking issue with the bequests to fund the hospital, nor the small amounts left to Dora Kelly and R.C. Webster, but he never would have left family out of his will. One thing for sure, he would not have left such a large estate to Ruby and Albert. Ruby had a good life after he took her in, but everyone in town knows she was nothing more than a housekeeper, a servant."

It's obvious that Ruby is upset. She stands and starts to insult Louisa, but Chipperfield pulls her back to her seat and he whispers something in her ear. It feels good to me to see her face the truth! I hope the jury believes Louisa.

Boyer has no further questions. Chipperfield stands and he adopts a professional tone when he addresses Louisa, "Miss Murphy, your brother told you about a will that he had prepared some years ago. Can you state with assurance that he did not arrange for a new will?"

"I can state with assurance that my brother had nothing to do with preparing the will in question. First of all, it is poorly handwritten. Joseph was an attorney; he would have insisted that a formal document be prepared. Also, he would not have agreed to some of the terms of the will. I believe this was the result of a clandestine scheme between Albert Taff and Ruby O'Grady who will inherit the bulk of the estate. The doctors who supposedly witnessed the signing went along with it because of the bequest to fund the construction and maintenance of a hospital."

Chipperfield returns to his seat, looking frustrated. Louisa is excused and they announce a break, so I hurry from my seat to the bathroom. When I come out, Anna and John are talking to Louisa in the hallway.

John smiles when he sees me coming, "There she is! What did you think, Dora? Louisa was the lead witness. We think she made a good impression on the jury."

"Miss Murphy, your purple coat and toque are so pretty. You looked so elegant up there. I think everyone was impressed except Ruby."

Anna chimes in, "It was funny that Chipperfield had to sit her down. Louisa, this is confusing for Dora, though. She's listed as a defendant, but she's really on your side. I explained that you are not objecting to monies left to her, but she's concerned about what might happen to her if the will is set aside. You and I need to talk."

"There's nothing to talk about. In the end, the court will decide where Dora is to live."

"Well, she asked if she could live with us. We would like to take her in, but we simply do not have the room. I told her I would talk to you."

Louisa's mouth drops, "Are you suggesting that she might live with me? I'm sorry, Dora, you are a very nice girl, but you can't live with me. I am an old lady who is used to living alone. There's really no room in my life for a young girl like you, and I'm not willing to change the way I live. Anna, you know me. I have my friends and I want to be free to travel."

I walk with my head down, trying to control my tears when we return to the courtroom. Boyer calls Nurse Mattie Havermale to the stand. Chipperfield jumps up, "Objection, your honor, Miss Havermale is a medical professional and…"

Judge Thompson cuts him off, "Objection overruled. Miss Havermale, will take the stand."

"Miss Havermale, you were Mr. Murphy's nurse, is that correct?"

"Yes, but only during the day shift."

"When were you first assigned to attend Mr. Murphy?"

"He fell ill on Christmas during the evening. I was called to relieve the night nurse the next morning."

"And you worked days every day until you were dismissed on January 17, is that right?"

"Yes, sir."

"Why were you dismissed?"

"Mr. Taff said he was ordered to dismiss me by Mr. Murphy's sister, Louisa Murphy. They switched the night nurse, my sister Maude, to days because Miss Murphy wanted a male nurse at night."

"Is that the only reason you were dismissed?"

"That's what I was told."

"You administered medications to Joseph Murphy, did you not?"

"Yes. I gave him what the doctor ordered."

"How often did you administer medications to Mr. Murphy?

"I don't recall. My notes were destroyed a few days after I left Mr. Taff's employ."

"Why were your notes destroyed?"

"Mr. Taff told me to burn them. He said they would not be needed, that they were private matters."

"Was Mr. Murphy conscious when you arrived for your shift on December 26?"

"I don't recall."

"Mr. Murphy's attorney, Albert Taff, hired you. Is that correct?"

"Actually, Dr. Nelson called me to the Murphy home. However, Mr. Taff paid me for my services."

"Regardless, you must have some memory. Was Murphy conscious or comatose when you arrived?"

"I don't remember."

"During the time you cared for him, was Mr. Murphy conscious at any time?"

"Sometimes. Most of the time he was sleeping."

"You were instructed to bar visitors from Murphy's chamber. Is that correct?"

"Yes."

"Who issued those instructions?"

"Ruby O'Grady told me that Dr. Coleman ordered no visitors."

"Do you remember a time when Mr. Murphy's ward, Dora Kelly, came to his chamber?"

"Yes. I returned from the bathroom and she was standing over him, calling his name. I told her to leave the room."

"That's all? You just told her to leave? Or did the two of you have words, and didn't you slap her?"

"I told her to leave, that she was not supposed to be there. She argued that she would only stay a few minutes. I'm not used to young people talking back to me so, yes, I did slap her."

"Do you think that could be the real reason you were dismissed?"

Mattie looks down at her lap and she doesn't answer.

"No further questions. Counsel, your witness."

When Nurse Mattie Havermale steps down, she looks the other way as she walks past Anna and me to sit in her seat.

Boyer calls Anna to the stand. She puts her hand on the Bible to be sworn in.

"Mrs. Moss, your maiden name is Murphy. Were you related to Joseph L. Murphy?"

"Yes. Joseph was my first cousin."

"And you were close to him, were you not?"

"We became very close in later years. He and I were the only ones left from our family in Canton. We got together during holidays and we often went to church together. My husband, John, and I went to the house immediately when we heard he had fallen ill. The doctor had ordered no visitors and at that time, we understood, thinking he needed his rest. One of our concerns was his ward, Dora Kelly, that she might be upset, so our attention that night was mostly on her."

"So, after his attack on Christmas Day, he was sick for a month before he died. When were you allowed to visit him in his chamber?"

I've never seen Anna cry before, "Never. I was not allowed to see him. I pleaded with Ruby, but she didn't care that I was family. She continued to bar me and others from his room."

"Others?"

"Neighbors and friends, and even Dora Kelly, who lives in the house, was not even allowed to see him."

Boyer takes a hanky from his pocket, and he hands it to Anna, "You must have been very upset."

"Upset is not the word. I was outraged, but Albert Taff told us Ruby was in charge, so there was nothing we could do. I could not reason with her."

"Your witness, counsel."

Chipperfield asked from his chair, "Mrs. Moss, you called Louisa Murphy the night Joseph Murphy fell ill, did you not?"

"My husband, John, called her the next morning."

"And when she came to visit, she was allowed to visit her brother in his chamber. Is that right?"

"She was not allowed to visit Joseph, she pushed past Ruby who was guarding his room, but she said it was pointless to try to talk to him because he didn't even recognize her."

"Objection! Hearsay!"

"Sustained."

January 28, 1908 — Dear Diary, The trial started today. It was very dramatic. In the hall, Louisa made it very clear she wouldn't let me live with her, so now I am even more concerned that I may not have a place to live if the will is set aside. Louisa says she likes me, but she doesn't want me. I'll stay in Canton, though, even if I have to get a job and leave school. And what about the $3,000? I need that money so I can find Jack and Louis! The judge keeps looking at me, so I try to be calm. Maybe he's wondering where I should end up. I hope he has a plan. More trial tomorrow. R.C. said he will pick me up so we can get there early. Everyone is telling me not to worry, but I'm worried about testifying, too. Boyer said he is just going to ask me about Ruby barring visitors. He told me not to volunteer information, to just answer the questions truthfully. Mrs. Blackahy is nice, she invited Anna, John and R.C. for supper, the best cornbread ever, but she's kinda strange. There was an extra place setting tonight at supper. When no one else came, I asked who it was for. Mrs. Blackahy said she always sets a plate for her husband in case he decides to come home. It's a little weird because she's a widow! I don't know what's scarier, the thought of a dead person at the supper table or a crazy lady who's waiting for her dead husband. She seems nice, but I decide to push my chest in front of the door since I'm alone in the house with her at night. After Anna and R.C. left, I heard the creaking of Mrs. Blackahy's rocking chair until I fell asleep.

I peeked around the corner of the door leading to the parlor, and she was just humming and reading her Bible. She seems happy but I think she's lonely here. We don't have anything to talk about, so I'm glad that I brought my books. As long as I can see Anna and R.C. every day I can get by. I'm saving up stories to tell Rex when I see him in a few weeks. Signed, Dora Kelly.

The Governor

Wednesday, January 29, 1908

We are supposed to be in court at nine, but the courtroom is already packed when we arrive at eight o'clock. We're lucky to have reserved seats. Ruby and Albert are talking to Chipperfield. I try to wave at her, but she turns the other way. Every seat is filled, and people are standing in the back, but the room is unusually quiet.

I hear my name called and look up. Mr. Boyer takes my hand, and he leads me to the witness stand. My knees are shaking as I walk up three steps to the witness box. I'm high above the crowd and all eyes are on me. I turn to face Mr. Boyer, "Miss Kelly, would you please state your name and age for the record?"

My voice is shaking, "Dora. Dora Belle Kelly. I just turned 14 on January 7."

"Miss Kelly, you were Joseph Murphy's ward, and you live in his house, is that correct?"

"Yes."

"When did he take you in?"

"He came to the orphanage a few months before my ninth birthday."

"For the record, the orphanage was the Illinois Children's Home and Aid Society in Chicago, Illinois."

"Miss Kelly, what was your relationship with the decedent, Joseph Murphy?"

"I was kind of scared of him at first, but he took good care of me

Mr. Murphy had kind eyes, and I liked him. We had some fun times and long talks, so I learned to care for him."

"You said you learned to care for him. What does that mean? Did you love him, or did you just take care of him?"

"I guess I loved him. I did take care of him, especially when Ruby got sick."

"Would you please tell us what happened the night of December 25th?"

"I was home alone with Mr. Murphy; Ruby was out with her friends. Mr. Murphy collapsed going up the stairs, and I couldn't get him up. I ran across the street to R.C. Webster's house for help. He helped me get Mr. Murphy to his bed. Then he called Doc Nelson."

"At that point, Joseph Murphy was very ill, was he not?"

"They said he was. I was not allowed to see him."

"Did you try to see him?"

"I kept trying to go to him, but they wouldn't let me in his room. One day, I waited for Nurse Havermale, the day nurse, to go to the bathroom, and I sneaked into his room. He looked terrible. His face was pasty white, and his eyes were open, but he was just staring at the ceiling. I don't think he saw me."

"Dora, tell us what happened next."

"Nurse Havermale came back, and she caught me in his room. We had words and she knocked me over. She told me to get out of his room and not to come back. I looked down at Mr. Murphy and I think I saw a tear from one eye, but he didn't say anything. I don't know if he understood what had happened. I left the room because I didn't want to upset him in case he did understand."

"So you left the room and went downstairs. Was Ruby O'Grady there?"

"Yes, I was crying, and she noticed my face was swelling, but she didn't say anything. No one said anything until Anna came the next day, and she saw my black eye. She yelled at Ruby for not protecting me."

"You are referring to Anna Moss, is that correct?"

"Yes."

"Your witness."

Chipperfield does not question me. I get to my seat and Anna pats my leg, "Good job, Dora. We're proud of you!"

I'm proud of me too. I can't believe I did it without crying. I just sat up straight and told the truth like Mr. Chipperfield told me to. I'm sad because Mr. Murphy is dead, but I'm glad that I had a chance to tell everyone about how the nurse slapped me. They were wrong to keep people away. Mr. Murphy must have thought no one cared.

Boyer calls Maude Havermale to the stand. She says the same things her sister did, except she tells more details.

"There were times when he was awake, but he slept most of the time. The doctor ordered drops because they wanted him to rest."

"I assume you must have formed a professional opinion of his state when you took care of him. Was he comatose at times?"

"Sometimes, yes, and there were times when he surprised me, and his eyes opened."

"You said you gave him drops. How often did you administer the drops?"

"I can't say. I destroyed my notes. Mr. Taff called me few days after the assignment ended and he told me to burn my notes."

"Did you find that unusual? Are your notes normally destroyed?"

"No, but I assumed he had his reasons."

"Well, you seem to be a bright young woman, you must have established a schedule. You can't remember the frequency of his medications?

"I can't say with certainty."

"Miss Havermale, were you on duty at 2:00 a.m. on January 14, when Mr. Taff presented a will to Mr. Murphy for signature?"

"Yes, I remember that night well, because that was a very long night."

"How so? Tell us what happened."

"Well, usually after everyone goes to bed it's quiet. But the night before, Mr. Taff and the doctors arrived at eight o'clock as usual."

"That's Doctors Coleman, Nelson and Schoeles. Correct?"

"Yes."

"Please continue."

"The doctors talked to Mr. Taff and Ruby O'Grady on the landing outside Mr. Murphy's chamber for quite a while, I'd say about 30 minutes. I could tell there was something confidential being discussed, so I just stayed with my patient. Then Dr. Coleman asked me to step out. He instructed me to hold off giving Mr. Murphy his medications until further notice. He said they wanted Mr. Murphy to be alert so they could talk to him."

"What medications were you giving him?"

"I don't recall."

"But they were drops to keep him calm. They made him sleep. Is that correct?"

"Perhaps."

"So, what happened after that?"

"Dr. Coleman made frequent trips to Mr. Murphy's room to check his vitals. It was close to one o'clock when he left the room and announced to Mr. Taff and the other doctors that he had Mr. Murphy set up and ready to go."

Taff's lawyer stands. "Objection, nurse-patient privilege."

"Overruled."

"Those were his words? Set up and ready to go?"

"Yes, then everyone came to Mr. Murphy's bedside, Albert Taff, Ruby O'Grady and the three doctors. Mr. Taff handed a paper and pen to Mr. Murphy, and he asked him to sign the paper at the bottom of the page."

"Did anyone read to him, the contents of the paper he was to sign?"

"No."

"Did Murphy seem to be aware of what he was signing?"

"Objection!"

"Sustained."

"What happened when he was asked to sign the paper?"

"Mr. Taff told him that it was okay, that they had talked about it. I thought it was strange because Mr. Murphy just kept hanging onto the paper like he wasn't going to let go. Mr. Taff finally got him to scribble something on the bottom, but Mr. Murphy held onto the paper for dear life. Finally, Taff had to pull the paper from his hand."

"Do you think Mr. Murphy would have continued to hold onto the paper if Taff had not pulled it from his hand?"

"It seemed like he would have."

"No further questions."

Chipperfield has just one question, "Miss Havermale, during your employment at the Murphy home, there were times when Joseph Murphy was awake. Is that correct?"

"Yes."

"That's all I have for this witness, your honor."

John takes us to the Stafford House for dinner during the recess. What a place! White tablecloths and napkins with China plates and crystal glasses at each place. John and R.C. help Anna and me to our seats, high back chairs with red velvet cushions. I put my napkin on my lap and wait for Anna to tell me what to do next, but waiters are already on their way to our table, carrying trays of food high above their heads. I'm hungry and I know we have to get back to the courthouse, so I'm eating fast.

Anna puts her hand on my arm, "Slow down, Dora. John ordered the food before we left our room this morning, so we have time."

I finish my mashed potatoes and gravy, and since this is a fancy restaurant, I decide to eat my fried chicken leg with a knife and fork. I try to fork the chicken, but it slides across the gravy on my plate and the chicken leg flies across the table, landing on John's lap!

Anna sees that I'm embarrassed because everyone is laughing, "Dora, it's alright to pick a chicken leg up with your hands when you eat it." She uses her napkin to return the chicken leg to my plate. I pick it up with my hand and down it in short order. I look around the room to see if anyone might have noticed my accident, but no one is looking our way.

We return to the trial and Mr. Boyer is questioning William Ferguson, the night nurse. He seems much nicer than the other two. When the lawyers ask him about Mr. Murphy, he describes it much more fully.

"When I arrived, I consulted with Nurse Havermale. I found it interesting because she said there would be times when he would be awake, but during the times I cared for him, he was never conscious."

"But you said you gave him drops. You administered medication even though he wasn't conscious?"

"Yes. You just put the tip of the dropper in the corner of his mouth."

"Did you wonder why you were giving him drops, supposedly to keep him calm, when he was already unconscious?"

"Yes. But I just did what the doctor ordered. I assume he had his reasons."

"Mr. Ferguson, is it your professional opinion that Mr. Murphy might have been over-medicated? Did you question the dosage or the frequency of his medications?"

"I don't question doctor orders."

"What medicines were you administering to him?"

"I can't say. My notes were destroyed, as ordered by Mr. Taff."

"Your witness."

Chipperfield approaches the witness, "you say Mr. Murphy was not conscious. Can you say with assurance that he never regained consciousness even if for a few minutes?"

"I did not see him regain consciousness. He was very ill."

The door to the courtroom opens and there are heavy footsteps in the back of the room that echo off the wood of the judge's bench and the witness stand. Whoever it is must be a very large person, or there is more than one man walking towards the front. I lean towards Anna, peeking to see who is approaching.

Boyer stands and walks to greet the men, "Governor Yates, thank you for coming."

Boyer is shaking hands with the governor who is wearing a dark blue suit with velvet lapels, and a vest and ascot just like in the picture books. He's accompanied by two policemen and another man dressed in a dark suit. At first, I think he's winking, but he just has small squinty eyes. He has a full head of dark curly hair and a downturned mouth, almost like he's frowning.

The Governor looks my way, and he nods without smiling. He takes a seat to our left and the other men find seats in the back. Anna whispers in my ear, "The Governor was a good friend of Joseph's."

When Boyer calls Governor Yates to testify, and he tells about finding out about me!

He says, "The last time we met, he spent some time telling me that he was going to take in a new ward, a young girl, from the orphanage. He said he was making a will in case something should happen to him, so she would be cared for."

"Did he happen to mention any of the other benefactors?"

"He mentioned several times in the past, that Canton needs a hospital, and he said he was going to leave monies to build and maintain the hospital. I didn't inquire, but I assumed the remainder of his estate would stay with family."

"Did he talk about his family?"

"Once, he mentioned he had two sisters in Quincy, and a cousin in Canton. He spoke fondly of them."

Flashbulbs from cameras are exploding until the judge brings down his gavel, "Gentlemen, this is a courtroom and I demand respect! There will be no more photos taken of the Governor or any other witness during this proceeding. Violators will be found in contempt of court and will be escorted downstairs to a jail cell."

Chipperfield approaches, looking down with his right hand in his back pocket, "Governor, that last meeting with Joseph Murphy was years ago, was it not? Before he took Dora Kelly in?"

"Yes, it was at a dinner at the Palmer House in Chicago in November of 1902."

"So, you really don't know whether or not a new will was made after that meeting."

"No, sir, I do not. However, at that time he did say he felt good about a new will, that he had everything taken care of."

"Thank you, Governor. No further questions."

January 29, 1908 — Dear Diary, Today was the second day of the trial. Chipperfield said Anna and I did good. I was so proud of myself for speaking up without crying that I almost giggled. Governor Yates testified this afternoon and he looked right at me and said that Mr. Murphy wanted to take care of me. Some parts of the trial are interesting, but some parts are really boring. Days are long when you have to sit on a hard bench all day. I'm glad that Anna and John are here. They took R.C. and me to a hotel restaurant for dinner. It worked out nice - I wore my new rose colored velvet dress on the very day I testified, then we went to a fancy restaurant, and I saw the Governor. I think R.C. is supposed to testify tomorrow. After supper, Mrs. Blackahy showed me the rest of her house. She has a big green parrot in the back room. She laughs when he curses. He keeps saying "dammit, where's Homer?" over and over again. She doesn't seem so creepy now that I know her better. I hope Anna and John will stay for the rest of the trial. I would like to go home, but I want to be here to find out what happens. I can't trust Ruby and Albert to tell me everything. Who knows what will happen to me when this is all over? I'm tired, so I'll worry about it later. I'm going to sleep after I push my chest against the door. Signed, Dora Kelly

Thursday, January 30, 1908

Boyer waves R.C. to the front, when we arrive early the next morning, "R.C., you will be the first witness so why don't you sit up front, next to Dora?"

R.C. looks uncomfortable sitting in the witness box. I think he has too much starch in his white shirt because he keeps running a finger between his neck and the collar. Still, he looks nice all dressed up in a suit and bow tie.

"Mr. Webster, what was your relationship to the decedent, Joseph Murphy?"

"Uncle Joe and I were close friends. We were neighbors, I live across the road, and I helped around the homestead, taking care of the horses and such. Sometimes he had me go out to his farm."

"You refer to him as Uncle Joe, but you were a paid worker, were you not?"

"Yes, sir, but over the years we became close. He not only cared about me, but he always asked about my wife, Mary, and our children. One time he took my son, Dickie, with him on a business trip to Quincy. On occasion, we would be invited to his house for dinner."

"Please tell us what happened Christmas night, 1906."

"We were cleaning up the dishes after supper and Dora, that's Dora Kelly, came pounding on our door. She was so hysterical that I had to help her into the house. She told me that Uncle Joe was ill, that he fell on the stairs. I ran to his house and found him unconscious on the steps. He was a big man, but Dora carried his feet, and I was able to lift him to his bed."

"What happened next?"

"I asked Dora where Ruby was, and she told me Ruby had gone to a party with her friends. I couldn't believe she would leave a young girl like Dora alone to take care of him since he just had another attack a few days prior. I went to the phone and called W.D."

"W.D. is Dr. Nelson, is that right?"

"Yes, sir."

"Mr. Webster, were you employed by Joseph Murphy when he took Ruby O'Grady in?"

"Yes. She delivered milk to his house. She was pitiful, she always had a dirty face and scraggly hair. She was eight years old at the time. Her family still lives across town, but they are poor. Uncle Joe took pity on the girl, and he took her in. My wife cleaned her up and got rid of her lice. Uncle Joe clothed her, and he gave her a nice place to live. She had everything she could want or need."

"So, he cared for Ruby."

"He cared for her, but I wouldn't say he cared much about her. He told me that he believed God sent her to him to be taken in, that it was the Christian thing to do. At first, she did small chores around the house and as she got older, she became his housekeeper. They got along fine, but after Dora came to live with them, things got tense. Ruby started chasing around and all they did was argue."

"Objection, your honor. Move to strike the comment Miss O'Grady was "chasing around.""

"Sustained."

"Well, she was out partying with her friends on Christmas Day when Uncle Joe fell ill. Another thing, there were times she wouldn't allow Dora to go to school because she wanted her to do the cooking and cleaning. She turned mean towards Dora and she was ungrateful to Uncle Joe at the end."

"After you helped him to his chamber, when did you next see Joseph Murphy?"

"In his coffin. Ruby kept everyone from seeing him." R.C. chokes up, "I would like to have had a chance to say goodbye. I loved him, and so did a lot of other people she kept away."

I'm crying, and Anna's crying when the judge brings down his gavel for a recess.

We go to the bathroom so we can compose ourselves. The trial has already resumed when we return to the courtroom.

"Mr. Webster, during the nine years prior to taking Dora Kelly in, Ruby O'Grady lived alone in the house with Joseph Murphy, did she not?"

"Technically, yes, but he had hired help come in to cook and clean until Ruby was old enough to take over household duties."

"How long was that?"

"Cain't really say. It sort of happened gradually. She did more and more as she became older until, one day, they didn't need a housekeeper or cook."

"Was Miss O'Grady a paid servant?"

"Not that I know of, but she lived a privileged life. She could call for me whenever she wanted to go downtown to Dobbins for shopping. There were no limits. She could charge anything she wanted to Uncle Joe's accounts, including fancy clothes and candy at the sweet shop. I frequently took her to the seamstress who sewed her dresses."

"You said the situation became tense after Dora Kelly arrived."

"Well, not right away. At first, Ruby and Dora seemed to get along. They would go shopping together and I think Ruby enjoyed having a young girl in the house. That changed, though. Ruby had always been resentful that she was not allowed to go to school. She saw Dora making friends and going to school, a life she never had. Then Uncle Joe started to tell people around town how much he cared for Dora. At times he would pull Dora onto his lap to read books to her. He called her his baby. Ruby became jealous and spiteful, referring to Dora as the Princess!"

"Well, possible jealousy aside, now Ruby had two people to care for."

"Not really. In fact, Ruby was sick for months the year before Uncle Joe died, and Dora did everything. She took care of Ruby and Uncle Joe, in addition to cooking and cleaning. After that, Ruby pushed more and more work onto Dora to the point Dora could no longer go back to school. I overheard Ruby scream at her one day that Dora was no better than she, that she did not need to go to school to learn how to cook and clean."

"How did Mr. Murphy react when Ruby and Dora argued?"

"Oh, Ruby didn't say anything when he was around. They had a big blow up, though, Ruby and Uncle Joe. Uncle Joe wanted some things to be private, but I can say he didn't like Ruby's boyfriend, said he could find someone more suitable. It really got tense when she started staying out all night."

"Your honor, I have no further questions for this witness."

Chipperfield challenges R.C., "Mr. Webster, I'm confused, you didn't live in the house, so how did it so happen that you overheard these arguments?"

"I was in the house doing janitorial work every day, so sometimes I heard Ruby yelling at Dora. Uncle Joe told me about the blow up with Ruby. He was heartbroken, said she disappointed him. He was most concerned that word would get around town."

"Well, things were as tense as you described, and Dora was doing all of the work, why did he continue to allow Ruby to live in his house? I would think she must have done something, or he would have kicked her out. Right?"

"I know there were times when Ruby took credit for Dora's work. Also, Uncle Joe had compassion – he wouldn't have kicked Ruby out when she was sick. He kept telling her to help Dora. Dora never complained but I could see it was hard for her to keep up. I think he thought Ruby was helping, but she wasn't.

Mr. Stead, the Illinois States Attorney, testified next about the legal status of the will. He said it has not been filed with the state, so I assume my life is still up in the air.

After a recess, the judge addresses people in the courtroom, "Ladies and gentlemen, the plaintiffs' attorneys have advised that they have presented all of their witnesses, so we will adjourn until tomorrow at ten o'clock when the defense will present their case."

The Truth

Friday, January 31, 1908

"Hrumph! I want it understood that today we will get down to business. My wife is having a tooth pulled this afternoon, so I will be going home by four o'clock. I will appreciate it if counsel will stick to the point. Also, opposing counsel should limit their objections. Mr. Chipperfield..."

"Thank you, your honor, I call Albert Taff to the stand. Mr. Taff, you were Joseph Murphy's attorney, but you and he had a long - term relationship, is that correct?"

"Yes, sir. My father died when I was two years old, then my mother died two years later. Uncle Joe took me in when I was four. I lived with him in his house until I finished law clerking."

"So, he raised you like a son."

"I wouldn't go so far as to say he was like my father. More like an uncle. I called him Uncle Joe."

"But you must have developed feelings for one another over the years."

"I was very fond of Uncle Joe, and I will be eternally grateful for all he did for me. I think he loved me. When I was little, he bought me toys and he played with me on his knee. Sometimes at night, he would tuck me in, and we would read a bedtime story. Every summer, he took me with him on business trips to Quincy. Of course, our relationship became more formal in later years, it was yes, sir and no, sir. Without a doubt, we respected one another."

"He also took in a young girl, Ruby O'Grady."

"Yes, but much later. He kept telling me about this little girl who delivered milk, that she was always dirty and wore ragged clothes. He said he was concerned about her welfare. He finally went to her father and said he would take her in. When she first came, I could hear her crying at night, but that stopped, and she settled in. It was for the best, she had a better life."

"So the two of you lived with Mr. Murphy, sort of like a family."

"I guess you could say that. Like me, Ruby called him Uncle Joe."

"As Joseph Murphy's attorney, you prepared his will and you presented it to him on January 14 before witnesses, but some of the witnesses stated that he already had a will on file. Why did he make a new will?"

"I penned his new will from memory. Some months prior, I had just returned from Quincy to look at some property that he later purchased. We had a long talk after dinner, and he told me changes he wanted to make. When I presented it to him for signing, I reminded him of that conversation."

"So, to the best of your memory, you simply followed his instructions."

"That's right."

"Your witness."

Boyer bounces out of his chair, and he almost runs to the witness box.

"Mr. Taff, did you read the will to Mr. Murphy before he signed it?"

"No, I didn't feel there was a need to. The will was in accordance with his wishes. You must understand, Uncle Joe was very ill, so we were trying to handle matters quickly."

"Is that why you instructed the nurses to destroy their records? You were trying to close matters as quickly as possible?"

"Uncle Joe was a very private person, and there was no reason to maintain those records. I assumed the doctors' medical records were adequate, so in the interest of ensuring privacy, I instructed the nurses to burn their records."

"Mr. Taff, as executor, you have been paying Joseph Murphy's creditors and other expenses, including substantial sums to Ruby O'Grady on legacy. Correct?"

Albert seems surprised that Boyer knows about the monies paid to Ruby. "Yes, sir, that's true. I recently had a conversation with her, advising her to cease drawing from the estate until this suit is settled. Of course, she is still living in the house, so I will continue to pay her household expenses, and she is entitled to a monthly stipend to cover expenses for the girl, Dora Kelly."

"With servants, I understand. Are the servants paid by the estate?"

"Ruby's the lady of the house, now, at least until this suit is decided. The janitor, R.C. Webster and the farm hands are paid the same as before Uncle Joe died. I don't believe Ruby actually has a housekeeper. Dora Kelly is doing the cooking and cleaning."

"No further questions."

We stay in our seats for the ten-minute recess. "Anna, how did he find out about Ruby taking money from the estate. I didn't tell him. Ruby threatened me if I told. I don't want any trouble."

"Pshaw! I wouldn't worry about it. What can she do to you that she's not already doing?"

I decide not to say anything more. I don't want Anna or anyone else to know about the night I gave Mr. Murphy his medicine. Ruby's glaring at me. I need to tell her that it wasn't me. I didn't tell!

Doc Nelson's testimony is kind of boring. The judge needs to call a recess so I can talk to Ruby! Chipperfield only had a few questions for Dr. Nelson. He's calling Ruby to the stand. Please, God, don't let her say anything!

Ruby stands and she walks with her head down to the witness box. "Anna, where did she get that dress?"

She's wearing the high-top boots she wears when we go to the farm, and they touch the hem of a plain flour sack dress. She never dresses like that!

"Miss O'Grady, tell us about your relationship with the decedent, Joseph Murphy."

"Uncle Joe and I were very close. He took me in when I was eight years old. My father delivered me to Mr. Murphy's front porch and told me I had to stay with him. He said he had enough to worry about, taking care of my mother and my sister."

"So, Joseph Murphy raised you like a daughter, correct?"

"Yes. He provided for me. I had everything I needed, even a room of my own off the kitchen, but it took me a while to get over the fact my mama and daddy didn't want me."

"On Christmas night, 1906, you were out with friends. When did you find out Joseph Murphy was ill?"

"When I came home the next morning, there were several buggies in the dooryard, so I knew something had happened. I was shocked when W.D. told me how sick he was. I knew Dora, that's Dora Kelly, was able to take care of him. Of course, I would have stayed home if I had only known."

"What exactly did the doctors tell you?

"Like I said, W.D. said he had a heart attack, that it was very bad, and he was to have nursing around the clock. When Dr. Coleman advised he was not to have visitors, Albert put me in charge, said I was not to allow any visitors to enter his chamber."

"So, you were just following doctor's orders by keeping everyone out of his room?"

"As much as I could. They gave his sister, Louisa, a brief visit. Then there's the time Dora sneaked into his room. I got into a lot of trouble over that."

"You got in trouble for what she did?"

"Yes, sir. I got yelled at by Anna Moss for not protecting Dora. Can you believe it? When she was being disrespectful? Then, Albert yelled at me for allowing it to happen."

"You loved Joseph Murphy, did you not?"

"Cain't say I loved him, but in the end, I was grateful he took me in. No one asked me if I wanted to live with him, but I learned to care for him. My real papa lives across town. I worked hard for Uncle Joe, though. It was really hard after his attack. Albert put me in charge, and I had to do everything. I not only had to look after the nurses and make sure he was cared for, but there were people coming in and out, so I had to greet and take care of guests. (Sniffle) His sister lives in Quincy and there was no other family to go to for help. Dora saw how hard I was working, so she helped a little bit."

"Your witness."

Boyer talks while he approaches the witness stand, "Miss O'Grady, what was your understanding when you came to live in the Murphy home?"

"I don't understand the question. My papa sent me to live in his house. He said it would be a better life for me."

"Well, did anyone give you a reason for Mr. Murphy taking you in?"

"No one told me, but Papa said he liked having children around."

"Did you go to school?"

"At the beginning, but the year I turned twelve, our housekeeper left. I had to drop school so I could cook and clean."

"But you had a lot of privileges. You had nice clothes and you purchased goods at Dobbins on Joseph Murphy's account."

"Yes, he kept clothes on my back. I saved the print flour sacks. Six of the same print was enough for a summer dress."

"According to Dobbins' records, before Dora Kelly came to live in his house, you were buying nice fabrics including silks and velvets and you recently ordered a party dress from New York. In fact, you've purchased dresses within the last two weeks, have you not?"

Ruby doesn't answer, she looks at Chipperfield, but he does not offer assistance.

"Ruby, how many dresses have you purchased in the last two weeks?"

"I can't remember."

"Eight. Eight dresses, including one woolen dress, two silks and a velvet, a slight step up from the flour sack dress you're wearing."

"Miss O'Grady, this here paper is from the 1900 census of Canton, Illinois. Would you please read this line for the jury?" He points, "This line, right here."

"Ruby O'Grady, 16, servant."

"And the line above it?"

"Joseph L. Murphy..."

"So, the census report was for people living in Joseph Murphy's house. It seems the die was cast from the beginning, Mr. Murphy took you in, knowing he would eventually need a new housekeeper. It says right here, you were a servant."

"No one told me I was a servant. I just did what I was told. Uncle Joe made sure that Albert was educated and, today, he's a big lawyer. Girls are different,

I had to quit school so I could cook and clean. I took care of that man for years. I'm entitled to get what I can."

Boyer has anger in his voice, "Ruby, is that why you went along with this scheme to scam the estate, because you are entitled to do so?"

"Objection, your honor!"

"Sustained. Mr. Boyer's last sentence will be struck from the record, and the jury is to disregard that statement. It's not been proven that a scam took place."

"No further questions. Thank you, Miss O'Grady."

"Court is adjourned until nine o'clock tomorrow."

Ruby storms out of the courtroom. I push my way through the crowd, trying to catch up with her. She must know that I didn't tell. I look down to the end of the hall where she and R.C. are talking. I hear RC say, "Dora didn't tell anyone about the funds you've been drawing from the estate. I was the one who told Boyer. I was fixing a floorboard in the back room and overheard your conversation with Taff. Then I confirmed it with Taff, who is a family friend. You just need to back off and don't you dare do anything to hurt Dora. There's more I could tell, so just keep that in mind. Start being nice to her, Ruby. She is a good girl."

R.C. waves at me. Ruby just looks away. We put on our coats for the cold walk to Mrs. Blackahy's.

"Dora don't worry. Ruby's not going to say anything."

"But how did you find out?"

"I overheard you talking, and I was the one who told Boyer. She can't do anything to me, but this proves she will go to any length to get the homestead!"

We say our goodbyes on the front porch. And I smell something horrible – we must be having sauerkraut for dinner! I hate sauerkraut, but she's already putting supper on the table. I'm hungry so I make a meal out of the sausage and warm bread and butter. I tell her I'm not feeling well and excuse myself, leaving the sauerkraut on my plate.

I've been chilled all day, so I put on my nightdress and go to the bathroom to take a warm bath. I sit on a stool, and lean forward, touching my forehead to the rolled edge of the tub. The heat of the water creates steam on my face, and I start to cry. The tears fall like rain that will not end until the clouds have passed. I take my nightdress off and step into the warm water. Finally, there are no more tears, but I can't stop wondering what's going to happen to me. Oh, well, I'm not going to know the answer tonight. I slump down until the water comes up and tickles my nose. I laugh, thinking about Rex. Someday, the two of us will find Jack and Louis.

The Verdict

Tuesday, February 4

Dr. Coleman is on the witness stand for two days. Tuesday is the second day of Chipperfield's examination of the witness. The crowd has thinned out, and John had to go back to work, so it's just Anna, R.C., and me. R.C. moves up front to sit next to me.

Chipperfield continues, "Dr. Coleman, were you present to witness the signing of the will on January 14?"

"I was, along with Doctors Nelson and Schoeles. We witnessed the signing of the will, and we all signed affidavits to that effect."

"Is it a fact that Joseph Murphy held onto the papers after signing the will, that he would have continued to write and sign repeatedly as long as the papers were in his hands?"

Chipperfield talks in a monotone. After listening to him all day yesterday, I'm bored and only partially paying attention when Dr. Coleman almost yells an emphatic, "No!"

"Dr. Coleman was the will prepared during the evening while you were there?"

"No, Mr. Taff brought the will when he arrived the evening before. The reason we had to wait was to allow the effects of the medicine to dissipate so he would be cognizant for the signing."

"Was there any mention as to why a new will was needed, and who's idea it was to write a new will?"

"I was not made aware of the reasons behind preparation of a new will. However, to the best of my recollection, Dr. Nelson consulted with Albert Taff and Ruby O'Grady, and they decided to make a new will."

"After Murphy was alert and ready to sign the will, did anyone ask him if he did not intend to remember his sisters?"

"Your honor, unless it is absolutely necessary, I prefer not to answer that question."

Judge Thompson rules, "That's a fair question. The witness will answer.'

"I personally asked that question. Several times during his illness he manifested a strong antipathy towards his sisters, and he even told me to keep Louisa out of his house. When she came to his room, he pretended to be unconscious. He refused to recognize her, and he would not talk to her"

"Your witness, counsel."

Boyer jumps up from his chair, and he struts past the jury towards the witness box.

"Dr. Coleman, the nurses have testified that Mr. Murphy needed medication to keep him calm. What medicine or medicines were administered?"

"Laudanum drops. The doses and frequency were intended to keep him in a calm state. At no time was the medicine given, sufficient to cause delirium or coma."

"Dr. Coleman, can you please enlighten us, why was Joseph Murphy under constant medication? Why was he given drops, even when he was unconscious?"

"I wanted him to be maintained in a steady, calm state. I did not want him to become confused and agitated."

Drops! He was unconscious and they gave him drops? The same drops I gave him? Ruby lied to me! I didn't make a mistake! The drops were supposed to make him sleep. I didn't do anything wrong!

I look up and smile at Anna, I whisper, "I'll tell you about it later."

"But you did bring him out of his coma the morning of January 14. I assume your reasons outweighed your concern about Joseph Murphy's physical or mental state. Dr. Coleman, are you aware that some authorities consider Laudanum to be antiquated and relegated to times past?"

"Some doctors have their own opinions."

"And are you aware that some authorities have published papers contending that Laudanum can have an adverse effect, that it can actually slow the heart down and precipitate death?"

I am aware of those journals. However, another prestigious expert, Dr. James Woods, authored a paper disputing those reports. In fact, he referred to them as quackery."

"Dr. James Woods, is he the renowned expert who said all men who reach the age of 60 should be chloroformed? I'll withdraw that question, your honor. Just commenting. No further questions." Boyer continues, "Your honor, it's obvious that the original will could provide insight and could answer many outstanding questions about the contents of the new will. I would like to file a motion that the first typewritten and signed will be produced."

Chipperfield stands up and both attorneys approach the bench. "You honor, the original will is not in the possession of my clients."

"Well, where is it? What about his attorney, Taff?"

"He does not have it."

"Mr. Boyer, I agree with you that the original will would be beneficial, and the fact that the defense contends they do not have it is suspect. Mr. Chipperfield, I want you to talk to your clients and you should instruct them to do everything possible to find that will. We will adjourn until Thursday, to allow time for someone to find and present the original will."

Tuesday, February 4 - Dear Diary, What a day! The trial is recessed until Thursday. Something about trying to find a lost will. Dr. Coleman's testimony took two days. Today, he said the purpose of the Laudanum drops was to make Mr. Murphy sleep. That's what happened when I gave him the drops, he fell asleep. I didn't do anything wrong. I guess I shouldn't be surprised that Ruby lied to me about it being my fault. I told Anna the whole story, how Ruby said she would tell on me if I told anyone about her drawing funds from the estate. I've been afraid to say anything out of fear that she would tell the judge I had over-medicated Mr. Murphy. Anna was shocked when I told her. She said she was glad that R.C. had gone to Boyer, but she thinks the judge should know so he can make sure I am protected. She's going to talk to Boyer. I feel better, even though I still don't know what's going to happen to me. Mrs. Blackahy is calling me for supper – have to go! I hope there's no sauerkraut tonight! Signed, Dora Kelly

Monday, February 10

Every seat in the courtroom is taken, and people are standing in the back, waiting to hear the verdict. The newspapers reported that they couldn't find a will, which means the jury has to decide.

We are in our assigned seats and the newspaper reporters are seated to our right. There's a group of women all dressed up in their church clothes and hats, some with big brims, others are toques with feathers. I have to control my laughter – they don't even know our family. Must not be a lot to do in Lewistown.

The whispers die down and silence fills the room. Then, it's almost as if the room shifts and the floorboards groan as the jury walks slowly to the jury box, with their eyes focused directly on the judge.

The bailiff passes a piece of paper to the judge, "Gentlemen of the jury, you have not been able to agree on a verdict? This is a serious matter. There are people on both sides waiting for a decision so they can go on with their lives. Mr. Foreman, are you close to making a decision? If I send you back for additional consideration, do you believe you can reach an agreement?"

"Don't hardly know. It's not just one person that needs to be convinced, there are disagreements on more than one issue. We've tried to come to an agreement, but every man on the jury has strong opinions, and I don't see them changing their minds."

The judge brings down his gavel as he dismisses the jury. The journalists are clamoring to be the first out the door of the courtroom, knocking chairs over in their haste. It's hard to tell what Ruby is thinking but those of us who are defendants gather around Chipperfield to find out what to expect next.

"This is not necessarily bad news. So far, the will is still intact. It's too early to predict, but there might be a new trial. If so, they will have to make their case before a new jury."

Louisa appears to be angry, and it looks like Anna and Boyer are trying to calm her down.

Anna talks all the way, during our walk to Mrs. Blackahy's, "when they get back to Quincy, Boyer wants to meet with Louisa in his office. I don't think she has the stomach for another trial, and the only other option is to propose a settlement."

"So, am I supposed to go back to the house to live with Ruby?"

"At least for now. There's no change."

It's only ten o'clock, so we decide to gather our things so we can get to Canton before dark. I thank Mrs. Blackahy and we leave for the cold ride to Canton. Anna and I are sitting inside the carriage, and we hear R.C. encourage Jenny to go faster while shaking the reins. Jenny snorts, her breath spewing steam into the air. Neither one of us feels like talking, so we just relax in the warmth from our blankets. I have a lot to think about. At least for now, I have a place to live, but I know it won't be easy living with Ruby with him coming in and out. The swaying motion of the carriage makes me sleepy, so I try to sleep most of the way.

I wake up as R.C. stops the carriage in front of Anna's house. Rex and John are waiting for us on the porch. Rex waves, "Dora, I'll see you tomorrow after school."

Ruby is waiting for me in the kitchen. "Dora, Albert says the appraisers are finally coming. Albert said we just need to make sure the house is clean."

"What will they want?"

"They will inventory everything, all of the household goods, furniture, China, everything to assess the value of the estate for tax purposes. I suppose they will count every knife and fork! By the way, they will be going through your room, so if there is anything personal you don't want them to see, then find a place to put it. Just don't hide anything important". She doesn't wait for me to answer. "Oh, by the way, Jim and I are going to get married on March 11. It will just be family and a few friends. I'll order a cake from the bakery, but I trust you will be here to set everything up, and you will serve punch and take care of our guests after the ceremony."

"Does that mean Jim will be moving in, or will you live at his farm?"

"This is going to be our house, so he will be living here with me."

"But it's not been decided...."

Ruby cuts me off, "Where we live is not your concern. Just you get everything ready!"

February 10, 1908 — Dear Diary, The trial ended today, sort of. The jury couldn't decide so I have to wait to see what's next. After I got home, Ruby told me we have to get ready for the appraisers. I have a right to return to school. Maybe I can just help after school. I was surprised when Ruby told me she and Jim are getting married on March 11. She expects me to do everything for her, set it up and serve and clean up. I pretended I was mad, but actually, I will enjoy doing it. She already has it in mind that this is her house, so he will be moving in after the wedding. I'm tired from the trip, so I didn't feel like arguing, so I just came to my room. I know I'm being a mope, but I don't care. Rex is coming tomorrow after school. He's my best friend so I can hardly wait to tell him what happened at the trial. Signed, Dora Kelly

The Settlement

Ruby and I eat our porridge in silence. I brought my book to read while I eat breakfast, so I don't have to talk to her. Mr. Murphy told me it's rude to read while eating a meal, but I decide it's better than arguing. I look up to the heavens and send a silent prayer, "Sorry, Mr. Murphy."

After we finish eating, Ruby goes to her room, leaving me to clean up the kitchen. The phone rings, breaking the quiet. Ruby comes out of her room, running to answer the phone, "Hello. Yes..... Yes....., that's fine, I'll be there at three."

"That was Albert. Chipperfield believes we should offer a settlement to avoid another trial. We're meeting at three in Albert's office. R.C. will be there. You don't have to go unless you want to."

"That's okay, Rex is coming after school. Besides, if R.C. is going, I don't think I need to be there."

R.C. pulls onto the dooryard to give Ruby a ride to Albert's office, and Rex arrives a few minutes after they are gone. I can't stop talking. I tell him everything. The trial, about Mr. Murphy's friend, Governor Yates, about Ruby's threat and how she lied, blaming me for over-medicating Mr. Murphy. We laugh when I tell him about the parrot, the flying chicken leg, and, R.C. confronting Ruby, telling her she can't do anything to him. He asks me a million questions, and he makes jokes that make me laugh, even though I'm worried about what the settlement might be.

I lean into his shoulder. "I learned one good thing. Mr. Murphy signed a contract that says I'm supposed to go to school, and according to the will, Ruby has to live by the contract. Yesterday, though, she told me the appraisers are finally coming next week, so I won't be able to go to school, because I have to help with cleaning and getting everything organized. She said they'll rummage through everything!"

"Everything? What about the chest in the cellar?"

"I forgot! How can we hide it?"

"You can't. Let's go down and look inside to see what's there. Then we can decide what to do."

We go out back and down the cellar stairs. I wonder if anyone has been down here since we were here last 'cuz cobwebs hit our faces with every step.

"Wait here. I'll get the broom and some matches for the lantern."

Rex sweeps the cobwebs with the broom, and we feel our way to the dark back wall until he lights the lantern. The air smells musty and damp like wet clothes that have been sitting in a bag for a long time, but as we approach the chest, the smell of parfum is so strong I can taste it.

"Rex, I don't remember it smelling this bad. I'm getting a headache."

"Yeah, let's just hurry and get out of here."

We loosen the clasp and lift the lid of the chest. Rex carefully removes the uniform jacket, laying it across the railing by the steps. I lift a christening gown of tatted lace with a ribbon sash. It's yellowed with age.

"I wonder who this belonged to. Do you think it was his? Mr. Murphy's?"

Some of the lace on the hem falls apart into my hand as Rex takes the gown to gently lay it on top of the jacket. "Careful, it's falling apart."

It looks like all that is left are some pictures and old newspapers, but when Rex brings the lantern closer, I see a calico horse laying on top. His mane and tail are made of yarn, and he's missing one eye. I wonder and try to imagine Mr. Murphy as a little boy.

Underneath the toy horse is a picture frame with a portrait of a woman. "Rex, look, isn't she beautiful? Who do you think she is?"

"Don't know, but she must have meant something to Mr. Murphy because so far, everything in this chest seems to have a special meaning."

Rex glances down at the newspaper headline. "Wait a minute!" He lifts the yellowed paper, carefully unfolding it so we can read it.

Heiress Suffers Fatal Fall

"Says here:

> *Miss Catherine Dupres' died yesterday from a tragic accident at the annual Du Page County steeplechase competition. Miss Dupres, who was well known as an accomplished horsewoman, was planning a June wedding. Her fiancé, Attorney Joseph L. Murphy of Canton, could not be reached for comment."*

"Rex, know what? Just before he died, Mr. Murphy staggered out to the landing. I think he was delirious, but he was calling for someone named Catherine. This must be her!"

"Wow! He must have really loved her."

"But he never told us. Let's ask your mother, she'll know. What should we do about the chest? I don't want people rummaging through it and ruining everything. Besides, I doubt this has any value except to family. Ask your mother and father what we should do."

We return our finds to the chest, taking care to keep everything in the same order as they were before. Rex covers the chest with the blanket, and he turns off the lantern. As we approach the steps, a sunbeam bounces through the window, and the tiny dust particles that hover along the ceiling explode into tiny bubbles that are all colors of the rainbow. They float through the air and shed light into every corner of the room. I have a warm feeling, almost like someone is hugging me, and I'm not afraid. I look at Rex and I can tell he feels the same way. We laugh and close the cellar door behind us, and he puts his hand on my shoulder to make sure I'm all right.

Everything's ready for the appraisers. What a mess! Ruby had us stack stuff everywhere. She told me to just pile all of the pillows and bed linens on the beds, and other things are stacked everywhere on the floors in the parlor and dining room. There's hardly room to step around. I didn't have to move any of the furniture, but I had to empty all of the cabinets and drawers. All of the China and fine silver are stacked on the dining room table, and the kitchenware and pots and pans are stacked on the kitchen table. Mr. Murphy's law books are heavy, so Rex organized them for us, against the wall at the bottom of the stairs. He said he did it for me. Good thing, 'cuz he didn't get so much as a thank you from Ruby. Problem is, we have to put everything back when the appraisers leave.

Ruby is heading to the parlor to let Albert in, when I come downstairs.

"Good morning, ladies. I assumed you may not have had breakfast, so I picked up some pastries from the bakery. They will be here in a half hour, so we have time for some coffee or tea and scones before they get here."

I'm starving, but there really isn't any place to make breakfast. We take our cups of tea and some scones, and we sit on the bottom steps of the stairway.

"Albert, what are they going to do when they get here? What am I supposed to do?"

"There's really nothing for you to do now. You and Ruby have already done everything. I'm here to supervise the appraisers, so if they ask you any questions, don't send them to Ruby. Tell them to see me."

The doorbell rings. "They're here!"

There are three men, one to work on each floor. When I come out of the bathroom, one of the appraisers is digging through the dresser drawers in Ruby's room. I hurry up to my room. No one told me they would be looking inside dresser drawers. I thought they would only appraise the stuff that we set out.

When I enter my bedroom, a man is counting the stockings in my drawer, one by one. I'm embarrassed so I don't say anything, but I run downstairs to

Ruby. I pull her by her elbow into the pantry, "Ruby, he's going through my drawers, looking at my stockings and undergarments!"

"I told you. You should have hidden them somewhere. You could have boxed them up. Anna would have kept them for you until they leave. I'm as upset as you are. They shouldn't be looking at our personal belongings. They said it will only take two days then they'll be out of here."

"You're no help! Where's Albert? I want to ask him."

"Did I hear someone mention my name? What's wrong?"

"No one told us they would go through our drawers. The only thing I have in my dresser are my undergarments, and there's a man pulling everything out!"

"What about you, Ruby? Do you have anything to hide in your dresser?"

"No. just my undergarments and night dresses."

"I'll take care of it."

"When you get back, I have an invoice to give you for the work I did to organize everything for the appraisers."

Albert looks at me and I shrug my shoulders. He goes upstairs and I hear him talking to the men. He returns to the kitchen, "They say that they're done going through the drawers. I told them to just leave your things out because they left a mess. You will probably want to put your things away the way you want them. Now, let me see that invoice."

I notice the sheet of paper with handwriting, that Ruby hands to Albert. His eyes get big, and he looks shocked! "$1,783.00? You can't be serious! How'd you come up with the amount? Did you just pull it out of the air? The thought that you would expect payment of any kind never crossed my mind, but this is an exorbitant amount!"

"I don't know, and I really don't care what you did or did not expect. This was a lot of work, so I expect to be paid."

Albert looks at me. I shrug. I know nothing about it. I want to tell him that Rex and I were actually the ones who had to move and organize everything. Ruby just keeps taking more and more. I bet there won't be any money left for my inheritance by the time she's done. Maybe Albert can help me to find a job.

Friday, February 14, 1908.

I found a letter on Mr. Murphy's desk that Ruby had left behind. Louisa accepted the proposed settlement. Louisa and Anne receive a cash settlement of $30,000 each, and each side agreed to pay their own legal expenses. $40,000 was awarded to the Physician's Club of Canton to build and maintain a hospital in Canton. Albert Taff will receive $9,000 plus numerous rental properties in Canton, and R.C. Webster and I are to receive $3,000 each. Ruby O'Grady has been awarded the homestead and the rest of the estate including tracts of land in Minnesota and Iowa; a 300-acre farm on the Spoon River; numerous houses and lots in Canton, and 1/3 interest in business blocks in Quincy, plus considerable investments. I'm to be her ward until I get my inheritance. I feel terrible.

I know I won't get my money for a long time, so I go up to my bedroom and cry for a while, and then decide I will do my best to stay here because there's nothing to be done about it, and I want to stay in Canton. Daddy used to say, *Is ait an mac an saol.* Life is strange. Now I know that's really true.

CANTON DAILY REGISTER: CANTON, ILLINOIS, FRIDAY, JANUARY 25, 1907.

JOSEPH L. MURPHY

Another Old and Prominent Citizen Finishes Life's Journey Friday Morning.

TWICE ELECTED MAYOR

More Than Forty Years a Member of Fulton County Bar; Aged Seventy-six.

Joseph L. Murphy died at 10:15 o'clock Friday morning, at his home 339 South First avenue. Death was due to fatty degeneration of the heart, and followed an illness of about six weeks.

About 10 days before Christmas Mr. Murphy over-exerted himself while on a visit to his farm on Spoon river, and a day or two later he experienced a severe attack of heart failure, from which he was relieved with difficulty. He recovered sufficiently to be able to leave his bed, but in arranging his business affairs preliminary to a proposed trip to California he again overtaxed his strength, and a relapse followed from which he failed to rally.

Joseph Leopold Murphy was born in Mount Rock, Queen's county, Ireland, July 22, 1830, and came to America when about a year old, with his parents, Mr. and Mrs. Richard Murphy.

Richard Murphy on his mother's side was descended from the Fitzgerald family, prominent in Irish history, and by another branch of which family the famous old castle of Kilkenny is still held.

In America the Murphys settled first in Uniontown, Penn., remaining there about six years, after which they removed to New York city, from which city, after a short residence, they came to Illinois, settling first near St. Augustine, where they lived about a year, coming from there to Joshua township, Fulton county.

Richard Murphy's death occurred [illegible] and the [illegible] ly moved to Canton.

Joseph L. Murphy attended school in Quincy and later was a student at College Mound, Mo., for two or three years. He read law in the office of Warren & Wheat, in Quincy, and was admitted to the bar in the early '60's.

Returning to Canton, Mr. Murphy engaged in the practice of his profession in partnership with Parley C. Stearns for two or three years, after which this connection was severed, Mr. Murphy continuing in the law business without an associate until 1865, when he entered into partnership with G. L. Miller, the business being conducted under the firm name of Murphy & Miller. This continued five years, after which Mr. Murphy retired from active practice to give his attention entirely to his private business affairs, which had by this time assumed large proportions.

For many years Mr. Murphy resided with his mother and sister on North First avenue, just south of the present site of the Nazarene church. His mother died in January, 1874, and about three years later Mr. Murphy purchased several lots on South First avenue and erected the home in which his death occurred.

Mr. Murphy was unmarried. His near relatives living are two sisters—Miss Louisa M. A. Murphy and Mrs. Annie Hopkins—both of whom reside in Quincy. Miss Murphy has been at the home of her brother in Canton for several days. Mrs. Hopkins is spending the winter in California, and owing to poor health may not return east to attend the funeral. Three brothers and two sisters are dead.

John and James Murphy, of Canton, and their sister, Miss Margaret Murphy, who makes her home with Miss Louisa M. A. Murphy in Quincy, are children of a cousin of the deceased. Another cousin, Joseph Ledwith, and several second cousins, named Fitzpatrick, reside in New York.

Miss Mabel Martin, daughter of Mr. and Mrs. John Martin, residing on West Hickory street, has been raised and educated by Mr. Murphy, of whose household she has been a member since her eighth year.

Three or four years ago Mr. Murphy contracted with the authorities of an orphans' home in Chicago, to care for and educate until her twenty-first year a little girl, Dora Kelly, now about 10 or 12 years of age, and who has since that time been an inmate of his home.

Mr. Murphy was a Republican in politics and always took a deep interest in political matters. He was mayor of Canton for two terms, in 1871 and 1872, and served one term as alderman, in 1880. He was a member of the Canton lodge of the Masonic order.

Mr. Murphy leaves a large estate, including tracts of land in Iowa and Minnesota, a farm of about 360 acres on Spoon river, numerous houses and lots in Canton, and a third interest in business blocks in Quincy, besides a considerable amount otherwise invested.

FELL ON ICE.

Injury Which May Be Very Serious Sustained by Mrs. Malstrom Thursday Evening.

Mrs. Edwin Malstrom was one of a skating party at Van Winkle lake Thursday evening, and is the victim

TODAY'S MARKETS

Prices and Prospects in Chicago— Receipts of Live Stock at Union Yards.

QUOTATIONS AT PEORIA

Prices Paid by Canton Dealers for Stock, Grain and Other Farm Produce.

Greenwell & Company supply the Register with this report of today's Chicago and Peoria livestock markets:

Chicago.

Receipts hogs, 24,000.
Held over, 4,345.
Light, $6.45@$6.70. Mixed, $6.45@$6.72½. Heavy, $6.45@$6.75.
Receipts cattle, 2,000.
Receipts sheep, 7,000.
Prospects: Hogs, 5@10 cents higher. Cattle, steady. Sheep, steady.

Peoria.

Hogs $6.45@$6.60 at opening of market today.

GRAIN MARKETS.

Prices of Corn, Wheat [illegible] today [illegible].

T. A. Grier & Company, Chamber of Commerce, Peoria, furnish this report of the Chicago and Peoria grain markets this afternoon:

Peoria

Corn—Receipts, 84 cars. Market steady and demand good. No. 3, 41½c; No. 4, 40½c; no grade, 39. Oats—Receipts, seven cars. Steady with good demand. No. 2 white, 35@37½c, No. 3 white, 36½@37.

Chicago.

Corn—No. 2, 41½@42½c; No. 3 yellow, 41½@42½; No. 3 white, 42½@43; No. 4, 40@41½; no grade, 38@40. Oats—Standard, 37@37½c; No. 2 white, 38½@39; No. 4 white, 37@ 37½; No. 3, 36½@37.

LOCAL MARKETS.

Canton Markets Are Paying for Stock, Grain and Produce.

Hogs, $6.10@$6.25.
Cattle—Butcher steers, $3.40@$4.—50. Feeding steers, $2@$3.65. Heifers, $1.75@$4.50. Cows $1½@$15. Calves, $2.65@$5.65.
Corn, 37½ cents.
Oats, 34 cents.
Wheat, 65 cents.
Hay, $15.
Straw, $6.
Eggs, 23 cents.
Butter, 25 cents.
Turkeys, 12 cents.
Chickens 7½@8 cents.
Ducks, seven cents.
Lard, 10 cents.
Country lard, 11 cents.
Cabbage, 1½ cents a pound.
Potatoes, 50 cents.
Parsnips, 1½ cents a pound.
Turnips, 50 cents.

Funeral.

The funeral of Jacob Wolf will be

tor. In his last illness she was his comfort and stay, and in his will it is announced that she is the chief beneficiary.

Three years ago an orphan girl, Dora Kelly, was taken from a Chicago orphanage and given a home by Mr. Murphy, who agreed to care for her until her 20th year. In his last will he also provided for her. The two sisters, Miss Murphy and Mrs. Hopkins, both of Quincy, are his only near relatives.

Mr. Murphy amassed a fortune estimated at more than $150,000.

The funeral was held yesterday afternoon from the residence in charge of the Masonic lodge. ~

1/28/1907 Daily Journal

THE ILLINOIS RIVER'S RAPID RISE CEASES.

Havana, Ill., Jan. 28. - The exceedingly rapid rise of the Illinois river and tributaries, the Spoon, Sangamon and Mackinaw, which for the past 25 years has not been surpassed and which for the past ten days has wrought destruction in all that was in its path and the path of its flood has ceased.

The levee separating the Illinois river from Fulton county is safe, and, for once in the past ten days the terror, which reigned in every part of Fulton and Mason counties, has abated. The large cakes of sharp ice, however, which are floating down the swift currents, are responsible for a feeling of danger. ~

2/1/1907 Quincy Journal

SISTER TO MAKE A BITTER FIGHT

TO RECOVER SHARE OF RICH BROTHER'S ESTATE - MISS LOUISA MURPHY

Of Quincy Declares Her Brother Was Off mentally When he Made His Will.

The Fulton County *Ledger* of Canton, Ill., says:

Miss Louisa Murphy, of Quincy, who was called to Canton a few days before her brother, J.L. Murphy, died, is not satisfied that her brother was mentally competent to make his will when he did, and has commenced proceedings to have the will set aside. She has retained O.J. Boyer to look after her interests, and probably one or two other attorneys will be employed.

Miss Murphy claims that she was not notified to come to her brother's bedside until Monday, Jan. 14, the day after the will was made. She reached here early Tuesday morning, Jan. 15, and declares after her arrival here her brother's condition was such that she scarcely had an intelligent word from him. Consequently, she does not think it possible that her brother was right mentally when he executed his will.

Miss Murphy declares that her brother had always contended he would never make a will, and she states that no member of the family ever made a will.

Nothing was left to any of his relatives. Mrs. Hopkins, a sister, is in poor health, and is in California

and was therefore unable to attend her brother's funeral. John and James Murphy, of Canton, and Miss Margaret Murphy, who resides with Miss Louisa Murphy, in Quincy, are second cousins. Several cousins reside in New York.

Mr. Murphy left an estate estimated to be worth from $150,000 to $250,000. The first sum is the estimate placed upon the estate by A.E. Taff, the executor under the will, also one of the principal beneficiaries, while Miss Louisa Murphy claims it is worth nearly $250,000. It consists of about 1,200 acres of land in Iowa and Minnesota, some Fulton county lands, the handsome home place in Canton, about a dozen tenant houses in this city, and a one third interest in two or three business blocks in Quincy, among them the Newcomb hotel, and several residences in that city. ~

2/6/1907 Quincy Daily Journal

SIMPLY CAN'T GET A PREACHER

TO TAKE THE PULPIT OF THE CHRISTIAN CHURCH AT CANTON, ILL.

Canton, Ill., Feb. 6. - Another pastor has declined the call to the local Christian church. The Rev. N.T. McConnell, of Deland, was called to the local pastorate, but after considering the matter for two weeks, finally decided to remain with his church at Deland, as his congregation was unwilling to release him. The local church is having a strenuous time selecting a pas-

ABOVE: Sisters Contest Murphy Will. Quincy Journal

LEFT: Illinois Governor Richard Yates

VOLUME XVII—NUMBER 200.

CANTON, ILLINOIS, FRIDAY, JANUARY 25, 1907.

TO FOUND A HOSPITAL

Forty Thousand Dollars of His Fortune is Bequested by J. L. Murphy.

LAST WILL AND TESTAMENT OF DECEASED

Substance of Its Provisions—Information from Source Reliability of Which There Is No Cause to Doubt—Most of Large Estate to Adopted Daughter.

By the will of Joseph L. Murphy, whose death is chronicled in another column, the city of Canton receives FORTY THOUSAND DOLLARS for the purpose of building, equipping and endowing a public hospital.

Though, as yet no will has been read, it can be stated from authority which there is no reason to doubt, that a will exists, that this amount for a hospital is one of the bequests, and that it is made with only one condition: That the erection and equipment of a building for this purpose and the setting aside of a portion of the bequest as an endowment fund is entrusted to the Canton Physicians' Club in co-operation with the executor of the will, Attorney A. E. Taff.

Other bequests which are understood to be made by the will are:

To Dora Kelly, the young girl whom Mr. Murphy a few years ago brought to his home from a Chicago orphanage, $3,000.00.

To R. C. Webster of Canton, $1,000.00.

To A. E. Taff of Canton, a section of land in Iowa, several houses and lots in Canton and $9,000.00.

To Miss Mabel Martin, a first bequest, taking precedence of all others, of the home on South First avenue and $9,000.00, and the residue of the estate after all other bequests and expenses have been paid.

As far as can be learned, none of the testator's relatives are beneficiaries under the will.

The total value of the estate is estimated at $150,000.00.

Details of Will: Bequest to Found Canton Hospital — Canton Daily Register

BELOW: Hospital Ground-breaking

The Original Graham Hospital

Emergency Room Entrance, Graham Hospital — Canton, Illinois

PART FIVE

A New Life

"Some pursue happiness, others create it."
Unknown

Movin' On

February 19, 1908

Ruby and Jim are drinking coffee at the kitchen table when I come downstairs for breakfast. I can feel the tension in the room and figure they are arguing, so I turn heel and start to go back to my room, but Ruby calls me back.

"Dora, we've been waiting for you. Sit down and have some tea. You can eat later. We need to talk. So, it's been decided, you and I will continue to live together in this house. I guess we need to lay down some ground rules. I know what you've been thinkin' since you heard about the contract, but don't go getting' any big ideas. This ain't goin' to be a free ride. You'll have to earn your keep."

I figure I have nothing to lose. "You're not my mother, and according to Albert, I'll just reside here. The only space that is mine is my room, everything else is yours, but you don't own me, and you can't tell me what to do!"

Ruby starts to interrupt, but I cut her off, "I'm not finished! Ruby, we don't always need to agree with one another, but if we're going to live together, we need to find ways to get along. You said you will be hiring a housekeeper; I assume you mean your sister. Where is she?"

"Don't concern yourself with my sister. What she might do will be my decision, but she wants to go to school, and she has to help my mother at home."

I feel a knot of pain and anger swelling in my belly. Her sister wants to go to school? So, do I! I decide it's best to end the conversation right now. We can talk later when I'm not so angry.

"Ruby, I'm not hungry, so I'm going up to get dressed. Let's find time later to sit down and agree on a list of things for me to do after school and on weekends."

I'm dusting the piano when I hear someone knocking on the kitchen door. It's Rex! I try to appear calm while a tingle runs down my back. I open the door, smiling.

"What are you so happy about? I know, Mother says the secret to being happy is going what you love to do, and you love dusting, right?"

"Silly, I'm just happy that you came by! I didn't know you were coming."

Rex lowers his voice, "Where's Ruby? I talked to my parents."

"Let me get my coat."

We leave for a walk up the street. "They want to take the chest to their house. They want to move it sometime when Ruby isn't here. Sometime when my father's not working."

"They'll probably go out tonight with their friends. They go out every Saturday. I'll call you when they leave."

Once Ruby and Jim leave, I call Rex and I watch out the window. Soon, Rex and John are pulling onto the dooryard with a wagon. Toby prances up to the house, and he snorts when John pulls the reins. Rex jumps down and he starts walking to the back of the house. Toby starts to follow, and the wagon is still rolling, until Rex grabs his bridle while telling him to stop, but the wagon continues to roll, gently nudging the horse's rump.

Rex laughs, "See what happened? See what you did to yourself?" He tells Toby to stay put while he ties the reins to the railing.

I run ahead to light the lantern, and it only takes a few minutes for John and Rex to load the chest onto the wagon.

"Thank you, John, and tell Anna I said thank you for allowing us to keep the chest at your house."

"Tell her yourself. Get your coat so you can come to our house for supper. Anna wants you to be there when we open the chest."

February 21, 1908 — Dear Diary, Rex and John came for the chest, and then we went to their house go for supper. We opened the chest and Anna was overcome with emotion. Funny, it didn't smell like before, and I didn't have any eerie feelings, so I guess the spirits, whoever they are, were happy to be out of the cellar. Anna said the jacket was from a wounded soldier who was walking home from the war, but he only got as far as their front step. They fed him and tried to care for his wounds, but he died. She said all of the Murphy children, Joseph, Louisa and Anne, wore the christening gown. The lace was tatted by their mother. The horse was Mr. Murphy's constant companion until he had to give it up to go to school, and we were right, Mr. Murphy never got over losing Catherine. She said they were a sought-after couple. He was an upcoming attorney, and she was beautiful and outgoing. They were invited to all of the fancy parties. Anna said she would take special care of the chest and its contents, and she will make sure it stays with family. Signed, Dora Kelly

March 11, 1908

I have never seen Ruby so excited and happy than she was on her wedding day! Maybe she'll start being nicer to me if this lasts! She's upstairs with her girlfriends, putting on her dress. The house looks great! She ordered bouquets of white roses and baby's breath for the table in the parlor and for the sideboard in the dining room. She even has pots of white tulips on the front porch.

Ruby let me decide how to set the dining room up for the reception. I put the lace tablecloth on the table, and the wedding cake in the middle of the table is so tall I can't reach the top. I'll need help when it comes time to cut the cake. I polished the big silver punchbowl and matching cups, and I set out a stack of blue willow plates for the tea sandwiches. I'll put the plates with pink roses out later for the cake. The white basket that I use to store Victoria's clothes is perfect to hold the bouquet of linen napkins. I'll let her think this was a lot of work, but I really had fun doing it.

They're coming down the stairs. Her friends come down first, wearing matching pink ankle length dresses, then Ruby comes out of her room, and she strikes a pose at the top of the stairs on the landing. She must have ordered her dress from Chicago. It's really pretty, ivory lace with a ruffled neck and a short train. Her short-cropped hair is covered with a lace cap that's attached to a long veil. I notice she's wearing the pearl necklace that Mr. Murphy gave her last Christmas.

"Ruby, you look beautiful!"

"Well, thank you, Dora. So nice of you to say so."

Her friends clap and squeal with excitement as she walks slowly down the stairs.

"Do you have everything ready? I want everything to be perfect when my guests arrive after the ceremony. Knowing you, you must have forgot something."

Silence creates its own sound as it floats across the room. All eyes are on me.

"Nope, I made a list, so everything's ready. Come see your cake in the dining room."

They go to the dining room, and I can hear the oohs and aahs. R.C. is out front with the carriage so I go to the parlor and wait for them to leave.

"Well, I guess everything's ready." They put on their coats, and they leave – finally! Silly me for thinking she could be nice.

Since I'm serving the punch, I had Helen make me a new dress from powder blue crepe fabric I bought at Dobbins. This is the first time I've worn heels, so I carry them down the stairs and sit on a kitchen chair to put them on. One look in the hallway mirror, and I wish Rex was here to see me.

They'll be here soon, so I fill the silver trays with the tea sandwiches from the bakery. Let's see, there's cucumber sandwiches, chicken salad made with crustless bread, and tiny pastries with cream cheese and strawberries. Yum! Think I'll have just one, she'll never know. Just as I pop one in my mouth, I hear a commotion outside. They're here! I chew fast, trying to down the thick cream cheese and strawberry in one swallow. The door opens and I gulp!

I greet the guests at the door, showing them where to put their coats, then I hurry to the kitchen where R.C. is waiting to help me fill the punch bowl with pitchers of mixed juices that I prepared. He pops the cork sending a signal that the champagne punch is ready.

R.C. hurries out the kitchen door and I go to my station in the dining room. Everyone is having a good time, and people are so nice to me when I hand them their punch. One of the bridesmaids, the prettier one, whispers, "Dora, this is very nice. I know it was a lot of work, but you should be proud."

"It's okay. I liked doing it."

March 11, 1908 Dear Annie Rose,

I hope all is well with you and your new beau. Tell me all about him. What does he look like?

Ruby and Jim were married today. I was in charge of the reception at the house. It was nice and her dress was pretty. The cake was so tall it almost toppled over when his mother took the top tier off so we could cut the cake. I didn't say anything, but I had to work hard not to laugh. Everyone but Ruby was nice to me, and I had fun doing it. I just wish Rex could have been here, though, to see me in my new heels. We are special friends, like you said. But I'm still not sure what is going to happen, because I haven't been able to go back to school. What will he see in me in a few years? I'm sure there are a lot of girls who like him, too.

Have you ever worn high heels? I felt very grown up, but I couldn't wait to take them off after everyone left.

Jim moved in right away. Can you believe he dropped satchels and bags of dirty clothes on the kitchen floor, when I was trying to clean up from the reception? "These need washing, Dora." Oh, well, this is my fate, I'll just have to learn to be more tolerant. I miss you and hope we can find a way to get together soon.

Love, Dora

Finding Family

Albert is waiting for me when I arrive, "Good Day, Dora, nice to see you. Let's go into my office. What brings you here today?"

"Anna suggested that I talk to you about my situation. Actually, it's not been too bad. The love birds stick to themselves, and I've been spending a lot of time at Anna's. We just try to stay out of one another's way. Ruby just lies around all the time. She's getting bigger every day."

"That's right, she's with child. When is the baby due?"

"Next month, maybe before Christmas. The problem is she thinks I'm her housekeeper. At the funeral luncheon, she said her sister was taking over, but the only time I've seen her was at their wedding, so I'm left to do all of the cleaning. Another school year has started, my friend, Rex, is a sophomore and I haven't even made it past fifth grade. I've lost another year because she won't let me go back. You said the contract said I am supposed to go to school, but it's one excuse after another. First, I had to help get ready for the appraisers, then there was the wedding, and now she has a baby on the way. I can only imagine what she has in mind after the baby is born."

"Have you tried to talk to her?"

"We argued right after the will was settled. We really haven't talked since, other than her ordering me around. She always tells me not to get any big ideas about school."

I'm trying not to cry, but I can't help it. I wipe my nose on my sleeve, and Albert gives me his hanky, "Don't cry, now. I'll talk to her. I want you to feel that you can come to me but truthfully, there's little I can do. I can't force her to do what's right. I guess we all knew it would be hard for you to live there, but that's your only option for now. I have an appointment coming up soon, Dora. Come by anytime."

December 18, 1908, Dear Diary, nothing has changed since I talked to Albert. He never got back to me, so I guess he just doesn't care. I went to Anna's house for Thanksgiving. Ruby invited her mother, father, and sisters, so I had to make a big dinner for six people before I left. I made sure I was gone before they arrived because I don't want to see her sister. I've been busy getting the house ready for Christmas, too. R.C. brought a big tree and some evergreens. I'll decorate the house just like we did when Mr. Murphy was alive. The special ornaments that he brought from Ireland have special meaning, and I remember his smile when I gave him the red and green paper chain. I'll put it in the center of the tree, just like he said. I thought Ruby would get into the Christmas spirit and help, but all she does is lie around and mope. She wears my patience, but I hold my tongue. I remember when Mama was carrying Louis, she was up every day, working and taking care of Jack and me. Not Ruby! But there are some bright spots. Anna and I are going Christmas shopping tomorrow.

I need some ideas what to get for Rex and Harold. I'm going to sign off for now 'cuz I'm sleepy. There's a lot to do for me and my friends, and even more to do for Ruby and Jim. Right now, I count the months and years. I can't wait for the time when I can count the days. Signed, Dora Kelly

I wake up to loud screams, so I run down to the landing. Jim is running ahead of me, down the stairs.

"Jim, what's wrong? Is it the baby?"

"Can you call Doc Nelson? She's hysterical, worried that something's wrong like last time."

"I'll call the doctor. Put some pots of water on the stove, and I'll get some towels and linens for the nurse and doctor."

I hear another scream. "There she goes again. You'd better get up there. I'll call the doctor and get everything ready."

After Doc Nelson arrives with Nurse Havermale, I go to my room to put on a work dress and apron. There's really nothing I can do, so I decide to make tea and coffee in case Jim wants some. Finally, Ruby lets out one loud scream, then I hear a baby cry. Jim comes running down the stairs, "It's a boy! Can you believe it? I have a son!"

The nurse calls down for more water and towels, and I can hear Ruby. I can't tell if she's laughing or crying. Either way, the baby is okay, and she must be okay if I can hear her voice.

I walk slowly up the stairs after everything quiets down, and I tip toe to the door of their room. Nurse Havermale hands me the basket of soiled linens. Seeing Ruby with the baby sleeping soundly under her arm brings back memories of an almost forgotten time when Louis was born. Ruby seems so happy, and I don't want her to see me crying, so I put the basket down and run up to my room.

I hear the front door slam and it's time to make dinner, so I start down the stairs. When I reach the landing, Ruby calls me to her room.

"What do you think, Dora?"

I look at the infant, and there are no words to describe the feeling I have for this little person I don't even know.

"Do you want to hold him?"

"But he's sleeping!"

"It's okay. Babies sleep a lot. You won't wake him."

I lift the warm bundle and hold him close while he nestles his way into my heart. He's not Louis, and he will never replace my brothers, but I know I will love him. I think he will bring joy to this house.

December 22, 1908

Jim's sitting at the kitchen table when I come downstairs.

"Want some coffee? Just made it."

"No, thanks. I drink tea for breakfast. You're up early, is Ruby awake?"

"I hope she's sleeping. We were up and down with the baby all night. I feel like shit!"

"I'd like to help, but he's nursing. I was going to talk to Ruby, but it's probably better that I talk to you. I'm not going to be here to serve holiday dinners. I'm going to church Christmas Eve with Anna and her family, and she's invited me to spend the night so we can be together Christmas morning. I told her I'd bring a mincemeat pie, so I'll do some baking for you, but I won't be here to serve any of the meals."

"This is a bad time, Dora, with her just havin' the baby. Doc said she's supposed to stay in bed for ten days. She's not going to be happy. Seems to me you're being kind of selfish."

"I'm not selfish, Jim. If I was, I wouldn't do half the things I do around here. I'll make some things ahead that you can heat up. Maybe her sister will help out for a couple days."

"You know her sister. We've tried to get her to help a couple times, but she's no help. I suppose there's no changing your mind."

"Jim, Christmas is not the time to be arguing. I'm going to Anna's like I said. You'll have to make your own plans."

He puts his head down and he brushes his hair back from his forehead. "I'll have another cup of coffee, then I'll go see if she's awake." He perks up when he hears a cry upstairs. "Well, sounds like Little Eddie is awake, so I guess she'll be awake."

I make breakfast while he goes up stairs, and I take a breakfast tray with oatmeal and warm milk to Ruby. I hesitate at their bedroom door. She's nursing the baby, but she waves me in. I guess Jim hasn't told her yet.

Christmas Eve, 1908

Ruby and Jim are at their usual place, drinking coffee at the kitchen table when I come downstairs.

"Goodness, you're up! I thought you had to stay in bed."

"I decided to just come down for meals. What are you going to do today?"

"Well, after I make breakfast, I'm going to bake pies. Are you having anyone over tonight or tomorrow?"

"My mother called; they are stopping by. They want to see the baby, but they won't be staying to eat. It will just be Jim and me."

"I'll make a couple extra pies in case you want to have dessert while they are here. Thought I'd make mincemeat and apple, my Christmas present to you and Jim. Wait, I have something upstairs."

I come downstairs with a little package tied with a blue ribbon. "Here, I got this for the baby."

Ruby pulls the ribbon. She looks away but I think she actually sheds a tear.

"I hope you like them. The lady at Dobbins told me they were knitted by a woman across town. They looked small when I bought them, but his feet are so tiny. I guess he'll grow into them."

"They are really pretty. I really like the blue ribbon ties. But, Dora, I must say, I'm very disappointed in you. How can you leave us at a time when we need help?'

"You always need help, Ruby. And I always help. Please, I don't want to argue, it's Christmas. I'm going. My mind is made up."

Later that afternoon, I pack my pies up and set theirs out. R.C. takes my satchel and the pie basket, and he ushers me to the carriage. I feel like a queen!

John waves at us when we enter the sanctuary. He's saved a pew since there are nine of us. Like every Christmas Eve service, the church is beautiful with candles, the tree, and red poinsettias banking the altar. Seems the same, but it's not. I miss Mr. Murphy. I miss his baritone voice when we sing Silent Night, and there weren't any presents under the tree when I left the house. I close my eyes and pray. I pray for Ruby, Jim and the baby, that they have a nice Christmas and I ask God to bring peace to our house in 1909.

The service ends at midnight, and I'm sleepy. It's a short ride to Anna and John's. I'm sitting next to Anna, facing Harold and Rex. Rex breaks into a knowing smile but he doesn't say anything. Harold surprises me, though, "You look real pretty tonight, Dora, in that red dress with your matching headband."

"Thank you, Harold. Everyone looked nice tonight, even Dickie with his navy knickers and red vest. I think Mary sews her children's clothes."

"They are nice people. R.C. was a good friend of Joseph and he's our friend, too. Real friends are hard to come by."

John pulls the carriage close to the porch, so we don't have to walk through snow. Anna hurries to the kitchen to make cocoa. She has a bed made for me on the couch in the parlor, so everyone sits around the kitchen table. I'm facing the door to the parlor and notice the chest, set against the wall with a portrait of Mr. Murphy above on the wall. It looks like she polished it. I'm so glad it's here, safe with family.

Rex laughs, "I guess Dora's tired."

I hear my name. I'm having trouble keeping my eyes open. "I'm sorry. I got up early to bake and I made a pot of chicken and noodles for Jim and Ruby. I think I am tired!"

"Of course, you are, and it's one o'clock in the morning. We all can use some sleep."

"Oh, Mother! It's actually Christmas. Can't we open presents now?"

John laughs, "We'll open them in the morning. Your mother has planned a special breakfast, so we'll eat first. Let's call it a night."

I remember going to the bathroom to change into my night dress, but I'm so tired, I don't remember anything after that. I must have fallen asleep as soon as my head hit the pillow.

It sounds like a mouse is scurrying across the other side of the room. I sit up in time to see John sneaking a small present onto the tree. He looks at me, putting his finger to his lips, telling me to be quiet. Rex and Harold must have heard their father, because I hear two thuds, as their feet hit the floor.

I go to see if Anna needs help and the boys come to breakfast, partially dressed, pants, no shirts. Harold is skinny but it's the first time I noticed, Rex has muscles and a few blonde hairs on his chest. I'm embarrassed and look away. I don't want Anna to see me looking.

"Boys, you need to wear shirts when we have company. Sorry, Dora, I try to teach them."

"It's okay, Anna, I had brothers."

"I know, but they were little. My boys are young men. Everything's ready, so let's eat. The boys are anxious to get to the presents."

Rex and Harold go upstairs and put on shirts, and then we all pitch in for ourselves, getting coffee and tea, while Anna puts some boiled eggs and a warm plum kuchen in the middle of the table.

"Wow, Mother! This is great!"

"Oh, Harold, you've had kuchen before. It's perfect for Christmas morning, though, little bother and we can hurry to the presents."

The kuchen is delicious and I'd like another piece, but I'm already the last to finish and the boys are waiting for me so they can leave the table.

I go to the parlor and move the bedding, so we have a place to sit. Rex and Harold are on the floor looking at name tags.

"Look, Father, this one's for you!"

John tries not to smile, but I can tell he's pleased, "From who? Can't be Santa, Anna told me I'll probably get coal this year."

The room is filled with laughter as we all open our gifts. Anna really likes the Home Sweet Home sampler that I made for her and John, and the chess set I bought for the boys turned out to be the ideal gift. I don't have a gift to open yet, but still, there are two packages under the tree.

"Oh, Dora, we forgot you! Oh, well, I'll try to remember next year!"

"Rex Moss, give Dora her presents. You're such a tease!"

Rex hands them to me one at a time. The first is a small leather purse from Anna and John, and the present from Rex and Harold is a notebook and a pencil case for school. I thank them, knowing I may not be returning to school.

Suddenly, it's quiet as John stands to take the last gift off the tree.

"Here, dear, this one's for you."

Anna opens the tiny box, "Oh, no, John, you must take this back. It's too much!"

"No, I want you to keep it. You do so much for the boys and me, and I have watched you help Dora and Louisa to deal with all the turmoil. You deserve it, and I want you to have it. You can wear it when we go to church."

"Look, Dora." She holds the box so I can see the ruby brooch. "It will be lovely with my black wool dress. Thank you, John."

When Anna and I are cleaning up the breakfast dishes, she asks, "How are things going, Dora? We think of you a lot. Is Ruby treating you well?"

"About the same. We get along, but we don't talk much and I can feel the tension. I talked to Albert about school, but that was a waste of time."

"You're still not going to school?"

"With Ruby, it's one excuse after another. First the appraisers, then the wedding, now Little Eddie and she's in bed for now, but she seems to think I'll be her housekeeper forever. I love the baby, though. He's so cute and he snuggles when I hold him."

Anna looks at John and he nods, indicating they will talk later.

Christmas Day, 1908, Dear Diary, I had a wonderful Christmas at Anna and John's. Rex and Harold tease me a lot - makes me miss my brothers and mama and daddy even more. What with all the work I'm doing for Ruby and Jim, and me not going to school, I hardly see Rex, so this was special. I wonder where my brothers are and what they did for Christmas. I'll find them someday. Hopefully, they are in happy homes with families. Anna asked, so I told her everything. She did say she was surprised that Ruby let me spend the night, but like Albert said, I just live there, I'm not a servant. Anna and John gave me a leather purse for Christmas that matches my coat. I've not had a purse before, so that was special. Rex and Harold seem to think I'll be back in school, so they gave me some school supplies. I've about given up on that idea, though. It was good to get home so I could hold the baby, but I don't know what I would do without Anna and John. Signed, Dora Kelly

The Kuchareks

Saturday, January 9, 1909

Anna's having a dinner to celebrate our birthdays. I'm outgrowing my clothes, so I decide to wear my Christmas dress again. Oh, well, it's no matter, I haven't grown too much, so my new dresses mostly fit.

Ruby asked me to change Little Eddie's diaper before I go. I can't wait to get out of here, even for a few hours. I've been washing diapers and cleaning poop all day. The whole house smells when I boil his diapers. I just hope I don't smell, too.

The baby is fussing, so I pick him up from his cradle and lay him on the cot. The second I take his diaper down, he shoots a stream of pee that drips down the front of my dress!

"Darn it, Eddie! Now look what you've done."

Ruby enters the room, "What's wrong? What can a baby possibly do to upset you?"

"He peed all over the front of me, and I don't have another dress to wear. I told you, I've outgrown most of my clothes."

"Well, go clean up and find something else to wear. I'll finish here. Next week, get some fabric from Dobbins and take them to Helen. Get enough for three dresses."

John and Rex are in the dooryard waiting for me when I come downstairs.

I put on my coat and leave without saying anything.

Thank heavens Anna fixed a simple dinner of roast chicken. I haven't been very hungry after all of the food during the holidays. We're sitting around the table after the meal, just talking, mostly about the boys' school projects. Rex's ears turn red when John tells me Rex is the top of his class in wood shop.

Then, the subject changes to my least favorite thing to talk about. "How about you, Dora, you still want to go to school, don't you?"

"Of course, but I've pretty much given up. Ruby always has work for me to do, so I have to stay home."

"Father, what can she do?" Rex turns to me, "Dora, think about it! Seems to me you have to start sometime. How about you get ready, and Monday morning I'll come by to walk you to school?"

Harold chimes in, "Yeah, you have to start sometime. She'll probably yell, but what can she do?"

There! There's a dress that fits in the back of my chifforobe. I'll go to Dobbins after school.

I'm waiting in the kitchen with my coat on when Ruby comes downstairs. "You goin' somewhere?"

"I'm waiting for Rex. He's going to walk me to school."

Ruby's eyes get big, and she explodes, "You must be kidding! You have things to do here. I never told you it that you can go to school."

"I can do chores after school. Besides, you're not my boss and the contract said I am to go to school. I'll go to Dobbins for some fabric after school."

Ruby yells up the stairs, "Jim!"

"What, Ruby?"

"Get down here!"

As soon as his foot hits the bottom stair, she starts yelling, "Look at her, she's defying me again! She says she's goin' to school, leaving me to cook dinner and take care of the baby. You set her straight!"

I open the door to let Rex in. "What's going on?"

Jim answers, "Ruby's upset 'cuz Dora wants to go to school. She cain't go, though. She has things to do around here."

"Too bad, she's going to school with me!"

Jim's face turns red, and he grabs the collar of Rex's shirt, and he pushes him up against the wall, "Look here, you little twerp, don't come into my house and start issuing orders. I said she has things to do here! Got that?"

"Jim, please let him go. He didn't mean anything. Rex, you go on. He's right, I have work to do here. Maybe I can go tomorrow."

"But they always have work for you to do. You should be in school."

"I know, but it's just not worth it. Just go!"

Rex storms out of the house, and I close the door, watching him all the way as he walks down the street, talking to himself. I hang up my coat and when I return to the kitchen, Ruby and Jim are sitting at the table, waiting for breakfast.

I fry up some bacon and eggs while Jim makes coffee. No one talks while we eat, the only sound is the scratching of spoons scooping yolks off the plates. The baby's awake and crying, but I just finish the dishes and go directly to my room. There's leftover chicken soup, so Ruby can warm it up for dinner.

I wait until I hear them go to their room, then I put on my coat and run across the road to R.C.'s. I could walk, but it's cold, so I ask him to take me downtown to Dobbins.

"What's goin' on, girl? Are you alright? You look upset."

"R.C., we had a big argument when Rex came to walk me to school. John grabbed him by his collar and shoved him up against the wall. I was so scared! I thought he was going to hit him. I told Rex to go on, that maybe I will go tomorrow, but they will never let me go to school."

"He grabbed Rex? A boy? He's out of his mind. I'll talk to him."

"No, please, you might make it worse. I'll just do what I'm told. At least she said I could take some fabric to Helen. I've outgrown most of my dresses."

"Then I'll talk to Taff. He needs to do something before someone gets hurt."

"You can try, but I've already gone to him. He said he would talk to Ruby, but nothing happened."

"Well, here we are. Just take your time and find something you really like, then I'll take you to Helen's."

Ruby's waiting in the kitchen when I get home. "Where have you been, across the road spreading lies?"

"You said I could go to Dobbins. Helen's going to sew three dresses for me. Two will be work dresses and the other one can be for church."

"Well, I came downstairs so I could talk to you. We're having a party Saturday night, so you'll have to make some food, maybe some sausages and rolls. Go to your room after you set everything up, or go over to Anna's if you must. You're not invited. You just need to get things ready. By the way, I noticed the stairs need dusting. You know what needs to be done."

Monday, January 13, 1909, Dear Diary, Big argument today. Rex tried to stick up for me, but John grabbed him by his collar, and I was so scared! I just told Rex to leave, and he stormed out. I hope he's not mad at me. I can't see how this is going to work. I cook and clean to avoid arguments, but the more I do, the more they depend on me. I'm nothing more than a servant with nowhere else to go. Signed, Dora Kelly.

I spend the night at Anna's, and we all go to church the next day. The pastor's sermon is all about finding happiness. I'll pray to God to help me, but I wish Ruby was here to hear what Pastor said. She's never happy.

R.C. drops me in the dooryard. The house is quiet when I enter the kitchen. They must be sleeping in. The house smells like alcohol and cigarette smoke, and there are plates with food on the kitchen table. I pinch my nose and dump the food into the garbage can. There's an apron hanging on a hook by the pantry door. I put it on.

I decide to gather all of the dirty dishes before I start washing. There are dirty plates everywhere, on the steps and in the parlor. Someone spilled a plate into the cushion of the settee. It's taking me a minute to take it all in, then I start carrying the dirty dishes to the kitchen. I reach under the settee to pick up a plate, and it's a one of the China plates with blue flowers, broken into four pieces.

I'm so angry that I don't even try to be quiet when I wash the dishes, pots, and pans. They have to hear me, but all's quiet upstairs. After everything is finally clean and put away, I take a small basin of soapy water to the parlor. I hear them come downstairs while I'm scrubbing the seat cushion of the settee.

Jim's rattling around, making coffee, then he sits at the table, holding a lit cigarette in his hand, to his forehead.

Ruby has her head in the Frigidaire. "Dora!"

I go to the kitchen.

"Do we have eggs? We need something to eat!"

"Yes, we have eggs. Sorry I didn't have time to make biscuits. I've been busy."

"C'mon, Ruby, give the girl a break." Jim seems more interested in keeping things quiet than keeping the peace.

"Did you know something spilled on the seat cushion of the settee? I'm hoping it won't leave a stain. I can't believe you allowed this to go on in Mr. Murphy's house!"

"It's not his house anymore, it's my house, so it's none of your business."

"But I'm the one who has to clean up after you and your friends."

I have no desire to eat after cleaning up the smelly mess, so I go to my room and stay there all day.

I hear Ruby and Jim arguing when I come downstairs the next morning, so I stop to listen from the top step of the landing. Ruby's yelling while Jim's trying to be calm.

"I don't know. He just said some men in suits hammered a stake in the ground out front, with a sign that I have 24 hours to pay up or I'll be evicted."

"For what?"

"C'mon, Babe, just give me a check. You don't need to worry your little head; I'll take care of it."

"A check for what, Jim?"

"They say I owe back taxes."

"But I've been giving you money all along. I knew you owed taxes and that you had some debt, but you told me you had paid everything down. You lied! What did you do with the money I gave you? How much do they want?"

"I've had expenses, Ruby, it's gone. They want $500.""

"Expenses for what? I've given you more than $2,000. How could you spend that much money?"

"Let's see, I had to have something to wear to the wedding, and all of my clothes were wearing out. I've been buying refreshments for the parties, then I had to get a wedding ring."

He walks behind her to put his hands on her shoulders, and he kisses the back of her neck. "You do like your wedding ring, don't you?"

Ruby shrugs her shoulders, and she brushes his hands away. "Don't come near me when you're hung over. You still smell like whiskey! Another thing, what about the Thursday night card games? How much money have you lost at cards? Jim, I have been trying to tell you, we're in trouble! You need to work so you can start bringing in some money."

"I know, sweetheart, and I have plans. Let's not fight. Just give me a check so we can just be happy. I remember how beautiful you were on our wedding day. I think of you all the time."

Ruby starts to yell, "Jim, listen to me! We don't have it! Do you realize what it takes to live here? I just received tax bills for all of the real estate we own. They all want money, the County, Quincy and the States of Iowa and Minnesota, and I haven't paid anything on our accounts for some time. I keep waiting for Dobbins and the grocer to say something. What little money we get from the farms hasn't covered our spending. It's all on me. Just what do you do around here?"

Jim stands up, kicking his chair across the room and he slams the door so hard the glass almost breaks, "Bitch!"

Ruby's crying, and I don't want her to know I heard, so I go back to my room.

Ruby is nursing the baby while I clean up breakfast dishes the next morning, when Jim appears at the kitchen door. He goes to the closet to hang up his jacket and Ruby starts yelling before he even returns to the kitchen. She startles the baby and he's screaming, so I take him from her arms to the rocking chair in the parlor.

"Where were you last night? You've been drinking! Did you do anything to try to stop them from taking the farm?"

"What did you want me to do? I didn't have money to pay the tax bill."

"Did you go to the bank so you could try to talk to them? They might have given you a loan."

"It wouldn't have made a difference." He goes up the stairs to their bedroom, and he slams the door. After a short while, he comes down and he goes to the barn to hitch one of the horses to the wagon. Ruby watches until he disappears down the road.

She comes into the parlor, angry. "His farm will be gone by sunset. Don't you say anything, Dora! You have no idea how it is. Give me the baby and clean up the kitchen."

I don't know whether to feel sorry for her, but I do what she says.

I go to Anna's knowing I'll come home to a mess. The parties are getting worse. Over and over, I've washed all of the plates, except for those that are broken. Today, I go to the dining room to put plates away in the China closet, but the glass on one of the doors is broken. A shard of glass falls down, barely missing my arm. I jump back and it crashes to the floor, exploding into a hundred pieces.

I go to the phone, "R.C. the glass in the China closet door is broken. Can you fix it?"

R.C. comes right away, in time to see some of the mess. "How often does this happen?"

"Most Saturday nights, except sometimes they go to someone else's house. I'm not invited so I go to Anna's. R.C., they are disgusting people! They are breaking all of Mr. Murphy's nice things, and when they do, they don't even bother to pick up the mess. They leave it for me to do when I get home. I'm the only one who cares about anything in this house. I feel bad for Little Eddie when I'm not here. I can only hope they look after him, so he doesn't get hurt."

"I'm sorry, Dora, sorry for you. Let me get the rest of the broken glass out of the door. I'll be back to repair it after I get a pane of glass. I'll send the bill to Albert with an explanation, so he knows what's going on. I'll make sure that he talks to Ruby."

Jim comes downstairs while R.C. is repairing the China closet.

"Morning, R.C. I'm glad you're here. You know, Ruby's been on my case to start doing more to help with the finances, so I'm going to take over the Spoon River farm."

"How will that help? The farm's always been profitable. Don't see how you can make it better."

"Well, I'll be reducing the payroll. I plan to let Jeremy go, and I'll take over the management."

"But he's been with Uncle Joe for more than twenty years! This is what he gets for being a loyal employee and turning a profit? Anyway, why are you telling me? Are you planning to fire me too?"

"No, no, we need you. Besides, Murphy left money to pay a janitor in his will, but I was hoping you will go to the farm with me, when I tell the hands about the changes I am making. I made a list."

"You mean, you want me there when you fire Jeremy? Sorry, but you're on your own. He's been a friend for more than twenty years. How long have I known you? A few months?"

R.C. looks at me, and he winks. I run to the parlor so John won't see me laughing. It is so funny to see Jim back down from R.C. I hope Albert makes Ruby back down, too, or there won't be any more money left to live on!

Graham Hospital

March 30, 1909 — Dear Diary, I'm so excited! I received a formal invitation to the hospital groundbreaking. Anna received one too and she said it's an honor to be invited. They didn't send one to Ruby, so she's miffed, but she insisted hers will come in tomorrow's mail. It will be a cool day so I'm just going to wear a nice dress with my church coat and matching hat. Anna said to wear boots 'cuz it will be muddy. Mr. Murphy would be so pleased. Signed, Dora Kelly

April, 1909

I peek out my bedroom window, R.C. is waiting in the dooryard. I hurry down the stairs and Ruby has her coat on. "Are you going out?"

"I was about to ask you the same thing. I'm going to the groundbreaking, you can't go. You have to stay here to watch the baby."

"I'm not babysitting! Besides, I was invited. You weren't!"

"Of course, I was. The invitation just got lost in the mail. Jim and I are going. The baby's sleeping and there's a bottle in the fridge for his ten o'clock feeding."

"Sorry, Ruby, I'm going! It's up to you if you want to make a fool of yourself. Call your sister." The wind catches the door, and it slams behind me.

The ceremony is brief. Albert, W.D., Dr. Coleman and the Mayor man shovels. Ruby and Jim arrive late, and they stand behind the crowd. Albert is shaking hands while he works his way through the crowd towards Ruby and Jim.

When he reaches them, he looks more stern than friendly. "How are things going? I heard you sold the farm. I thought the farm was thriving, why would you sell it when you need income?"

Ruby doesn't answer. "Oh, there's Dr. Coleman. I must say hello."

I look down and she's wearing her dress shoes. They walk towards Coleman and the mud makes a sucking sound, tugging at her shoes. Dr. Coleman sees her coming, so he turns away, brushing her off.

Anna and I decide to go to the tearoom. Jim helps Ruby trudge through the mud to their carriage.

Ruby's sister is there unpacking many suitcases when we get back to the house. I don't say anything, but it looks like she's moving in. Hopefully, she'll lend a hand. Otherwise, she will just be one more person to clean up after.

Anna called to let me know Louisa is coming for the cornerstone ceremony. There's no room for her to stay here, but Anna said I needn't worry 'cuz she'll be staying with the Conklins. The Ladies Auxiliary is serving cake and coffee after the ceremony, so I have to get there early to help set up.

There's a smaller crowd today than there was at the groundbreaking. Other than some doctors and a newspaper reporter, it's mostly close friends and family.

John walks over to talk to three men who are Freemasons like Mr. Murphy. Everyone stops talking and the only sound is a bird chirping in the Oak tree. The Grand Master starts the ceremony by applying a golden square and level to the stone. "My Lord Bishop, the stone has been proved and found to be 'fair work and square work' and fit to be laid as the foundation for this hospital."

The other man, a Bishop, spreads cement over the stone with a silver trowel that has a pearl handle. He gives the stone three knocks with a mallet, and he declares the stone to be duly and truly laid.

Louisa steps up and she hands some papers to be enclosed in the cornerstone. The Chaplain of the Masonic Order reads a prayer,

> *"May the Great Architect of the Universe enable us as successfully to carry out and finish this work. May he protect the workmen from danger and accident, and long preserve this structure from decay; and may He grant us all our needed supply. Amen. So mote it be."*

We step into the temporary building for refreshments.

"Anna, that was really nice. Louisa, what were the papers for?""

"The papers were Joseph's biography. They will be enclosed in the cornerstone for historical reasons. You're right, Dora, this was very nice. Joseph would be pleased."

May 6, 1909

It's the first meeting of the hospital Ladies' Auxiliary. They invited Anna and me to join! I feel like a grownup. Everyone seems to know one another, and they are all talking at once. Not knowing what to do or what to say, I just smile and nod and listen. The Chairlady explains the charter for the new organization and our mission to raise funds for the hospital.

We are eating cake when two ladies come to talk to Anna and me.

"Miss Kelly, and Mrs. Moss, we're so glad that you came. Is it true what they are saying, that the Kuchareks are having wild parties at their house?"

Anna intercedes, "I don't believe Dora wants to participate in town gossip."

"Well, we also heard that she was sick for six months before Mr. Murphy died. What did they say was wrong?"

"As I said, Dora has no interest in gossip."

"Well, it really doesn't matter since the house is being sold."

Anna, seems as surprised as I am. "Who told you the house is being sold?"

"Why, it's all over town. The Plattenbergs are such nice people. Their parties are so elegant, the right kind of parties, if you know what I mean. They'll know how to entertain in such a lovely home."

"Dora, let's thank these lovely ladies. We must take leave. R.C. is waiting."

Anna and I can't believe what we've heard! I can't wait to talk to Ruby when I get home. She's on the back porch, putting some clothes in a box.

"Guess what, Ruby, a lady told Anna and me that you're selling the house. Is it true?"

"Oh, yes, I guess I should have told you. We're moving to a smaller house, so it will be less work and money to keep up. It's really cute, white with a white board fence out front.

"Why didn't you tell me? Will I have a place to stay?"

"Of course, don't you remember? I'm stuck with you until you're 21. We'll only have two bedrooms, so you'll have to share a room with the baby. Don't worry about it. I'll let you know when we're moving. It will be next week or the week after. Maybe you'd best start packing your room, and the kitchen and dining room as well."

Leaving the Homestead

May 13, 1910 Dear Diary, We've moved! Ruby officially sold Mr. Murphy's house today, and we moved across town to a smaller house. Ruby's sister has the maid's room to herself, so I have to share a room with Little Eddie. It's not a bad house, but I miss Mr. Murphy's house and having my own room. I cleaned the floors of the old place after everything was gone. Before I left, I closed the door and leaned against it with my eyes closed. For a minute, I remembered all the good times there, and It was almost like I was living them again, like R.C. carrying me upstairs to my room the night they brought me here, and the smells of the holidays, the turkeys, pies, and the melting wax from the candles. I cried when I closed the kitchen door for the last time.

Like expected, Ruby's sister is no help. At least, she packed and unpacked her own things, but she did little else to help with the move. It would have been nice if she had watched the baby while we were packing and loading the wagon. She goes to school, then she sleeps late on the weekends, so she's just more work for me. She's looking better, though. Her hair is clean and brushed, and she has new dresses and shoes. I can tell she's been at the Sweet Shoppe, 'cuz she's getting fat! She must eat a lot of candy. I need some summer dresses, but Ruby says we don't have the money. Maybe that will change now that we're in a smaller house. It's been a while since I heard from Annie Rose. I suppose she's busy with her beau. I'd like to have a beau, but I don't go anywhere to meet boys my age and I haven't seen Rex for a while because of the move. I hope I can go visit them all soon. Rex is my best friend, and his family are my family. I don't know what I would do without them. Signed, Dora Kelly

I'm unpacking dishes in the kitchen when Albert pays a surprise visit to talk to Ruby and Jim.

"I don't know what's going on, but your creditors have been calling me. What's happening, Ruby?"

Ruby tires to shrug it off. "Don': worry, Albert. As you can see, Jim and I have been making some changes to reduce our expenses."

"Did that include firing Jeremy? Have you factored in how much will that cost you in income? Also, I've also been tracking how much you're paying your father and sister to work around here."

"I'm a farmer, so we don': need a foreman. I've already made some changes. Sold some of the animals so I could buy feed. The price of seed went up this year, so I had to cut corners."

"You might not know, Jim, but Jeremy had a long-term relationship with the people at the elevator, and he was good at controlling costs when prices increased. He never sold or bought an animal unless Uncle Joe told him to. How are you making decisions? Are you and Ruby keeping any books?"

"What's it to you, Albert? We don't answer to you."

"To some extent you do, Ruby. As executor, I still have to pay your employees. The money is dwindling, Ruby. I'm willing to work with you as an advisor when you and Jim are making major decisions, but you need to control your spending and Jim needs to find a way to replace the income lost when they took his farm. Otherwise, I will have to start selling off more assets."

Albert starts to leave, so I ask him if he will give me a ride to the grocer. I don't need a lot, just a short list, so I can walk home after I pick up staples.

After he drops me off, I shop from my list, glad to be out of the house. I put my food basket on the counter, "Good afternoon, Mr. Turl. I also need a bag of sugar."

Mr. Turl doesn't say anything, he just goes to the backroom, and I can hear him talking to his wife. When he returns, he says regretfully, "I'm sorry, Miss Kelly. I can't let you charge more until something is paid on the account."

I can feel the blood rush to my head. I don't know what to say, so I just turn heel and run out of the store. I'm not crying, I'm just furious! Why didn't Ruby say anything when she knew I was coming here? I know she said she needed to pay on the account! Anna said Ruby is a wealthy woman, so why can't she pay her bills? I lean against a tree behind the store until I calm down. As long as I'm downtown, I may as well go to Dobbins for some gingham so I can sew curtains for the kitchen.

Mrs. Lowell is waiting on a customer, so I go to the back of the store to look at the fabrics. They have several ginghams, but I want yellow. I turn to walk to the front and notice there is a yellow and white gingham tablecloth on another table, just the right size to cut for our curtains, and I'll probably have some left over.

Mrs. Lowell sees me walking to the counter, "Excuse me, Miss Kelly, I need to make a phone call. I'll be just a minute."

I'm waiting, but I have a feeling that Ruby's behind on her account with Dobbins, too. I can hear Mrs. Lowell talking to someone; after a few minutes, I decide to leave. I'm almost out the door when Mrs. Lowell returns.

"I'm sorry, Miss Kelly, that was Mr. Dobbins. Mrs. Kucharek's account has been closed. Tell her we will re-open it when she pays the last bill."

I leave the tablecloth on the counter and walk quickly out the door with as much dignity as I can.

Ruby and Jim are sitting at the kitchen table when I come in the door.

I'm still so angry! "What's going on? They closed your account at the grocers. And at Dobbins! What are we going to do if we can't buy food? It's not just about you, you have a baby to worry about. Also, your sister is living here! You must have known! I can't believe you didn't you say anything when I asked Albert to drop me at the grocery store. They said they will re-open both accounts when you pay the bills. When will that happen?"

"They shouldn't have said anything to you. They should have just called me. How I pay my bills is not your concern."

"What were they supposed to do, Ruby? I was standing there with merchandise. Mrs. Lowell was nice, but I was so embarrassed! Even if you pay the bills, I don't know how I can face those people again. You are shameless! You can go for groceries next time or send your sister. At least it will give her something to do. I'm tired of all this. All we do around here is argue, and no one ever says I'm sorry. I'm going to my room. Fix your own supper!"

July 20, 1910

Somehow, Ruby is caught up on the bills. I've become used to living in this new house. No more wild parties, either. I take care of the baby and keep the house nice, and stay out of Ruby and Jim's way.

We're having a nice summer. The house is a lot less work, so I decide to take Little Eddie out back to play in the yard. At first, he chases his ball, then he sees the sandbox. I try to keep him out of it because he gets sand in his mouth and everywhere. The sandbox is under a tree, so the sand is cool. He grabs fistfuls of sand, and he laughs and shakes his head when the sand runs through his little hands. I think his diaper is dirty, so I lean over to pick him up and take him inside, when he shoves a handful of sand in his mouth.

"No, Eddie! Don't eat the sand, it's dirty. Yuk!"

He just laughs. He doesn't seem to mind that his diaper is dirty and full of sand. He's such a happy baby. Surprising with all the yelling that goes on. I tickle his bare tummy and pick him up. He's laughing so hard he hiccups. I brush the sand off his legs and bottom and take him inside.

August 31, 1910, Dear Diary, this summer has flown by, and except for the 4th of July, it seems every day has been the same as the day before. My life is pretty boring, except when Rex comes by. We like to go on long walks so we can talk, and he holds my hand. Sometimes we just sit in the grass and I pick four-leafed clovers for him to take home to Anna. He keeps wanting to take me for ice cream, but I feel a little uncomfortable. I don't want to be around all those schoolgirls that like him so much. He's going back to school next week. He'll be a senior this year, then he'll graduate. I can't believe it! He says he wants to be a carpenter, but he'll probably have to work at the factory. I wonder if he'll want to keep spending time with me after he graduates. He invited me to go to some graduation parties, but I'm not sure I fit in anymore. All I do is work and he has a more interesting life than I'll ever have. I don't know. He'll probably always be my friend, but our experiences are so different now. I'm lucky to have him as a best friend. Oh yes, Ruby's pregnant again. She's not sick, this time, but she uses it as an excuse so I have to do all of the work. Little Eddie is walking, and he gets into everything, so I really have to watch him. I don't know where they're going to put everybody in this little house. They will probably put the two children in the same room, but then where do I go? On the couch in the parlor? Five more years of this until I get my inheritance, and I'm always worried that I may not even have a place to sleep. Sometimes it seems like it might actually happen! Every day just blends into the other. I guess this is my life, for now. Signed, Dora Kelly

March 17, 1911

Jim's on the phone talking to Mr. O'Grady. "It's another boy, Reilly Logen! He'll be lucky - born on the Day of the Festival of St. Patrick. He looks just like Eddie!"

I gather up all of the soiled linens and put them in a tub of cold water. Good thing it's nice outside so I can scrub them and hang them on the clothesline.

Jim and Ruby have the newborn in a cradle by their bed, for now, so she can nurse him at night. After I scrub the linens, I'm supposed to go to Anna's for supper. She wants to start planning for Rex's graduation. It's been a while since I spent time with them, because Ruby has insisted I stay close to home. They'll be angry, but I think I'll just go. I don't care.

Rex is sitting in the porch swing waiting for me. When he sees me walking up the street, he runs to meet me. "I know you and Mother have plans, but my friends, Matt and Esther want to go to the moving pictures after supper. They're fun and I want you to meet them. Would you like to go?"

"Let's ask."

Anna is putting a pot on the table when we enter the kitchen. "I was just going to call you. Rex, go tell Harold and your father that supper's ready. John bought a radio, so all they do is sit with their ears next to that box. I'm hoping they have some programs for women, but it's so new. Most of the time, it's just world news."

"Rex wants to go to the moving pictures after dinner. If we go, we have to leave at 6:30. Do you think we can be done by then?"

"Of course. I just want to talk to you about the graduation dance."

Harold runs into the room, grinning. "Mother, that radio's fantastic! We were listening to music all the way from Pittsburgh!"

"That's amazing! Isn't that amazing, Dora? I guess I'll always know where to find you, at least 'til the newness wears off. Let's eat so Rex and Dora can go out with their friends."

Anna and I talk while we do the dishes. "Has Rex said anything about the dance?"

"He might have, I'm not sure. I wasn't sure I could go. He said we might be going to some parties."

"I wasn't sure if you knew. He should have asked you directly. If you want to go, the dance will be formal, so I was wondering if you would like to go shopping for some material, maybe a satin, to take to Helen. I don't have a daughter, so I would like to pay for your dress."

I go to her and we hug. "I so much want to go! Thank you!"

"We should go tomorrow as she will be busy sewing dresses for other girls. Now, be on your way. You don't want to be late for the moving pictures."

Matt and Esther are waiting for us in front of the theater. "Esther, Matt, this is the girl I told you about, Dora Kelly. Dora, we all hang out after school, and the four of us will go to the graduation dance together."

Esther seems nice and I can tell that Matt really likes her. She's little like me, but she has dark hair that's naturally curly. She smiles and she takes my hand and we step aside to wait for the boys to buy tickets.

"I've been wanting to meet you, Dora. Rex talks about you all the time."

"Really? What does he say?" I can't imagine there's much to tell.

Rex grabs my hand and waves two tickets. "C'mon, Kid, let's go inside."

We find seats in the back. Matt takes Esther's hand, so Rex holds my hand. The film is *The Last of the Mohicans*. I try to follow the story but there's no sound and Matt and Esther whisper and giggle the entire time. A lot of what I do see is violent, so I close my eyes or turn to Rex to talk. Still, we have a good time.

Rex walks me home, holding my hand all the way. There's a sliver of a moon that looks like a clipped fingernail. As we approach the house, Rex pulls me under the shadow of a tree.

"I really had a good time tonight. Did you?"

"Yes, and I like Esther and Matt."

"And I really like you, Kid! Can I have a goodnight kiss?"

I tap my cheek with my finger, and he kisses me on the cheek, then he steals a second kiss on my lips. I can feel the blood rush to my head. "I have to go, Rex. I'll see you later."

I can hear the baby screaming as I open the latch on the gate. I open the door and Eddie is standing in the middle of the room, sucking his thumb, watching Ruby and Jim make out on the sofa. I hear Reilly crying in his cradle. They look up when I slam the door.

"How long have you been spying on us?"

"I wasn't spying on you. I just got here."

Ruby sneers a little. "We'll deal with you tomorrow. You went out without permission. For now, put Eddie to bed, and take care of Reilly. Can't you hear him?"

I pick Eddie up and go to their room to check on the baby. He's fine, he just needs a diaper change. "C'mon, Eddie, you can help me."

I let him carry the diaper and I lay a towel down on the bed so I can change his baby brother. "Phew, Reilly, you're a little stinker!"

Eddie laughs and he runs to the parlor, "Reilly's a little stinker!"

Jim sits up, "Eddie, go tell Dora you need your nightshirt. It's time for you to go to bed."

Once the children are down for the night, I return to the parlor.

"What's wrong with you two? Who's the grownup around here? Who watches the children when I'm not here? Eddie was watching the two of you! Have you no shame?"

"Where have you been, Miss High and Mighty? Chasing around town with your buddy Rex and his friends? There wouldn't have been a problem if you had been here to watch the kids. Jim and I are entitled to some time alone."

"Oh? Really! I'm not a servant and I'm not your babysitter. I love Eddie and the baby, but they are your children, not mine!"

I return to our room and go to bed. Eddie climbs in with me and we snuggle.

March 17, 1911, Dear Diary, I saw The Last of the Mohicans with Rex
and his friends, Matt and Esther. I hope we'll be friends. Rex walked
me home and kissed me on the lips! I don't think anyone saw us, but I
guess I wouldn't mind if they did! And to think, I used to think women
got pregnant from kissing! I know that's not true, anymore. I think I
love Rex, and I think he might like me. Since we first met, he's been
my best friend. I hope he loves me, too. We might not kiss again, but I
hope we do. What if we don't? He probably kisses other girls at school.
He is really handsome. I can't wait to see him again, and I'm going to
the graduation dance with him. We'll see what happens! I hope I can go
-- I had another argument with Ruby when I got home. She was making
out with Jim, ignoring Reilly, who needed to be changed, poor kid, and
Little Eddie just stood there sucking his thumb while he watched them on
the couch. Ruby blamed it on me. She said I should have stayed home to
watch the babies. I doubt they would have been smooching in the parlor
if I was home. It seems we are all living on top of one another. This
house is too small and my life here is unbearable. I'm not sure I can
wait until I'm 21 to leave! If Ruby says I can't go to the dance, I'm just
going to sneak out. Anna will help me. Signed, Dora Kelly

May 20, 1911

Esther told me to come early to her house so we can do one another's hair.
She's becoming such a good friend! We even shopped for lipstick together
to wear for the dance when we were buying satin for our dresses. She said
her mother has our dresses hanging on the doors of the chiffarobe, ready to
put on. I didn't tell Ruby about the dance, she never has anything nice to say
and I don't want anything to ruin it. She would just find a reason I can't go. I
just told her I was going to Anna and John's to help them. I don't care if I get
in trouble later.

"Here, Dora, I emptied a drawer for you so you can put your things
away. Matt and Rex are supposed to be here at 6:30 so we have plenty of
time to get ready."

We spend the whole afternoon doing our hair and talking about boys. "Has Rex ever kissed you?"

I look down, a little embarrassed. "He did, didn't he? I thought so. I can tell, he really likes you."

"Do you and Matt kiss, too? I know he likes you."

"Of course, silly! But you and Rex are different. The way he looks at you is special."

I don't know what to say so I just smile. I hope she's right. She helps me put on my dress and then my lipstick. I can't believe how grown up I feel! I hope Rex likes how I look.

Mrs. Onel knocks right before the boys are supposed to be here. "Are you ready, girls? Now you stay up here until they come so you can make a grand entrance down the stairs. Just be careful in those shoes so you don't fall."

I put my matching headband on and lean against the wall so I don't wrinkle my dress sitting down.

Esther and I look at one another, and we giggle. Our dresses match perfectly, satin with sweetheart necklines, hers green and mine blue.

"You look amazing!"

"Dora, you look great, too! We'll know when Matt and Rex see us come down the stairs. Ohhhh, there's the doorbell!"

Mrs. Onel comes upstairs to get us. "Now, take your time."

Esther goes first. Mrs. Onel comes back, "You should have seen the look on Matt's face! Your turn, dear."

I hesitate at the top of the stairs and walk down, holding onto the railing with one hand, and my skirt with the other so I don't trip. Rex meets me at the bottom step and he holds out his hand to help me step down.

"I brought you a corsage. I hope you like roses."

Mrs. Onel pins our cosages to our sashes. "Well, I see Mr. Moss is waiting outside in the carriage. You musn't keep him waiting. Go on now, have a good time!"

Matt boards first and Rex stays on the ground, so they can help us into the carriage with our long dresses. They must have planned it – I wonder who told them how.

Sunday, May 21, 1911, Dear Diary. Rex took me to his graduation dance last night, and it was a fairy tale evening. There was punch, so we sat at a table and talked most of the evening, but we danced a couple slow dances. At first, he seemed to be embarassed when he put his hand around my waist, but he noticed the other boys and before I knew it, we were waltzing around the room. I'm so darn short, that I was looking at his stomach! I hadn't danced before, but I was okay following his lead. He said Anna showed him how to waltz. Afterwards, John drove us to Esther's house. We held hands all the way, but John was obviously watching us so they just thanked us for coming, and hurried back to the carriage after walking us to the door. Esther and I were so excited that we had a hard time getting to sleep. She said Matt told her she looked pretty. I didn't tell her what Rex said to me, but he said, "Kid, you are beautiful tonight!" It was a special evening, and I want to keep some things to myself. I will always remember what he said to me, even if I have to leave Canton or he decides to marry one of the girls in his class who are always hanging around him. Today, I go back to being a maid. But at least once in my life I know what it means to be treated like a real princess. Signed, Dora Kelly

Rex's graduation ceremony is nice. I'm a little uncomfortable though. The girls keep looking at me, probably wondering why they haven't seen me for such a long time, and why he took me to the dance instead of them. I wish I could graduate, but that will never happen now.

Anna and John are so proud of Rex. John chuckles and sits up extra straight when he gets his diploma. He looks so tall and handsome up there on the stage! He's even taller than the principal!

I can tell, Rex is embarassed by all the attention. After the ceremony, he grabs my hand. "C'mon, Dora, let's go talk to Matt and Esther."

We had fun, but it's always back to work for me. It seems I'm always tired. I

wake up in the middle of the night, feeling Little Eddie's hot hand on my arm. "Dora, I sick."

I sit up and turn on the light. He's burning up with a fever and he has red splotches all over his face. I lift his nightshirt and the splotches are all over his body. I don't know what to do, so I go to Ruby and Jim's room and shake Ruby gently so Jim doesn't wake up, too.

I talk in a whisper as we walk back to our bedroom, "I think he might have the measles. He's feverish."

We take him to the bathroom, and he cries the entire time while we sponge cool water all over his little body.

"This will have to do until we can call W. D. in the morning."

Ruby goes back to bed, leaving me with a sick child. I pull a clean nightshirt over his head, and it seems he's not quite as hot, but he's still crying. I wrap him in a blanket and take him to the rocking chair in the parlor. I hum a lullaby and hold him close and before long, he goes to sleep, but when I stop rocking, he stirs, so I just keep rocking.

I don't know when I stopped. We're both sleeping when Ruby comes to check on us at daybreak. "You sat up all night with him? Goodness! Let's see if he'll lay in his bed."

I don't get much sleep the next few days. Eddie's fever breaks on the third day, but whenever I sit down, he crawls onto my lap and he lays his little head on my shoulder.

After a few days, Eddie is finally back to himself. When he's awake, he runs around the house in circles, kitchen, bedroom, parlor, and kitchen again, over and over. Baby Reilly is cranky, though, so I decide to take a break with a cup of tea while he's finally napping.

I hear him squeak soon after I sit down, and head to the bedroom, knowing he's awake. He feels hot when I pick him up. I look under his nightshirt and, sure enough, he has red splotches on his tummy.

"Ruby, Reilly has the measles! No surprise, but here we go again."

Reilly's measles aren't as bad. He has a rash on his stomach and a small spot on his face. His fever is gone the next day. It's funny to see him happy and gurgling with his red eyes and a big red splotch on his right cheek.

Jim brought a tree home from the farm and Ruby has the boxes of decorations setting out when I come home from Esther's. The tree's not very big, only about as tall as I am. He has it sitting in a bucket with water, and tied to a hook on the wall so it won't fall down I get a small quilt from the babies' dresser to put around the bucket so it's not so ugly.

Nothing needs to be said, we just start putting the ornaments on the tree. It seems strange putting Mr. Murphy's special ornaments on a small tree in this house. The trees in the house on First Street reached the ceiling, and they were beautiful, even without decorations. Here, we put an ornament on every branch, the more fragile ornaments near the top and out of reach of little hands. Little Eddie is excited, squealing and running around, so I guess it's worth it. They don't have a fireplace mantle, so Ruby puts some candles and greens with pinecones on the parlor table by the window.

"The house smells good, Ruby."

"I know, the smell of evergreen puts me in the Christmas spirit. We're having a small Christmas this year. Jim's been building some toys for the children, but there won't be any presents for anyone else this year."

"Don't worry about it. I'm going to Anna's anyway, so just worry about you and the babies."

"The only time I miss living at Uncle Joe's house is Christmastime. He always made sure we had a nice Christmas. I miss him at Christmas, don't you?"

December 23, 1911, Dear Diary, I'm going to Anna and John's tomorrow for Christmas Eve service and I'll spend the night so I can be there Christmas morning. Ruby seemed a little sad after we put the tree up. I didn't say anything, but I felt like screaming at her! How can she say that after all the problems she caused and the grief she gave him during the year before he died? I can't wait to get out of here tomorrow. I'd like not to come back, but I would miss Eddie and Reilly. Ruby didn't do anything when they had the measles, she left all the caring to me. I love them, so I didn't mind, but I would be afraid to leave them with her alone for too long. What a mother!

I made Christmas gifts this year so I didn't have to ask for money to go shopping downtown. I knew I wouldn't get any if I did ask. Nothing special, I cross stitched a sampler for Anna and John, and I filled two Mason jars with fudge for the boys. I'll wear the bracelet and necklace Rex gave me. I hope he notices how much I appreciate them. My birthday's coming up, one more year behind me, and one year closer to freedom! Signed, Dora Kelly

The Suffragettes

Monday, March 4, 1912

R.C. called. He's coming with Mary for a visit! Ruby and Jim took the kids to the farm to see the new baby calf, so I called Rex to see if he wants to come over, too. I made a pitcher of tea; they should be here any minute.

Rex comes bounding up the porch steps at the same time R.C. pulls onto the dooryard. I set the sugar bowl on the table, and pour four glasses of tea.

"This is really great, Dora. Hits the spot! Rex, Mary has something she wants to talk to Dora about. Let's you and me go outside. Dora said the window in the garden shed is cracked, so I need to measure it to buy some glass."

I watch them walk out back, while Mary takes a newspaper out of her bag.

"Dora, look at this article. Thousands of women marched in Washington yesterday, in a Women's Suffrage Parade. They want us to have the right to vote!"

"Oh, my goodness! Do you really think that can happen?"

"They say it will if we all start speaking up. Even Uncle Joe told R.C. that women held the country together during the war, and we should be allowed to vote. I'm hoping the educated men in this country will support us. I met a woman in the drug store, and she told me she's in town to talk to us about a march they're organizing right here in Illinois. There's going to be a meeting tomorrow night. Why don't you and I go?"

"I'd like to go. Where is it?"

"It's at seven o'clock at the Presbyterian Church."

"You bet, I'll be there! What about Anna, and Esther and her mother?"

"She said to invite as many as we want. I think my sister wants to be there, too."

Mary and her sister come with the carriage to pick me up. Mary has the reins.

"Where's R.C.?"

"Well, we'll have a full carriage after we get Esther and her mother, and I decided if we want the right to vote and to be independent, then I should be able to get us there and back!"

We are still laughing when we pull up in front of Esther's house.

Esther boards first, "What's so funny?"

"Mary's driving!"

Mrs. Onel hoists up her skirt to board the carriage, "So she is! Let's go, Mary!"

March 6, 1912 — Dear Diary, A bunch of us went to a rally yesterday about a movement to stand up for women to have the right to vote. There weren't any lights on the main floor of the Presbyterian church when we arrived so we thought it had been cancelled, then we heard voices in the basement. The basement was packed with women and they were setting up more chairs. There was a reporter from the Canton paper, so Esther and I leaned against the wall in the back where we could see and hear everything, but we wouldn't be noticed.

They showed photographs of the march in Washington, and the speaker told us how important it is to keep up the momentum all over the country. They are organizing a march on the capital in Springfield and the speaker said they might have another in Chicago. Esther wants to go and I'd like to go, but I will need the train fare plus a little extra for meals. I'm not sure I can do that. I know Ruby would never give it to me. It's not the first time I wish they paid me. Women were signing up. We talked to others in our group and decided to take some signup forms, but we need to talk about how it would work. Signed, Dora Kelly

I don't have time to linger over my diary, so I start supper, thinking all the time about what it would be like to vote! I'm up to my elbows in flour, making noodles when I hear Rex at the front door. I motion for him to come in.

"Hey, did you just get off work?"

"Yup, came here right away. We need to talk."

"About what? You seem upset about something."

"Mother said you want to go to that women's march in Springfield."

"I haven't decided, but I'm thinking about it. I'll need train fare."

"Well, I don't think you should go."

"What? Are you kidding? You came to that conclusion without asking me why I would want to go? I'm disappointed in you, Rex Moss. It's exactly like they said last night! Women like me have been trusting men to do what's right and pass a bill that would give us the right to vote, but we've been naïve. Oh, sure, it was alright for women to take over men's work and take care of farms and families during the war, but we're too stupid to vote? I had already realized I can't go but all of a sudden after talking to you, I just might change my mind. It seems to me that women like me need to take charge of the issues, if change is to happen."

"Dora, I'm not saying that I disagree with a woman's right to vote, but do you really think it will make a difference if you, just one person, decides not to go? You never know what will happen at a rally like that. I read what happened in Washington – there was a mob that attacked some of the women! If the others decide not to go and you go by yourself, you won't be safe. Even if you go with friends, what if you get hurt, or if you get lost in the crowd? Springfield is a long ways away. I just don't want anything to happen to you."

"I'm perfectly capable of taking care of myself, Rex Moss. I'll let you know when I make a decision. Now, go on home. Your mother probably has supper ready, and she must be wondering where you are."

I hurry to clean up the table and wash my hands, then I call Esther while the broth is coming to a boil for the noodles.

"Know what, Dora? Matt was here and he basically said the same thing. He doesn't want me to go."

"Why do they think they can tell us what to do? Were you going to go?"

"I haven't decided. Mother said she would give me the money if I want to go, but I wanted to talk to you before I decide."

"Well, first of all, we can't let them tell us what to do. We're not married, they are just friends. Of course, I'd never admit it to them, but they might be right. What if we go and something happens, they would never let us forget it."

"So, what should we do? I hate to give in."

"Well, I don't have the money, so I had already made up my mind."

"I know! They said they might have a march in Chicago. Why don't we tell them we decided to wait and see what happens in Springfield, but we're thinking about going to Chicago. That way we can take a pass on Springfield without giving in."

"Good idea. I probably can't get the train fare anyway. The marches are important, but right now for me, it might be just as important to stand up for myself."

I haven't heard from Rex since he was here on Wednesday. That was our first fight, but I thought he'd be over it by now. We usually get together on Saturday nights since the graduation dance, so maybe he'll call or just show up. I did tell him I would let him know when I made my decision. Maybe I should call him. I don't know what to do.

It's too cold to sit on the porch, so I take my book to the easy chair in the parlor. I look up when I hear the wind and rain hit the window. Rex is standing on the porch, soaking wet!

"Get in here! I'll get some towels."

"Thanks. That rain is really cold!"

While he's drying off, I get a blanket from the closet, and he wraps it around his shoulders. We stare at each other, but we don't know what to say.

Finally, Rex breaks the silence. "I'm sorry, Dora. I'm not sorry for being concerned about your safety, but I shouldn't have talked to you that way. Mother told me I should have said it better."

"I'm sorry, too. We should be able to disagree, but we had a fight instead. I was going to call you. I talked with Esther about it. I'm not going to Springfield. We might go to the march in Chicago, though. It's really important to us."

"Well, if you decide you want to go, I'll pay your train fare, but you need to have a plan in place in case you become separated."

"Deal. So what are we doing tonight?"

"Do you want to just go out for sodas with Esther and Matt? It looks like the rain has let up, so we should probably go before it starts again."

"I'll get ready."

Esther and I keep reading the paper to find suffrage news, and we call whenever we find a story. Finally, the papers report that the march in Springfield was a minor success. Less than 500 women marched which was impressive considering it was cold and rainy. We're disappointed because the organizers decided not to schedule a march in Chicago at all because not enough women came to Springfield. I wish Esther and I had gone, instead of waiting!

It's June, and it's already hot! It's going to be a hot summer. I get up early while it's cool to get the inside work done, then I take Eddie outside to play in the yard. The water in the washtub is warm from the sun, so he can play in the water.

Eddie is really a cute little boy. He tries to run but he has trouble keeping up with his chubby little legs. Rex and Esther call him The Shadow, 'cuz he follows me around everywhere, and he cries when I leave.

"C'mon, Eddie. I made you a little pool. Want to play in the water?"

He takes off running and giggling, knowing I will chase him. "See, I caught you again! You can't get away from me, you little dickens! Here, let's get your clothes off so you can play in the water."

Ruby comes out the back door, "God, it's hot!"

"Can we just have a cold supper tonight? There's leftover fried chicken and potato salad."

"I don't care, but I ain't cookin'."

She sits down but we don't talk, so I pick up my book to read. It's a perfect summer day, the only sounds are birds chirping and Eddie splashing and talking to his self.

A deep voice breaks through the silence, "Hello! Dora, are you out here? Oh, there you are!"

Rex opens the gate to the backyard and he stoops next to the washtub. "Hey, Eddie, look what I made for you, a little boat! See, it floats!"

Ruby sniffs. "That was nice of you, but Jim make toys for the boys."

"I didn't mean - you know, Ruby, I made it for him because I like him. Everyone likes Eddie. He's a good little kid."

"Just don't go telling people we can't take care of our own kids."

"Why would I say that? Ruby, I really wish....."

I grab his hand. Ruby's never going to let this go. "C'mon, Rex, let's go for a walk. Ruby, can you watch Eddie for a little while?" I don't wait for her to answer.

Rex and I just keep walking and talking, until I realize we've walked to his house.

"Want to come in? I'll walk you home after supper."

June 27, 1912 — Dear Diary, Anna didn't know I was coming for supper tonight, but she did say I can come anytime. Rex told her about his run in with Ruby. Anna said she had planned to give the boys' wagon to Eddie and Reilly, but now she's changed her mind. She said she's been planning a fourth of July picnic by Canton Lake with Esther's mother. I didn't say anything, because I doubt I can get away. I feel a little sad, because I haven't been to a fourth of July parade and picnic since I left Ullin. I bet Aunt Maggie and everyone will go to the park as usual. I wonder if mama will be going, too.

I came home early 'cuz Rex has work in the morning, and I knew Ruby wouldn't be pleased I stayed away so long. It was worth it — we had a lot of fun. Ruby and Jim didn't say anything when I came home. I went to our room and the babies were already asleep. Eddie's hair was damp, and Reilly had a heat rash on his neck. I opened the window, hoping to let in a breeze, but the air was dead and the room smelled like sweat. I won't get much sleep tonight if it doesn't cool down.

I'm going to call Esther in the morning to see if she and Matt want to go swimming after Rex gets off work on the 4th. I'm going to take the day off, even if I have to sneak out! Man, it's hot as all get out! I hope it rains soon. Signed, Dora Kelly

I can't believe Ruby and Jim gave me the day off today! I love the 4th of July!

The parade kicks off promptly at ten o'clock. Canton's parade is much bigger than the one in Ullin.

First in line is one of those new Runabout cars. "Rex, who's that?"

"He's the mayor. Look! There's Matt playing the trumpet."

A group of soldiers in uniform follow the marching band, there are little boys walking behind, waving flags, and P&O has a platform wagon with some farm equipment.

"See, Dora, that's a plow on the front, and the bigger one is a harrow. That's what I work on."

"Look how pretty the horses are!"

A lady with a long dress is riding side saddle on a white horse. He trots his back end forward towards me, then he drops a pile of manure directly in front of me. It's steaming, and with the heat, it really stinks! We laugh and choke at the same time.

"Can we leave? I think I'm going to throw up!"

"Sure, it's about over anyway. C'mon, Esther, let's find Matt. Careful where you walk."

Anna is setting up the picnic when we arrive, but Rex and Matt head for the diving board. Esther and I tip toe in so we don't get our hair wet, but the guys make a big splash when they hit the water. We look at one another and laugh, we'll deal with our hair later. For now, the water feels great!

The Blizzard!

October 30, 1912.

We had a fun summer, then all at once after Labor Day, summer collapses into fall. Eddie's all excited because Jim brought a small pumpkin from the farm. I have everything set out on the kitchen table to make his first jack-o-lantern.

"So, Eddie, do you want a happy pumpkin or a sad pumpkin?"

"Can he have a scary face?"

"We can try, but I always seem to make a happy pumpkin. Are you sure you want him to be scary?"

Jim hears us talking, and he comes into the kitchen, "He wants a scary face! This isn't a girl's pumpkin, it's Eddie's pumpkin, so if my boy wants a scary face, then that's what he gets. Right Eddie?"

"Okay, what will a scary face look like?"

We decide he should have a big mouth with jagged teeth and mean, diamond – shaped eyes. Eddie draws a mustache with a black crayon, and I draw two bats on each side for ears.

"There, what do you think?"

"Funny, but not too scary."

Jim butts in, "He'll be scary at night when he's lit with a candle. You'll see. Oh, by the way, this letter came for you in today's mail."

As soon as I see the envelope, I know it's from Annie Rose. I haven't heard from her in a long time.

October 20, 1912.

Dear Dora,

I've been wanting to write to you, but I have been so busy. I'm working at a local dry goods store, and most of the time when I get off work, I go out with my friends. I wish you could meet them. You would like them. I don't seem to get much accomplished, but I enjoy what I am doing, and time passes so fast.

You might have heard, Theodore Roosevelt was in town and he was shot while campaigning. They say his wounds were minor, but it happened near our store, so we were scared when we heard gunshots, and the newsmen interviewed my boss.

I hope all is well with you. Are you still hanging out with Rex? I wish we could get together so you can tell me what your life is like, now that you have moved. Please write back! I'll try to be better at writing.

Love, Annie Rose

November 8, 1912

It's the first really big snow of the year! We are hunkering down because of the blizzard. The newspaper says there were hurricane force winds on the Great Lakes. The snow has drifted in front of our door, so we can't get out. The babies don't care, they're playing with their toys where it's warm in front of the fireplace, but Jim will have to find a way to get more wood from outside because it's getting colder and colder.

The phone rings, and I can hear him talking. "So, what do you want me to do? I cain't even get out the door. I ain't coming out there in this weather!"

Ruby comes into the kitchen with a runny nose and hacking cough. ""This cold is driving me nuts! What's going on at the farm?"

"Oh, we've lost some livestock to the storm. Norm said we lost some sheep and a couple hogs, and he thinks we most of our chickens got blown away or crushed. The chicken coop collapsed from the weight of the snow, and he found some dead chickens and chicken feathers all over the yard, and on the outside wall of the barn."

"So, what do you have to do?"

"Nothing I can do. I can't even get out the front door! Once it stops snowing, I'll call R.C. to come dig us out. We need to get some wood for the fireplace, though, or it's going to get pretty cold in here."

I can't believe he just settles in near the fire with a blanket instead of going to take care of the farm. Mr. Murphy would have tried to help, or called someone. Mr. Murphy cared about the farm.

The snow doesn't let up for weeks, and Jim doesn't get to the farm at all. We only get out every now and then to bring in firewood and to shop in town. They stay close to home, though, and I do all the errands, which is fine with me, because that way I get to see Rex every now and then.

Thanksgiving is just roast chicken for the five of us, a simple dinner. It's a cold winter, and we're doing our best just to get through it.

December 24, 1912

I'm really depressed with all of the snow. We really didn't have a Thanksgiving, and now it looks like I will be here with Ruby and Jim for Christmas, which is hardly Christmas at all, without a tree or decorations because Jim seems content to just lay around the house most of the time.

I'm at the back of the house doing the washing when I hear bells in the dooryard. It's R.C. with his horse and a sleigh!

"Come on in out of the cold! Where did you get the sleigh?"

"Rex told me P & O had one parked in a shed out back, so I called them. I'm going around town, taking people to be with their families and, tonight, I'm picking up some ladies so they can go to church together. It's been fun! I feel like Santa. So, young lady, gather your things. I'm taking you to Anna and John's for Christmas!"

Thursday, December 26, 1912 — Dear Diary, I had the best Christmas ever! R.C. drove me in a horse and sleigh with jingling bells and lots of laughter to Anna's and John's on Christmas Eve, then he brought me home after supper last evening. It was so good to get out into the world and spend time with family! I had been shut in because of the snow, but just in case, I made Christmas gifts fror everyone, and it's a good thing. They always have nice gifts for me. Rex gave me a music box. As much as I hate the snow this year, R.C. made me love it for a day! Signed, Dora Kelly

My Friends!

Spring, 1913. It's exciting to see green grass starting to grow, and crocus peeking through the snow in the shade. Rex and I have had cabin fever, so he suggested we ride out to the farm to see the work Jim and his hands are doing to repair the damage from the blizzard. There's still a chill in the air, but it feels good to be outside and to feel the fresh air. They've started plowing so there's the aroma of fresh black dirt.

It looks like they have finished the cleanup, and they are just putting a roof on the new chicken coop. Rex ties up our horse and wagon, and we go looking for Jim.

He's in the barn. "Hey, you two. What are you doing here?"

"Dora told me about all the damage, so we decided to come out to see how you are progressing. I brought my toolbox in case you need help. Besides, it's a nice day, so it was good to get out."

"Well, as you can see, the chicken coop is almost done. Cleaning up all of the debris was a lot of work. Before the storm, I had two horses, three milk cows, a bull, six sheep, and 22 hogs. The cattle were outside when the wind hit. The bull broke through a fence and the cows followed, so they were running loose down the road. One cow was killed when a tree fell on her. A neighbor saw the others and he took them to his barn, or they would have frozen to death. Biggest loss was the sheep, they disappeared probably through the broken fence, and I lost all of the chickens. Never found the sheep. They're stupid animals! They're just about done with the chicken coop, but thanks anyway. You'll have to bring Dora out next week; I'll be picking up a shipment of baby chicks at the farm store."

"Gee, we're really sorry. I didn't know it was this bad or I would have come out sooner."

"Yeah, how are you going to recover from all this?"

"Well, little lady, I haven't talked to Ruby yet, but we will probably need to sell some of our properties. She won't be happy, so don't say anything yet.

Let me handle it. On the good side, it will be less taxes that have to be paid."

No surprise, Ruby doesn't take the news sweetly! When I wake up the next day, I can hear talking and Ruby is yelling. I can hear them right through the door. I shush Eddie and distract him with a toy so I can listen.

"You're always complaining about paying taxes. Let's sell off the property in Minnesota. It's too far away, so it's not easy to manage."

"I know, but it's one thing after another, and you're always coming to me for money!"

"The snowstorm was no one's fault. We suffered a loss, so now I have to dig us out of it."

"Alright, I'll agree to selling the lots in Minnesota, but that's it! And you'd better use the money right this time! No more gambling! We don't have much left, Jim, and we can't afford to waste anything."

Ruby and I are washing clothes the next day, thinking Jim is out at the farm. The sheets are hung on the clothesline, so I pick up the basket to go into the house when I hear a horn honking.

We go to the front of the house, and there's Jim, driving a red Model T Runabout.

Ruby is surprised, "Who's is that?"

"It's ours! Figured you and me can drive it up to Minnesota to sell like we said. We've never had a vacation."

"Jim, we're selling property because we need money, and you bought an automobile? How much did you pay for it?"

"I talked the price down. Don't worry your little head about it. I figured it all out. You just get ready to go. Thought we'd leave Friday morning so we can be there on Monday. C'mon, I'll take you for a little ride! You'll stay with the boys, right Dora? Thata girl."

Friday, April 4, 1913 — Dear Diary, Jim and Ruby left for Minnesota this morning, leaving me to take care of Eddie and Reilly. They just assumed I would be here. Jim's been riding around town in his new automobile all week. He's like a little kid with a new toy. I'm not sure when they're coming home, but Rex said he would come for supper tomorrow since we won't be able to go out with Esther and Matt until they get back. Albert stopped by this afternoon, said he heard Jim had bought an automobile. He didn't seem happy, and he was really upset when I told him they are on their way to Minnesota to sell more property. I felt bad for Jim when he told us about all he had lost from the storm, but I don't now. It doesn't make sense to me, to spend money when you need to sell something to get money! For once, Ruby's making sense. It's just one more thing that happens around here, and it's always something. I can't wait to be free. Signed, Dora Kelly

Ruby and Jim have been gone for a week. It's a good thing that Eddie and Reilly are good babies, and no one gets sick. Ruby calls to let me know they will be home on Sunday afternoon. I tell Esther I plan to have food prepared for them to eat, so I can leave as soon as they get here.

Jim honks the horn as soon as they enter the dooryard. He comes in the front door, carrying their bags with Ruby right behind, asking, "Where's my Little Eddie?"

I leave for Esther's house without asking about their trip, or whether they got a good price for the property. She'd probably tell me it's none of my buiness anyway.

The rest of spring and summer is fun. I try to stay away from the house as much as possible so they can have family privacy, and I really don't want to be around to hear them arguing, which they do all the time now, usually about spending money and needing money. As long as I can get the supplies on account, I just stay out of it.

I spend most of my time between Esther's house and Anna's, and I'm with Rex when he's not working. Sometimes he stops by the house when we're going out, and he plays ball with Eddie. Eddie reminds me of Louis when he's chasing the ball.

Rex said Jim has been teasing him when he comes to see me. They had words the other day after he told Rex that he knows what Rex is after. Rex said he wanted to punch him in the nose. I know it's not like that with Rex, but Jim is so crude. I just hope he doesn't say anything to me.

August is almost over. We're going to the lake with Esther's family on Labor Day.

September 9, 1913

Anna calls to tell me Louisa called her this morning. Mr. Murphy's sister, Anne, fell down the steps last night and she died from a broken neck! Anna and John are going to Quincy to make the arrangements, since Louisa can't get here in time. I decide to go over to their house and make supper for Rex and Harold while they are gone. I'll be sure to clean up, so they have a nice homecoming.

It is in the papers for a while, because they had a coroner's inquest to determine if her death was an accident! I read it aloud one day at breakfast.

"Anne E. Hopkins fell down the steps at 8:25 p.m. Her caretaker, Anna Kirk, called neighbors for help. It was gruesome sight and they assumed she was dead, so they carried her to a lounge. Dr. Beirne brought a priest with him who administered last rites, and he detected some heart activity, but she died a few minutes later. The caretaker told them that she witnessed the fall."

The coroner's inquest was held the next day at the home, and Dr. Beirne was jury foreman. One of the questions before the jury was, considering all of the wounds and the position of her body at the bottom of the steps, was this an accidental fall, or was she pushed? At the inquest, the caretaker changed her story. Instead of her witnessing the fall, she said they went to their separate bedrooms about eight o'clock and she heard Anne turn the lock on her bedroom door. She said she didn't know that Anne had come out of her room, and she did not know that she fell until she heard her body hit the bottom step.

"Mrs. Hopkins was old and feeble, and I think she fell when she reached to lower a shade. It was horrible! I found her at the bottom of the stairs with her head halfway under her chest, and she was bleeding profusely from her right eye."

Dr. Beirne testified to the extent of her injuries. "She apparently fell headlong. Her right leg was fractured, and she hit her head on the radiator at the bottom of the stairs. It's my opinion that this was a tragic accidental death."

Based on the doctor's testimony, the jury ruled the death was accidental.

Ruby said, "That family is just stupid about lawsuits. I'm glad we're rid of them."

September 20, 1913

It's Saturday, my evening off! Rex and Harold will be here in a few minutes. Robin Hood is showing, so we are going with a bunch of friends. Harold has a girlfriend. She's pretty, but he's so shy around girls that he doesn't talk about her much. Rex says she's nice, but it will be interesting to see what she's like.

Esther and Matt are waiting for us outside the theater. Harold introduces his friend, Emma. She doesn't say much, seems she's shy too. How did they ever start talking to one another?

We're in our seats waiting for the film to start. Matt and Esther are holding hands, and Rex reaches for my hand. Rex leans over and whispers, "Look at Harold!"

He's just looking straight ahead, frozen with his hands folded between his knees. "This is fun, isn't it, Emma?"

Emma says she's having a good time, but she doesn't seem comfortable either.

After the movie, we stand outside and talk a few minutes. Matt asks Rex, "So, what do we do now?"

"Heck, I don't know. We can't go home too early 'cuz Mother and Father invited friends for supper. Emma lives down Main, so we could go with Harold to walk her home."

Emma's house is past Greenwood Cemetery. We've walked this way before but not at night. There are a lot of trees in this neighborhood and fallen leaves have built up along the wrought iron fence surrounding the cemetery. It's cloudy, so there's no moon and it's pitch black. Rex pulls me close to make sure I don't trip and fall.

Suddenly, we hear a crunch, like footsteps in the leaves. All of us stop and stand still on the sidewalk. We start to walk, and there it is again.

Rex calls out, "Hello! Who's there?"

No one answers so the boys look through the fence, but they don't see anyone. We all take off running, and we run all the way to the gate to Emma's house. Harold walks her to the door, Rex and Matt laugh when they see them shake hands.

"That's my brother!"

September 20, 1913, Dear Diary. We went to a movie tonight with Esther and Matt and Harold brought a new girlfriend. We decided to walk her home and it's really dark and creepy at night, and something was haunting us or following us from the cemetery! Just as we got to the gate of the cemetery, we heard footsteps in the leaves, it even scared the boys! No one said anything on the way back home, but as soon as we came to the cemetery fence, Rex grabbed my hand and we all took off running up the street. Rex and Harold had to stay out late 'cuz Anna and John had company for supper, but I had to come home early. I really feel bad for Anna. It's really horrible what happened to Mr. Murphy's sister. I don't know why the newspapers have to report all the ugly details. Everyone in town is talking about it. Some say the Murphys are cursed. After reading the papers and hearing footsteps in the cemetery, I'll probably have nightmares. We had fun, though, so I'll just think happy thoughts. Signed, Dora Kelly

Our Way!

Summer, 1914.

Esther and I have become best friends. She broke up with Matt but she has a new beau, Ryan. He's nice, but Rex and Matt are still best friends.

Life with Ruby and Jim is even more difficult. I'm an adult now, still sharing a room with two little boys. They fight all the time, and don't seem to care who hears it, me or the children. Every day the house seems smaller. I get out of the house as much as I can, but it's not very often. Esther and I plan picnics sometimes, but Rex has a job, so we can only get together on the weekends.

I turned 20 in January, so less than a year to go. I still don't know what I'm going to do. One thing for sure, I'm going back to school. I need schooling if I want a good job, and I'll need a job if I'm going to find my brothers and take care of them.

August is always hot, but tonight it's so hot I can't sleep, so I lie awake thinking about Jack and Louis. I drift off to sleep dreaming that the three of us are back in our bed, and Jack is nudging me to wake up. Then I'm really awake! Eddie is pushing me awake.

"Dora, can I sleep with you? It's too hot in my bed."

"It's hot everywhere, Eddie. Let's go out to the porch. Bring your blankie so you have something to lay on."

Ruby is cooking and setting the table when I come home from the ladies auxiliary meeting. There are two extra plates on the table.

"Are we having company for supper?"

"Oh, just a friend of Jim's and his boy. His wife died a few months ago."

I go to my room to change out of my church dress, and I hear the men talking when I return to the kitchen.

"Do you want me to help?"

"No, everything's ready. I guess you can pour the iced tea."

This is so unlike Ruby. Not only is she cooking, but she's put out the nice China. Maybe she's trying to impress Jim's friend.

Jim introduces me to Andy Weller when they come to the table. He sure didn't dress up to come for supper. His overalls have a hole in one knee. His son seems to be uncomfortable and doesn't know where to sit, so I tell him to sit next to me. Ruby puts a ham and a bowl of potato salad on the table and Jim starts to dive in when Andy bows his head and folds his hands to say grace. We never say grace here. I almost laugh when Jim freezes with his mouth full, pretending to pray!

At first, Andy seems nice, but then he starts to eat. First thing he does is to stick his finger in the potato salad for a taste. "Seems good, I'll have some." Then he grabs the bowl and spoons out a large serving. He and his son smack their lips when they chew, and they wipe their hands on their overalls when they are done.

They're not very polite, either! Even before everyone was finished eating the main course, Andy says, "Any dessert? My wife always had a cake or pie in the house."

"We have watermelon for dessert tonight. It's too hot to bake."

I clear the table while Ruby goes to the fridge for the watermelon. I don't want to be rude, but I just want to finish eating so I can go outside and sit on the porch to cool off.

They finally leave after a while. I wonder if Andy and his wife were included in the friends that partied at Mr. Murphy's house. He's so crude – most likely he's one of their friends.

There's a gentle breeze. Even though it's getting late, I decide to stay on the porch where it's cooler. I can hear Ruby and Jim talking. She says my name so I listen closer to hear what Jim is saying.

"He said he really likes her. Said she'll be fine to take care of the boy. He's also looking forward to getting her inheritance so he can buy some hogs."

I storm into the house. "What are you talking about? Are you two trying to marry me off? Forget it, if you are. I'll get my own husband when it's time. Another thing, that money is mine, and no one else's."

Ruby sneers, "It is time now, girl! You'd better start making plans 'cuz you ain't living here after you turn 21. You should be grateful that he's interested in you. He owns his own farm. I doubt you could do better. And you're certainly not staying here as our housekeeper! We'll find someone who's grateful to work for us and take care of the boys!"

It's pointless to try to talk sense to Ruby, so I just go to bed. I lie awake thinking, and decide to talk to Esther in the morning. It seems Ruby's right about one thing, I need to start making some plans.

As soon as breakfast is over, I tell Ruby I'm leaving and I'll be back in time for dinner. Mrs. Onel is shocked when I tell her about Ruby wanting to marry me off.

"How old is this man, anyway? She can't force you to get married if you don't want to. Anna and John would not stand for it, and I would speak up as well."

"Thank you. That makes me feel better, but you don't know Ruby. She is going to make my life so unbearable that I want to get out. Andy's son is twelve, but they didn't tell me how old he is. They just said his wife died."

Esther looks as angry as I feel. "Mama, I haven't told you how mean Ruby is to Dora. That's why she spends so much time at our house."

"Don't you worry your little head, Dora. Ruby can't force you into something you don't want."

September 8, 1914

Today is the first day of school. I decided I would go back this year, because if I'm going to make my own way, I need more education than I have. I don't want to be a maid or end up like Ruby.

I don't know what to expect, since I'm older, so Anna said she would meet me there. She's waiting for me in the superintendent's office when I arrive.

The superintendent is polite, but doubtful when he hears I'll need to repeat the sixth grade. "I don't know what to say, Mrs. Moss. It's good that Dora wants an education, but where can I put her? She's young but it doesn't seem right to put a 20 year-old woman back in grammar school."

He turns to me, "Dora, if I make you a freshman, do you think you can keep up? You're small and you don't look your age, so you should fit in."

Starting in high school is so much better than I hoped! I know I can read and do math, and I will do my best. "Mr. Wood, I promise you I want to learn and I will study hard so I can keep up with my classes."

"I believe you. It's settled then. I'll have Miss Turner, our counselor, help you with your class schedule today, then you can go to your classes tomorrow."

I get all the classes that I wanted. I'm most excited about literature. When I leave Miss Turner's office, Anna is waiting for me so she and John can drive me home with my books.

"Thank you, Anna, for coming with me and explaining everything to Mr. Wood. I can't wait to read interesting books again. I love to write, too!"

John looks proud. "Dora, you mean a lot to Anna and me. It wasn't your fault that you haven't been going to school. We are here to help you in any way we can."

The house is quiet when I get home, loaded down with schoolwork. Eddie and the baby must be napping so I decide to sit on the porch and look at my text books. I'm into Chapter Two of the literature book when a carriage pulls up to our gate. Ugh! Andy steps down and he's holding a bouquet of flowers.

I call to Ruby, "Ruby! Andy's here to see Jim."

Andy holds the flowers out to me, "Actually, I came to see you. I brought you some flowers."

I really don't want them but I say thank you anyway.

"I was wondering if you would like to take a ride out to see my farm."

"No, thank you, Andy. It's nice of you but I have to study. I'm in school, you know."

"Girls don't need so much schoolin'. Ruby says you're already a real good cook."

I pick up my books, leaving the flowers on the swing, and run into the house so he won't see me crying. He and Ruby talk for a few minutes then he leaves.

Ruby calls me to the kitchen. "What's wrong with you? He brought you flowers! You could have been polite. You are so ungrateful."

"I don't like him. He's too old for me and I have no desire to see his farm."

"Well, you'd better get used to it. You only have a few months to find a place to live and as far as I know, no one else wants you. Grow up!"

I slam the door behind me on the way out, and I run all the way to Esther's house.

Esther and her mother sit with me in the kitchen, and I try to calm down, but I am so scared. "That man, Andy, came to the house again, and he brought me flowers. He wanted me to go with him to his farm to visit. He said girls don't need school, that Ruby told him I'm a good cook! Ruby said I was rude. Well, maybe I was, but he is just – disgusting! She said I should be nice to him 'cuz no one else will want me when they kick me out."

Esther's mother takes my hand, and she gives me a hankie. "Dora, no one can make you get married, not even Ruby. Now go on home, and I'll talk with Anna and John. There are a lot of people who love you. Don't worry. Esther will call you later."

I run home to make supper, and by the time I'm chopping the onions I have calmed down enough to start thinking about making plans. Maybe I'll run away, or get a job, or move in with Esther until I can find a room. But I will never never never marry Andy!

I'm just finishing the dishes after we eat when Rex knocks on the door.

"Hi!"

"C'mon. Let's go for a walk."

Rex dives right in. Esther ran over to his house to tell him all about Andy and how upset I am. "What's this I hear about Ruby trying to force you to marry some older man?"

"Not only is he older, but he has a 12 year-old boy. He is planning to use my inheritance to buy some hogs!"

"You told them no, right?"

"Of course, I did, but they are going to kick me out in January and now I'm so scared, because there's no room at your house, and like she said, no one else wants me. I have no place to go."

Rex looks hurt and angry all at once. "Are you kidding? What about me? What about us? Dora, don't you know that I love you?"

I stop walking. He'd never said that before! I can't believe it. He turns me towards him and looks in my eyes. "And I thought you loved me, too!"

"Oh, Rex, I do love you! I've known I loved you for a long time, but I didn't know you felt that way. I know you're my best friend. But not --. I didn't know!"

He gives me a soft kiss. "Dora, don't you want to marry me? Let's get married! I want you out of that house. I have a job. It may seem rushed, but we have to do something. And if you love me...."

"Oh, yes! That's what I want! I hoped we could. I just didn't want to believe it, Rex. I told myself you were just my best friend. I thought I had to find a way to take care of myself, to fix this mess before you might want me!"

"Dora, I've wanted to marry you ever since the graduation dance. Didn't you know that? You are my special girl, Kid, and you always will be!"

I fall into his arms for a long kiss. He smiles and I smile back, then we kiss again. "Well, I guess we'd better tell Mother and Father that we're getting married. There's a lot to do. We'll have to find an apartment, too. C'mon, let's celebrate. Wanna share a banana split?"

Rex picks me up the next day after work. John is listening to the radio in the parlor and Anna is in the kitchen.

"Mother, Father, Dora and I have something we want to tell you."

Anna is standing in the doorway and John turns the radio off. Rex looks nervous. "Dora and I want to get married!"

"What? What's this all about?"

Rex stands straighter and he takes my hand. "I know this comes as a surprise, but Ruby and Jim are trying to marry her off to some old guy with a kid. We've grown up together, we've known one another for a long time, and we love one another, so I think this is the right time for us to marry."

John looks serious. "So you've decided to rescue Dora, is that it? Are you sure you're getting married for the right reason? Your mother will tell you, marriage can be difficult at times. The reason we've been married so long is we love one another. Do you really love her, Rex?"

"I do love her, and she loves me. I have a good job at P&O; we'll have to find an apartment, but I want to get her away from those people as soon as possible."

Anna bursts in with a huge smile, and reaches out for my hands. "Well, then, I guess Dora and I have a wedding to plan!"

"Thank you, Mother. Thank you, Father."

"Come now, you two, give your mum a hug!"

We sit around the kitchen table to make a list of things we have to do. We'll see about getting a marriage certificate tomorrow, then we'll talk to our pastor at the church. I go over to Anna and John's house as much as I can, but I want to keep Ruby and Jim in the dark and keep cooking and cleaning like nothing's changed. We want to make sure they don't do anything to interfere.

Rex takes a day off work the next day, so we can go to Lewistown for a marriage certificate. The lady at the counter smiles when we walk through the door. "Are you a bride and groom?"

"Yes, ma'am. My name is Walter Rex Moss, and this is my fiancé, Dora Belle Kelly. We're here for a marriage certificate."

"Good, I can help you, all I need are your birth certificates."

"Here's mine, but Dora doesn't have one. You see, Joseph Murphy brought her to Canton from an orphanage in Chicago."

"I'm sorry, but if she doesn't have a birth certificate, I can't give you a marriage certificate."

"Can't you make an exception just this once?"

"No, dear. I'm sorry. Come back when you have all your paperwork."

We are devastated, but I am determined to make this work. I spend the next two days with Anna at her house, making phone calls to see if I can find a certificate, but every call is a dead end. John talks to Pastor, but there's nothing he can do. Finally, as a last resort, Anna decides to call Albert to see if he can find anything in Mr. Murphy's files, but all he has is the contract with the orphanage. Anna says he wants to talk to Rex and me, so we get on the phone.

"Dora, Rex, I hear you want to get married. I'm happy for you and I want to help. We'll figure something out. Don't you worry. I have an idea that might work. I'll call you tomorrow."

I spend the next day trying to keep busy, but all I do is cry. By the time Rex comes to pick me up after work, I'm crying uncontrollably.

"What's wrong, kid? You should be happy – we're getting married!"

"We can't get married, and I'll never marry. You can marry, though. If you can't marry me, you will find someone else. I'm right back where I started, with no place to go and no one to want me!"

"But Albert said he would take care of it. Let's see what he comes up with. You and Mother are going to his office tomorrow afternoon. Don't worry, you're the only one for me. If we have to, we can go to another state where you don't need a birth certificate."

Albert greets us with a big smile when we walk into his office. "Hello, ladies, have a seat. Dora, I have a surprise for you."

He hands me a piece of paper. Across the top it says, "Certificate of Birth!"

"Where did you find it? Wait! This says I was born in DuQuoin. That's not right, Mama told me I was born at home in Ullin. DuQuoin is too far, she wouldn't have gone to Du Quoin!"

"Look, Dora, this is all you have, and it took some doing to get it for you. It doesn't make a difference where you were born. What matters is your birthdate and who your parents were. Just take it so you and Rex can get married."

"Thank you, Albert. I don't know how you pulled this off."

"Don't ask, Anna. It's done. Now don't forget to invite Neva and me to the wedding!"

October 14, 1914

It's my wedding day! I had been dreading it when I thought of Andy and his rude son, but now I am so excited I can hardly think! Mrs. Onel fixed Esther's room up. She said wanted us to have a special place to get ready. There's an array of cosmetics on the vanity, a full length mirror is hanging on the back of the door, and she put a vase of flowers on the dresser.

Esther helps me with my hair. "Are Ruby and Jim coming?"

"Heck, no. I didn't invite them. I didn't even tell them about the wedding. I made up so many lies and had to sneak around to set all this up! She keeps telling me to be more grateful, but there's nothing she or Jim can do! Can you believe, she wanted me to be home today to cook, 'cuz Andy is coming for supper. I said I couldn't, and boy was she mad!"

"Boy, are they going to be surprised! When are you going to tell them?"

"I really don't answer to them, but I guess they have to find out. Rex and I are going to the house tomorrow afternoon to get my belongings."

Mrs. Onel sticks her head in the door. "How are you girls doing? I want you to take your time, but we have to be at the church a few minutes ahead of time."

Esther and I look at one another, and we hug. "Well, Dora, I guess it's really going to happen. Wait to put on your lipstick so it doesn't get on your dress."

"You put your dress on first so you can use the mirror. Besides, I want to take time to see you in your maid of honor dress! Thank you for being my friend, and standing up with me. It will be small, but it will be a pretty wedding, don't you think?"

"Think about it! It's going to be perfect! With all the problems you had getting your marriage license, and we pulled this together in a few weeks."

"You mean Anna and your mother pulled it together. Oh my gosh! Esther you are so beautiful! That copper satin really sets off your eyes and, girl, you have such a figure. Wait 'til Ryan sees you!"

"Silly! I like my dress, but you will be the star today. C'mon, put it on! What's that you put in your shoe?"

"A four-leafed clover that I picked on my way to your house. Here's one for you..."

We arrive on time, at ten to two. Rex is waiting in the foyer with a bridal bouquet of white roses. Anna has a small bouquet of yellow roses for Esther.

I wait until he goes into the church and get ready to walk down the aisle. I feel like a princess in my tea length lace dress with a flower made of white satin, pinned to my sash. A lace headband sets off my blonde curls.

Esther sees Harold is already standing up front so she goes to her appointed spot next to Pastor Denham. Everyone is waiting for the ceremony to start, R.C. and Mary, the Onels, the Taffs, and Anna and John.

Then I go into the church, where Rex is waiting for me to walk me up the aisle. He can hardly speak. "Dora, you look so beautiful!" I blush, but I know it's true, and I can see how proud he feels.

"You look nice, too!" I feel just as proud as he looks, and we start walking together down the aisle, towards the small circle of our friends and family.

Rex looks down the aisle and he sees Anna waving us to come on down. He turns to me, "Well, Kid, I guess from now on, it's just you and me!"

If I were a bird, I would fly

so high into the sky that I

will catch a ray of the sun

like a golden ribbon for you to hold.

I will soar never letting go

of the other end until I find

two brothers taken, two brothers lost.

Together we will pull the ribbon,

landing on a soft field of clover.

Loving, never leaving, at peace forever.

~ Sandra McKay

Dora Kelly on Her Wedding Day

The Moss Family, Anna, Rex, Leonard, Harold, John, Circa 1922

Rex and Dora Moss, Circa 1964

John & Anna Moss
60 Years

Epilogue

This project was originally meant to be a booklet for family about my Grandmother Dora's childhood growing up in Mr. Murphy's house after her father died. Two years before she died in 1976, she told me she was writing the story of her life, so when my grandfather asked if there was anything of hers that I wanted, I asked for her writings. I took them home and put them in a bottom drawer where they remained untouched for more than thirty years.

Dora's writings surfaced when I was cleaning out drawers on a Sunday afternoon. I sat on the bedroom floor for hours, trying to make sense of the disjointed writings of a woman who suffered from dementia, and decided to take this on as a project. I spent ten days just piecing together parts of sentences so I could develop a transcribed version of her story, which ended after her father died and her mother was forced to give the children up. Still, it was an interesting story and my husband, Don, said, "you have to write it for her!"

Dora, "Little Grandma", had told us stories about growing up in Canton, living a privileged life with servants, including a driver and carriage, but all of her stories were about happy times. Whether she had repressed memory, or she simply wanted us to think she had a blissful life, we will never know. She did tell us that she spent her inheritance hiring a detective to find her brothers, but he only found Louis after he had been killed in a coal mining accident; she never knew what happened to Jack. She grieved for her lost brothers up to the day she died.

My research started at the Fulton County courthouse in Lewistown, Illinois where I found some documents, and they directed me to the Fulton County Historical and Genealogical Society, which is based in the Canton library. That is where I met Cathy Parsons. Cathy is a volunteer who, theoretically, does genealogical research in her spare time, but it soon became evident that research is her passion, and it must consume all of her time.

Cathy is a "digger". She uncovered volumes of documents, including newspaper articles about Joseph Murphy and testimony presented at the trial, down to detailed receipts of expenditures for purchases of buttons, shoes, and candy, not to mention $1.50 for a hired hand to take a calf to the farm. I owe Cathy a great deal of gratitude; without her fierce determination to dig deeper, the true story of Dora would have been lost.

Ultimately, those documents, along with Dora's writings and interviews of family members, became the basis for the novel. During the two-year research period, my husband and I made numerous trips to Canton, and we had the privilege of a walk-through tour of Mr. Murphy's homestead, an impressive three-story red brick house. We also visited Ullin Village which helped me to understand the layout of the village, and the locations of the Kelly cabin and Curtis Kelly's barbershop.

My intent was not to write with historical accuracy, but to weave a story based on a true story, backed with historical documents. Dora's life in Ullin Village was well-documented in her writings. Her relationship with her father and the events surrounding his death are among the many stories that are true. Other true events include Jack taking off to play marbles behind the train station. Ella did leave eight-year-old Dora alone to care for Jack and Louis, and several mishaps occurred, including the scalding of Dora's legs, which were the reasons the village doctor encouraged Ella to give the children up.

I have a letter from the orphanage, which was located in the Englewood section of Chicago, with the actual dates Dora arrived at the orphanage, and when she left with Mr. Murphy. R.C. Webster was Mr. Murphy's best friend and he worked around the homestead. Names of most characters in the book are accurate. Some are fictionalized, such as Dora's friends, Hannah and Annie Rose, and I changed a few names to protect people's privacy.

Mr. Murphy was extremely wealthy, a local equivalent of Bill Gates. He was known throughout the State, having served two terms as Canton's mayor, he was a personal friend of Governor Yates, and he ran for Secretary of State. Details, including his business trip with Dickie to Quincy and visits to the farm on the Spoon River were also documented. His heart attacks and events surrounding his illness and death, including the names of the doctors and nurses, are all factual. Dr. Coleman did instruct the nurses and the housekeeper to ban visitors from his chamber, and the will was reportedly signed at 2:00 in the morning shortly before he died.

Details of the trial and the testimony were extracted from numerous newspaper articles. The trial, termed in the newspaper as The Famous Murphy Will Trial was very high profile and Governor Yates and the Secretary of State were actual witnesses. There was no question that Mr. Murphy intended to bequest $40,000 for construction and operation of a hospital in Canton. While the Graham sisters, intended to raise money to fund construction of the hospital which, at that time, cost $20,000, that never happened, but with Mr. Murphy's bequest, they had the funding needed to proceed with construction of the Graham Hospital.

True stories and character names discovered in documents through research are too many to mention and, yes, the White Sox (at the time called the "Hitless Wonders") did beat the Cubs in the 1906 World Series! However, I had to draw on my imagination to fill in details that are hazy or missing, so the only honest thing to say is, A Place for Me, An Orphan's Journey Home, is a novel.

John Grafton Moss and Anna Murphy Moss were my great grandparents. While we could not confirm the connection, I talked to family members, and we all agreed that Anna was probably Joseph Murphy's cousin. Rex, actually Walter Rex, was my grandfather. He was a quiet man with a dry sense of humor, probably because he couldn't get a word in edgewise, as Little Grandma was full of spunk, and she always had something to say. She was 100% Irish, she believed in the little people, and she had an uncanny knack for finding four-leafed clovers.

I remember many happy times going to Canton to visit my great grandparents and Uncle Harold and his family, including grandsons, the Reffetts. One time we spent the night, and all of the children slept in the same bed, boys at the top and my sister and I at the bottom!

The reason I decided to write Dora's story for her is I want people to know the tremendous challenges that she and other children experienced at the beginning of the 20th Century. Dora pretended that she had a blissful life, but we discovered the real truth, and the real story was much more significant than the one passed down through family. She would have glossed it over and the real story would not have been told.

Finally, I wrote this story in the first person because I wanted to capture Dora's distinctive voice. At times, writing became emotional because of her suffering and how much she and Rex loved one another. Then, there were times when, for example, capturing my grandfather's character, it was just plain fun! Also, I had to imagine my grandparents' romance, but knowing they celebrated every year on their anniversary by sharing a banana split, the banana split scene was a given.

Acknowledgements

Writing this book has been an incredible journey, not only for me but for my husband, Don McKay as well. It was Don who told me I had to write my grandmother's story, but little did we know this would develop into a major project. Don has been with me every step of the way, when interviewing family, numerous trips to Ullin and Canton, and hauling groceries and luggage forty steps up a steep hill to a cabin so I could shut off and write. This book started with an idea then it blossomed. *A Place For Me* would not have happened without his encouragement and moral support.

Dora's story does not belong to me, it belongs to people in my family who knew and loved my grandparents. Everyone in my family, including Aunt Rose Moss and my cousins, Elizabeth Greer and Gloria Lewis, has been supportive of this project and for that I am grateful. I also want to thank my author friends, Vicki Tapia, Andrea Lyon, and Karen Dewitt for taking time to share their experiences and for their good advice.

Posthumously, I owe a great deal of gratitude to my grandfather, Walter Rex Moss, who trusted me with Dora's writings. He never asked what I planned to do with them, so I am humbled by the trust he showed in me.

I was privileged to spend many hours working with Cathy Parsons of the Fulton County Genealogical Society. Cathy fell in love with our story, and she continued to dig for more during the entire process. Documents that she uncovered transitioned this book from a small storybook for family, into a historical novel.

I want to thank Nick Halbert who is the current owner of Joseph Murphy's homestead for allowing Don and me to do a walk - through tour of the house. I had a warm feeling, knowing that my grandmother and Mr. Murphy had lived there. When writing, I visualized the scenes on the stairway and in the kitchen and parlor, because I had been there.

There are a number of people who contributed to this story by sharing their experiences and information, making it impossible to create a proper thank you, but thank you to everyone who has expressed an interest and enthusiasm for this project, including Tammi Medus, Executive Assistant to the CEO of the Graham Hospital, and Amanda Atchley of the Canton Area Chamber of Commerce who helped me to get started. Amanda was the first to tell me about Cathy Parsons. Linda Mikulich, Deputy Clerk – Vital Statistics at the Fulton County Clerk's Office let me invade her office one afternoon, allowing me to make numerous copies of documents. Sunnie Brookbank has followed the progress of the book from the very beginning. Sunnie and Dana Karstensen, my SEO consultant, participated in a brainstorming session that led to the creation of the title. My friend and colleague, Keith Corman, who is a railroad historian researched train schedules, and there were many phone calls with Terry Seward, Grand Master of Masons, State of Illinois, 2011 – 2013, who gave me an education on the history of the Masons, and a detailed description of a Masonic funeral.

Patrise Henkel is a true professional who quickly developed a vision to create the book cover design. Patrise also formatted the book, and she led me through the final process. Working with Patrise seemed effortless – she asked me for some ideas, and with little information, she did a quick turnaround with a winning cover and, suddenly, the book became real. I owe her a great deal of gratitude for her work and for turning the book into an exciting experience.

Marcel Proust once said, "let us be grateful to people who make us happy; they are the charming gardeners who make our souls blossom." That's Carol Burbank of Storyweaving! Carol is my editor and she we spent countless hours while she coached me through the writing process. Carol knows every twist and turn in Dora's story, and she always came up with the right touch, helping me to make this a better book while keeping in mind that this was a personal story and giving me the space to tell it exactly that way.

Sandra McKay

9 780996 656665